# EMPEROR

## John Fullerton

ISBN: 9798366467957

Book, cover design and editing by Socciones Editoria Digitale
www.socciones.co.uk

'Do not swallow the enemy's bait.'
- *The Art of War*, Sun Tzu, tr. Gary Gagliardi

# What readers are saying about *Emperor*

'This is bloody good - especially the fast pace and mastery of detail.'
**- Shyam Bhatia, author & war reporter**

'John is clearly a talented, accomplished and inventive writer – with a knowledgeable grip on the dark machinations of global politics.'
**- Toby Jones, editorial director, Headline**

'I was on the edge of my seat for most of the ride.'
**- Tom Vater, author & journalist**

'I thought this was a thought-provoking, timely novel, from a talented writer - he is a huge talent.'
**- Finn Cotton, senior commissioning editor, Transworld**

'Emperor is gripping, well researched and realistic...The characters, their actions and motivations are very believable and make the book hard to put down.'
**- Jaidev Jamwal, military analyst & journalist**

# 1

# November 30

## 08:42 China Standard Time, GMT +8

The weight of a stranger's leg flung across his thighs woke him.

He didn't know her name, but he remembered her. He recalled her smile, her moves. A graceful dancer. He remembered her hip in his groin on the dance floor and the memory aroused him once more. She had small hands, and he looked at them again on the pillows, the palms roughened and creased from manual work. The fingers were long and slim and turned up at the tip like Ottoman slippers. What trick of DNA was that unexpected refinement? He recalled through a mist of vintage *maotai* having taken hold of those girlish hands, turning them over and kissing those palms at some point of madness during the evening. On hearing her poignant tale - of youth, femininity, poverty and hard, endless graft to fill her family's rice bowl - he almost wept. He could see her in his mind's eye, bent almost double, digging and planting in all weathers. Conceived in soil, born in soil, wedded to it, to die in it.

She must have a name. If she'd told him, he'd forgotten it.

Wang found him these girls from the countryside - healthy, keen to serve, all Communist Youth League members, enthusiastic in bed, always cheerful, honoured to be fucked by the General Secretary.

Such cruel sweetness on a conveyor belt, none to be repeated.

Did this one know what her reward would be? Had she known beforehand? Would her family celebrate their newfound prosperity? Some did. Would she boast of their coupling? It was not unknown.

The capsule of *Wei-ge*, or Big Brother, the Chinese version of Viagra, had done its work despite the counter-effects of the *maotai*.

The Emperor relished her smell. It was almost overpowering and natural. It never failed to enchant. This was a clean, fresh smell of sweat and cunt and hair, a curious mixture of hormones better than any artificial scent, the Chanel and Arpege his wife and daughter liked so much.

He didn't say so, but he thought they stank like whores. Artificial scents and makeup were nothing but deceit. This one was no whore, though she had been bought in a manner of speaking, to serve the Party with her vulva. The Emperor had never heard of the poet *Nonnus*, but he would have recognised what he'd said of Dionysus: 'Mad for the women.' Nor had Qin heard of *Clement of Alexandria*, who said Dionysus was 'the one who touches the vulva'. Qin was neither Dionysus nor any other god, but he had known many vulvas one way or another as Emperor. It was his right as he saw it, his jus *primae noctis*. He cared nothing for gods or bodhisattvas. He knew himself to be mortal, a mere emperor in a long line of emperors, good, bad, and indifferent; in his case, the head of a dynasty he knew would only prevail by constant growth and expansion and meanwhile, when he had nothing better to do, he plucked vulvas like the seven strings of the *guqin*. He liked to pleasure his bedmates even more than he liked to be pleasured himself. He knew that it spoke of his advanced years. It excited him at a time of life when excitement, especially physical excitement, was a rare and diminishing thing.

Qin believed, of course, not in divinity but the march of history, of material destiny. It was his particular Marxist-Leninist destiny to give history a big effing kick up the arse toward a universal order of socialism with special Chinese characteristics.

He had noted she wasn't a virgin, this one. It was better that way and more fun. He hated it if they cried from pain or from fear of him, and Wang knew that. They needed to be bold in bed, enthusiastic, and willing to take and to give. He didn't mind if they were pretending as long as they were convincing.

Did Wang try them out first? It was a disgusting suspicion, and he pushed the thought away from him.

Qin disentangled himself. He didn't want to wake her. Instead, he liked to watch her sleep; the breaths coming even and deep. He wished he could sleep like that.

The evening had been a celebration of a sort. He had been happy, at peace with himself. Even Wang had noticed the Emperor's joyous mood. Qin had decided that was why. The decision would be seen as the Party's, but everyone knew it was his. The seven-man Politburo would vote unanimously, of course, because they always did, and he said they must, and they would do so today in his presence.

But it was his decision.

In little over sixty days, the People's Republic of China would be at war.

He would fulfil the Party's most solemn promise.

The cost in lives and treasure would be horrendous, but that was nothing compared to the cost of not doing so, of holding back, of cowardice.

Qin stood, walked across the room barefoot, found his swimming shorts, pulled them on, scratched his belly, his *laobandu*, or boss's pot, and threw a bathrobe over his shoulders.

He glanced back at the girl lying across the vast bed, a bed twice the size of a super king-size. It wasn't just his erotic playpen with one side raised for easier imperial fucking, a feature he'd had copied from the Great Leader's bed, now in the museum next door, but his worktop, too, piled high with books and papers, many of them *jiumede* or secret. Not that the girl would be interested, and she wouldn't dare read anything she wasn't supposed to. Her life would be forfeited if she did.

By the time he returned from his swim, she'd be gone. Chief bodyguard Wang would make sure of it. The Emperor would not see her again.

\*\*\*

Qin walked over to the edge of the indoor pool - the same pool where the Great Leader had humiliated Khrushchev in front of officials from both countries back in 1958. Qin had turned nine that year. He'd been born in the year of the Revolution. Except for the sleeping girl and Wang - chief protector, procurer of women, the best vintage *maotai* and his Dunhill cigarillos - Qin was alone. He was tall, broad and well-fed, so tall that his paunch wasn't that prominent. His skin was pale, his hair pitch-black, and he had enormous feet. Among his countrymen, his size was unusual, and he knew it gave him an advantage when playing his part in public, especially in front of crowds. This giant among men dropped his white cotton bathrobe on a poolside lounger. On a small table next to it was a pot of tea along with and a well-thumbed copy of one of his favourite books, Luo Guanzhong's *The Water Margin*.

Qin was thinking pleasant thoughts; that this was the greatest gift someone in his position could have, and that was to be alone, to be silent, to be freed from the burden of having to hear others chattering, and, above all, to enjoy the delight of not doing anything at all for as long as he chose and without challenge. Not even his wife and daughter could scold him or question him (he wasn't sure which was worse). Solitariness, silence and inactivity were nothing short of an ultimate liberty; an exquisite luxury enjoyed by the very few, by people he could count on the fingers of one hand - dictators all, for whom riches as they were commonly understood no longer had any meaning.

This was true wealth.

His face was flat and moon-shaped, his cheeks plump like a baby's, so too his neck, which was ringed with the lines of a man on the frontier of old age. Excluding sexual exertions, swimming every day in the pool, sometimes several times a day, was his only exercise. He swam summer and winter, for the pool was heated in the colder months, as it was today. Qin always swam alone. He knew only breaststroke and backstroke, but that was enough. Qin didn't like to get his hair wet for fear the pomade would run and make him look ridiculous, but he'd baulked at wearing a bathing cap because it too made him look silly. He reasoned people wouldn't respect someone comical.

Qin walked over to the steps leading down into the shallow end, holding his head tilted to one side, to the right. He did this so often that he wasn't even aware of it. He went down the steps into the cool water, hands out on either side. Holding his head this way helped to prevent the headaches his medical team said were caused by a brain tumour. So far it was benign, they said, and not a cause of immediate concern, but they had wanted to conduct more tests, something he'd refused. If they were right and the tumour was of no immediate concern, why then should he bother? If they were wrong, it was their own heads they should worry about.

The tumour was a state secret. Not even his wife and daughter knew or, if they did, they were careful not to say anything.

He knew what people called him behind his back, from his bodyguards to the most senior cadres. They called him Emperor. The Party's enemies used the term, too. They meant it as an insult, but Qin liked it. He liked it a lot, but would never admit it to anyone.

Even his daughter called him that - daring to mock him to his face.

He enjoyed the sensation of the water rising on his skin; the caress of it as it rose with each step. It washed him clean of the stench of sex, of the femininity of which he was sated, and returned him to his sense of his unsullied, masculine self. He waded deeper until the water reached his neck, then he launched himself forward - making no splash, easing himself into it. He swam slowly, sometimes for hours at a stretch without pause. No-one else was permitted in the pool and certainly not foreign leaders. It was his privilege to have it to himself. It had belonged to Mao, and now it was his. Mao had been proud of his ability to swim great lengths, yet he had only been capable of a kind of clumsy sidestroke. As Qin swam, he disengaged his mind, so that it floated free like his large body. It was the steady rhythm that made it possible. Thoughts thinned out; what had been a consciousness crowded with chatter, oppressed by worries and nagging doubts and petty resentments like an overcast sky, emptied until there was nothing but the sensation of moving through the water, and then the sensation of moving vanished, and it was as if he was suspended in space and it was the water that moved.

An empty mind was like a cloudless sky; it was rest beyond sleep.

Up and down he went, slow and steady. The water glittered. The tiles were sky blue. Of course, the temperature was the way he liked it. The first 40 lengths were the hardest; once he'd managed that, it all became so effortless. After 100 lengths, he lost count. It was the closest he would ever be to the sensation of flying. The swimming had given his shoulders, upper arms and chest excellent definition for someone his age - or so he thought when admiring himself in his bathroom mirror.

His Mona Lisa smile was still in place as he ploughed up and down, hour after hour.

Time and space disappeared.

What was time, after all? He owned time. He ate when he was hungry, fucked when he wanted, slept when he felt the urge - and that was seldom for more than a couple of hours at a time - and he often worked through the night. Night and day, they made no difference to him.

No-one questioned his habits, or the lack of them, except for the two official women in his life, and he had stopped listening to them long ago.

As he climbed out of the pool, all the thoughts came crowding back like a mob bursting into his consciousness, trying to elbow their way in, fighting for primacy.

There was a fresh towel on the lounger. His robe had been folded. The teapot had been refilled, and he noted with satisfaction that the book had not been touched.

His personal doctor from Group One Clinic had showed him the mist, the milky cloud in his head on the X-ray sheets on a screen. The image had frightened him, but he didn't show it. The truth of it was that he knew he did not have long. No-one said as much. Dr Lo wasn't brave enough to tell him to his face, but he knew. There was the one task that he had to undertake before he was crippled by pain; a promise the Party had made year after year, since the 1949 Revolution itself, and given it was over 100 years since the Party was founded, he could not allow his third term in office to end without fulfilling it. It was his destiny, and that of his Party. It was the very raison d'être of the People's Liberation Army and all training, all manoeuvres, had that one goal in mind.

Only the previous week, the annual Party congress had reaffirmed the commitment, but thanks to the Chairman and General Secretary (he occupied both posts), in much clearer, more forceful terms. Now it was time for the seven-member Politburo to turn that promise into reality.

China would be reunified.

And soon.

The date had been discussed and decided. Qin had decided it.

The Emperor's quizzical smile was still in place, his head tilted to one side in what looked to some like a conciliatory gesture. Right below him, under his big, white feet, below the tiles and several metres of reinforced concrete, was the new Strategic Command Centre, like a subterranean spider in the centre of its web of tunnels under the government complex in Beijing, the *Zhongnanhai*. Ultra-modern with immense screens on all sides and a vast central 'sand table' on which battles could be simulated, the multi-million dollar Control Room, equipped with the very latest technology - bought from foreign companies in the Netherlands and Germany - was his new toy. Qin was Chairman of the Central Military Commission and outranked marshals and admirals - even ministers. He would be in ultimate control of all operations, and in touch with all his country's command posts by fibre-optic links, while impervious to the enemy's nuclear and conventional strikes, invulnerable in the face of their cyber attacks, invisible and inaudible despite the ceaseless scrutiny of their listening and watching satellites, and countless enemy spies on the ground.

None of his predecessors had pulled it off. Most had never come close to trying.

Mao had planned such an operation, but had postponed it because of the war in Korea. The Americans had planned it, too, in 1944, but they had called it off because they lacked enough soldiers to take on the 100,000 Japanese occupying what was then called Formosa. The Americans had wanted a five-to-one superiority in numbers, but most of their forces were then still fighting the Nazis in Europe.

This time, there would be no postponement.

Two million soldiers and marines should be more than enough.

With such agreeable thoughts, the Emperor's headache vanished and for once, he could hold his head straight. Qin sat on the lounger and poured himself another cup of his favourite tea.

The Party would be victorious, and it would be his victory. His. His leadership, his gift to the Party, to the country, to the Chinese people, to the world - before the tumour in his head killed him.

# 2

## 10:53 China Standard Time, GMT +8

It seemed far too easy. It was also far too normal.

That worried her.

She was sure her back was clear. The question was: why?

Ding Pan had taken an early morning Air China flight from Beijing to Shanghai, a distance of 1,100 km or 684 miles, so early that it was still dark when she left her flat. She had bought a single, one-way ticket online with her Mastercard for the equivalent of around 70 U.S. dollars. Yes, she knew that the booking was recorded and could be checked. The alternative would have been a seat on the world's fastest passenger train, but that would have taken around six hours - using up most of the morning - against two and a half hours by air. That, too, would have required her to give her name and proof of identity, even if she had paid in cash. It would have been no more secure than flying. Pan wasn't doing the environment any good, but she also knew she needed to do this fast if she was going to stay ahead - and staying ahead meant staying alive.

Survival meant speed, and speed took precedence over her carbon footprint and her data trail.

From Shanghai's Pudong International Airport, Pan flew one way via China Eastern to Hong Kong, a flight time of three hours and twenty-five minutes, at a cost of 170 dollars. To save time and avoid delays - and aside from her winter coat - she had a carry-on bag with two changes of clothing, a few toiletries and a paperback of short stories by Lu Xun, Hu Shi and other writers of the revolutionary era. Safe reading.

The former British colony basked in afternoon sunshine, the glass and concrete high-rises crowded together like clusters of slender stalagmites winking up at Pan amid breathtaking scenery of blue sea and green hills. For a few minutes, Pan forgot her predicament and gazed down, marvelling at her next destination as the plane prepared to land at Hong Kong International Airport. Using her Chinese passport, she moved through passport control and customs without having to queue. No-one asked her anything. No-one appeared to pay her any attention, though - as usual - men, Westerners mostly, elderly and large lotharios, would stare at her legs, her tits, her hair. She'd never liked it, but she was used to it and paid it no attention. Ten minutes later, she was on the Airport Express light train and headed for Kowloon Station.

With no apparent purpose in mind, she wandered down Nassau Street in the neighbourhood known as Lai Chi Kok or Lychee Corner, stopping and gazing in shop windows - mirroring it was called - past Mei Foo Sun Chuen, Hong Kong's biggest private housing estate with its 99 towers, and took a turn around the pleasant Mei Foo park, ambling along the paths like a tourist without a worry in the world. Pan began to sweat, for after the deep cold of Beijing, the 22 degrees Centigrade of Hong Kong was positively tropical. She sat down on a park bench shaded by trees for a few minutes, placed her superfluous padded coat next to her, dug out of her bag a tourist map, unfolded and appeared to consult it before putting it away again and, after glancing at her watch, rising and disappearing into the Mei Foo Mass Transit station.

Still nothing.

Pan's back was clear, or so it seemed to her.

She muttered to herself, 'Is it going to be this easy - really?'

She felt like a bank robber who'd just got away with millions and couldn't understand why she heard no police sirens.

Ding Pan's next stop was the Foreign Correspondents' Club on Lower Albert Road in Central. To get there, she took two taxis, changing once halfway to her destination. She didn't go into the bar, but lingered in the foyer, producing a laminated ID card in the name of Niki Kawashima, and she asked the concierge in Cantonese if there was, by any chance, a letter waiting for her.

There was, though it took the man what felt like a century to find it - an A4 padded envelope, and by the feel, there wasn't much inside. A couple of news clippings or a contract, maybe. The address was handwritten in black ink - big, hasty capitals in downward strokes. The stamp showed it had been sent from Beijing four days before. Pan dropped it into her shoulder bag and asked the concierge to look after her coat for an hour or two. He gave her a key with a number. She turned on her heel and walked out into the late afternoon, down the hill to the corner, and hailed yet another cab, this time to the Central Post Office, a few blocks away. As she settled on the back seat, she glanced out of the rear window.

Still nothing.

On entering the building, Pan moved along a corridor lined on both sides with post boxes. These might seem expensive to rent, but for small companies a cost-effective alternative to setting up a physical office in a territory where space of any kind was so scarce - and costly. Hers, number 6122, was at the end, high up and almost out of reach, Pan being just five feet and one inch tall.

Inside she found another envelope, or rather a slim cardboard container not unlike those used by Amazon to despatch books to the company's customers. 'Marketing materials', it said on the back.

It, too, went into her bag.

She twisted her hair away from her neck and coiled it over her shoulder, using the movement to pause and look back.

In the main hall, she stood at a vacant counter and emptied the contents of both packages into a padded envelope and addressed it to a post box at the Dubai Central Post Office on Zaa'beel Street, for the attention of Ms Kawashima.

Ding Pan reminded herself she wasn't yet in the clear. Once at Hong Kong airport, she paid with a debit card for a seat in economy on an Emirates flight to Washington, D.C. with two layovers, in Bangkok and in Dubai - all told a journey time of 42 hours.

She had already made an overnight booking for a Ms Kawashima at Dubai International Hotel at the airport - a 'luxury executive room' with free Wi-Fi at the special discounted price of only 324.54 U.S. dollars. Well, it could be worse.

Pan perched on a stool at the bar in the departures hall and ordered coffee and mineral water. She used the time she had to watch people walking by or just hanging about. The scruffy Chinese guy with the baseball cap staring at the magazine stand, the mother bending down and fussing with a child in a pushchair, an elderly couple arm in arm, another Chinese woman in her twenties, alone, reading a paperback novel in English, her feet up on a huge green backpack.

Pan knew her precautions were clumsy, but amateurish as they were, they were preferable to the risks of carrying anything on her person - or among her few possessions - that might prompt an unhealthy interest in her as a traveller.

Once in DC, she'd set up a meet with her old school pal, Avery, known to her friends and associates as Ava. Pan would use all her powers of charm and persuasion, but she was confident Ava wouldn't let her down. Pan had done her research. Ava's skill set, her innate curiosity and her proclivity for all matters Chinese would get the better of her instinctive caution, for Ava was not a natural rule-breaker or rebel, and Pan was counting on her own proven skills at persuading people to do things that weren't logically in their interest. Ava was her backstop, her friend of last resort, in case something did go wrong.

If Pan survived that far, and reached her refuge on Massachusetts Avenue, she might allow herself to relax a little - even though she knew all too well that she was running from a sun that rose in the east, from the ticking of every watch and clock from Jakarta to Helsinki; she couldn't shake off the knowledge that every day, every night, hour, indeed every minute that passed was gone for good and never would return.

# 3

# December 1

## 11:42 China Standard Time, GMT +8

Qin picked out a navy *Zhongshan* suit, sometimes known as a Mao suit, though it was the republican leader Sun Yat-sen who had first declared it as official, formal dress for males. Mao's had been cheap, with the cuffs too long, almost covering his hands. But Mao was a peasant and didn't care at all for his appearance. He had worn his clothes and cloth shoes until they fell apart, relying instead on personal charisma - and terror - to impress. Qin's *Zhongshan* suits were of more modern design, custom-made of a blend of wool and mohair, or silk. He had at least a dozen - grey, black, blue and green - aside from the Western-style suits made by Hong Kong tailors, which he wore to greet foreign leaders. To his shame, Qin had fought in no wars, didn't know how to handle himself under fire or how to use combat weapons. He knew he would be the only one present at the meeting who wasn't in uniform, so this would have to do. It was smart enough, even luxurious. He pushed his feet into a pair of black leather loafers his wife had brought him from Velasca during one of her shopping trips to Milan.

A member of Qin's domestic staff (servant would be the inappropriate term, though that's what he was), a young man in white shirt and navy pants, laid the suit out for him. He withdrew backwards, bowing as he did so, like a valet in some royal palace. Qin used to tell them off for being obsequious, but it had made no difference, so he'd given up. He rather liked it. Didn't the Emperor merit some grovelling respect, after all?

To prepare himself and gather his thoughts, Qin helped himself to a cigarette, a Dunhill cigarillo, no less. None of that local rubbish for the paramount ruler, thank you very much. He walked around his cavernous office-cum-bedroom while smoking it, inspecting the disorder on his immense bed, half of which was given over to his books and papers.

Out in the corridor, one of his bodyguards had the lift ready, the door open. Qin dropped two subterranean floors. He enjoyed the sensation of weightlessness, of free-fall, appearing without warning in the command centre like a spaceman - or so he fancied - emerging from his shiny steel spacecraft like a teleported hero of a black-and-white television show he remembered having watched in childhood.

Everyone stood as he walked over to his high-backed swivel chair, a slight smile in place. Five of them, selected by Qin. An admiral, two generals, two public security and intelligence chiefs - the cadres stood as the Emperor took his place and nodded to them to be seated. He trusted them as much as he trusted anyone, and that wasn't much. At least they were all Red Princes - the sons of top Party cadres going all the way back to '49 if not earlier. Qin liked to keep it 'in the family'. It was how the system worked. You were loyal because there was no alternative. You were loyal to your parents and siblings, but would not hesitate to inform on them if the Party ordered it. That was the way it was in China, always had been. And because you were loyal to your parents, you were loyal to the Party. But the Party came before parents, of course. Everything you had, everything you were, depended on that sense of loyalty. The princelings lived in special houses given to them by the Party for life. The homes were in special, walled compounds guarded night and day. They and their children went to special schools from kindergarten on, they ate special food and wore special clothing, shopped in special shops, and attended special Party courses at university and, in return for their loyalty, took up the most important Party posts. With that came the special rewards: luxury foreign cars and drivers, household staff, bodyguards, money and lots of it.

They all, including Qin, belonged to the Red Aristocracy because they were the sons and daughters - and the grandsons and granddaughters - of the real revolutionaries.

He forgot for a moment where he'd put his speech, then found the sheet of paper in one of several jacket pockets. He smoothed it out on the console in front of him, cleared his throat and began reading from it. It was very short and had been penned by his chief speechwriter. He knew he was hopeless at making any kind of speech without having it written for him in advance. He had only to look up to see all the pale faces gaping up at him to forget everything in his head.

'Welcome. Welcome to the inaugural, bi-monthly meeting of the Strategic Command Centre. This is a moment of historic importance in our drive to reunification.' He paused, then found his place again with his right forefinger. 'We all know the Politburo have, in three recent meetings, agreed in principle the decisions and directions we will take in the weeks ahead. Under those Party decisions, the first war planning and coordination conference was held last Wednesday at Eastern Theatre Command at which rocket forces, PLA, PLAN, PLAAF, intelligence, security and city and provincial government were represented. A broad plan of action was agreed. You have the minutes of that session before you.

'I would ask each of you to report now on the concrete steps taken, and which are being taken, since that conference, and in accordance with the decisions made by the Party. Thank you.'

He sat down and rested his gaze on the model of the tear-drop island, with its ridge of mountains running north-south along the eastern half, that lay on the sand table in the centre of the room.

This was their goal, the missing piece of real estate that would make China whole.

Qin knew what they were going to say because he'd had to approve their remarks beforehand. It was a tedious process, and out of sheer irritation, he had found fault with them all and had made them correct them. It was going to be bothersome pretending to listen, too.

Colonel Sun of military intelligence, formerly known as PLA2 and now the Intelligence Bureau of the Central Military Commission Joint Staff Department, was in charge of the Strategic Command Centre. His job today was to ensure that the images on the big screens changed with each speaker, illustrating the work they described.

First, Wu Xian, 79-year-old head of the United Front Work Department, an intelligence organisation responsible for winning over overseas Chinese, summarised the opening salvo in the psychological warfare campaign. Wu was small and frail, and in ill health. He annoyed Qin with what appeared to be a hesitant, fussy manner, fiddling with his glasses.

Wu declared that among their African, Latin American, and Asian friends, Chinese diplomats were hammering home the need to respect one another's internal affairs and avoid interference - something most of them would appreciate and understand. It meant Taiwan, of course, and these leaders knew what was expected of them. To those powers likely to oppose or criticise reunification, Chinese-influenced outlets in the media and diplomatic circles repeated again and again the tangible benefits of sustaining good relations with Beijing, along with setting out the stiff penalties - in credit and trade - that would follow for failing to respect Beijing's right to conduct its internal affairs as it saw fit.

At the forefront of this global drive was the China Council for the Promotion of Peaceful Reunification, or CCPPNR, formed in 1988 to counter Taiwanese independence. A thinly disguised front organisation of the aforementioned United Front Work Department, the CCPPNR, promoted CCP propaganda. The chairman was himself a member of the Politburo's Standing Committee. No fewer than 91 countries hosted CCPPNR chapters, Wu declared. There were branches in most U.S. cities. The national headquarters in Washington was called the National Association for China's Peaceful Unification. In Chicago, it was the Chinese American Alliance for Peaceful Reunification and in Britain, it was the UK Chinese Association for the Promotion of National Reunification.

Qin was proud of his own active encouragement, in particular of the Sydney-based Australian Council for the Promotion of Peaceful Reunification of China, which had forged deep, personal links with Australian politicians and had made big donations to Australian parties across the political spectrum.

As Wu spoke, the screens showed a succession of Chinese ambassadors speaking in foreign capitals with Chinese subtitles.

Targets for this message included Tokyo, Seoul and Manila. Influencers on social media, friendly journalists and sympathetic politicians had mobilised in the United States and Europe, too, helped along with financial credit (and cash grants to grease the palms of those who could be bought outright) for new infrastructure projects.

Twenty-five ambassadors had shown they appreciated the peace-loving policies of the People's Republic of China. Twenty-three governments backed the Belt & Road Initiative. Three serving European prime ministers, six former U.S. generals, two former U.S. chiefs of staff, five former U.S. presidential advisers, twenty-three business leaders, two hundred and sixteen journalists, eleven 'think tanks' - all were prepped to issue articles and statements ramming home a single message: Beijing wanted only peace and security, and it had the sovereign right to defend itself against aggression, armed provocation and interference in its internal affairs by the lackeys of U.S. imperialism.

Taiwan, they would say yet again, was an internal matter.

Finally, Wu declared, in an offensive directed against the 'splittists' and 'counter-revolutionaries' on the island itself as well as their allies around the world, Beijing broadcast the single, simple and oft-repeated message that resistance was futile. This was backed up by increasing air and naval activity in the South China Sea and especially in the Taiwan Strait itself.

PLAAF planes and PLAN ships appeared on the screens.

Wu stated that there was already a probable majority in the U.S. Congress that took the view that relations with Beijing were too important to allow dissension over Taiwan's future to derail the global trade and financial system in which Beijing played so central a role.

Great strides had also been made since 2005 with Beijing's policy of 'ethnic Chinese participation in politics' or *juarez canzheng*, exploiting anti-Chinese racism and what the Party called a 'century of humiliation'. Wu also pointed out that ethnic Chinese supported by the Party were actively running for office in Canada, the UK, New Zealand, Australia, the United States and elsewhere.

Active measures were taken to silence terrorists too, such as the so-called dissidents and human rights activists of Chinese ethnicity. Taking pictures of their children on their way to school had proved a very effective tool in silencing the enemies of the Party. Photoshopping the heads of female lawyers and artists onto nudes, which were then posted to escort sites online, also had had positive results, along with thousands of phone calls made to the homes of wayward people of Chinese origin. These projects were being stepped up and widened over the Taiwan issue.

Qin struggled to keep his eyes open. Wu was such a boring speaker; in fact, he read out what was in front of him. No passion at all in the little creep! He would not return to the Centre, Qin decided.

Air Force General Zheng Chen was next. He was a big man, his camouflage fatigues exaggerating his size, making him look like an enormous bear. The general rose to his feet, leaning forward, hands flat on his desk, and glared around him as if expecting trouble. He spoke with some force and without even looking at his approved speech. He needed no microphone, and Qin noted he had kept it switched off.

Of 22 forward airbases in southeast China, Zheng declared, 16 were fully protected, with concrete aircraft shelters, buried command centres, ammunition and fuel bunkers. Runways had been extended and widened and eight additional runways built along with seven extra control towers.

The big screens showed completed shelters, then construction at other airfields where shelters were still being completed and runways extended.

Work proceeded day and night. Airport perimeter defences were also being improved, and reinforcements of militia and People's Armed Police were being redeployed gradually so as not to spark alarm among the civilian population. These units would be needed to prevent acts of subversion by terrorists - short-hand for Taiwan's special forces. All work on this should be finished within two weeks - with the help of private construction companies that had 'volunteered' to cooperate with the Party and government on a cost-only basis.

Qin smiled to himself. Corporations that did not 'volunteer' for the war effort would find themselves without credit, their debts called in, their executives imprisoned, their workers dismissed, their major shareholders snared in corruption trials. They would cease to exist.

Two new fuel farms had been built, and a third was close to completion, Zheng continued.

The huge silvery storage tanks appeared above their heads like giant Zeppelins, only these were planted in the ground, separated by high barriers of sand known as berms.

Frontline aircraft were being deployed to the southeast, squadron by squadron, while older types were being redeployed to reserve squadrons elsewhere.

More aircraft streaked across the screens, this time the new SU-35 fighters bought from Russia and deployed to forward airfields.

'In five days' time,' Zheng said, looking at Qin, 'our land-based, mobile nuclear missile forces will disperse to mountain and forest sites. This will be gradual, and carried out after dark mostly, but we recognise it will be impossible to conceal the move for very long. This will coincide with an official announcement of a limited nuclear test - a clear warning to our enemies who may attempt to use nuclear blackmail.'

No fewer than 290 new strategic missile silos had been built so far in the east, west and centre of the country. For public consumption, images of the work captured by satellite were described as wind turbines and all part of China's progressive march to 100 percent renewable energy.

The announcement prompted a round of polite applause.

With that, the bear stopped his growling and sat down.

Qin liked Zheng's forceful performance. The Emperor preferred facts and figures - stuff he could see and touch, not vague assertions.

Next, it was the turn of Admiral Jia Lihua, a mere youngster in his 50s.

'Refitting militia boats and commercial trawlers with military grade communications and radar has been completed with modifications completed on 30,000 units,' Jia declared. 'We are now switching to the accelerated production in eight shipyards of landing craft and the additional modification of civil shipping for amphibious purposes.'

Colonel Sun's technical team put up the previous day's video of yards constructing the ships night and day.

'Minelaying capabilities have been expanded in recent months, employing surface vessels and diesel-electric submarines. I would like to declare the PLAN ready to carry out operations for the planned phase of sea and air blockade.'

Jia paused, signalling a change of topic.

'Tomorrow, our four strategic nuclear ballistic missile submarines and four nuclear-powered hunter-killer subs will leave their Hainan bases and deploy to operational areas where they will patrol in full combat readiness in anticipation of the likely approach of advance elements of the U.S. Seventh Fleet.'

Archive video of Chinese submarines illustrated the point.

Another pause.

'From today, we, along with our PLA and PLAAF comrades, will begin a week of brigade-level amphibious exercises, including close air support, a key requirement being effective command-and-control and coordination of all the elements involved. Paratroops will practise drops behind enemy lines. Both soldiers and marines will take part.'

Jia sat down.

General Wang was the last, a sleek and well-fed veteran of the Long March. He spoke of the deployment of mobile air defences to the operational area, especially around airfields, ports and troop embarkation points. Aircraft were practising dispersal drills, as well as night operations, while drone fleets were moving from the interior to the coast.

Batteries of the latest S-400 surface-to-air missiles were already in place.

Qin needed another of those Dunhill cigarillos.

'I would like to invite you all now to hold an open discussion on any of the issues raised. You may speak freely. We are friends and comrades. Who wants to go first?'

The Emperor hoped no-one would, that they could wrap this up and go home.

Jia's hand shot up.

'Admiral?'

'If our operations are to be phased, as has been decided by the Party at the conference at Eastern Theatre Command, what then are the chances of achieving strategic surprise?'

Qin put on his most confiding smile. 'None.'

'Can you expand on that?'

'We want to boil this frog by degrees. We intend to bring pressure to bear little by little. Our intelligence is that a third of the island's armed forces want to negotiate a process of unification. They don't all want to fight. Another third wants to run away to California or Queensland. The remaining third wants to fight to the death. We want to help those who see sense. So, we must use pressure, increasing it little by little, forcing the enemy to respond to each sortie and patrol so that they're exhausted, mentally and physically, long before we attack.

'We want the Americans also to decide once and for all whether they want to go to war and shed thousands of American lives for this island so far away from their shores. Have the Americans not lost enough wars by now? Do they want another long war in east Asia? Do they have the stomach for it? So, we will not surprise them in a strategic sense. We want them to have ample warning of our intentions, to be persuaded of our determination to attack, occupy and subjugate the island and its inhabitants. There can be no bolt from the blue. The only surprises will be operational and tactical.'

Jia had his hand up again.

'Have we calculated the impact of hostilities on our country and people?'

Qin hid his irritation with that slight smile of his. It wasn't in the brief, and it was none of Jia's business.

'Lives will be lost, Admiral. Families will grieve. The quality of life for the survivors will deteriorate - for a while. Our economy will stall. The global financial system will be shaken. The prices of commodities - and especially crude oil - will increase on world markets. Did you see the price of crude this morning? At home, there will be suffering, make no mistake. Of course. That is war. War is suffering. But our Party made a solemn promise in 1949 to reunify China and our Party has renewed that pledge every year since and that is what we will do, regardless of cost. It is expected of us. History demands it. The Party demands it.'

Demanded by the Party, and Qin was the Party, and the Party was Qin.

The Word was Qin.

There were no more questions.

Qin was the first to leave.

He would need his coat, scarf and gloves. He would have to leave the warmth of his official Red Flag limousine to walk a short distance in the open to the Great Hall of the People, where protocol required that he present awards to a couple of *da bizi*, Big Noses. With that thought, the headache returned. He would have much preferred do it all by video link, but then medals weren't digital, not yet anyway.

Bloody foreigners!

# 4

## 11:00 Eastern Standard Time, GMT -4

Eleven thousand, one hundred and forty kilometres from Beijing and twelve hours behind, Ava wore her 'don't fuck with me' look. Even her friend and senior colleague, James Halberton, had been heard to mutter that Ava's mask would freeze the balls off a camel. Not that there were any camels or indeed camel's testicles at their Adams Morgan office in Washington, D.C., at least none Ava was aware of, but it seemed to her to be a snarky reference to her first National Security Agency (NSA) posting of 18 very long months in what had been the NSA's least popular foreign locations: Area 82 at Bagram outside Kabul.

It was Thursday in DC. Outside, the sun struggled to provide the world with any warmth. It was winter; the days were short and cold. She should have been cheerful, and she wasn't sure why she wasn't. It couldn't just be the weather. After all, she had a rare byline in The Guardian. That was something, at least. She sat down at her desk; unlike some, she didn't like clutter. It was crowded quite enough, with two computer monitors and three telephones. It wasn't unlike her desk at the NSA, in fact. She kept her stuff neat. Everything had its place. The China Room itself was chilly because computers liked it that way, but Ava didn't. She kept a wool sweater, a scarf, and a rug at work to cope with it. She blamed the goosebumps and frozen toes on sitting still and staring for hours at those screens.

As for Area 82, despite the dust, heat and flies of summer and the sub-zero winters, it had turned out to be a blessing in more ways than one. She'd volunteered, and that had been marked a positive, if naïve, first step on the career ladder. For another, she'd seen the place grow from two sites - code name ICE CENTER - one for the Americans, the other for the Norwegians, the latter a cheerful, humorous bunch who threw better barbecue parties than the home side - into a Regional Cryptologic Centre with 25 staff from nine nations.

She'd learned so much. She'd seen at close hand the RT-RG in action: the NSA's Real Time Regional Gateway that processed massive quantities of metadata and churned out targets almost instantaneously, so much so that it accounted for some 90 percent of military kills in Afghanistan.

It saved ISAF lives, preventing ambushes, IED and sniper attacks. Or so she reassured herself. She had wanted so much to believe that her work was beneficial.

Didn't everyone want that?

Sure, RT-RG had been a shot in the arm for NSA staff, a real morale raiser - they could see for themselves that they were making a real difference on the battlefield.

There were wrong kills. Too many wrong kills. Inevitably, in Ava's view, without corroboration from humint, meaning old-fashioned human intelligence, but that would have been almost impossible because of it not being a priority. The Americans didn't try to do it anymore, and where it was feasible, thanks to the Brits and other European partners, humint would take too long to be much use. When the CIA had made the effort, the results were disastrous. For example, the case of the double - or triple - agent named Humam, who succeeded, despite warnings that were ignored, to blow himself up, killing Jennifer Mathews, the CIA sub-station chief in the Afghan town of Khost, four other Agency officers, a Jordanian intelligence operative, plus two private security guards.

Ava had taken the lesson on board. Insufficient checks, a lack of preparation, inexperience, poor agent handling skills and a rush to recruit someone in al Qaeda's inner circle were all factors in the disaster.

Intelligence collection nowadays was hard and fast. Ava knew it had to be; it was how the politicians liked it and it was what they were willing to pay for. There wasn't the budget or the patience for much else. Politicians didn't take a long view of anything, not even climate change. Tell them you're going to recruit someone close to Putin and it will take five years and cost four million dollars, and they'd give themselves a hernia laughing at you as you made your way to the exit one last time, clutching a cardboard box of belongings while your embarrassed colleagues looked the other way.

She'd worked on an exchange project at the UK's GCHQ at Cheltenham and she knew that the Brits had it worse. They struggled on a tiny budget under the non-leadership of a buffoon of a prime minister who could barely tie his own shoelaces on a good day. Even so, the Americans had pumped in millions to keep the Brits stumbling along in Washington's wake.

Despite the pressures, the UK intelligence community - and in this instance it meant the Secret Intelligence Service or SIS - tried against the odds to maintain their tradition of human intelligence gathering and sometimes they surprised even themselves by succeeding.

Ava's personal gain of having served in Area 82 - Ava had seen neither Taliban nor camels firsthand - was that as a junior analyst on a starting salary of 91k a year, she'd learned how to deal with the sexists and racists in the U.S. Department of Defense. Ava was not someone who could or would melt into the wallpaper; she was female, young, in terrific shape. Ava was also a tall redhead, and some guys found the combination intimidating. She was not in any way submissive. That and the fact that she was seen as a so-called intellectual because she was a linguist with a postgrad degree in international affairs.

But there were episodes she'd prefer to forget but couldn't - stuff that lay just below the surface and that, try as she might, she couldn't bury. The NSA was implicated. So too was she. The 'kill list', the drone strikes, the so-called night raids.

Ava quickly gained a reputation as someone who would take shit from no-one, regardless of rank. Her confidence had been reinforced by three years of classes in jiu-jitsu, a form of street fighting applicable after only three to six months of training, depending on the level of personal commitment - and Ava's commitment to whatever she chose to do was total.

The final gain was that she had been included in a unit citation for Area 82's work. The National Intelligence Meritorious Unit Citation, no less.

Not long afterwards, though, she left the NSA. It had been a hard decision, upsetting to herself and to her employers, at least for a while. But she was sure she'd done the right thing, and that she was doing the right thing now. She worked for herself as a freelance analyst, including a retainer with this bunch.

She assembled the package she wanted Halberton to see. He didn't look especially busy and Ava judged it a good moment to get his attention before something else more important came up. She sent it to him and followed it up by going over to him in person. Nothing like the personal touch.

'Take a look, please.'

'What are they?' His ginger eyebrows met in the middle when he frowned.

'IMINT from 0230 local time this morning. Standard photo-optic pass over southern China. This is Fuzhou port, southeast mainland. Handles around 35 million tons of foreign cargo a year.'

'OK. So - the shipyard is all lit up at night and it looks busy. Why?'

'One moment. A little later, same thing at Ningbo, which handles 198 million tons of foreign trade cargo a year.'

'Again - why?'

'Your question's a good one, as always.' They smiled at one another. James had hired her straight off - almost the moment she stepped out of the NSA for the last time. He'd told her she had the skills and the experience they needed at Cincinnatus.

'They're working 24/7. Looking closer at another image, this time in daylight, we can see it's not shipbuilding or any major structural work. The ships - boats - appear to be quite small. That's because they're fishing vessels. Trawlers.'

'And?'

'So I picked a couple at random from the US Navy's unclassified database, got a couple of other images, such as this one. It shows a PRC trawler a year ago. And this - a week ago. Same vessel. See the difference?'

'Should I?'

'Look at the antennae.'

'Got it. You're saying –'

'I'm saying they're installing military grade comms on their fishing fleet, their militia boats first. That radome is new. And then there's something else I dug up from our friends in Taipei. It first appeared in Taiwan Daily and I tracked it back to a Taipei University study. Seems the researchers somehow got hold of a partly redacted report from their National Security Bureau people. Seems the NSB runs networks in the major Chinese ports or on the ships. Coast watchers.'

'Humint. Agents.'

'Right. So this is a media report of an academic study which is based in turn on a summary of agents' reports, saying the PRC is calling in all older militia vessels and civilian fishing trawlers for a major refit of communications and radar.'

'That's about it, James.'

'Good work, Ava, even if it is third hand. Presumably it was leaked to make the point. Anyway, it's the corroboration we need for this to fly. Any idea how long this has been going on?'

'According to the university report, three weeks - and still being rolled out at other ports, such as Zhoushan and Xiamen. Same thing's happening all along the southeast coast.'

'Ava, I have to ask. Sorry. Devil's advocate and all. So why do we care? Does any of it matter? To us?'

'If you were chief of staff of the People's Liberation Army Navy (PLAN), James, and you were planning a blockade of Taiwan in the future, wouldn't you do this? Wouldn't it be essential, given how they use their fishing fleets to extend their hold on the South China Sea? It's a dark fleet, and deniable.'

'And this? It looks like fireflies in the dark.'

'Shipping last night right across the South China Sea.'

'Wow. I never imagined it would be so crowded.'

'It's a vast area, but busy enough so you can make out the blank areas, right?' She moved the cursor. 'There and there - and there, too. Like an eclipse, or black holes, only several at the same time.'

Ava reminded herself that her boss was a mathematician, a talented one, and this was not his field. It wasn't hers, either.

She continued, 'We can see these vessels - and there are all sorts, from oil tankers to container ships - because they have an automatic identification system or AIS. What we're definitely not seeing down there are the Chinese fishing fleets, including both militia boats and intelligence ships disguised as trawlers. Why? Because they've turned off their AIS beacons. Sometimes, it's because of illegal fishing, in others because they're intruding into other countries' exclusive economic zones and would rather we didn't notice. It's now more general and systematic. They've gone dark as they do every night and have done so for the past several months. They must be under orders to do so - I'd say it's some new standard operating procedure.'

'I didn't know linguists knew this shit.'

'Even dumbass linguists like me have to know enough to get by, including something of your world of algorithms. Now I'm going to show you a radio frequency or RF satellite image.'

He pointed at the screen. 'What are those?'

'The missing Chinese fishing boats, militia vessels, coast guard patrol boats and spy ships. Hundreds of them. And look where they were - a few hours ago.'

Ava pointed her cursor at each of what looked like a rash of glowing rice grains.

'Mischief Reef. Those you can see are using L-band and VHF communications. The location lies within the Philippines EEZ, but the Chinese have built up an artificial island and they've put in an airfield, a helipad, hangars, observation towers and radar, as well as missile shelters. Construction is still going on. AIS beacons on those boats have all been switched off.'

She moved the cursor. 'This is Whitsun Reef. Last February, 200 plus Chinese vessels anchored nearby, claiming they were sheltering from bad weather. The boats used a VHF Direct System Calling or DSC not associated with any vessel, so they were under the international community's radar. Fishing? I don't think so. Most of them have since left, but not all.'

Ava plunged on with her report, hurrying in case her boss tired of it. 'They're all part of the People's Armed Forces Maritime Militia. Co-ordinated from the centre, but built, crewed and hosted by regional and provincial authorities. They're not registered centrally, so Beijing denies responsibility for harassing our ships and those of other nations. It's a sort of maritime guerrilla force, some 20,000 strong.'

'Twenty thousand vessels - are you kidding?'

'Right. And the number is growing when there are already more fishing boats than fish in the ocean.

'And over here. See? The Scarborough Shoal, scene of a standoff between the Chinese and Philippines in 2012. Again, when you use the Hawkeye360 RF satellite imaging - it's unclassified, by the way - we can see vessels that have switched off their AIS beacons. These are in fact two Chinese coastguard patrol boats, the *Zhang Gun Hai Jing* 3502 and Chinese Coastguard vessel 3302.

'Finally, the artificial Subi Reef. Here we've the Chinese Y-8Q and KQ-200 anti-submarine and KJ-500 radar command aircraft - along with anti-submarine and troop-carrying helicopters. They're now a permanent feature, it seems, according to U.S. Defense News.'

Halberton grunted, scratched his stubbled chin. 'I'm convinced. So we have ourselves an indicator. An indicator of what I'm not sure. Let's get it out there. Keep your report tight, but let's have all the images with captions and I'll run it up the flagpole. Great work. You can write this up for The Washington Post or the LA Times. Let's see if they bite. I saw your Guardian piece, by the way.'

One of Ava's phones was ringing, and eventually she picked up.

'Yeah. Who is this?'

'Hi, Ava. You sound fierce. Bad timing? Should I call back later?'

'Do I know you?'

'Guess who?'

'Jesus. I do know that voice. Don't tell me you're calling from Beijing.'

'I'm in Dubai, sweetie. I'm calling you from the airport. I'm heading your way. Let me buy you dinner to make up for lost time. My treat.'

'Pan, is this really you? It's been forever.'

'It is indeed me, yours truly. When can we meet?'

'Sounds urgent. You can make an appointment with my secretary. Sometime next month seems a distinct possibility.'

'Hilarious, bitch. Shall we say six tomorrow…?'

Ava frowned, working out what day it was tomorrow and puzzled by her long-lost school friend's urgency. She estimated the flight time from Dubai was around 15 hours.

In the meantime, James was as good as his word. Before Ava and Pan had finished their call and had arranged to get together, he had posted Ava's offering on the website and despatched it to their subscribers, even before the cookie break, but that was the last either Ava or Halberton heard about it. She tried the papers he'd mentioned, but they weren't interested. But as Lord Tennyson wrote a long time ago, theirs wasn't to ask the reason why, only to do - and die.

# 5

## 14:50 China Standard Time, GMT +8

Lord Cabritta was a thin, irritable-looking Englishman. A powerful figure in the UK Labour Party, he was a rightist known as a Blairite - whatever that might be - and gay. Not that Qin cared one way or the other about some peevish, foreign faggot's sexual perversion or his politics, although Qin despised gays and felt an instinctive loathing for their kind. With this one, blackmail wasn't necessary. The Western world was in terminal decline, as was well known in the Party, and its leaders were both dissolute and weak, so this craven creature was no surprise. What mattered was the English visitor's prominence as a member of the 48 Group Club, the work of three secret members of the Communist Party of Great Britain. It was an organisation that had supported the CCP over the years. It still helped shape UK public attitudes towards China and had proved to be an important means of gathering political and military intelligence through its members' *guanxi* or personal contacts in Whitehall and Westminster.

Cabritta had been groomed by Beijing's ambassador to London and had been told during their several private meetings that the Briton was so special because he alone understood China and the Chinese and their place in the world. Only someone of his enormous intellect and social stature could be relied upon to get the message across. It was ego that fuelled Cabritta's ambition, and PRC intelligence had over the years perfected the art of flattery to win over the weak in mind and body.

Immaculate in a double-breasted suit and silk tie, Cabritta made a few remarks in English. He read from a note, expressing the desire for stronger relations between the two countries' political parties and pledging his county's commitment to building a 'golden era' of UK-China relations.

The phrases could have come straight out of the pages of that morning's China Daily. Perhaps they had.

Qin, his quiet smile in place, head tilted to one side, pinned the award to Cabritta's lapel. They shook hands and stepped back. They nodded and smiled. Qin had an urge to wash, or at least wipe, his right hand after the brief physical contact. The *bai pi gou*, white-skinned pig, stank of cologne. He told himself that he could afford to wait, to be polite, for this effete foreigner could be counted upon to make all the right noises when the war began. The award would help ensure he wouldn't shirk his duty in the Party's hour of need.

Next was a Frenchman, another *lao pengyou* or 'old friend' of the Party. Former prime minister Jean-Pierre Raffarin was reported to have started the prestigious France China Foundation. In 2005, while on a state visit to China, he had endorsed a law allowing China to invade Taiwan.

Qin pinned the Friendship Medal to the Frenchman's suit.

They smiled, nodded, shook hands, turning to face the cameras. Raffarin almost bowed.

Another distinguished vassal pledging obedience to the Red Emperor.

Such wonderful overseas friends who knew their places!

Qin spoke a few words. He said the medals were a special honour awarded for exceptional loyalty to the cause of the Party and the people.

His duty done, Qin retreated to his *Zhongnanhai* pool. The first snow of winter squeaked underfoot. He loved the sound and its special smell, maybe because the air was cleaner, or then again, it might have been the scent of the pines. It was a clear day, without smog, and the world seemed so still and beautiful. He walked alone along the edge of the lake, his breath leaving little clouds of steam behind. His bodyguards were deployed in a loose semi-circle, keeping pace but never getting too close. He would wash his hands at last, swim, take a nap, then face his wife and daughter over supper at the family villa on the nearby Jade Spring Hill.

***

Qin finished most of whatever was in his bowl, realising as he put down his chopsticks and sat back on his chair that he'd forgotten what it was he'd eaten. His tongue explored teeth and cheeks to discover what it was. He detected a hint of garlic and oyster sauce and the inevitable grains of rice, but other than that, he was none the wiser. He looked up and saw that his wife was watching him as if he was some rare species of animal she didn't recognise.

They hadn't spoken during the meal. Only their daughter, sitting between them in the centre of the long table, had attempted normal conversation. All she elicited with the polite, 'How was your day, Dad?' and 'hope all's well with you guys,' was the grunt of acknowledgement from her distracted and grumpier-than-usual father and a worried half-smile from her mother, who plucked at a Tiffany diamond bracelet.

'Excuse me.' Grace got up, furious, and threw down her napkin.

They watched their daughter flounce out of the room.

Qin noticed several things about his wife. She'd been to the hairdressers. She was wearing something new from Chanel and a Bulgari necklace, chunky and luminous, and doubtless very expensive. He was sure he'd not seen it before.

'Delicious,' he said, though he remembered nothing of it. His tone was sarcastic because he knew - as Emperor it was his business to know - that she only played with her food because she'd hosted two multi-course dinners already that evening, the first a formal affair with her most valuable business *guanx*i at the Michelin-starred Lei Gaden on Jinbao Street, where a single serving of fish cost 500 U.S. dollars - or the equivalent in renminbi - and the second, a more relaxed affair for friends and family, at the Grand Hyatt's famed Yue Ting Restaurant.

Red Princelings and Princesses loved to frequent five-star hotels and treated them the way Westerners made use of private members' clubs.

She would have gone on to a third dinner engagement if Qin had not let it be known, via Wang, that the Emperor was returning home for a rare family meal.

Meng Bing was powerful in her own right. What he didn't know, nor did he care to know, was how much she was worth. Millions, for sure.

Her name was her own, as was the custom in China for *tai-tais*, married women, but everyone in China knew who Meng Bing was - the wife of the Emperor - and as such, her name was like a very exclusive brand, a political Gucci or Balenciaga, to which she had sole title. If a multi-million dollar construction project needed planning permission - say 150 seals or so-called chops - Meng Bing's association with the project would ensure it sailed through the tiers of officialdom without obstruction, saving a fortune in bribes and many months, if not years, of delay. Or it might be a loan for a new highway, a seaport, a bank consortium. He knew she didn't invest a penny of her own or the family money in any of these schemes, but in return for her goodwill and her name, she would take the customary thirty percent of everything, of all revenue, and before tax. There were no written contracts, no signatures, no notes. And when the profits flowed, she directed them into the accounts of her relatives and friends, not her own.

The dependable Wang kept him informed, but more often than not, Qin was too busy playing his role of Emperor to listen to accounts of his wife's complicated deals. They no longer interested him.

Meng made her first millions when Ping An Insurance went public, and the shares rocketed. He wondered if she'd been badly stung by property giant Evergrande's huge debt and a crash in the stock's value. If she had burned her fingers, well, it was just tough. It was her own fault for playing the big capitalist. He felt no sympathy.

A proportion of her profits went abroad. She called it her safety net.

What she didn't know was that her husband knew well that some of it - so far, over two million dollars - had been paid into the accounts of her relatives in Taiwan: a younger sister, an aunt, two uncles.

'I want to talk to you about something.'

Qin waited, head to one side, the headache pounding away.

Here we go.

'There are rumours,' she began, then hesitated, watching for his reaction, but there was none. 'Rumours, you know, that something out of the ordinary is being planned by the Politburo. I heard as much this evening. My friends were chatting about it and asked me if I'd heard anything. I pretended I didn't hear. Something military.' She paused, as if summoning up her courage.

'Involving Taiwan.'

He looked back at her, quizzical smile in place, feeling as if the top of his head was about to explode.

He spoke in a low voice, not out of concern for his wife's anxiety but because of the pain in his head and neck. 'You know how rumours work in this country. Pay no attention. People who spread rumours are like those who light fires in the wilderness. They are troublemakers. Black hands - don't upset yourself.'

Not a denial, merely the usual put-down.

'The Hong Kong media…' She twisted the bracelet.

Qin raised a restraining hand. He was trying not only to restrain his wife but also his own temper. 'The Hong Kong media have been infiltrated by our enemies who take advantage of the special status of the territory. They spread lies about us. It's an infection, like a virus. They want regime change. That's why we have the new National Security Law. The editors and journalists who peddle this rubbish…'

He couldn't continue. The pain had spread down his jaw and into his teeth.

But she didn't stop, damn her.

'The South China Morning Post said only this morning that an area in the west of the Leizhou Peninsula was cordoned off to traffic for two days because of "live-fire" exercises. Did you see the article? According to our own media, a naval detachment under Southern Theatre Command conducted an amphibious landing exercise in the South China Sea in the early hours of this morning. It involved,' - here she paused, recalling the terms, 'an amphibious transport dock, helicopters, air-cushioned landing craft, whatever they are.'

'It's the PLA's profession to practice,' Qin answered. His voice was calm and little louder than a low whisper, a clear danger sign. 'It's what they do.' He pushed his chair back, readying himself to make a speedy departure.

Meng was undeterred, or it was possible she didn't notice how terrible he felt. One quality that Qin had found so attractive in the early days of their marriage had been her driven, focused and almost blind ambition. It was ambition that had kept them together, his and hers, not romance, as they climbed the Party ranks in tandem. No longer. Now he was paying the price, or so it seemed to him.

'The Hong Kong paper said the PRC has conducted 20 naval exercises involving elements of island capture in the first half of the year, far exceeding the 13 carried out during 2021. I have the clipping here, if you want to see it.' She reached down for her handbag at her feet.

Qin didn't.

The much respected South China Morning Post, now owned by Alibaba - which had removed the paper's Chinese-language website - was allowed a certain latitude because it was useful to the Party for it to be seen by the naïve as still independent. This tactic was called 'big help with a little badmouth' or *xiao ma da bangmang*.

She placed her forearm on the table, hand flat, pointing in his direction. It was a physical gesture of appeal and one that seemed almost affectionate, a reminder of their relationship as it once was. There had been a time when they'd both reached forward across that same table and held hands, when words had been unnecessary.

'Promise me something, husband. Promise me the Party is not taking China into a war. If only for the sake of Grace and the rest of our family. Please. Promise me. If you can't, then we should tell our relatives and close friends they might be better off going on a long holiday - a very long holiday - to the States or Australia. They'll understand.'

He was taken aback, quite shocked. Qin saw she was pleading with him, begging him. For once, he realised, it was no act on her part. Meng was a senior Party cadre in her own right. Whatever she'd heard, it had made her afraid - more afraid than her fear even of the Emperor in one of his bad moods - and he knew it was rare for his wife to be afraid of anything or anyone - except him, of course.

She was doing it for her family on the island. No doubt about that.

Qin stood up, gripping the armrests for support and unable to speak. His head felt like an enormous egg with a delicate shell, and if he wasn't careful, it would shatter.

He fled the dining room. The Emperor pushed past a surprised server carrying a tray, staggered into the cloakroom, slammed the door and locked it. He leaned over the basin, breathing hard and sweating. He turned both taps on full and threw up his supper, whatever it had been.

# 6

# December 3

Pan seemed surprised, but not disapproving. 'You quit?'

'I did.'

Ava sensed Pan already knew she'd changed jobs.

'I didn't think they'd let you go. You know that once you're in, you'd have to stay or something, at least until you'd finished your contract.'

'Nope. I wasn't on contract. They asked me why I was leaving and I said I was sorry, but I had other plans, and that was it. They thought it odd, I suppose, but that's all. I didn't make a big deal of it. I just wanted out.'

The two friends had met up in a basement bar they both liked on Logan Circle called the Crown and Crow. They enjoyed the laid-back vibe, the friendly staff, the Victorian decor and the extensive selection of cocktails. There were plenty of good eateries to choose from a stroll away.

The neighbourhood was a great place to be - the park like an oasis in the centre with its grass and trees and the equestrian figure of Union General Logan himself, the imposing Victorian townhouses around the circle, their historical facades lit by the streetlights, the colourful pavement forecourts of the restaurants and bars with their hanging flower baskets and picturesque lighting, the crowded tables and the gusts of laughter and music, made even more festive by the frosty air and the approach of Christmas.

Pan frowned, as if she was unhappy about Ava's news. 'They paid well, though, right? What are you doing now?'

'The NSA did pay well. I'm no longer in government, that's for sure.'

Ava did not want to talk about Afghanistan. Not with Pan, not with anyone. She did not want to talk about how it had affected her. Ava did not want to discuss targets selected by the NSA's monitoring and, in particular, about one attack on a village of 36 people, of whom only one survived, a badly wounded child. She did not want to replay any of the images in her mind. She wanted, above all else, to forget, to move on.

If only she could.

Pan was still talking. 'Private sector? One of those big corporations that works with the NSA but twice the pay, right? Booz Hamilton is one I've heard of that employs dozens of ex-NSA folk. Smart move.'

'Something like that. Now that's enough about me, what about you, Pan?' Ava didn't mention that her salary had dropped since her move, and that she was slaving away for a tiny outfit that was all but broke, stumbling from one contract to the next.

'Still singing for my supper,' Pan said with a smile. 'But it helps pay the fees.'

'So when do I call you doctor? Or professor?'

'When I'm old and grey, I guess. Not any time soon, that's for sure.'

They took their drinks and moved into the lounge section, settling side by side on a comfy sofa. Ava stretched out her long legs and cradled a Cuke Mule - lime, ginger beer and cucumber vodka. Well, vodka anyway. Pan had opted for a Wasp's Elbow - gin, maraschino, lemon, cardamom honey. She kicked off her shoes and curled her legs under her.

Pan's questioning was relentless. 'So the name of this outfit you're with is what?'

'Cincinnatus.'

'How do you spell that? No, don't bother. Explain.'

'It was one of Edward Snowden's aliases when he first reached out to journalists. Lucius Quinctius Cincinnatus was a Roman patrician and a soldier around 2,500 years ago. On the face of it, I suppose we'd call him right-wing, conservative. He opposed giving equal rights to the plebeians. Ordinary folk like you and me. Seems rather an odd choice for a whistleblower's nom de guerre, but some historians see him as a model of civic virtue. He resigned his absolute authority, along with all the perks, and went back to farming after achieving victory over invaders. He's also said to have quelled a pleb revolt and once he'd done that, he again gave up his powers as dictator of Rome and returned to his simple life.'

I'm being a bore, but she did ask, Ava told herself.

There were worse things to talk about.

'But you yourself must have hated Snowden, surely? Didn't the Department of Defense declare Snowden an enemy of the state?'

'Well, the Army did. And of course, the NSA kinda sees him as a traitor even now. I don't. In fact, he's part of the reason I quit. To me, he's a brilliant computer geek who risked all to stand up for moral principle. He's my idea of a true patriot, in fact.'

'Wow. That's a refreshing viewpoint. Good for you. But I still don't get it, Ava. Why?'

Ava wanted to relax, not go over old ground. She took a deep breath. 'Look. Okay. The NSA was listening to everything millions of Americans were saying every day, every hour - on their cellphones, on the Internet, in their emails. Billions of calls and messages. It was illegal. They lied about it, of course. And it was all so unnecessary.'

'Understandable, though, no? It was an emotional response to 9/11. The entire country was in no mood for compromise, for the niceties of morality. Not then. Everyone was feeling kind of hysterical, remember? And if you recall, it was the lovely President Bush who instructed the NSA to bug the American population without a warrant - back in 2001 and long before you joined the spooks.'

'Listen. Pan. There was this guy, Bill, at the NSA, the technical director. Back in the analogue age, he was mastering something no-one else knew anything about: metadata. Bill realised he didn't need a code to break an encrypted message, that the metadata would provide a back door. He was the pioneer, and he put it to good use. Bill predicted the three-day Middle East war in 1967. He forecast the 1979 Christmas Eve Soviet military invasion of Afghanistan. With a small group, he took this further with digital algorithms - by developing a computer program code-named THINTHREAD.'

'I'm not sure you should tell me this stuff.'

'Hey, don't worry, Pan. It's not classified, not any longer. Even Netflix is streaming a documentary about it.'

'Okay, if you say so.'

'Bill's particular algorithm could cut through billions and billions of irrelevant metadata scooped up by NSA satellites and land-based signal intelligence stations worldwide. THINTHREAD could have identified and stopped 9/11 in its tracks. It also had protections built into it for civil rights - such as the right to privacy. But the NSA shut it down. The people who ran the NSA wanted power and money. They wanted big deals, even if it meant ditching something effective and cheap as THINTHREAD. When 9/11 happened, the NSA chiefs saw the attack as a financial goldmine. They knew there were huge corporate profits to be made by outsourcing. THINTHREAD was a threat to both the huge NSA budget and the corporate contracts dished out with federal money. Bill's team was broken up, and despite his brilliance, Bill was driven into retirement. Millionaires were made after thousands of Americans lost their lives. No, Pan, Snowden's one of my all-time heroes, and as for the NSA management... Well, what can I say? That I regard it now as a criminal enterprise mired in graft comes pretty close.'

'Do they know that's how you see them?'

'Of course they don't. Not that they care. Unlike Snowden, I'm no threat. My opinions don't matter and I don't. I'm just an average American, raised in an average home by average parents in an average town and now I have a kinda average job.'

'I have seen a couple of your bylines, by the way. They're what prompted me to get in touch. I thought it must mean you were no longer with the federal government, but I wasn't sure. And let's be clear: you're in no way average.'

'Snowden is way out of my league, honey. He might have been self-educated, but he's brilliant. I'm a mere linguist, remember?'

Ava drained her glass. 'Same again - or something different?'

'It's my round,' Pan said, jumping to her feet. 'And I'll choose.'

'Be my guest,' laughed Ava, and sank back into the cushions. Her friend must have landed that same afternoon, but she gave no sign of being tired after her long flight. What Ava was determined not to do was confide in Pan about her experiences. It was too upsetting, too painful - and she was sure Pan wouldn't understand. Why should she?

***

Ava and Pan had agreed on Le Diplomat on 14th Street. Ava called ahead, and it turned out a table for two was available. Pan chose the petit plateau of fruits de mer. She said that was all she wanted. Ava, who liked to eat well, picked the duck. They shared a bottle of Chablis.

They talked films and books, about old friends, school pals half-forgotten, about London. It was inconsequential stuff, the things people liked to talk about because it was familiar ground, made them feel comfortable and restored a measure of their old rapport. Anyone listening in would have found it dull girl talk.

'You remember what they used to call us back at school?'

Ava did. 'The Red and the Black - your black hair, my red. And my freckles. After one of my all-time favourite novels, too, but I guess those kids had never heard of Stendhal.'

In fact, Ava didn't know that much about Pan. They had been classmates at an expensive private day school for girls in the west London borough of Hammersmith called Godolphin & Latymer. It had been a great school that achieved excellent academic results. Unlike so many private schools in the UK, it didn't cull those who seemed unlikely to make the best grades. Once they'd accepted someone - and the entrance exam was formidable - the school stuck with them and helped them through the usual ups and downs of adolescence to do the very best they could. It was loyal to its students. After all, the parents were paying huge fees for the privilege. For three years, Ava and Pan had shared a sense of humour, a love of books and a loathing for hockey - and then they had gone their separate ways but kept in touch with cards and the occasional call or text message. That was pretty much it.

Ding Pan wasn't Pan's real name, Ava knew. If she had a real name, that is. It was the Chinese name one of her Chinese 'uncles' had given her, or so she'd told Ava back in school. She was born in China of Japanese parents, and she had both Japanese and Chinese names, switching from one to the other at will as she tried her best to melt into the background of whatever country she found herself in, especially as the Chinese Communist Party spent a lot of time and treasure fostering hatred for everything Japanese, churning out anti-Japanese books and films every year, while the Japanese suspected that 'Niki Kawashima' wasn't 'pure' Japanese but was sullied by Chinese impurities. She was, of course, fluent in Mandarin, Cantonese and Japanese and their linguistic ability was something else they had in common. Pan also had a show business name for her singing career as well. Sabine Lee (or Li) had a talent that had proved sufficiently successful to pay her rent and the fees for her postgrad studies. Ava remembered Pan saying at some point that her paternal grandfather had been a Japanese-American and had been interned during World War Two on the West Coast, hence her U.S. citizenship.

Ava often wondered about Pan's political views, if she had any.

And there was that family tragedy that Pan never talked about.

'So you're working for the Asia-Pacific Security Program, right?'

'Uh-huh.' Pan didn't like discussing herself any more than Ava did.

'Based where?'

'Here - and there.' Another guarded response.

'Where's there?'

Pan gave in with a sigh. 'The Gortyn-Tsinghua Center for Global Policy. In Beijing.'

'Wow. Tsinghua is famous. The best university in the PRC, it's said. That's impressive, Pan!'

'Yeah? We bury anything controversial in academic jargon and double-talk. You should listen to some of our public podcasts. They'd send you straight to sleep. Talking a lot and saying nothing is an art form. I'm already an expert in obfuscation, believe you me. I know how to dodge ideological bullets.'

Ava recognised the remark as deflection so typical of Pan.

'So your job is - what?'

'Senior fellow. I've got my doctorate at last.'

'Jesus, that's brilliant, Dr Pan!'

'I'm glad you think so, my dear.' Pan raised her glass of Chablis. 'To the brilliant pair!'

They drank a toast to each other.

Ava thought Pan would make a terrific spy. Was she one?

They were so different in appearance. Pan was petite, quick on her feet, fiery, with long black hair that seemed almost luminous, prominent cheekbones, epicanthic eyes, a smashing smile and a natural squash player. She was gorgeous. Ava was tall, languorous, with impossibly long legs and quite clumsy - at least, she thought she was clumsy compared to her agile former schoolfriend. Ava was a striking redhead with very white skin and freckles on her nose. She kept her hair short. She gleamed with athletic good health and vitality, and she'd been a talented basketball player at school and university, even if she said so herself.

'So where's your office, Ava?'

'Adams Morgan.'

'Trendy!'

'So they tell me.'

'Then explain to me, please, what this Cincinnatus does.'

'It's an open source intelligence, or OSINT organisation.'

'Whatever that is.'

'You must know, Professor.'

'If I knew, I wouldn't ask.' There was a flash of steel in that retort.

'Imagine that your foundation comes under cyber attack in Beijing. It happens to the best people, I assure you. So you ask us to help you fix your operational security or OPSEC. We do this by carrying out a reconnaissance of your websites and your communications, your servers and so on. We use programs such as Mitaka, Spiderfoot, Darksearch.io, Intelligence X, yeah? Maybe you know them in your own line of work. We pinpoint any vulnerabilities. We report these to you and then, if you want, we fix them. Can take days, weeks, months.'

'I get it. And right now you're working on something China-related?'

'Right, but if I told you the details, I'd have to shoot you.'

Pan rolled her eyes. That old cliche, for Chrissakes.

'It's about Exclusive Economic Zones in the South China Sea. There's a lot of reading to do, and quite a lot of computer analysis. I look at open Chinese sources, especially maritime and military commentaries. My current project is for a Singapore bank with extensive shipping and maritime interests.'

No-one knew mainland China better than the Singaporeans.

Ava drank coffee, Pan preferred tea.

They asked for the check - or bill, as Pan would have it in UK English.

'I've a confession to make,' Pan said after a long pause.

'I thought you might.'

'You knew?'

'All I know, Pan, is that you don't go out of your way to see an old friend out of nostalgia or because you feel sentimental about your old school. It isn't you.'

'Ouch. Touché.'

'True though, right?'

Pan insisted on paying. Ava put up a fight, so they split it rather than spoil the evening by bickering.

Pan confessed. 'OK. You're right, I guess. I'm not sentimental, it's true. Someone I know needs help. I thought of you. I made some checks, ok? You have the language skills and the experience. This contact is very senior, very powerful, and he has something very important to say. He won't go to the Americans and he won't go to the British. Or the Japanese. Or even the Australians. He doesn't trust them. He wants it made public, but he has to protect himself. If he was revealed as the source, or suspected as being the source, it would mean his arrest, torture and execution - and that goes for his family, too. Assuming he has one.'

'Christ. Another Snowden. A whistleblower.'

'Something like that. Only he's a senior member of the Chinese Communist Party and close to the General Secretary.'

'Qin. Party General Secretary, Chairman of the Central Military Commission and President. A hardline autocrat who's shutting up shop as far as the West is concerned and reimposing total Party control over nearly everything. A real bastard if we can believe what we read.'

'Right. That's what Fox News and CNN would like us to think.'

'Where do you come into all this?'

'I'm the messenger. I'm desperate, Ava. You're the only person I trust and who can handle this. We haven't got much time. You'll need an air-gapped computer, a laptop, whatever, and I'll provide the rest.'

Ava didn't want to get involved. No way. She knew that much.

'Your friend could defect,' she said. 'He could get exit visas for himself and his family for a holiday someplace in Asia and keep going and not return. Kuala Lumpur might be a good choice. Or Bangkok. He wouldn't be the first. If he's as important as you say he is, the U.S. government would protect him, provide him with a new identity, give him a job and a home.'

'He's not a friend, but a contact. He wouldn't get away with it. Not in his case. He's a *gaogan*, a high-level official, a member of the Red Aristocracy. You know these people. Born into wealthy Party circles, they qualify for the top jobs. No way they'd let him go. They'd track him down. That's what they do. Let's say he takes his family on holiday in Cyprus, then he vanishes when he leaves his hotel to buy cigarettes or to take a stroll on the beach. No-one would be the wiser. He would vanish - for good. He doesn't trust the Americans or the UK. Even if they did as you suggest, the information he has would be kept secret by the Americans because they see their relationship with Beijing as too important to jeopardise over some defector. That's why he wants it made public before anyone can shut him up and put a lid on it. It's urgent, and he doesn't trust any government to publicise it. He's right not to.'

'Do you know what this information is?'

'Up to a point. And he doesn't want to defect. He wants to stay where he is and continue to report on what's going on. I call that brave - even foolhardy.'

There it was. That was what this meeting was about - the drinks, the ambience, the food. It was all about this mysterious, nameless person and his secrets. Pan had sought Ava out not out of friendship but because she was seen as being of some use after her apprenticeship with the NSA and now that she was getting play in the media with her research.

Fucking nerve!

'Why don't you distribute the material yourself?'

'Because I'd be arrested or thrown out of the country. I'm watched. We all are in Beijing. All foreigners. You do know, don't you, that there are 600 million surveillance cameras in the PRC? They use facial recognition. I'm monitored the moment I go out of my front door. They listen to our phones, watch us online. The neighbours are tasked to watch us. Same goes for cleaners and drivers. In China, you never open up to people, not even people you count as friends. I'm especially suspect because of my mixed background. That's why I need you to do this for me, Ava. I can't trust anyone else. I can't. There isn't anyone else - if there was, I wouldn't be begging you because that's what I'm doing. I'm begging you and I'm sorry, okay?'

Pan looked upset.

Ava listened to the appeal in silence, both embarrassed and annoyed.

'What's he like, your source?'

'I don't know, to be honest, other than that his material is first rate.'

'What do you mean, you don't know?'

What the fuck was this?

'We've never met. I know nothing about my source - his name, age, marital status, his job, his Party position. All I know is that he has the most incredible access.'

'That word incredible - it's too incredible. How can you expect people to take it seriously if you can't name your source, or at least provide some detail? And why do you assume your source is male? This could be a provocation to discredit you, your work and the institution you work for.'

Pan raised her hands, a gesture that seemed to express a desire to placate, to appease Ava. 'Almost everyone above a certain level in the CCP is male. It's a patriarchy. I can think of only one minister who's female. It's the way it is.'

'So you expect publishers and readers to accept at face value contentious material from an unnamed source? You expect me to?'

'You'll see. Anyway...' Pan's voice dropped, and she looked upset. 'If you won't do this, say so.'

Ava would not admit it, but as much as she didn't want to get involved in this madness, she was intrigued. Maybe because it was mad and Pan had figured as much.

'So what are you asking me to do, Pan? What do you want?'

'Do you have an air-gapped laptop?'

'I can get one at my office.'

'Take these. It's a plug-in Hardware Security Monitor or HSM along with the 256-bit master key on a plug-in card. The HSM has an anti-tampering device built into it.' Pan opened her left hand and there they were. She had come prepared, having assumed her friend would comply.

'I can see that. What's on it?'

'Crypto for the messages.'

'Pretty Good Privacy - PGP?'

'No way. This is much better. It's ChaCha.'

'I thought it was a dance, like Salsa or something.'

'Hilarious. If you use AES, it's fine - but it's a block cipher and someday someone will find a way in. ChaCha is a stream cipher and unbreakable. It's also fast. You'll be able to decrypt the stuff from my contact, translate it, then copy it onto another thumb drive, insert it into your usual computer and try to get it out there on the web. I'd aim for The Intercept. The Project 2049 Institute, too. UK Declassified is another. Media Lens. Asia Times. Fair. Truthdig. I'm sure you know better than I who'd want this. Your Cincinnatus website and its subscribers, if you can do so without getting into trouble with your boss. Your contacts in the ROC. The Taiwanese might substantiate some of it, at least. I'd suggest widening the market. Facebook. Instagram. Twitter. People won't believe it at first, but they will. Independent Chinese media, such as Tang Dynasty News, might like it. With some, you'll have to be careful. Reuters, for example, is far too close to the CCP's Xinhua News Agency. The same goes for Bloomberg - they're compromised. So is your Guardian newspaper. We have to hope we're not too late.'

'Too late for what?'

'Only the next war, my sweet, coming our way soon.'

Ava lost all patience.

'What the hell are you talking about, Pan?'

# 7

# December 4

## 10:10 Eastern Standard Time, GMT -4

Pan sat in a yellow wing-back armchair, her favourite, feet tucked under her, looking out of the third-floor sitting-room window at the drifting snow. It was, she realised, a Saturday, so there wasn't much traffic inside the Beltway. The local news reported stoppages and roadworks on the 1-66 in Arlington, but nothing else seemed to be going on. No one out there knew - or if they did know, they probably didn't care - that it was the first day of the countdown to a war that could consume them all.

It was Day 59, yesterday having set the clock ticking on the Taiwan invasion if Pan's informant was to be believed. Pan certainly did believe, or she wouldn't have placed herself knowingly in jeopardy. She might have done better pushing a pin into a map and at random, picking one of the smallest of some 25,000 islands in the Malay Archipelago, for example, but they'd still find her, she reasoned, given time and the effort required to do so. They had the resources, and they weren't stupid. How much easier it would be for her pursuers to locate her here in the Kawashima family's Washington home. Once her father's and now hers.

She kept it the way she remembered it, adding nothing, taking nothing away. It was what realtors called unmodernised and Pan wouldn't have it any other way. A cleaner came once a fortnight, that was all, and vacuumed and dusted. It was rather grand, as apartments go, and sparsely furnished. A four-seat sofa in pale blue, the armchair she was sitting on, a round, drop-side Regency table, a huge Martial Raysse abstract worth a fortune - bought long before the artist became well known - above the fireplace, a standing light in one corner, a chandelier, and that was it. The only decoration - it wasn't really a decoration - was a large hardwood antique Buddha from Myanmar, still gilded in gold leaf. Her parents' old teak bed in the main bedroom, a Persian rug of blue and pink on the floor, and in the kitchen a battered table and three kitchen chairs (what had happened to the fourth?). Her own bedroom wasn't much better, a small double, a bedside table and lamp, a cream rug in the shape of a cloud from her childhood, a cheap white chest of drawers stuffed with her gear.

Mock-Gothic on the outside, art nouveau inside, the building had an eccentric charm about it. The stairs creaked and the old, rather uneven parquet floors inside the three-bed apartment creaked, too, as if they were conversing together. The walls were oak panelled, even the marble-topped bathroom furniture seemed ancient, and the copper pipes never failed to gurgle and shake like thunder. There were still the old Delft tiles on the bathroom walls and the huge, ungainly taps were Victorian.

They'd guess that Pan would make a run for home.

She told herself she had done what she could. It would be up to Ava to find the courage to follow this through. There was nothing more Pan could do, or so it seemed. She'd broken the link, and there was no reason why they should connect Pan with Ava.

Then there was the news.

Pan couldn't resist it, even now, using her online Kawashima identity to scan the latest.

- Li Yundi, China's 'prince of the piano' has been abruptly boycotted and banned from posting online after police announced his detention on suspicion of soliciting a prostitute. Whether he had done so wasn't really the point. The charge wasn't a big deal - it would usually lead to 10-15 days in administrative detention, but the arrest and Weibo ban on Li - despite, or because of, his having 20 million followers - followed a pattern seen with other celebrities who ran foul of sensitive political issues.

- The European Parliament voted in a landslide to adopt a report on Taiwan that urged urgent preparation of a bilateral investment deal - despite a Beijing envoy's strenuous efforts to influence the vote.

- Taiwan unveiled the first generation of a battery-powered exoskeleton suit that could enhance the physical endurance of soldiers and increase mobility.

- The People's Liberation Army warned of its determination to crush any attempt to separate Taiwan from the mainland after it carried out beach landing and assault drills in the province directly across the Strait from the island.

- Japan had sent mobile electronic warfare units to Taiwan to monitor activity in the Strait, bringing the number of Japanese forces on the island to around 250 personnel.

- Taiwanese President Tsai Ingwen said the island and the mainland should not be 'subordinate to each other' in an apparent rebuff to President Qin's call for peaceful cross-strait reunification.

- Fifty-six PLA fighter jets - the most in a single day so far - entered Taiwan's air defence identification zone following months of such flights.

- Taiwanese Defence Minister Chiu Kuocheng said Beijing would be 'fully able' to invade Taiwan by 2025.

- Satellite images revealed China was upgrading and reinforcing its major air-bases - Longtian, Huian and Zhangzhou - along its southeast coast close to Taiwan, indicating Beijing may be stepping up its plans to take the island by force.

No shit, Sherlock!

- The PLA was training military nurses using a boat simulator to prepare them for combat involving an island landing.

- Chinese and Indian military commanders were deadlocked over the best way to pull back troops from a strategic area in the Himalayas.

Etcetera.

Pan decided she would not venture out of the apartment. She was under siege. There was enough to eat in the larder - cereal, rusks, tinned tuna, ham, cheese and fruit, pasta, bottled pesto, beans. As soon as she'd reached home after the dinner with Ava, she'd torn off her clothes and taken a shower. Thankfully, the hot water system still worked. She'd pulled on a pair of pyjamas she found under her pillows and slept a solid 10 hours.

When she needed the lights on, she was careful to first draw the curtains.

As she polished off a bowl of granola and powdered milk in the kitchen, the doorbell rang from downstairs. Again. And again. She heard a male voice, in English, out on the doorstep. 'Hello? Hello?'

Pan ignored both buzzer and the voice.

\*\*\*

Pan started on one of her father's books, social anthropology and a fascinating but dense account of the lives of hunter-gatherers and the first urban centres in pre-history Mesopotamia, but she felt drowsy and slept again until the afternoon, telling herself it was jet lag.

She longed to call someone, anyone, if only to hear a friendly voice, but she resisted the temptation. She would have liked to have spoken to Ava, to ensure everything was okay between them, and so she could be reassured that Ava was still on track to carry out her tasks as Pan had so carefully explained.

She thought about going out, venturing to a nearby brasserie for a decent meal, or just to the corner shop run by a friendly South Asian family to buy fresh milk, bread and eggs, but she decided against it, though it would have made her feel so much better to see a smiling face and exchange a few words, even for the half a minute or so that the transaction took to complete.

It was cold. Pan pulled on a sweater and leggings.

She drew all the curtains, then put on the lights to cheer herself up. With a wool blanket over her knees, she sat down in her armchair and picked up a collection of Tolstoy short stories. Pan called it literary comfort food.

She still felt as remote as a lone Arctic explorer.

It was that sense of isolation and loneliness that prompted Pan to run to the front door of the apartment when she heard knocking and scratching.

She looked through the peephole, but all she could see was a dim outline.

'Who is it?'

'Is that you? I heard some noise earlier and wondered who it was.'

'Who is this?'

'It's Mr Lund. Your neighbour in 312. Remember? Is everything alright?'

His voice was weak and kind of trembly.

'Hello, Mr Lund. So sorry to have disturbed you.'

'Not at all. Not at all. You're not disturbing us. Can you open the door? I can't hear you.'

Mr Lund started knocking rather feebly at the door again.

He was worried, poor old fellow.

Pan unbolted the door, unlocked it, dropped the chain.

She was about to open it, pulling it towards her, but what occurred next was so fast, so unexpected, that she couldn't grasp what was happening.

The door was driven inwards from the outside with such force that Pan lost her balance and started to topple backwards into her own hallway. She didn't see the elderly pensioner, Lund, or Mrs Lund, but she glimpsed the form of two strangers, male and bulky in their winter coats, but that was all - just a glimpse. Next came a blow out of nowhere - a fist that exploded in her face, striking her jaw and right cheekbone, snapping the former and cracking the latter.

As Pan's feet left the ground and she crashed to the floorboards, brilliant lights flashed in her brain and went out.

# 8

## 10:16 China Standard Time, GMT +8

The Emperor floated. He lay on his back, his back arched, arms and legs outstretched, chin up, water around his face like a nun's cowl. His eyes were open, although there was nothing to see unless he moved his eyeballs to the right. A figure stood there, a man in white and black.

Outside, it was freezing.

Wang was waiting for him. Qin said nothing. Wang was the figure Qin had glimpsed, the bloke in black pants and white shirt, hands clasped in front of him. Silent, respectful, alert like a soldier standing at ease. He'd removed his long, padded coat and fur hat because it was so warm in the pool area.

Qin paddled with his hands, so he turned, slid over onto his belly and touched the bottom of the pool with his toes.

'We'll have tea,' he said. 'Get yourself a cup.'

Wang Zhenrong was chief of his innermost circle of bodyguards. He wore two hats; one was that of a senior member of the Central Commission for Discipline Inspection (CCDI), the highest Party control agency for protecting the leadership and fighting corruption and malfeasance within the Party - and it was also Qin's primary weapon of choice for purging the system of malcontents and removing potential rivals. The other was that of a brigadier-general of the Central Security Bureau, which came under the *Gong'anbu*, or Ministry of Public Security. There were three layers in the Emperor's guard force at the *Zhongnanhai*. Wang was head of the first CCDI layer, then the 1,000 armed bodyguards of the Central Security Bureau. They patrolled the paths, walkways, gardens and lakes of the complex, then the outermost ring - deployed at the gates and outside the high red walls - was formed by patrols and static posts of armed troops from a special PLA battalion garrisoned nearby.

'Sit.'

They sat on the lounger, side by side, the small table with the teapot and cups before them.

'You play mother,' said Qin. 'My hands are wet.'

Wang obeyed.

'How is the weather out there today?'

'Five below. Could be worse.'

'And your family? How are they?'

'Well, thank you.'

Qin grunted. He could imagine it on the streets and was glad he was where he was and not sliding and slipping on icy pavements.

'So, tell me your news.'

'We have them both in custody.'

'No trouble?'

Wang shook his head. 'No trouble.'

'The families?'

Wang put down his cup. 'As you'd expect, chief.'

'And how did our friends react when they were detained?'

Wang thought for a moment, took a deep breath.

'Well. Let's see. Li Lijun went quiet, said not a word. He was calm. Hugged his wife and children, put on his coat, hat and scarf - and went out with us to the street as if he was on his way to work, except it was 3 a.m. We didn't even need to cuff him. You might say he was polite and dignified. That was that. Easy.'

Li was a former vice minister and former head of Unit 601, the security force charged with the active suppression of the Falun Gong movement.

'What about our other pal, Shi Zhengua?'

'Altogether different, that one. Yes. Tried to pull rank. When that didn't work, he shouted for his bodyguards - who'd already been taken care of and ordered to stay clear - and swore at us. Lots of abuse. Called us bandits, bastards, merce- naries. Spat at us. He tried to act the bully. We had to hit his knees with a baton and once he was down on the floor, squealing like a stuck pig and with a nose- bleed, we cuffed him, then four of our people dragged him to the van. His wife was screaming, too. You might say it wasn't an easy arrest, but once we had him in the van, he quietened down soon enough.'

Shi was a former head of the Public Security Bureau in Beijing. Qin hadn't expected him to go quietly. The man was a thug, after all.

They were both members of former general secretary Jiang Zemin's circle, a powerful network of *guanxi* that Qin was determined to isolate, then break. These two would be held in the CCDI's unofficial prisons, and a long way away from anywhere of any significance. It would be a message to the rest of them.

'Think they'll co-operate?'

'Oh, yes, chief, everyone co-operates in the end,' Wang said. 'At least, the intelligent ones do. They want to live, and they want their families to do so, too. They don't want to lose everything, after all. They've so much to lose as we remind them.'

General Wang showed his teeth, a wolfish leer.

'Good. We'll keep them locked up for six months to a year, depending on how long they take to see sense. Then we'll bring them to court and charge them. Serious violations of discipline. Overweening political ambition. Arbitrary disagreements with central Party guidelines. Creating and spreading political rumours. Get the picture? They'll confess to a conspiracy to undermine the Party - and beg the court to be merciful. Then they'll apologise to the Party. We will be lenient; they'll get ten years. If not...' He didn't have to spell it out. If they failed to confess and show remorse, they'd disappear for good, shot in the back of the head, their remains thrown in a ditch somewhere in China's most remote mountains or deserts. Their families would be tossed out of their Party homes, too.

'Let's have more tea. Then take a couple of hours off, Wang. Go home to your wife. You must have been up all night. We don't need you until this afternoon.'

\*\*\*

Qin recognised it was a problem, though, and hard to finesse. Someone like Jiang Zemin might be ancient and long retired, but he and many others like him still had residual power as rallying points for ambitious men who sought greatness, who disagreed with Qin's leadership, who saw their path blocked by Qin's authority. The Emperor tried to separate and fragment these bubbles of dissident influence. Allowing them to coalesce would be a fatal error. He permitted the survivors of the previous generation to keep their Party privileges, their homes, their family wealth, but he did his best to strip them of their influence, to isolate them, and that was hard to do. Two years earlier, the Emperor had approved a magnanimous gift of 12 million U.S. dollars to every surviving national leader for their service to the Party. The lesson he wanted them to take on board was that if they were sensible and reasonable, they'd enjoy their advantages, but that they should leave it at that and forget all about politics.

Shi and Li had not been content with the trappings and had wanted power for themselves. Being a senior cadre and reaching the position of vice-minister wasn't enough. Now they had had their wings clipped, and it would send a powerful message to their Jiang Zemin pals: you can venture out of line only so far, comrades. Jiang Zemin himself was untouchable, of course. He might not have even been aware of the sedition rising like a tide around his ankles and the use of his name as a 'roof'.

Most of the Red Princes and their offspring were corrupt one way or another, and those few that weren't, well, they were easy to fix. Faked accounts, false allegations by a vulnerable associate or informer, something buried in the family history, a criminal act by a key ally or retainer - the CCDI never failed to cook something up if Qin ordered it.

There used to be a storage facility in the *Zhongnanhai* packed to the rafters with secret files on Party cadres. All it had taken was a telephone call to one of the archivists to have it dusted off then placed on the Emperor's desk. Or bed, in Qin's case. Nowadays, it's all digital. Wang would have whatever Qin needed almost instantly on screen at the tap of his index finger on a keyboard.

The difficulty was that this system - the *guanxi* networks of the Red Aristocracy - had been Qin's own route to unchallenged, absolute power. He'd been born into it, raised in it, moved up the ranks by manipulating the same system to his own benefit and out-manoeuvring his rivals. Qin knew the game and excelled at it. He'd risen as a crafty, bureaucratic in-fighter, and he maintained his power through the connections he'd built himself as he rose in the Party, through old debts owed and paid, favours bought and sold in committees and across boardroom tables. He couldn't sweep it all away because to do so would be to cut off his own legs, so to speak, leaving him friendless, isolated and without support - he'd find himself in the very position he wanted for everyone else. The Red Aristocracy had to be preserved. There was no practical alternative Qin could see, but these Party networks had to be tamed, trimmed, kept in line, subjugated - and from time to time, crushed and culled. Now and then he had to send a message by cutting off a branch or felling a particular tree in the forest of ambitious cadres. Li and Shi were the latest sacrifices to Party unity, to Party authority, to Qin's own survival as Emperor.

And Wang, head of the Central Security Bureau's 1,000 imperial 'bodyguards', was his chief enforcer. Which made him doubly dangerous.

Qin knew also that Wang's Central Security Bureau had acted as kingmaker in the past. It too was not something an Emperor could afford to forget.

***

Qin wouldn't travel by helicopter. He didn't trust the machines. He preferred road or rail, even on his rare foreign trips - but if time and distance were the issue, then he'd fly by fixed-wing aircraft. Qin didn't have his own plane, unlike his Western counterparts. Putin had an entire fleet of them, something Qin thought vain and absurd. Qin didn't believe in ownership of such expensive toys because he thought it a waste when they sat idle in their hangars. It also sent the wrong environmental message, and what personal ownership would say about him, even if he was Emperor.

His usual practice was to borrow an aircraft when he needed it from Air China, and they had two Boeing 747-400s available if the General Secretary needed to fly somewhere. They and their crews were vetted by the *Gong'anbu* for each mission, and one or the other plane would be refitted with a living area, a bedroom and an office. When not required, the two Boeings reverted to regular passenger flights.

Today, he was expected to drop in on one of the Hudong–Zhonghua shipyards in Shanghai in his capacity as Chief of the Central Military Commission.

He was driven to the airport in a black Hongqi L5 - a luxury, four-wheel-drive, four-door limo, flying the national flag. There were three of them, all armoured and identical in every way, two of them packed with his armed bodyguards, led by Wang himself. Only Qin always chose at the last possible moment which of the three he would use. They'd open the rear passenger door of the first, but he would ignore the courtesy and stride past over to the second or the third, or confuse everyone by changing his mind and going into reverse, heading back to the first, always ensuring that he kept his bodyguards on the hop, dodging from one Red Flag limo to the other and having to run to get on board in time as the column moved off.

Sometimes he sat in the back, sometimes up front.

It wasn't a whimsical decision. He knew his life might depend on it.

The three limos were followed by more close protection officers in two chase cars.

His convoy never stopped at traffic lights, of course.

Sitting in the rear of the second limo, Qin was carried along through an underground road - a six-lane highway - from the *Zhongnanhai* to Beijing International Airport, and the three limos drove without stopping onto the runway to the foot of the steps leading to the waiting Boeing, while the chase cars held back. Other officials - the armed forces chief of staff, the navy chief and the minister of defence - were already waiting.

He had prepared a pep talk for his audience at the shipyard.

Two hours and twenty minutes later, Qin stood - now changed into a short-sleeved shirt and open collar - at a lectern in the Pengu yard, surrounded by the clatter and clang of industry hard at work in a firework festival of acetylene torches. Shipyard and maritime officials stood around him, along with Qin's fellow passengers. Ranks of PLAN sailors in immaculate white uniforms stood at attention on the dock. Red flags fluttered above their heads from the blue-painted cranes and lifts. A dozen of Wang's armed bodyguards in dark suits formed an outer perimeter.

The occasion marked a watershed of sorts. First, the *Hainan* had completed her second round of sea trials and was now on active service in the South China Sea. Her successor had that very day finished fitting out and was about to put to sea. Most important of all, Qin was about to launch the third in class and he started by announcing - he was actually smiling - an order for the fourth.

China's Type 075 Amphibious Assault Ships were formidable, each displacing 40,000 tons with a full-length flight deck for helicopters, a flooded rear deck to float off amphibious tanks and troop carriers, and room for at least a battalion of marines for a beach landing.

There would be no shortage of work in the shipyards, quite the opposite. Aside from modifications to the fishing fleet and militia boats and construction of new landing craft, the pace of warship building was astounding. Only the previous week, the PLAN had launched the last of its 056 class - in all 76 corvettes in 10 years. The day of Qin's visit also marked the launch of the second in China's new class of large guided missile destroyers, each displacing some 13,000 tons.

Qin handed over a seal of the amphibious assault ship's commission and then a navy standard to the commander, the grey bows of the third ship in its class towering above them and providing them with shade from a blazing Shanghai sun.

'Word hard, work fast,' he growled over the microphone to the sailors and a selected group of shipyard workers in red safety helmets. 'The country depends on you. The Chinese people are depending on you. The Party depends on you. All of you. Each and every one. Do not shirk your duty. Do not cut corners. Do not let your families and your workmates down. You should do your best work. China will soon be put to the test. You will soon be put to the test. We face a battle for our survival and our ultimate victory depends on your skills - on you and no-one else.'

Qin had learned from Trump to keep his speech short and very simple. Simple truths, simple words, resonated with the masses.

No mention of Taiwan, of course, but everyone knew what he meant.

Nodding and smiling, Qin moved through the crowd, feeling the headache stir. He was sweating and hoped his hair dye wouldn't run down his face or neck. It was a balmy 18 degrees Celsius in Shanghai. He glanced over at Wang. Wang understood; the Emperor was uncomfortable and wanted to go home to the *Zhongnanhai* and his precious pool. Now.

# 9

# December 6

Deep cold swept into the northeast United States overnight on Sunday. Howling gales brought down power lines, sweeping the streets of DC with stinging flurries of horizontal snow and hail that piled up faster than the ploughs could clear it. There was no way Ava was going to cycle to work, and peering out of her window into the murk she saw few motorists about.

Ava hadn't heard from Pan over the weekend. She'd put off calling her friend because she hoped that business of secret messages from some unknown CCP source would evaporate without further discussion. She thought she'd made it clear that she wasn't all that keen to help, and that with a little time and distance, the message would sink in. Ava hoped Pan could find some other way to get whatever it was out in public.

Good manners got the better of Ava once she'd braved the blizzard, stumbled through the glass doors of the Cincinnatus office, said a hearty good morning to the receptionist, unwound her scarf, removed her woolly hat and finally settled down at her desk, keeping her long coat on and wrapping her blanket around her knees. She told herself she should at least thank Pan for having arranged their reunion. It had turned out to be a very enjoyable evening together, and it had been great to see her again. Perhaps they'd talk now without mentioning 'it'. Yes, Ava hadn't given Pan a definitive answer, only hinted at her reluctance. On the one hand, it did sound fascinating - China was her primary subject of interest, after all - and she didn't want to refuse her friend. Ava was fond of Pan. Though there were too many unanswered questions. If she was honest, she couldn't help but resent the fact that Pan had sought her out after such a long separation, less out of friendship than her potential usefulness in whatever this was. Could be she

was being petulant, even selfish, but Ava did feel a little let down, as if her friendship had been abused, especially as the project seemed so risky in all sorts of
ways.

Why didn't Pan tackle it herself? If being in Beijing was too great a risk, why
not take a leave of absence and work on it Stateside, given its importance?

She tried twice to get through, but Pan's mobile seemed switched off.

Pan had told Ava she was staying in her family's old place on Massachusetts
Avenue NW. Pan didn't rent it out because she said she wanted to use it from
time to time on her rare visits to the States. She'd passed on the street number
to Ava: 1143A, adding that it was an old-fashioned apartment, complete with
wood-panelled walls, creaking hardwood floors, and a wrought-iron balcony.
She'd joked that it had a slow and noisy museum piece of a lift she was afraid to
use in case it collapsed or got stuck while she was in it.

It took Ava a little while, but during her lunch break - it being too miserable to
venture outside - she found a landline number.

She was taken aback when a male voice answered. Ava explained who she was
- she didn't give her name but said she was a friend of Pan's, and the voice - to
Ava's considerable shock - identified itself as belonging to Pan's father, but she
gave no sign of her confusion and dismay. Ava also discovered that Pan was
indeed staying there, or should be, and that this man who said he was her father
had returned from his trip on the Friday morning, earlier than planned, a detail
Pan had omitted to mention.

Except, of course, as Ava knew perfectly well, Pan had no father.

'She didn't come home on Friday night - or Saturday morning,' said the gruff
voice in English with a distinct accent. 'I haven't seen my daughter all weekend.
Have you spoken to Pan? Have you seen her, had a coffee or whatever? Do you
know where she is?'

'No, I'm sorry. I haven't seen Pan or spoken to her at all.'

'Do you have a number, please? An address?'

'I'm sorry.'

'I forgot your name. You're...'

Ava cut the connection.

During this anxious exchange of lies, Ava watched a UPS courier approach
her desk and drop a padded envelope into her in-tray. It was addressed to her,
and she scrawled her signature on the courier's hand-held screen. She noted its
point of origin: Dubai.

The front door to the apartment on Massachusetts Avenue was open. The place had been ransacked. Soft furnishings - the sofa cushions - had been slashed open and torn apart. So had the wing-backed chair and mattresses on the three beds. Papers were scattered everywhere, drawers had been pulled out of the chests in the two bedrooms, the contents dumped on the floor. Plates and other crockery had been smashed in the kitchen along with a jar of mustard, another of tomato sauce and several cans and packets of food trampled underfoot. All the shelves and cupboards had been cleared, the contents swept onto the floor. Even the curtains had been ripped, the blinds pulled down, the television smashed.

The old-fashioned cistern above the toilet had been broken, and water streamed down the bathroom wall. The shower curtain had been torn down, the bath mat and rolls of toilet paper tossed in a corner along with soap, shower gel and nail brush, skin cream, shampoo and towels. Detective Kramer gazed about him, shaking his head. 'Whoever it was, they were in one hell of a hurry.'

They were also thorough, Ava thought, squeezing out toothpaste, face cream and shampoo.

After examining the front door, Kramer announced it appeared to have been opened by someone on the inside.

'Someone was here and let them in.'

Of Pan, there was no sign.

But Ava, poking around in the bedrooms, found the bag Pan had been carrying on the Friday night, what was left of it. It had been emptied, and the seams ripped apart.

Several floorboards in the hall had been torn up. Insulation around the boiler had been pulled out and thrown around.

The glass and frame of the big abstract in the sitting room had been smashed.

'Check this out,' said Kramer. He used a biro to sift through some of the scattered papers, including a diary, a notebook, a calendar - and the remains of two passports, one Chinese and one Japanese - in the names of Ding Pan and Niki Kawashima.

Kramer pulled on a pair of latex gloves. He held up a colour print of Pan he'd found, apparently fallen from a silver frame that now lay flat on a side table along with a cluster of other family portraits among shards of glass.

'Is this your friend?'

Ava said it was.

The detective and Ava perched next to each other on a windowsill.

'You say Pan had no father? How come?'

'We were at the same school in London. I think we were 13, in our second year at Godolphin and Latymer. Pan was called out of our first set English class. I learned later that her parents had both been killed in a helicopter crash - here, in the States. I seem to remember it was in Oregon. It's not something you easily forget, and I don't think Pan has ever really gotten over it. She never talks about it.'

Kramer said, 'But you didn't let on when you spoke to the guy today who was impersonating Mr Kawashima?'

'No, I didn't. He was improvising. Quick thinking on his part - but he didn't know Pan's family history.'

'Quick thinking on your part, too. Did you use a landline or a mobile?'

'Landline.'

'And you didn't give your name?'

'No.'

'Tell me about your relationship with Pan.'

Ava recounted their friendship, starting with their schooling in England, then the long intervals, right up to, and including, their evening at Logan Circle on Friday night.

Kramer watched her as she spoke and he said nothing until she'd finished. 'You had no contact all that time - until Friday night?'

'Except for the occasional birthday and Christmas card or the odd note and email.'

'How did you meet up?'

'She called me on my office phone, a direct line.'

'So you were in touch before Friday?'

'The day before.'

'That's it?'

'I tried calling twice today, but she seemed to have switched off her phone.'

Kramer kept the questions coming. 'Was she upset about anything? Was anything at home or at work bothering her at all? Money? Boyfriends?'

'I don't believe so. If she was upset, she hid it well.'

What seemed like a long silence followed, finally broken by Ava.

'She told me she wasn't seeing anyone.' And in case Detective Kramer didn't get the point, she added, 'Romantically or sexually. Pan wasn't into one-night stands.'

In case it was on the detective's mind.

But maybe that, too, wasn't true any longer and Pan had changed, as people do.

Kramer looked at Ava. 'Okay.' He sounded doubtful, though.

Kramer called someone on his cell, summoning help. He looked as if he hadn't slept or shaved in twenty-four hours. He was wearing jeans, brown work boots and a thick jacket. Perhaps he was coming off duty from some all-night job in the freezing cold when he'd been ordered to drop by, saving someone else from having to make the trip in such lousy weather. He had accepted a mug of York-shire Gold tea - Ava found one mug intact and a packet of the tea, unopened, in the kitchen - and he needed it by the way he gulped it down.

'I think I got everything we need right now,' he said. 'These folks will take over.'

Police technicians had entered in white suits, masks and shoe covers, putting up lights and photographing the debris. Another pair were searching for prints. Someone else was spraying what Kramer said was luminol near the entrance, apparently to reveal any bloodstains.

Kramer pocketed his phone, the picture, and his notebook.

Ava considered herself a good citizen. She was about to tell Detective Kramer, as she thought she should, about Pan's proposal, about the flow of sensitive ma-terial Pan claimed to have from a highly placed but unidentified source in the Chinese Communist Party. It seemed relevant, or it could be relevant. She told herself it would be wrong to withhold something of this nature, no matter how daft it might seem, but something made her hesitate. It was Pan's insistence on confidentiality, her mention of the risks the source was running, her determina-tion not to deal with government - any government - and her express wish to make it public. Ava reasoned the DC police were unusual, indeed unique, in that they were local, state and federal. That term federal bothered Ava, as she was sure it would Pan.

She said nothing about it.

'Over here,' said one of the forensics team. He pointed to the floor inside the front door.

Kramer went over to him and they looked down. They muttered to one an-other, heads together, Kramer glancing back at Ava as if to make sure she hadn't heard whatever it was they'd said. Kramer stepped away, and the technician placed markers around the spot before taking samples with what looked like a cotton bud.

'Blood spatter,' Kramer said. 'Not a lot - but enough for DNA, I guess.' He went into the bathroom and found a comb. In Pan's bedroom, he found a hairbrush, too. Both went into evidence bags.

Something else.

'It's a tooth,' Kramer said. 'A molar.'

Ava's one thought was for her school friend.

What have they done to you, Pan?

***

Ava forgot about the package - the Jiffy bag, as it was called - until she saw it still lying untouched in her in-basket when she returned to work. Before sitting at her desk, she took possession of the air-gapped laptop that James had set aside for her - a 2014 reconditioned Apple MacBook Air. She dusted it off, then put it and its charger in her shoulder bag and dropped in the package without opening it.

She couldn't wait. She had to know. There wasn't much work to do. By 3 p.m., she'd finished the task set by the Singapore bank and filed her report. James wouldn't mind because she'd completed the project ahead of time. She left a note on his desk. 'Working from home', she wrote, adding a single x. Outside, the blizzard had relented, but snow still fell, silencing the city, and it was already dark.

Once back in her tiny one-bed condo, she cleared the table in the living area - a table she used for meals and work - poured herself a glass of California red, set up the laptop and cut open the package with kitchen scissors.

It seemed empty. Ava felt a momentary panic when she inserted her hand, feeling for the flash drive and finding only what seemed to be an empty cassette box wrapped in two sheets of newsprint from a month-old copy of the Financial Times.

But it was there after all, a thumb drive. Not an effective hiding place, Ava thought, but it might do in the face of a cursory inspection. Ava thought she must have misunderstood; she had thought Pan would supply this material, but it had come directly via some sort of intermediary in Dubai, who must have repackaged it. Which meant that Pan had passed Ava's details on to the intermediary, if not the source himself, and that Pan had been confident that her friend would collaborate regardless of any misgivings she might have.

You've got a bloody nerve, Pan.

She wanted to use Ava and whoever was in Dubai as cut-outs to avoid leaving her footprints - and fingerprints - all over this. The ruse hadn't worked, though.

First, Ava uploaded the ChaCha program from the flash drive Pan had given her.

Then the hardware security module and finally the thumb drive from the package.

As the lines of compacted code melted back into Mandarin script, Ava scanned the lines of content. There were dated notes, sometimes comprising several paragraphs, in other cases a single line or two, not unlike entries from a diary.

Some looked official.

She forgot the time. She forgot everything except the Chinese script rolling up the screen in front of her.

As she scanned the contents, she realised she'd opened a contemporary Pandora's Box that not even the Greek author of the original myth, Hesiod, contemporary of Homer, could have dreamed up - this time curses with special Chinese characteristics.

Ava remembered the glass of wine. She found it without looking, by feel, lifted it to her lips without tearing her eyes away from the text, then drank it all in one.

Fuck, Pan, what have you done?

# 10

# December 7

## 09:05 China Standard Time, GMT +8

Qin had work to do, but he stayed in bed, or on it. A folding bed table made of bamboo straddled his legs, which were covered by a white sheet, while his back rested against several large pillows. Next to him was a stack of official papers two feet high. The contents were already approved and carried the Politburo seals or chops - but his signature was required. It was an unfortunate chore, because he'd much rather be enjoying a three-hour-long swim in his pool.

At least the heating was on.

The first document was straightforward. It approved the purchase of a Russian heavy attack helicopter, the naval version, known as the Ka-52K 'Black Shark' produced at Primorye Kai in the Russian Far East, along with advanced avionics. The order was for 32 of the enormous machines to fill a gap because Beijing's own shipboard versions of the Z-8, Z-9 and Z-20 would not be ready in time. There might be a second order for yet another Ka-52K batch in a matter of weeks. Moscow needed the money to maintain its military industries. The Chinese needed the weapon system for deployment on their three Type 075 landing helicopter dock assault ships, and eventually the fourth, because the vessels would play a central role in the capture of Taiwan and its outlying islands.

Taken together with the recent purchases of Russian Su-35 fighters and the S-400 SAM missile system, the latest deal Qin initialled had brought the two countries closer than ever since the falling out between Mao and Khrushchev.

Next was a sheaf of documents approving curbs on corporate profits and setting out redistribution of those same profits into new infrastructure projects. These included ambitious annual plans for the construction of social housing. Property developers were the primary target.

He signed a memorandum approving a new property tax despite opposition by some senior cadres who stood to lose out.

Qin picked up another file to be initialled, this time on the breaking up of IT firms that had become too big for their boots in the view of the Politburo. In Qin's view.

China had become far too unequal. Inequality on such a scale was dangerous. It posed a threat to the Party and its leaders. Qin knew it, had absorbed the advice from the only adviser he ever listened to, a member of the Politburo's standing committee, General Song. A defector from Taiwan, a genuine hero in Qin's opinion, veteran soldier Song was right. It was time the Party reasserted itself in all things. There could be no aspect of a Chinese citizen's existence that was not determined, monitored, weighed, regulated and assessed by the Party. That included shareholdings, boardroom politics, banking loans and debts, as much as it did literature and childbearing. Of course, Qin recognised - as did Song - that Deng Xiaoping's 'opening' to the West and its market all those years ago had been a brilliant masterstroke. It was a gamble that had paid off, luring immense sums of investment capital into China, pumping fresh blood into a moribund system on the point of collapse. The benefits were obvious. Over a recent five-year period, China had accounted for 28 percent of global economic growth, twice that of the United States.

But now that capital was available and flowing through the veins of a vigorous economy, growth was assured and half a billion people had been rescued from poverty, it was time to shut the gates, and stamp out the infectious poison that had spread like the plague, imported along with that same investment capital from a dissolute West and its insatiable, neoliberal financiers.

Qin learned from Song - and from Mao's legacy, of course - that social stability depended on one thing: fear. Fear and its twin, hate. They went hand in hand with incentives such as a minimum wage. Song's solution was simple. The Party would impose terror. It would do so in such a way that it became routine, inevitable - the way humans accepted with varying degrees of awareness that they were mortal, that they and their loved ones would die, that night followed day, that everyone would fall ill and that old age would be the fate of every golden youth. So it would be with terror.

This was far more subtle and omnipresent than the Cultural Revolution.

It would be injected into people's minds. Infants would imbibe it with their mother's milk and would learn, in due course, the ruthlessness and competitive spirit they would need to cope with it - and apply it to themselves 24/7 once indoctrinated.

The Party might enjoy a kind of inner democracy, or at least consensus, even liberty of a kind among equals who followed Party discipline, thanks to this 'self-policing'. It was right that members who stayed the course were rewarded with material privileges for bearing the heavy burden of their immense duty to humankind, to history. While these Party members, members of what was in essence an initiatory cult, could watch themselves and one another, having been 'baptised' in the rites of terror so that it seemed as essential to life as breathing, the masses on the outside had to be held in check by the Party.

Governed.

Watched.

Terrorised.

How else would a Party of 100 million members dominate - and lead - a mainland population of 1.5 billion?

***

After all that pen-pushing, the Emperor had a treat in store. He loved watching videos. Qin particularly enjoyed nature programmes because he found them so relaxing. He liked nature as long as he could watch, but not take part. Ugh. Swamps and jungle? Mountains and deserts? No thanks. Reptiles and bugs frightened him, and so did the ocean, but on screen he found it entertaining and calming.

But this was going to be something special, and it was nothing to do with the wilderness or climate change. He decided it should wait until after his swim. It was something to look forward to.

Feeling refreshed and renewed but pleasantly tired by the time he emerged from the water at 2.30 p.m., Qin settled back on his bed in front of his big screen, full of anticipation. He called for chocolate ice cream and, once it arrived, Wang sorted out the CDs supplied by the *Gong'anbu*, the Ministry of Public Security, handed him the remote and left him alone.

What the Emperor was about to view was restricted, but selected sections would be shown on national television in the evening as a prime example of foreign aggression and terrorism. Pour encourager les autres.

Five people stood in line, three men and two women, wearing yellow high-visibility gilets with horizontal reflective panels on their chests.

Two uniformed police officers flanked each prisoner, one on either side, the police wearing white gloves. Female officers guarded the female prisoners.

Their wrists were manacled.

They looked pale and haggard, almost bloodless, which was to be expected, but other than their corpse-like appearance, they looked unmarked at the distance of perhaps thirty feet. No sign of bruises or contusions. Qin stopped the video, tried to enlarge it. It was impossible to tell their ages, though they seemed to him to be in their 30s and 40s, but one man was clearly older than the rest, maybe in his 50s. All five looked straight ahead, somewhere at a spot above the heads of the three judges, the latter seated on a raised dais. The prisoners didn't move or so much as glance at the video camera recording the proceedings. They didn't speak or look at one another.

Qin dipped his spoon in the ice cream.

The video proceeded. This was a ceremony of great legal solemnity, and Qin recognised that each of those present had a role to play, including members of the public attending the hearing.

A large, coloured portrait of Qin with his quizzical smile hung on the wall above and behind the judges' bench, gazing down with benevolence on his people.

The chairperson of the court read out her judgement in a clipped, unemotional voice of authority, and she enunciated every word with care.

All five accused had confessed to spying for China's enemies, specifically the counter-revolutionary, splittist regime of *tu fei*, bandits, in 'Chinese Taipei'. All five had begged for the Court's mercy, and each had apologised to the Party and the people of China for their crimes against the state.

She paused, drank water from a glass. It was time to pass sentence.

'There is only one sentence that the People's Court can bestow for the crimes of treason, espionage and collaboration with a foreign power's intelligence services, the foreign power in this instance being the United States of America and its client regime of counterrevolutionary saboteurs in Taipei.

'The accused are sentenced to die, the sentence to be carried out immediately.'

The spectators clapped in unison like clockwork puppets and after five claps, one for each of the condemned, they fell silent. Their expressions were impassive. It was impossible to know what they thought or felt.

The same went for the guilty. Blank faces. Silent.

Qin had almost finished the ice cream. He licked the spoon.

He wondered if they'd been dosed with tranquillisers.

It would be popular on television if only because opinion polls showed that ordinary Chinese - non-Party members - were very much in favour of the death penalty, especially for corruption and violent crime.

The accused turned about, along with their escorts, a well-drilled manoeuvre by the look of it. None was heard to cry out in protest, scream in fear, faint or throw up. They had been rehearsed for this legalistic theatre. Now they dropped their heads onto their chests, ashamed of their actions, no doubt. The escorts grabbed the guilty by their collars, forcing them to bend forward.

They'd known what was coming.

Who dared say the People's Republic didn't follow the Rule of Law?

It wasn't quite over.

Change of scene: a street appeared on which there was little normal traffic, but with an unusual number of armed police in long padded coats and caps guarding two large white vans with smoked windows parked nose-to-tail at the kerb.

One of the condemned was marched along the pavement to the first van, his escorts gripping him by the elbows and the scruff of his neck, forcing his head down. He didn't have a coat, and he shuffled along in what appeared to be prison slippers. He must have felt freezing. The door slid open and gloved hands at the end of arms, clad in what were presumably medical coats, pulled him on board. He seemed to stumble, regain his balance, then vanished as the door slid shut.

The process was repeated with the second van.

The street was silent. There was no sound. Winter itself seemed to hold its breath. The police cordon was still in place, the officers stamping their boots and clapping their gloved hands together to keep warm.

The sky had that muddy look presaging more snow.

Two minutes passed.

It was time for a quick pee, so he stopped the video with the remote and climbed off the bed.

He was back to see the process repeated. Two more prisoners entered the vans.

Finally, the last, a woman.

The two death vans pulled out and drove away.

The police withdrew and after a few seconds, traffic returned to normal. It was as if nothing had happened, only a bad dream.

The executions by injection had taken around twenty minutes. Qin was hungry again. He wanted pork and sticky rice. He should have had the pork first, then the ice cream. That's what his wife would have said. But what the hell, he was Emperor and he could have what he wanted when he wanted it and how he wanted it.

# 11

# December 8

## 01:30 Eastern Standard Time, GMT -4

Ava sorted the texts into some sort of order. She noted that the first item - styled as an informal letter - bore the same date as the pink pages torn from the FT weekend edition of October 23.

She took the letter as her starting point. Two glasses of wine were followed by a mug of black coffee to help her focus when what she wanted to do was lie down and sleep forever.

*Dear Friend,*

*Before we begin, you and I, there are a few matters I should explain if only to make your task a little easier. This is an attempt - possibly futile - to introduce myself and what I represent without revealing my identity.*

*You might find this hard to believe, but I am no traitor. Nor am I a spy. I regard myself as a true patriot.*

*What do I mean by that? I am patriotic in several senses of that much abused term. I am loyal to my country. Okay, you might say there is no such thing as a contiguous country called 'China' - only an idea dreamed up by nationalists and later Communists in the 19th century, so how could I be loyal to something that doesn't exist? I would argue that China is much more than real estate, and a great deal more than a political concept. It's a culture, or several intertwined cultures, with a long and tangled history, a history of civilisations and intermittent barbarism, of immense creativity and authoritarian terror, of conquest and colonial exploitation, of flourishing science and art, and also periods of abysmal ignorance and terrible suffering. It embraces several languages and dialects, philosophies and religious traditions.*

*That is what 'China' means to me, and it embraces not merely the mainland but wherever Chinese people are to be found who identify as Chinese, who speak and live the lives of Chinese in all their many, many forms.*

*Second, I am a loyal member of the Communist Party of China. Loyal yet disobedient, undisciplined, a dissenter in Party ranks. A rebel against centrism. I accept that. It's true. I would argue that I have a greater loyalty to the truth than preservation of my willingness to toe the line for the sake of status, wealth, family, personal safety. I am putting the interests of the Party above my own. That is loyalty.*

*If my crime is to think for myself, then I plead guilty.*

*What truth, you ask?*

*The truth is that if General Secretary Qin continues on his present course, the Party will be destroyed, the country fragmented and plunged into anarchy of the most violent kind, that hundreds of thousands, if not millions, of Chinese lives will be extinguished, while the rest of the world will endure an economic blow, the likes of which have never been seen before, causing immense suffering among the weakest sections of humanity.*

*Although I don't know you and never will, I propose I become your 'source', your 'CCP source', your 'source close to the CCP Politburo', your 'informed source', your 'security source' - in short whatever terminology your capitalist media will accept. That's all - nothing beyond that. No name. No location.*

*Our course is perilous. I can't pretend otherwise.*

*I cannot do this alone. I need your help, my invisible friend, before I am caught, and it costs me my life, which it will.*

*We have little time. Sixty days from December 3. Fewer by the time you read this.*

*Your task: to reveal everything I send you, to distribute it as widely as possible, to make it known globally, but you must follow my rules of attribution and avoid all contact with your country's special services because we both know they will suppress this.*

*Can you do that? Will you help in trying to preserve peace?*

First thought: this was a lie, a gigantic hoax, a deception, a deliberate provocation, not unlike those email scams from Nigeria. Second thought: the anonymous author was an attention seeker, a frustrated bureaucrat indulging in his own fantasies, playing a fucked-up game, messing with Pan's life and hers.

A certifiable egotist, for sure.

There was no third thought, for Ava fell asleep on the sofa.

*\*\*\**

Four hours would have been enough. Ava would have dragged herself into the shower, made herself coffee, and staggered off to work, a little late to face a normal working day, or an almost normal day, given her preoccupation with the files that were now on her air-gapped laptop and which she knew she couldn't share with anyone, not even James.

It wasn't to be. An immense and constant hammering on her door woke her, and it seemed as if someone was trying to break it down, combined with the continuous ringing of her landline phone in the hall and her cellphone, which lay next to the laptop.

Ava made it to the hall, leaned against the wall. Her voice emerged as a croak. 'Who is it?'

There were two people outside. The closer to her door she recognised as Detective Kramer, the second a stranger who was standing back. Kramer had been doing the hammering. Ava opened her door a crack, keeping it on the chain.

'Ms. Shute? You remember me? Detective Kramer? We need to talk.'

'Who's that with you, Detective?'

'Agent Calasso,' said the woman, edging closer. 'FBI.'

'Okay.' Ava felt like shit. 'What do you want?' It sounded stupid. It was stupid.

'We need to talk about your friend,' said Kramer. 'But we'd rather not discuss it standing here. Can we come in and talk inside?'

'One minute.'

Ava turned away, leaving the door open but still on the chain, took the laptop into her bedroom, and slid it and the flash drive under her pillows, returned to the living room and straightened the sofa cushions. She took the wineglass to the sink in the kitchen area and returned to wipe down the coffee table.

One glance at herself in the hall mirror told her she not only felt like shit but looked it, too. Her red hair was standing up as if she'd crawled through a bush backwards.

Ava was also ravenous.

'Okay.' She held the door open. Kramer walked straight in, but Calasso entered more cautiously, looking around at the condo and its contents, the pictures, the wall of bookshelves, then up at Ava herself who towered over the visitors.

'Heavy night?'

Ava didn't reply.

'You live here alone, Ms. Shute?'

'I do. There's not enough room for anyone else, as you can see, except a pet mouse or hamster, and I'm not into pets. Sorry. I'm being facetious. I'm not awake yet. I worked all yesterday and most of last night, and thanks to you guys I've had little more than two hours of sleep. So I'm kinda muzzy.'

'Sorry about that. This won't take long.' Agent Calasso didn't sound in the least sorry.

'Can I see some ID, please? I don't need to see Detective Kramer's.'

Agent Calasso held up her badge. Ava peered at it, nodded.

The visitors sat side by side on the sofa where only a couple of minutes earlier Ava had been snoring her head off.

'Can I get you guys some coffee? Or would you prefer tea?'

Kramer and Calasso exchanged looks and Ava thought it meant they'd like to accept, but were unwilling to admit it.

'Looks like you need it more than we do,' Calasso said. 'So yeah, thanks, we'll take a coffee. Right, Kramer?'

'Sure,' he said, but he didn't sound keen.

Calasso was small and bird-like with dark, unruly hair pinned back from her pale face and a prominent nose that gave her a predatory but not unattractive look. She wore a grey suit, white blouse, practical ankle boots and no jewellery Ava could see, except for a wristwatch. She was probably carrying under the jacket, Ava thought. Age: late 20s, low 30s. Intelligent face. Hard eyes. Altogether, Calasso was definitely FBI.

'Then I'll make us all coffee,' Ava said and went over to the kitchenette, which was separated from the living room by a counter piled high with files - and more books. 'We can talk while I do this,' she added.

Calasso began, 'I understand you work for something called Cincinnatus, that right?'

'I do and it is.'

'What is it you do there?'

'My job description is that of senior analyst.'

'What do you analyse?'

'Pretty much anything they ask me to. I specialise in China. Is this about me or about Pan?'

Kramer broke in. 'Thing is, Ms Shute, this isn't just a missing person incident, all right? It's now a national security matter and a possible homicide, which is why Agent Calasso is here. I mean, don't get me wrong, we're not giving up on your friend's disappearance. We'll keep going on that, I assure you, but the Bureau will take the lead.'

Ava was too busy concentrating on filling her cafetière to respond at once.

'Cream? Sugar?'

The visitors shook their heads. 'No thanks,' they said in unison.

Ava brought them their mugs, then fetched her own.

It was Colombian, dark and strong.

'What happened?'

Kramer was about to respond, but Calasso got in first.

'You were with the NSA, yeah?'

'I was. Three years.'

'You had quite a record for someone who was there only a short while. Why did you quit? Seems like you had a promising future.'

'I like working on my own. What's this got to do with anything?'

Calasso didn't answer, but asked another question. 'Ms Shute, I gotta ask, given your professional interests - have you personally had any contact at all with the Chinese embassy or consulate here in DC? Or any Chinese Communists - or any Chinese person who might turn out to have Communist sympathies?'

'Of course not. No.' Ava felt her temper rising in her chest and throat.

'So you've been to no Chinese embassy party, no cultural event, nothing organised by some Chinese cultural organisation?'

'No.'

'Have you received funding from any Chinese organisation, such as a university?'

'No.'

Kramer jumped in. 'Couple of things we should mention. First off, we're actively searching for Pan. We think she was at home. For some reason, she opened her front door and was attacked. There was enough blood for us to confirm it's a match for the DNA we found on the hairbrush we took from the bedroom and the comb in the bathroom.'

They watched for Ava's reaction. There wasn't one.

'Your story on Pan's parents checks out. Did you know the late Mr Kawashima was a wealthy businessman?'

No response.

'Of course we're checking with neighbours, CCTV on the street and there's an alert out nationwide.'

'You're telling me she's dead? That's what you're saying. Right?'

'We aren't saying that, no.'

Kramer and Calasso exchanged looks.

Calasso took up the narrative. 'The academic institution in Beijing, where Pan worked, was raided by police on Sunday. Well, police assisted in the raid, but we don't know who else. Security would be my guess. Our guy at the Beijing embassy is pretty certain it's the Ministry of Public Security - I guess their equivalent of the FBI. They confiscated all electronic devices - computers, cellphones - and they took away all the paper files. No-one was at work, except the janitor and they left him alone. Place was pretty much cleared out.'

'Arrests?'

Calasso shook her head. 'Not that we've heard.'

'They're looking for something real important,' Kramer said. 'The Chinese authorities, I mean. We're concerned about Pan having whatever it is they want. We're worried…'

Ava understood. 'That Pan is being held against her will. If she's alive.'

'Right,' said Kramer, nodding. Ava noticed he'd taken a small sip of his coffee and hadn't touched it since. Agent Calasso seemed to have enjoyed hers. Her mug was empty.

'Let me get you some tea,' Ava said to Kramer. She'd remembered rather late that Kramer had preferred tea.

'I'm fine, thanks.' Kramer looked embarrassed.

All this - the FBI visit, the theft, the incident in Beijing - suggested that the encrypted files received by courier and now decrypted and copied on the air-gapped laptop under the pillows in Ava's bedroom might be genuine, after all.

For some peculiar reason she couldn't fathom, Ava felt cheerful about it. Could it be because Pan had been telling the truth? It wasn't a trick, some fiendish shit-stirring, Communist Chinese or nationalist Chinese disinformation plot.

'And Pan herself - you've heard absolutely nothing - nothing at all?'

'No,' said Agent Calasso. 'Nothing so far.'

'There's been no demand for ransom, no threat? Nothing?'

Calasso shook her head. Kramer looked down at his own feet.

'You've checked the airports, of course, and the hospitals?'

'We have,' Kramer said. 'We're still looking.'

'We're going to take this public,' Agent Calasso said. 'We're distributing a press release and a recent image of Pan today - national television, newspapers, radio, the usual websites. Your cooperation would be appreciated, Ms Shute, and I say this because something tells me you know more about this than you're willing to admit.'

Ava knew that when someone went missing, the first hours were critical. Pan had been missing since Friday night. It was now Wednesday. Four days had gone by and this was the fifth. The more time passed without news, the more the chances of finding Pan alive slipped away.

# 12

## 12:07 China Standard Time, GMT +8

'Did you hear that?'

Wang frowned in puzzlement. 'No. What?'

Qin didn't answer. Ever since he'd climbed off his bed that morning Qin had heard whispers. Someone was whispering, a persistent voice in his ear. For him alone, he was sure of it, but no matter how hard he listened, no matter how quiet it was, he couldn't make sense of it. At first, he'd actually turned around a couple of times to make sure no-one was standing behind him, whispering over his shoulder. Qin could hear the odd word and phrase, and the confiding cadence. He wasn't even certain if the whisperer was male or female. He'd ignored it for a while, especially during the video of the trial and execution of the enemy spies, but sometimes it felt like someone leaning forward and breathing hard on his cheek. It was a damn nuisance.

Who the hell did he or she think they were?

They walked side by side, Wang and the Emperor. Wang, who was wearing his Ministry of Public Security uniform, black pants and tunic with plain navy tie and white shirt, the rank of brigadier-general in silver on the black epaulettes, would try to hang back, thinking that it was not his place to walk next to Qin but a step or two behind. He, no doubt, thought that proper for a subordinate strolling around with the General Secretary.

Qin would stop and wait for him, and he grew annoyed.

'Keep up, Wang, for heaven's sake. I can't talk to you or hear what you say if you dawdle behind me.'

It was bad enough having a phantom whisperer lurking there.

Someone had cleared the snow from the paths around the two lakes in the *Zhongnanhai*, but now it was icy and more perilous than before. The lakes themselves had frozen over and the resident ducks were standing about on the ice, looking disconcerted and uncomfortable without water to paddle about in. The weak sun was shining. Leafless willows bent down to the ice as if bowing. Qin thought the scene was pretty as a painting. He had wanted to walk after watching the video because he needed to clear his head of the whispers - but it wasn't working. Somehow, he felt it was Wang's fault though it was clearly irrational to think so.

'I wanted to ask you something, Wang.'

Qin had thought of another reason to take a stroll with Wang.

'Of course.'

'About my wife.'

There was a long pause. They walked side by side now, and Qin noticed they were actually in step, their fur-lined boots crunching on the film of ice coating the paving stones as if they were soldiers marching to a drum.

Qin let Wang suffer in silence. This wasn't something he'd want to discuss at all. The perils were all too obvious, even for the head of the Central Security Bureau.

'You're familiar with the term *bai shoutao* or "white gloves", yes?'

'Of course.'

'So. Who's performing the role for her nowadays?'

The briefest hesitation before Wang answered. 'Tsai Chen.'

'Tell me about him.'

'I can bring you the file - or send it.'

'If I want the fucking file, I'll ask for it. I asked you to tell me.'

The Emperor had a powerful urge to slap Wang's cheeks.

'Young. Smart. Educated partly abroad.' Wang reached for more words. 'Outgoing, sociable, reputation as an effective middleman and negotiator with all the social skills required of someone in his role.'

'Where was he educated?'

'England. Master's in Business Management. He co-operated with the relevant department, *youguan bumen*, while there.'

Wang meant this Tsai had helped the *Guoanbu* - foreign intelligence - in some way. Or the United Front Work Department. Either way, it meant the same thing: spying. 'Family?'

'Ordinary Party members. Not one of us, if that's what you're wondering.'

Which translated as not one of the Red Aristocracy.

'So an ambitious, bright lad come out of nowhere.'

'Of course. That's usually the case with his sort. On the make with little to lose.'

'*Guanxi?*'

'Nothing special, as one might expect.'

'No links to our old friends Jiang Zemin and Zeng Qinghong?'

'None that we know of.'

'You seem very sure.'

'We checked.'

'Did you now?' There was just a hint of threat in Qin's tone.

Silence, except for the sound of their boots.

'Is the fellow corrupt?'

'No evidence he is.'

'But you'd find something if I asked you to.'

Silence.

'Is he fucking her? Or I should ask, is she fucking him?'

'I'll look into it.'

'No. You won't. You already know. Well?'

Qin glanced at Wang. The old devil had gone red in the face, especially the big earlobes that hung down both sides of his head like a Buddha.

Qin stopped and turned to face Wang, blocking his path and forcing him to halt.

'Yes,' Wang said. He looked sorrowful. He nodded his head and avoided meeting Qin's eyes. 'Yes. It's true. Nothing regular. Just occasional encounters. He keeps an office right next to hers, see, calls himself Madam Meng's corporate manager. There's a sign on his door saying just that.'

'Married?'

'Yes.'

'Children?'

'No.'

'I want images of them together in bed. Audio, too. Video. Stills. The lot.'

They'd walked around the smaller of the two lakes. The *Zhongnanhai* complex formed a rough trapezoid shape. Its high red walls protected an area of 250 acres, approximately 1.7 km long and between 600 and 700 metres wide.

'This Tsai must take a cut, though, mustn't he? As a middleman?'

'I guess so,' said Wang.

'You guess? Find out what the arrangement is, how much he makes, what he does with it. Does my wife know what he makes and how he makes it? And yes, send me his file.'

'Very well.'

'Did Madam Meng take a big hit in the Evergrande property mess?'

'She must have.'

'Wang, you're no fool and neither am I. I want chapter and verse. Not vague responses from you, of all people. You know why I don't intervene and why I don't shed any tears for those greedy investors who've lost their shirts in the property market. It's because of certain families involved, certain circles...'

'Yes, boss.'

Qin meant Jiang Zemin and company.

That was the odd thing about the *Zhongnanhai*. It was the home of so many leading political families, not only those of the first echelon but also the relatives of deceased and retired national leaders, who were permitted to keep their official homes indefinitely. And the families of current Party leaders too, of course. These homes were also where these same leaders worked. Qin was unusual in that his family lived in a separate villa outside the enclave. What was also odd was how little the people who lived and worked in the *Zhongnanhai* socialised. People didn't go to parties or social gatherings in one another's homes even though they were in such easy walking distance. Neighbours didn't have dinner parties or get together for a few drinks and a barbecue. Even the children didn't mix much. Qin never saw kids from different families playing games or sports in the place. Their parents discouraged it.

He thought there must be too much suspicion, fear, rivalry, competition and bad blood - bad blood that no doubt went back generations in some cases.

If his wife was getting too close to the wrong people, Qin would have to pull her up short. Wang would provide him with the details. If it came to that, this fellow Tsai could serve as a useful whipping boy and his abrupt departure would send a lesson to Meng Bin. As for her and Tsai going to bed together, so what? What did Qin care? Tsai would see it as being to his advantage to sleep with his boss, while Qin's wife would gain some sexual satisfaction from fucking a healthy young male. It saved Qin from having to carry out his conjugal duties. No, sex wasn't the issue. It didn't matter in the least except for possible future leverage.

What mattered, what always mattered, was power.

They were close to the *Zhongnanhai*'s main entrance, Xinhua Gate, guarded by troops who stamped and turned like battery-powered dolls, kitted out in their best winter dress uniforms. But they weren't toys that they carried. Their automatic weapons, with bayonets fixed, weren't merely for show. The rifles were loaded, Qin knew.

Across the entrance was a huge red sign with gold script that read: Serve the People.

Qin wondered if anyone believed that anymore.

The sibilant whispers had ceased, but Qin felt a slight tremor, a rumbling, below his feet. Somewhere down there was the six-lane highway that ran along a tunnel all the way from the Great Hall of the People out to Beijing International Airport and back. It was the route taken by troops who'd suppressed the 1989 uprising in Tiananmen Square. They'd poured out of the Great Hall like a swarm of invaders, taking everyone by surprise in the dark.

Time to retrace their steps. The icy, still air was making Qin hungry.

'By the way, did you see my article in today's Jiěfàngjūn Bào, the PLA Daily?'

Wang looked flummoxed. He'd been taken by surprise by the sudden change of direction in subject.

'No, boss.'

'It's headlined "The Party Commands the Gun". You should read it, Wang. I insist you read it.'

'Of course.'

'You'll see why I insist. It's an important message.'

'Yes, boss.'

The Emperor had signed the article, but he hadn't written it. It had been put together on his orders by Propaganda Department staff with an intended audience of PLA, as well as security and police commanders.

'How long have you commanded the Central Security Bureau, Wang?'

'Four months.'

'Four months. That's right. There have been five changes in command over the past year and you were the last. Do you know why I promoted you?'

Wang said nothing. He knew, of course he did.

'Read the article, Wang. Then you'll know. Let's just say that cliques of police officers, soldiers, or whatever, who think they're invulnerable and who conspire to take over the state by force will not be tolerated.'

Wang said nothing, no doubt he was digesting the meaning behind the words.

'Perhaps you remember some of these names. Sun Zhengcai. Ling Jihua. Guo Boxiong, Xu Caihou, Zhou Yongkang. Do you want more? I have many names. You know them, yes?'

'Yes, chief.'

'I bet you do. Unlike you, Wang, I knew them all personally. Politburo members, advisers, generals, security chiefs. People who'd risen high in the Party, occupying trusted posts with important responsibilities of state. But they wanted more, always more, and they thought they could plot my overthrow behind my back and replace me. We must be on our guard, Wang, night and day, because there are always jackals prowling around, filthy, disloyal scavengers looking for weaknesses they can exploit, seeking power for themselves. It's human nature to be greedy.'

'Of course.'

'Do you think I was wrong to have Lai Xiaomin executed? For corruption? A banker and senior cadre, if you remember. Convicted of stealing hundreds of millions. Was I too severe? Did I go too far? What do you think, Wang?'

'I couldn't possibly say.'

'Of course you couldn't. I understand. That's why the article is written for you, Wang. For you and others like you, so that you understand. If I fall, so do you.'

Qin was the Party. The Party was Qin.

'Don't let me down, Wang.'

Qin commanded the gun, no-one else, and his finger was on the trigger.

\*\*\*

There was a working session that evening chaired by Qin at the Strategic Command Centre. This time no-one was in uniform; they followed Qin's example in wearing their unassuming work clothes - the black, long-sleeved jackets with zipped collars. All electronic devices had to be handed in on entering the premises, Wang's men presiding over the metal detectors and ID scanners.

They took their places, faces solemn. No-one smiled or called out a greeting to the others. Everyone seemed preoccupied with their own thoughts.

Discussion centred on the issues of sea and air control. Admiral Jia Lihua was at pains to explain these concepts, and he set out for his comrades the reasons it was not realistic to think of having either for extended periods over the entire operational area. Instead, air and sea control would be imposed only when necessary and over a limited area for a limited time. Control would be tightly enforced and concentrated. Anything beyond that would be unrealistic and absorb too many resources.

Jia used diagrams to illustrate his argument. He walked over to the model of the island of Taiwan to show what he meant.

Qin asked him how sea and air control was coordinated with so-called denial of access to the enemy, and the admiral explained how it worked.

No-one was sure who the enemy was. Would the Americans intervene at once, or would they delay their response? Would the Australians and Japanese join in immediately or at all? What of the South Koreans and the Indians? The conjecture rippled around the conference this way and that, and finally dried up without a conclusion. Qin listened, observed, did not contribute.

In his capacity as chief of the Central Military Commission, Qin had a secret note distributed to participants about the phased nature of the approaching conflict. The first phase, that of propaganda, had already begun, and he reminded those present that the 60-day countdown to the war of reunification had begun on December 3, five days previously. As Westerners would have put it, the train had well and truly left the station.

General Zheng had a question. Was there a figure for the projected casualties for the invasion force and, if so, what was it? Not civilians. Not Taiwanese or mainland Chinese. Just the invasion force itself.

Qin answered, though he was certain the old veteran knew the answer better than he did. 'We expect the attacking forces will sustain approximately 150,000 casualties in the first 48 hours.'

The Emperor didn't mention that this was at the lower end of estimates, and that it precluded any use of nuclear weapons.

He rose to his feet and led the way out of the chamber, Wang close behind him. The rest waited, watching him pass. He used the palm of his right hand to pat his hair, reassuring himself it was still in place, that the gel and pomade did the job they were supposed to do. He was proud of his full head of hair. There was no question of his ever going bald. He'd even look pretty good in his coffin at his own state funeral, he decided. For Qin, heading up in the lift to his pool for a swim before supper, nuclear weapons and the casualties of war were forgotten. There were reasons to be cheerful, after all. The whispers had vanished, and he remembered it was dance night again.

# 13

## 09:22 Eastern Standard Time, GMT -4

Ava called in sick, saying she wasn't feeling too good. It wasn't true, though she needed sleep. The real reason was the flash drive and its contents. James didn't doubt her; he was sympathetic, thanking her for her work on the Singapore bank project and suggesting she take a day or two to rest up. That only made her feel guilty for lying to him. The weather was awful, though. On second thoughts, why not take the week? He said she deserved the rest after working long hours and weekends to get it done.

'Hey, I'll see you Monday,' he said. 'I want you fighting fit, okay? I've got something right up your street this time. You're gonna love it.'

James didn't say what it was, and she didn't ask.

Ava called Detective Kramer on his direct line, but there was no answer. She left a message asking if there was any news about Pan. Ava sent a text with the same message to his mobile number. She didn't try calling Agent Calasso because she didn't want to get herself entangled with the Bureau more than she already was, if only because she had a guilty conscience for having lied by omission.

No response from Pan's home phone, either.

She went to work.

The first message in the sequence after the mysterious contact's letter of self-introduction comprised 10 succinct, numbered paragraphs - like an NSA intelligence report. Ava had deciphered it, copied it via the flash drive onto her air-gapped Mac, translated it, then sat back to digest the contents with the help of her third coffee of the day.

## *JOINT TAIWAN ATTACK COMMAND HOLDS FIRST SESSION*

*1. Eastern Theatre Command held a special meeting on November 24 at Nanjing, Jiangsu. Thirty-three cadres attended. The plenary session lasted three hours, with a break for lunch.*

*It was chaired by the deputy chief of the Central Military Commission (CMC) with the assistance of the Joint Staff Department.*

*2. Regional commanders of all armed services were present, along with Party secretaries at regional and city level. Rail, road and air transport chiefs attended for part of the plenary session, along with port authority leaders. Chief executives of private and state logistics organisations took part in some discussions, along with senior Peoples Armed Police and Public Security Bureau commanders.*

*3. The meeting agreed with a CMC proposal to rename the Eastern Theatre Command the Joint Taiwan Attack Command (JTAC) with immediate effect.*

Joint Taiwan Attack Command Centre? Really? Oh, hell. Ava hoped it wasn't real - but she also hoped it was because yes, it was, selfishly, pure gold. An exclusive that was far too exclusive. If this was true, if this was genuine, it was scary, too. But how to prove it, how to corroborate any of it?

Ava got to her feet and stalked around her apartment. The NSA, the CIA and the rest of them would spend a huge amount of treasure and even sacrifice lives for this. If it was true, that is. And if so, then this was the strongest indicator yet of an invasion plan. She turned about in the tiny kitchen, went into the bathroom, scratching her head, and somehow ended up standing in the living room, looking around her, thinking she needed to do some housework. The place was a mess. Fuck it, who cared about dust and a sink full of dirty dishes? Well, Ava did. She made another circuit, listening to snatches of raucous music from next door, the squeak of floorboards from the condo above, a gigantic sneeze from someone out in the corridor. There wasn't much room for wandering around because the place was only 48 square metres. She dropped to the floor, face down, stretched out and counted 42 press-ups. It made her feel a little better, but not much.

I'll go to the gym later, she told herself.

She took several deep breaths. Pan, what have you done? What am I doing? Back to the air-gapped laptop.

*4. The meeting reviewed and approved Politburo decisions relating to the reunification of China. A special vote of thanks was passed unanimously in the leadership of General Secretary Qin for guiding the Party and country on the path of resistance to foreign aggression, blocking interference in China's internal affairs and enabling reunification.*

Great stuff. Only problem, comrades: Taiwan has never been ruled by the CCP, so the 're' prefix was inaccurate and misleading. Never mind, we'll go with the unification part.

*5. Special measures to limit civilian traffic by rail, road and air and to allow greater capacity for military reinforcement were discussed and agreed in outline. For example, rail is to carry 120,000 tons of fuel, munitions and rations over the next 40 days. Reductions in civilian movement will be gradual to avoid public alarm, minimise inconvenience and prevent provoking foreign interest and will therefore begin immediately.*

*6. Discussion also took place on the increased dangers of foreign espionage and terrorism and the countermeasures required.*

Right. The People's Republic of China was so peace-loving that it was going to mount an invasion of another country motivated by self-defence in the face of aggression. Not unlike the good old USA's policies in Iraq and Afghanistan. Got it. No-one's perfect.

*7. Committees were established to study the issues discussed and to report back ahead of the next meeting in two weeks' time, especially on the issues of logistics, transport, storage and security.*

*8. One issue dominated the proceedings, and that was timing. While support for the General Secretary's decision, by the Politburo, to mount the assault on February 1, the Chinese New Year, thereby achieving a high level of operational surprise, was unanimous, participants noted it was not without problems, especially regarding weather.*

Terrible syntax aside, they can't be serious. February 1? That was only a few weeks away, for Chrissakes.

Fifty-five days and counting.

*9. PLAAF and PLAN commanders went into some detail about the difficulties posed by a winter attack, but CMC and Joint Staff representatives pointed out that the date was for planning purposes. It was provisional on a break in the weather, allowing the assault and invasion to take proceed with a high probability of success. Formation of a meteorological sub-committee was approved, and it was required to provide weekly forecasts to the CMC on all matters relating to weather in the operational area.*

Madness, total madness!

Ava told herself that even she, an American female and civilian with no first-hand experience of East Asia, knew it would be tantamount to mass suicide. A mid-winter assault would be disastrous. It was certain to fail, and at a terrible cost. Rough, big seas racing down the Strait, unpredictable tides, gale force winds, thick fog, short days and a rocky coastline.

The invading troops, if they ever reached the Taiwan beaches alive, would be seasick, exhausted, wet and frozen and in no shape to fight their way onshore.

This wasn't a replay of D-Day in 1944 and a summer, 21-mile crossing of the English Channel.

This was 100 miles of sea. In winter.

The unknown author's notes followed one more paragraph:

*10. Participants agreed that amphibious assault formations would come under a forward joint command post at Fuzhou in Fujian, currently the PLA Army Theatre HQ, and with immediate effect.*

*Notes: The full minutes of the meeting run to seven pages, and are top secret, each file numbered with a distribution list of 72. This is my summary of the proceedings, along with an appendix with the names on the distribution list. I was not present, but I had access to the minutes long enough to take notes and record the names. Some topics mentioned will be dealt with in greater detail. I know what you're thinking. How can you corroborate this? How can you check? How do I know it's true? Given 72 copies, and assuming each recipient on the list probably has at least 10 friends and family, that's a potential 720 sources. All you have to do is find one who will talk. Don't use Skype!*

Whoever he or she was, the bastard had a sense of humour.

***

Ava had to decide where to hide the flash drive and the air-gapped laptop. The flash drive was small and easy to conceal, the laptop less so. Whoever searched her condo and her office would presumably be trained, such as the FBI, and they'd know all the likely hiding places. She couldn't keep either item in the condo, and the China Room at Cincinnatus wouldn't be much more secure. It would put Cincinnatus and its staff at risk, particularly her colleague James because they worked together on China-related projects. There was only one solution: it would have to be storage, with a combination lock, and she'd have to be careful she wasn't under surveillance when visiting the site.

It took her a few minutes online to find a place at 1420 U Street NW: a secure, indoor locker measuring nine square feet and rented out for only 23 dollars for the first month if she booked online. It used a keypad to lock and unlock, but she'd have to avoid using her own phone or laptop to book and pay. Obviously.

If she used one of her cards, it would show up on her bank statements and for the moment she couldn't think of a way around it. Maybe she'd have to turn up in person and pay in cash, but it would be more than double the online price. There were also CCTV cameras installed on site and - if the online images of the place were any guide - over the reception desk and in the corridors, too.

Sunglasses, a baseball cap, a wig. Nothing she could do about her height.

It required more thought.

Ava would make copies of everything and hide those, too.

Still in her pyjamas, with a chunky pullover over them, Ava made herself an omelette. While she ate, she logged into her normal laptop and checked her work emails. There seemed to be nothing of any importance, nothing that required an immediate response, but there was plenty of news, this time from Taiwan. The country was upgrading its reserve and conscript forces. It had requested the United States to speed up a delivery of F-16 fighters. The first of a new class of mine warfare vessels had been launched, and Taiwan's destroyers were being upgraded. The first new anti-submarine warfare helicopters were entering service. There were also images of Taiwan's indigenous anti-shipping cruise missiles. It was reported that an American special forces contingent was in Taiwan helping to train the island's defenders.

On the opposite side, the propaganda war was heating up. The Party's China Daily had photographs of battle tanks packed into a roll-on, roll-off or RoRo ship, the type that would be essential in loading and unloading armour during a Taiwan invasion. In another China Daily report, a PRC foreign ministry spokesperson condemned what he called the bellicose actions of the United Kingdom in sending a frigate through the Taiwan Strait, and he mocked the UK for following in Washington's wake, while a PLA official described the passage of the Richmond as a publicity stunt.

Meanwhile, Ava couldn't fail to note much discussion in international media of the intrusion of 149 PRC aircraft into Taiwan's air defence identification zone over four days - the biggest single intrusion yet, ostensibly to test Taiwan's air defence responses. Ava knew how this worked, a push-pause tactic, testing the defender's sortie times, making the approaches from different angles, trying to wear down the defending pilots, making them edgy and tired, and observing whether they slowed down in their reactions. It was a useful way to gather data about Taiwan's radar installations, too.

Hong Kong's SCMP newspaper quoted a mainland magazine, Naval and Merchant Ships, as saying that the PLAF's recent drills in the South China Sea were designed to prevent other military forces from coming to Taiwan's aid in the event of an attack. The PLA's ability to attack Taiwan was constrained by the so-called second island chain - the islands in the western Pacific Ocean, which included the US base on Guam. An attack on Guam would lead to a prolonged conflict with the United States, it added, while Washington could deploy B-1B and B-52 strategic bombers. Yet China might have a trump card after all if its second aircraft carrier could get close enough to Hawaii.

Ava clicked through one news report after another.

The theme was constant - the PRC was readying itself for conflict. It had unveiled its new CH-6 multi-role drone, capable of high speeds at high altitude, carrying 450 kg of missiles, sensors and radars. The huge WZ-7 drone, the Guizhou Soar Dragon, with a length of 14 metres and a wingspan of 24 metres, would be used in maritime and border reconnaissance roles. An Australian analyst, Malcolm Davis, was quoted by the SCMP as saying the two drones would provide forward intelligence of US naval forces, cueing China's long-range strike capabilities to attack them in what he said was known as 'anti-access and air denial'. Another aircraft unveiled at the 13th China International Aviation and Aerospace Exhibition in Zhuhai, Guangdong, was the electronic warfare version of the J-16 fighter: the J-16D, described by China Daily as being capable of reconnaissance, strike and defensive operations - and said by Wang Yanan, editor-in-chief of Aerospace Knowledge magazine, to act as a 'power amplifier'.

It would, he said, 'disrupt the enemy's radar and other electronic apparatus of ground-based air defence networks, detect their locations and then launch anti-radiation missiles to eliminate them...'

By now, all this technical gibberish had given Ava a headache.

If all that wasn't enough, Suzuki Matsuo, commissioner of the Japanese defence ministry's Acquisition, Technology and Logistics Agency, warned in a Washington talk that the United States and its allies were on the brink of losing their military technological edge over China.

There could be no doubt where all this was headed.

The question Ava asked herself was what she would do about it.

Where the fuck are you, Pan?

Fifty-five days to go.

***

Inaction was not an option, so Ava put together a brief report to run by James so he could post it on the Cincinnatus website. It was a way of testing his and others' reactions to such controversial information from a single, unnamed source:

## PRC ESTABLISHES TAIWAN INVASION COMMAND

*A source close to the Chinese Communist Party (CCP) has told Cincinnatus that the mainland's Eastern Theatre Command's role has been upgraded and renamed the Joint Taiwan Attack Command (JTAC).*

*The senior official, who spoke on condition of anonymity, told Cincinnatus that JTAC's first meeting was held on November 24 at Nanjing, Jiangsu. It was attended by service chiefs and both regional and city Party secretaries under the authority of the Central Military Commission and Joint Staff Department.*

*He said additional formations were assigned to JTAC from other regional commands, and it was understood that JTAC would have operational control of any military operations involving Taiwan.*

*Amphibious assault operations would fall under the PLA's Army Theatre Headquarters at Fuzhou, Fujian, which was now designated as a forward joint command post, he added.*

Enough. Ava kept it short and held back the best and most contentious aspect so far - the timing of the invasion - until later.

This was a trial run.

She had written it up on her usual laptop and she sent it off as an attachment to an email message with a single line: What do you think of this, James?

And hit the 'send' button.

Ava sat back on her sofa, closed her eyes. The response followed four minutes later, a beep on her cellphone.

'You're supposed to be resting, Ava.' James Halberton sounded tired, bothered. 'What is this? Who is this? I'm talking about your source.'

'Sorry, James. Can't discuss it on a mobile.'

A deep sigh from the other end. 'I'll call you on your landline. Wait one.'

Moments later, they had reconnected.

'Look, Ava, I know you can't reveal your source publicly. I accept that, alright? But I need to know. Cincinnatus needs to know, okay?'

89

He was grumpy, that much was clear, and she didn't want to make his bad mood worse, but Ava had no other option.

'It's not okay, James. No-one gets my sources. Don't you trust me by now?'

She said the last bit in a high, hurt tone because it had worked before.

'Of course I do, Ava. Goes without saying.'

'Then what's the problem? Put it out.'

She could hear him breathing over the phone. He was thinking, weighing what he called the cost-benefits, and she was sure he was anything but pleased by her 'exclusive'. Ava knew James was not someone who liked to argue if he could avoid it. He was a pushover, really, despite his disgruntled demeanour.

'Will there be more from this source of yours?'

He should have been pleased, even excited, definitely not irritated.

'Yes.'

'Listen. I'll post it. Happy now? No byline. No point in sticking your neck out. But if it turns out to be bullshit disinformation or a hoax, you're done here. Is that clear? Do we have a deal?'

'That's a deal, chief.'

He liked to be called that.

Ava couldn't help wondering how long it would take her former employers at the NSA to notice the material on the website, and when they did, what they would do about it.

# 14

# December 9

## 09:35 Eastern Standard Time, GMT -4

Cincinnatus was in the news that morning, national and international. It gave Ava quite a start, and she tried to soothe her nerves by telling herself that there was only one thing worse than having an exclusive story, and that was being alone with it for too long.

She needn't have worried. Her saviour took the unlikely form of the Pentagon. A spokesperson for the U.S. Department of Defense, asked the previous evening, during a routine media conference by a Philadelphia Inquirer correspondent, about the reported setting up of a Taiwan attack centre, confirmed the Cincinnatus report without naming the organisation, but began instead by correcting the journalist's terminology.

'I think you're referring to what they're now calling the Joint Taiwan Attack Centre. Right? Yeah, we know of its existence in Nanjing. Until recently, it was known as the Eastern Theatre Command. Its status has changed. You might say it's been upgraded. We did in fact observe unusual movement of high-level Chinese Party and military officials in and out of there on the dates mentioned.'

A flurry of questions followed from other media representatives and the spokesperson did her best to answer all at once with a single response. 'Okay, let me make this clear. Sure, we take this seriously. It's a matter of some concern and I assure you we're watching the situation closely.'

That was it - but it was all the confirmation Ava felt she and her employers at Cincinnatus needed to verify the mysterious Beijing source.

The questions then turned to the administration's response, but elicited nothing new in the United States' studied ambivalence towards the Republic of China in facing up to the threat from its huge adversary on the mainland. Would the United States come to Taiwan's defence at the outset of hostilities? Would the United States now step up arms supplies to the island?

The spokesperson had little option but to duck most of it.

She added the obvious; the Secretary of Defense was on record as saying there was intense competition underway for strategic dominance in the Pacific and that Washington would live up to its responsibilities.

That was the end of the Pentagon presser.

It was out on the wires overnight, too, of course - the Associated Press, Agence France Presse, Reuters, the German News Service and Bloomberg.

Ava flicked through the websites. Naturally, most papers on both sides of the Atlantic picked it up.

It was on CNN that morning, too.

Ava switched tv channels. Two elderly men, a retired U.S. Marine Corps commander named Miller and a former U.S. Pacific Fleet commander, an Admiral Blair, were discussing a possible war between the People's Republic of China and Taiwan.

'People gotta get one thing straight,' growled Miller. 'This ain't going to be no picnic. Back in '44 the beaches of Normandy were mostly wide and flat and extended for a continuous 50 miles. There wasn't much high ground. This is different. Most Taiwan beaches are short, narrow and overlooked by hills rising hundreds and, in some cases, thousands of feet. They've already got defences dug in those hills, even a gigantic underground airfield or two, and you must remember that because Taiwan is subject to frequent typhoons and tremors, most structures along the coast are already built of reinforced concrete.'

'Right,' said Blair. 'The Republic of China has around 190,000 regulars and around a quarter of a million reservists of mixed quality. We're talking a ballpark figure of 450,000 defenders. Conventional military wisdom is that an attacker needs a 3-1 superiority, but given the treacherous seas and weather, as well as the coastal terrain, I think it would be safe to say the attackers will want a 5-1 superiority - and that's two million troops, or more. Not all at once, of course, but that'd be the likely size of the ChiCom invasion force. It's never been done before. If it happens, and it's a big "if", it'll be a first...'

Miller again: 'I'm not saying it's impossible. But bear in mind the Communist Chinese troops will be mostly conscripts, poorly trained and led by officers without combat experience. The last time Beijing went to war was a short, sharp offensive against Vietnam in '79. The Vietnamese mauled them badly, the Chinese took unexpectedly heavy losses - I seem to remember a figure of around 37,000 Chinese dead and wounded - and while they did finally achieve their objectives, the PLA found that its command-and-control had performed badly.

Given the sheer scale and complexity of what's being contemplated now by the Communists, I think an all-out assault on Taiwan would be an unholy mess...'

'But not necessarily a failure,' said Blair.

'No,' Miller agreed. 'Not necessarily. But it would be very bloody and prolonged.'

James called to congratulate Ava, who couldn't speak because she had a mouth full of croissant. Instead, Ava was not someone to fail to seize any and every opportunity that presented itself - she hit the 'send' button on her second story while James was still talking and while she was still chewing and swallowing.

'Jesus, Ava, is this for real? Holy shit!'

'What do you think, James? That I made it up?'

'Hey, no, of course not, no. But this is the same source, right? Your very own "deep throat" in the CCP Politburo? Our bosses want to know. More to the point, our donors will ask the same questions.'

'I'm sure they do. Just run it, James, will you? There's more to come.'

'They're getting calls from the Administration, Ava.'

'I'm sure they are. They should be pleased.'

'I just had a call myself from the NSA public affairs office. They want to talk to you, invite you over for a friendly chat when you have time.'

'And what did you say?'

'That I'd pass on the message. What should I have said?'

'Nothing. That's fine, James, thanks.'

Ava wanted to drink her first coffee of the day while it was still hot.

## CHINA NAMES DATE FOR TAIWAN INVASION

*A well-placed source close to the Chinese Communist Party leadership has told Cincinnatus that General Secretary Qin has named February 1, the Chinese New Year, as the date for launching the invasion of Taiwan.*

*According to the source, the decision prompted muted criticism among senior military and political leaders because of concerns that extreme winter weather conditions are unlikely to favour a successful seaborne assault across 100 miles of the Taiwan Strait.*

*The source says General Secretary Qin subsequently clarified the secret decision by saying the date was provisional on a break in the weather that would allow for a successful operation.*

*Sea conditions in the Strait during the winter months are characterised by storms, high winds, huge seas and thick fog as well as fluctuating tides, raising questions about the physical ability of troops to storm ashore in the face of hostile fire after a long and rough crossing.*

*The source said the General Secretary's decision on the date was ratified by the Politburo's Standing Committee at a recent meeting of the new Strategic Command, chaired by Qin and located in a subterranean bunker below the Zhongnanhai government complex in Beijing.*

*Operational command of invasion forces will be located at the Joint Taiwan Attack Centre in Nanjing, Jiangsu Province, and will communicate with the Strategic Command by fibre optic links, the source added, while Qin reserved all strategic policy decisions for himself.*

*According to independent observers, optimal weather for a seaborne invasion would seem to exist in October, once the typhoon season is over and before winter weather sets in. This is the month when forces of the Republic of China would be most alert to the likelihood of an attack. April was also deemed suitable, except for the prevalence of thick fog at that time of year.*

That was surely enough. Ava had combined two of her informant's messages into one - and she preferred to keep her 'news' reports brief for maximum impact.

She was pretty sure her anonymous 'whistleblower' would agree with this approach.

Turning her attention to her borrowed air-gapped laptop, she translated the next message from her anonymous correspondent - the last on the flash drive. Would this be his last message? With no word from Pan, could Ava really hope for anything more?

Her mobile beeped. She ignored it.

A minute or two later it beeped again, and Ava turned it off without looking to see who it was.

The decrypted, translated message read:

## PRC PLAN OF ATTACK HAS THREE PHASES

*1. The PRC war plan to attack and occupy Taiwan comprises three distinct phases. The first comprises an air and maritime blockade, the second opposed amphibious landings and seizure of beachheads, the third will involve direct ground forces combat, the conquest of the island and the crushing of all remaining resistance.*

*2. PLA commanders regard the Taiwanese enemy as a tough, determined and resourceful opponent. They accept this will not be a four-day 'push-over' but a bitter and costly struggle*

*lasting weeks, perhaps months, in 'mopping up' operations in mountainous areas. They rec-
ognise the defenders will be well coordinated and will fight with modern weapons from well-
prepared, well-concealed positions.*

*3. The initial air and sea blockades will be carried out alongside cyber attacks, with priority
given to attacks on digital targets such as early warning radars. A massive electronic jamming
campaign - both active and passive - will be launched against Taiwan's air defences.*

*4. Deception will form a crucial part of the first phase, with fake radio chatter to mislead the
defenders, tricking them into believing that the PLA is massing forces in certain (false) locations, the aim being to encourage deployment of defenders' assets in the wrong places, exposing
them to PLA counter-attack, and to keep the Taiwan political and military leadership off
balance.*

*5. This initial digital and cyber offensive may last weeks before the bombing offensive begins;
this preparatory 'war of nerves' is designed to weaken the enemy's morale and confuse the
defenders.*

***

Ava showered and dressed, the latest report preoccupying her to the extent that she went through the motions of brushing her teeth and clothing herself unconsciously or, as she'd put it, doing so on auto-pilot. She sat down again and copied the last report onto a thumb drive and transferred the report to her usual laptop. She was about to write it up as a Cincinnatus brief to send over to James that afternoon when her landline started ringing.

It didn't stop, and finally Ava picked up.

'Hi.' Ava put as much hostility into that one word as she could. She didn't want to talk to reporters from other media. She didn't have the time.

'Ms Shute?'

'Who is this?' Ava still sounded brusque, but she recognised the voice.

'Agent Calasso, Ms Shute. Remember me?'

'What can I do for you? I'm kinda busy.'

'Oh yeah? I heard from your office you took the week off. Anyway, we'd like you to pay us a visit. Detective Kramer's here, too.'

'Today?' Ava glanced out of the window. It was raining, and the snow had turned to icy, filthy slush.

'Yes - right now. I don't want to talk about it over the phone, if you don't mind.'

'What's happened?'

'We have news, Ms. Shute.'

'What kind of news? News about what?'

'It's about your friend, Pan.'

'And?'

'It's not good news. I'm so sorry.' Calasso's tone suggested she meant it.

'Tell me.'

'You know where I work, right?'

'I do, but please tell me -'

Ava remembered only part of what Agent Calasso said; it was something about the Washington Field Office on 4th, but she missed the street number - was it 106 or 601?

'Can I expect you in, what, one hour?'

Calasso repeated her office details, but Ava wasn't paying attention.

'Tell me.'

'She's been found. I'd rather not discuss the details now. We'd rather see you in person if you don't mind, okay?'

'You found her? You found Pan? Where? Is she okay? Can I talk to her?'

'Fraid not, Ms Shute.' There was a long pause, so long that Ava thought she'd lost the connection. All she could hear was her own blood thundering in her ears. Agent Calasso's voice seemed to return but faintly, as if from a great distance. The words emerged slowly, with an awful formality. 'I'm sorry to inform you that your friend Pan is dead.'

# 15

## 10:25 China Standard Time, GMT +8

Wang was nervous. His hands tugged at each other, wrestling - so Qin thought - like rats in a cage. The Emperor pretended not to notice his visitor's discomfort. It rather pleased him; whatever it was, whatever Wang had done or not done, the Emperor was happy to have this severe and forbidding fellow squirm before him.

'Well? What is it?'

Qin was struggling to put on a tie and perfect the knot. He wasn't looking forward to welcoming a delegation from the Association of South East Asian Nations, but it was unavoidable - and an opportunity to rub in the message: 'Chinese Taipei' was part of China's internal affairs and its fate was not up for discussion. There had been no time for his lengthy morning swim, only a brief plunge and two lengths. That was one of the problems for the Emperor, any emperor, perhaps, and that was that life seems to comprise an endless succession of dreary meetings with dreary people.

Wang looked about him like someone who wanted to sit down but couldn't find a chair. There weren't any. He wouldn't dare sit on the edge of the Emperor's bed. Wang was a tall man, but he still had to look up at the Emperor, who was taller still.

For no reason, Qin wondered if Wang knew of the sex toys he kept under the bed-come-work table. Not that he cared.

'Yes?' Qin would not spare him.

'Boss, there's been a leak.'

Qin put a scowl on his own face. 'Where?'

'In Washington, D.C. I'm sorry to be the bearer of bad news, but the Ministry asked me to inform you.'

'Don't worry, Wang, I won't shoot the messenger - at least not until I've heard the entire message. Speak.'

Qin watched Wang in his bedroom mirror and saw him manage a weak smile. If this was an attempt at a joke on the part of the Emperor, it wasn't funny, not to Wang.

'Reports have appeared in foreign media of a plan - an alleged plan - to attack and invade Taiwan. These reports appear to be genuine. They give the date of the supposed attack, the various stages of the assault and details of the commands involved in executing the plan.' It had taken Wang some considerable effort to get all that out in succinct form.

Qin's expression did not change.

'And?'

'The reports in the Western media are based on a single, unnamed source said to be close to the Party. Here. In Beijing.'

'I see.' The Emperor was frowning because he'd had to tie the knot again.

'The foreign minister is preparing a statement denying the allegations.'

'No statement is to be made without my approval. Clear? The People's Republic doesn't respond publicly to malicious gossip from counter-revolutionary elements, real or imagined. This is no doubt a provocation, and we will not panic.'

General Wang nodded. He looked quite distraught.

'Call the minister yourself. Now. Anything else?'

'Colleagues from the Ministry of Public Security have located a possible origin of these lies. A woman working here as a researcher. Born in China to Japanese parents. She left her post in an academic organisation with no notice and flew to the United States shortly before the first report appeared. Our people found her, but not before two reports had already appeared in the media giving the timing and stages of the alleged operation. The reports were attributed to a so-called source close to the Party.'

'Where is she now?'

'She's dead. An unfortunate accident. She was restrained, but things got out of hand -'

Qin interrupted. He hated rambling explanations. 'That's careless. And stupid. Have our people in Washington been implicated in any way?'

'No. Not yet, anyway.'

'What do the U.S. authorities say?'

'Nothing so far. Except the U.S. Department of Defense, which confirmed to journalists the change of status of Eastern Theatre Command in Nanjing to the

Joint Taiwan Attack Centre. The Americans say they are watching the situation closely.'

'I bet they bloody are. And the Japanese? How have they reacted? Presumably the deceased had Japanese citizenship.'

'She did. Not a word as yet.'

'So the problem has been solved, the leak blocked?'

'That would appear to be the case, yes. If not the source of the leak, then at least the chain of communication has been broken.'

'So that's that. In a week, it'll be forgotten. The media will turn to something else to amuse themselves and entertain their readers. That gives us time to find the source if it exists at all, which I doubt.'

Wang said nothing, his fingers still grappling one another in frenzied combat.

'Why did you bother me with this, Wang? It's all lies. Disinformation. Ask the foreign minister to drop by, would you? Today, if possible. And no statements, no comments from us, no mention in Party media. We'll not overreact to this.'

Wang nodded and backed away.

Qin admired his silk tie. Frightening Wang had put him in an excellent mood.

*** 

The Emperor recognised that Chen Meilin was unusual in several respects. First, she was a woman in a very senior government post; second, she occupied an extremely sensitive position outside the Party itself. And then again, she herself was unusual. Tall, still attractive - so Qin thought, for a woman in her sixties - she'd been outstanding, even brilliant, as a career intelligence officer working under both diplomatic and illegal cover in what was often called the *Guoanbu*, a shortened version of the *Guajia anquan bu*. Communist China's intelligence and counterintelligence service answered not to the Party but to the State Council, which meant the government. It was, then, for historical reasons and in reaction to the excesses of the 'Gang of Four' and the notorious spymaster and sadist Kang Sheng, depoliticised. While loyal to the Party - that went without saying - it prided itself on its professionalism like no other arm of the Chinese state. Chen Meilin personified this approach.

The *Guoanbu* was bigger in budget and staff than the Russian SVR and the CIA's National Clandestine Service combined. It stood above political manoeuvring and purges. Those few Ministry of State Security (MSS) cadres who had been purged over the years had been removed precisely because they'd attempted to avail themselves of MSS intelligence resources to further their own personal or ideological aims.

For all these reasons, Ms. Chen had Qin's respect.

Among her achievements were several years' undercover work in the Middle East, the penetration of the British secret services with a highly placed mole and her execution - carried out in person - of several captured spies working for the U.S. Central Intelligence Agency. The executions were compulsory viewing for all MSS recruits, even now.

They walked in the open, shadowed by Wang's people but out of earshot. The sky was a scintillating blue, the only sound - aside from their lowered voices - the crunch of their snow boots on the ice.

'I heard about the Japanese woman,' Qin said.

'Some would say she was a sacrificial lamb.'

'So her death was in some way helpful?'

'The FBI will investigate, join the dots together—' Chen didn't finish the sentence but stopped, turned and looked out across the frozen lake, her gloved hands thrust deep into her coat pockets. Qin looked at her, noting that there was nothing expensive or unusual about the padded coat or the fake fur. She wasn't wearing mink, sable or fox. Aside from her height, her dignified bearing, she could have been anyone on a Beijing street. Qin approved of this ordinariness. Outward signs of status, of wealth, were not something this woman had ever cared about. It was a good sign, though dangerous. The incorruptible were highly resistant to pressure, physical and otherwise.

He wanted to ask if the dots the FBI joined up would give the Americans a full picture, an accurate picture, but he didn't want to sound stupid or too keen, too anxious.

Chen broke the silence. 'Public Security - *Gong'anbu* - is throwing everything they have at locating the source and neutralising it.' What she meant, but what Qin knew she wouldn't say, was that the death of the Japanese woman resulted from the Ministry of Public Security's overzealous - or clumsy - activities in DC.

'Who are you using?'

'A small team. Eighteenth Bureau. It conducts operations on U.S. territory, and, of course, the Fifteenth: Taiwan operations. Seven people selected for their ability and reporting to me. Unconnected with our embassy.'

'That's enough?'

'It's invisible is what it is, which is how we like it.'

Chen turned to continue their walk. She didn't wait for him. She didn't have to explain to Qin that intelligence wasn't conducted en masse; the MPS, as the county's national police agency, was something else. It was like comparing a stiletto with a blunderbuss.

Around them and behind, their protectors also lurched into motion, their breath forming a cloud of steam.

'There's more to come, though?'

'Oh, yes. In that sense, the death of the Japanese woman changes nothing.'

'You'll keep me informed.'

'Of course, General Secretary.'

She betrayed no signs of anger or annoyance at the MPS and her own MSS working at loggerheads on the territory of the main enemy. The *Guoanbu* - her service - was supposed to have primacy in all foreign intelligence matters, but it was Qin's predecessor who had restored a role for the *Gong'anbu* in overseas missions, inevitably leading to rivalry between the two, to say nothing of the duplication of effort this involved.

Qin said, 'Nothing recorded, written. No paper trail.'

Chen looked at the Emperor, then, eye to eye.

Qin had his answer in that unflinching look.

***

The Emperor emerged from the pool after a swim lasting two hours, relaxed and a little hungry. He demanded pork and noodles the way his kitchen staff knew he liked it. Everything he ate was specially grown or reared in a particular commune, tested in a laboratory, cooked by the vetted chefs in his own kitchen, then tasted by a team of tasters who were available around the clock in case he demanded midnight snacks or sudden meals at odd times of the day. Qin's food was therefore hugely expensive, given the labour required to produce and prepare it, but it was a precautionary process his chief bodyguard considered essential in securing the General Secretary's survival. It had been thus for his predecessors, also. It was a matter of national security.

While waiting for food, he summoned Wang.

'That place where the Japanese woman worked. What's the name again?'

'The Gortyn-Tsinghua Center for Global Policy.'

'Right. Has the investigation found anything?'

'No, chief. Nothing.'

'How many of the staff are in detention?'

'Two. Both Chinese nationals.'

'Return all the confiscated equipment. Do it tomorrow. Clean the detainees up, let them eat and sleep, and release them tomorrow. If they need new clothes, make sure they have them. I don't want them going home all messed up. Creates a poor impression.'

'Yes, chief.'

'The Center or whatever it is can reopen and resume work.'

Wang inclined his head and made as if to leave.

'I'm not done, Wang.'

'I want Tsai Chen picked up. Nothing recorded. Your objectives: to discover everything you can about his - and his employer's - links to Taiwan and the Taiwanese. Who are his friends? Who are his business contacts, his *guanxi*? Is he leaking secret material to the Americans? Is he helping his employer to do so? Is he a spy for Taiwan? Has he compromised my wife's security? All electronic materials at his home and work to be confiscated and examined in great detail. Got that?'

'Yes, chief.'

'No rough stuff for Mr White Gloves. Not yet, anyway. Continuous interrogation - sleep deprivation, extreme temperature, sensory deprivation, noise, stress positions. The usual. I want reports from you in person - daily. All other employees in Meng Bin's offices to be detained, too. Alright?'

'And Meng Bin herself?'

'My wife is to be left alone. But she must be monitored day and night electronically — and kindly put a surveillance team on her. Make sure they're the best. I want to know where she goes, who she sees, who she talks to and what she says. I'll want the transcripts. Oh, before I forget, Wang: you might see how Tsai reacts when shown the compromising material of him performing in bed with his employer. He'll know right away that if he wants to see the sky again in this life, he'll have to sing long and loud. It'll spare us and him a lot of time and pain once he gets the message. Okay?'

Wang nodded.

'Find me incriminating material, Wang. Genuine, not fake this time. Get the *Guojia anquan bu* on it right away.'

General Wang backed away.

The food arrived, and Qin snatched up his chopsticks. It smelled so good.

***

Qin, dapper in his Western-style business suit, welcomed the ASEAN guests in the Ziguan Hall. He said a few words of welcome. His voice was steady and without emotion - altogether a reasonable tone befitting a reasonable, confident leader of a superpower.

'My dear friends, we welcome you here today. It's good to see you all. I want to reiterate something many of you already know and have taken to heart. I want to stress to the international community, and especially the people of the Asia-Pacific region, that the Chinese people most earnestly desire peace. Only in peace can we all prosper and solve the world's problems; problems of poverty, of pollution, of global warming, of trade imbalances, of nuclear proliferation. China seeks peaceful cooperation with all. We hold out our hand in friendship without qualification, without conditions. There is nothing that cannot be solved with an attitude based on good relations and mutual respect. We do not seek conflict or rivalry - but we also reject hegemony by one world power, one international system that seeks to impose itself on all. This world power speaks of a so-called rules-based system, but what this means in reality is that they can get away with making up those very rules as they go along. This we don't accept. Instead, every community, every people, every nation, has the right to development. That is the basic human right we believe in and which we promote in all our policies. But know this, too, my friends: while we love peace, it cannot be at any price. We will not tolerate interference in our internal affairs. The Chinese people will not lie down and allow others to trample over them and destroy their values. We will defend ourselves against foreign aggression, against terrorism. We do not seek to interfere in others' internal matters, and we expect the same respect, the same courtesy, from others.

'Thank you. I wish you every success in your endeavours.'

Scattered applause. Qin smiled for the television cameras and photographers, though he felt a twinge in his head that made him lean to the right, an instinctive reaction to that malignant thing lying in wait inside his skull.

Xinhua would make a news announcement that afternoon that Qin was looking forward to seeing on television that evening. Four new satellites had been launched into space, yet another sign of China's technological prowess. They were, of course - as Xinhua would report - deployed for peaceful purposes. One was for improved monitoring of weather across the Pacific, the second carried a payload for agricultural purposes, the third, fishing and the fourth, monitoring road traffic.

They were nothing of the kind, as Qin knew. The only true fact was that four satellites had been launched, but the purpose was enhanced coverage of Taiwan and the Western Pacific. By the end of the month, Qin had been informed, there would be no fewer than six imagery satellites watching Taiwan and its adjacent waters, as well as U.S. carrier strike groups operating within 2,000 nautical miles of the Chinese mainland.

It was all part of the plan.

His mobile trembled in his pocket. He didn't have to look to know who it was. It would be his wife, Meng Bin. The raid on her office and the arrest of her young lover must be in progress. Would she scream and hurl abuse at him, or would she weep and beg him to call off the invaders? The odds favoured the former. The Emperor would not answer. He'd let her cool down before contacting her. There was little chance that the recordings of Meng's dalliance with her aide Tsai would have much impact on his wife - unless, of course, some of the most salacious moments were leaked to Chinese-language media offshore. It would damage her business empire, and that was something that would upset her. It was worth considering, but then there was their daughter and her feelings to consider.

# 16

## 12:07 Eastern Standard Time, GMT -4

Agent Calasso opened the door and stood aside for Ava. 'Can we get you anything? Coffee? It's out of the machine, but it could be worse. Right, Kramer?'

'I'm fine, thanks.'

Fine? What a dumb thing to say. Ava wasn't at all fine, but what was she supposed to say? What else could she say? Her stomach was a tight knot of worry and confusion. She kept her hands out of sight because she knew her fingers shook and she didn't want her hosts to notice their visitor's raised heartbeat. She couldn't do anything about the fact that her cheeks burned with apprehension.

Agent Calasso was her usual businesslike self, throwing off her black overcoat to reveal her grey suit, white blouse, badge at her hip, a 9mm semi-automatic in a shoulder holster. Ava thought she had the healthy, almost shiny, complexion of someone who worked out a lot, possibly a swimmer rather than a long-distance runner.

'Please, take a seat.' The tone was courteous, but firm.

Ava sat in one of two upright armchairs. It was an interview room of sorts, a grey sofa, the two single chairs, also grey, a plain black coffee table, grey carpeting. A photograph of the U.S. president on one of the cream walls. Blinds over the window, also blinds across the glass wall separating the room from the corridor. Kramer was there, silent and still, like part of the furniture. He stood by the door with a frown on his face, rubbing his stubbled jaw with his right hand. He wore a jacket and tie, and for the first time Ava saw he wore glasses she thought made him resemble a down-at-heel academic at some obscure college out in the sticks rather than a detective.

'So - what happened?'

Calasso sat down opposite Ava while Kramer stayed on his feet.

'Can we clear something up first, Ms Shute, if you don't mind, yeah? Where were you on the evening of Monday, December 6?'

Ava frowned, recalling the time. 'That's three days ago. Real shitty weather, if you recall. I talked on the phone with someone who falsely claimed to be Mr Kawashima, then I went over to the apartment on Massachusetts Avenue with Detective Kramer… right, Detective? We talked about Pan's disappearance since the Friday.'

'Uh-huh. Right. And on the Monday evening?'

'I took the afternoon off, went home and worked all night on my computer. I got about an hour's sleep when I was woken by you two pounding on my door, but I guess it was Tuesday morning by then.'

'Can anyone vouch for your being at home all Monday night?'

'I don't think so, no. Why?'

Agent Calasso dropped her bombshell. 'Your friend was discovered by the janitor below the balcony of her apartment early on Tuesday. She was lying at the foot of the building, among the bushes between it and the wall and railing separating the property from the pavement. There's a narrow space that no-one uses and it's out of sight from the street. It could only be seen from the apartment balconies on that side of the building if someone were to lean out and look down. Which is what the janitor says he did.'

'She'd fallen?'

'She jumped - or she was thrown,' Calasso said, shooting a glance at Kramer, who hadn't moved. 'Monday night, it seems, given the estimated time of death, though that could have been affected to some extent by the freezing weather.'

Kramer said at last, 'Likely cause of death: a broken neck. It was quick.'

'But,' Ava hesitated, then pushed on. 'The balcony is on the third floor, right? The vegetation would have helped break her fall. Surely—'

Kramer interrupted. 'We think she was on the roof, not the balcony.'

'What makes you say that?' Ava started feeling a little better now that she was engaged in trying to work things out.

'We understand that a couple of thugs went to the neighbouring apartment and threatened the old woman who lived there with a knife — they said they'd cut her unless her husband came out and tapped on Pan's door. Which he did. He had no other option. He identified himself. Pan must have recognised his name and his voice and opened up. That's how they got in. The old couple were terrified and fled back to their home and slammed the door. But they told us they heard people go up the last flight of stairs that lead onto the roof. They heard shouting. We reckon they tried to question her. Either she jumped off the roof to escape or they threw her. I guess we'll never know. There's a security door, leading out onto the roof, but residents have keys. There's a seating area and a few potted plants. If someone wanted to jump, they'd have to climb onto a four-foot wall. We've been up there with forensics.'

There was silence in the room. Calasso and Kramer both watched Ava. She stared down at the table, avoiding their gaze. She was trying to bring order to the chaotic flood of feelings and broken thoughts.

'Did the couple provide a description?'

'The intruders had covered their faces, but it seems they were foreigners.'

'Any specific accent?'

'No.'

'So I'm a suspect - is that it?'

Neither Detective Kramer nor Agent Calasso answered - not directly.

'We're treating this as a suspicious death,' Kramer said at last. 'In effect, a missing person incident has turned into a likely murder inquiry. We're waiting for the full autopsy report.'

'A murder inquiry with national security implications,' added Calasso. 'That's where you come into this, Ms Shute. It's why we want to ask you a few questions about Pan. There are some outstanding issues we don't get, and we thought you might help clear them up for us.'

'Okay. Sure. Glad to help.'

She wasn't.

'Thank you. Now you know your friend as Ding Pan, don't you? But it's not her real name. Can you explain?'

Ava took a deep breath. 'Pan was born in China to Japanese parents. She spent her first years on the mainland. Given the history and the hostility of many Chinese towards the Japanese, something the Chinese Communist authorities actively encourage, she had to adapt. She told me her so-called Chinese uncles gave her the name. I assumed local Chinese friends of the family who wanted to help protect the child. It involved adopting a Chinese persona with a suitable name. I believe her real name - her family name - is Niki Kawashima. At least I have no reason to doubt that it is - was - her real name.'

Calasso opened her notebook. 'But Pan has yet another name, one she uses in her role as a singer, right?'

'She does.'

'Did you know that as Sabine Li or Lee she had a week-long series of evening engagements at a five-star hotel near Fort Meade - close to your old place of work at the NSA headquarters?'

'I didn't, no.'

Kramer cleared his throat. 'She didn't invite you to one of her performances?'

'No.'

'You didn't know?'

'No.'

'Four Seasons. Pretty upmarket. Do you know it?'

'No. Not that I recall.'

'Did you know the jazz lounge where she sang is a favourite watering hole for retired senior NSA officers?'

'No, I didn't.'

'But you worked there - at the NSA. You must have known.'

Ava felt her temper rising, and she clenched her jaws to suppress it. 'I must remind you that most of my time with the NSA was spent abroad, and anyway, what retired NSA people might or might not do is not something that would concern me in the slightest. Strangely enough, Agent Calasso, I don't hang about hotel bars, either, seeking the company of NSA pensioners, or anyone else.'

Calasso was not in the least put out. 'Sabine Li or Lee, aka Ding Pan, aka Niki Kawashima, had quite a following as a talented jazz singer. Her reviewers compared her to Diana Krall. Maybe you heard of her.'

'Pan did say she performed as a singer and that she did it for the money to help fund her doctorate, which she now has - had.'

'Right. So she calls you out of the blue. You haven't seen each other in years, yeah? You went to a smart private school together in London. Godolphin something-or-other. I looked it up and the fees for the girls-only day school are currently around 23,000 sterling per annum. That's just over 30,000 U.S. A place for privileged kids from upper middle-class homes, yeah? So, what then - let me guess: you have a few drinks, you share a meal, you enjoy some pleasant talk about the old days? She quizzes you, like, about your new job.'

'Something like that, yes.'

'And why not? Perfectly natural.' Calasso walked to the window, turned, walked back, hands on her hips, edgy, impatient. 'But weren't you surprised by her approach, this sudden desire to make contact again?'

'Not really, I guess. Let's say I was pleasantly surprised. Intrigued.'

'Uh-huh. I can see that. Then, during this reunion, she asks you for a favour. She hands you something. Some papers, a file. She wants your help. In confidence. She wants you to place it in the media here in DC. Maybe kicking off by using the Cincinnatus website. She explains what you have to do and how. She says she can't - she's too exposed in Beijing and now that they're after her. Right?'

Ava looks at them both, the detective polishing his glasses on his tie, the FBI Agent getting into her stride, confident that she's onto something with this line of questioning.

'We've seen some of the stuff about China on your Cincinnatus website - yesterday and again today. It's real interesting. Let's see - signs that the Chinese Communist leaders are preparing to attack Taiwan and all based on some mysterious, unnamed source. What's the phrase? Close to the Chinese Communist Party? Yeah, that's it. No byline, but this is you, isn't it, Ms Shute? This is your speciality, and that's why your old friend Pan, or whatever her name is, emerged from nowhere and got in touch with you. That, and because she knows you used to work for the NSA. You're well qualified. You have high-level clearance even now. Oh, we checked. We did. You agreed to her request. She wanted you as a cut-out. That's the right expression, isn't it? A cut-out? Well, it's sure got the attention of the world's media. But it's Pan's material, isn't it? All the way from Beijing.'

Silence again.

Kramer again: 'When you both met, did she know she was in danger? Did she hint at being a target?'

Ava seemed deep in thought. She was asking herself the same question, casting her mind back to that evening on Logan Circle and 14th Street.

'She told me that in China all foreigners are under close surveillance.'

Calasso butted in. 'Not the same as being in physical danger, though. Or did she suggest she might be?'

'Not that I recall, no.'

'Didn't it occur to you then that you might also end up as a target?'

Ava did not respond.

'Tell me, Ms Shute, how long you think it will be before your former employers decide to take a closer look and seek some answers from you? We hear they're very interested to hear from you. In fact, they've asked us if we can help them get access to you and your place of work.'

'We're on the same side, Ava.' It was Kramer again, using her first name to make a connection. 'I understand you feel loyal to your friend, that whatever you both agreed was between you both, and that you keep confidences. I get it. Your loyalty does you credit. But we're all loyal Americans in this room. We've all served our country. You have. In our different ways, we still do. We all know our duty is to safeguard the public. We all want the same thing, don't we?'

'Do we?'

Calasso intervened, impatient with this appeal to a common cause. 'What did Pan tell you about her father, Ms Shute?'

'You mean, aside from his death?'

'Right. Aside from that.'

'I guess he was some kind of international corporate executive or consultant.'

'Did Pan tell you that?'

'She may have. I don't really remember.'

Agent Calasso had sat down again and leaned forward, forearms on her knees. 'Ms Shute, listen to me. Mr Kawashima was a wealthy man. Before his death 15 years ago, he brokered deals between Japanese and Chinese corporations. He was also a middleman between Taiwanese investors and the mainland, which had opened up to foreign capital investment. So yes, an executive and a consultant with big connections.'

'I didn't really know the details.'

Ava tried hard not to be seen to react to this information. What was Calasso getting at? That Kawashima had been a spy, an intelligence operative? Ava's mind was in turmoil, questions springing up in profusion. What name had Pan used at school? Well, it would have been Ding Pan. Or was it Kawashima? The more she thought about it, the less sure she became. It seemed such a long time ago. Whichever name she had used, Pan or her parents would have had official papers, or at least authorised translations of a birth certificate or something similar. She would have had a parent or guardian, a legitimate one, someone to take care of her after her parents died and until she came of age and could inherit. It had never occurred to Ava that Pan and the latter's identity were anything but genuine.

Calasso was on her feet.

'The friend you call Ding Pan, also known as Niki Kawashima and Sabine Li, was - we believe - working for a foreign intelligence service while in China. We've concluded that she followed in the late Mr Kawashima's footsteps, whether out of patriotism or loyalty to her dad - or both - we have no idea. But you might. You knew her as well as anyone.'

Ava snorted in disbelief. In fact, Ava was no longer sure what to believe, what was true and what wasn't.

'That's bullshit. She was brilliant at languages that's all. I've known her since school, for Chrissakes. Where's the evidence for this? You're guessing, making it up on the hoof.'

But who was Pan, even then, as a schoolgirl?

Did this mean that the mysterious Party source was a fiction - that this material had been manufactured all along by the Japanese with the intention of planting it in the U.S. media - the eventual goal being to push Washington off the fence regarding Taiwanese sovereignty and the island's defence in the event of a Chinese Communist attack?

The bulk of Tokyo's maritime trade was routed through the South China Sea - and most of that through the Strait, particularly oil imports. If the ChiComs forcibly 'reunified' Taiwan with the mainland, Ava reasoned, Beijing would hold a knife to Tokyo's throat. Japan would be seriously weakened, if not fatally, economically and politically.

Tokyo couldn't let that happen. It couldn't fight Beijing alone, but it would almost certainly join a U.S.-led alliance to defend Taiwan if it came to a shooting war. The Japanese constitution limited Tokyo's military posture to defence, curbing its ability to take any military initiative in the region.

Agent Calasso was still talking. 'Are you going to help us or not, Ms Shute?'

'You obviously know more than I do. The FBI is the leading counter-intelligence organisation…'

'Let's be quite clear,' said Calasso, her tone hardening. 'We can hold you on suspicion of murder, on alleged obstruction of justice, on suspicion of aiding and abetting foreign espionage activity. We can hold you on all or any of these and more - and trust me - you wouldn't get bail. Wouldn't it be so much easier - and less painful - to share with us what you know? You'd save everyone a lot of time and bother. And if you have important information, it's surely right to share it with us in the national interest.'

The national interest? Really? Ava had had enough. Fuck this. She'd done nothing wrong. These people were leaning on her and she didn't like it. She trusted neither Kramer nor Calasso. She jumped to her feet, towering over her interrogators - furious, tense and angry - not simply with the two people in front of her, but also at Pan for getting herself killed, somehow, and for putting her on the spot. *And* for allowing herself to be duped by Pan - if that was what had happened.

Instinctively, she adopted a ready position, left foot forward, knees slightly bent, hands open in front of her.

'I want my lawyer. Here. Now. And I'm gonna call my union rep.'

Detective Kramer sighed, rolled his eyes. He and Agent Calasso exchanged looks.

'Your union rep?'

'I'm a member of The News Guild, okay?'

'Sure,' Calasso said, smiling in a way that seemed more threatening than friendly, the steely kind grin someone might use when faced with a dangerous maniac. 'First, though, we'd appreciate it if you would identify the remains. Can you do that? We'll go with you. It won't take long, I promise. Then you can go right ahead and call your lawyer - before we take you into custody.'

'You threaten to arrest me, then ask if I can identify Pan's body as a favour? I'll tell you something for free, Agent Calasso. You're fuckin' weird is what you are and way out of line.'

Kramer looked sheepish. This was not going well.

'We're not going to arrest you, Ms Shute. Agent Calasso, she —'

'We just wanted to see your reaction,' interrupted Calasso.

'My reaction. You want my reaction. Here's my reaction: fuck you.'

Ava took a step forward. She flipped Calasso the bird, a middle finger thrust upwards, inches from Calasso's face.

Agent Calasso remained unperturbed while Kramer grinned at her.

'So, Ms Shute, now you've got that off your chest, will you or won't you identify your friend's remains?'

Kramer opened the door, Calasso strode out, Kramer followed, and they waited for Ava to join them.

# 17

# December 10

## 08:25 China Standard Time, GMT +8

Fifty-three days to go.

The countdown to invasion excited Qin. There was no doubt about it. Not that he'd ever say so, not to anyone, but he couldn't help feeling that it had boosted his vitality and his virility, both in bed and in the pool. Even his headaches were fewer and less painful.

He didn't float or meander up and down. He wasn't in a meditating state of mind at all. Today the Emperor was all action. He pushed himself hard, creating a disturbance in the pool's placid water, his head and shoulders submerging and rising as he used all his strength in his arms and back to surge forward, orchestrating that rhythmic movement with his legs and feet like some giant, pale frog in pursuit of its prey. It was almost the violent action of butterfly stroke, but not quite. His body seemed to respond to this push, almost lapping up the effort like a dog delighted to be let off the leash. In no time, he'd completed twelve lengths at speed.

Qin drove himself on, enjoying the effort to perfect his underwater turns at the end of each stretch.

The previous night, he'd risen to the occasion no fewer than three times with his anonymous young bedmate. The old man had life in him still. Qin didn't know if the Communist Youth League member, lucky to have been chosen by Wang for this most important task, had been shocked, appalled, impressed, or pleased. Shocked, almost certainly. Not that he cared much what she thought or felt.

It wasn't just her appeal, which was considerable, or the potency of the little blue pill.

Oh, no.

Qin was meant to rule. It was his destiny.

It was his destiny, also, to unify the country.

The Emperor would not shirk his duty in bed or in the forthcoming battle.

Halfway through his 20th length, happy in his watery dreams of glory, he glimpsed what he thought was movement in his peripheral vision, a blur of shapes and colour.

*Shit.*

Once he reached the far end of the pool where the water was deepest, he stopped, turned, arms resting along the ledge, breathing deeply.

General Wang and a woman, no less.

'Boss, it's your daughter –'

It was, too.

Qin waved an arm at Wang. It was not a greeting, but a dismissive sweep.

He called out, 'Wang - you can piss off.'

Why had the slippery bastard let Grace in? What had she said to get through? What excuse had she used? This was his exclusive preserve, and there were no exceptions.

The Emperor let go of the end of the pool, dropping back into the water and swam towards her, thinking about it. Had something awful happened? Watching her. Grace was tall for a Chinese and so - Qin searched his available vocabulary — glamorous. Her black hair was so long she could sit on it, he thought. She was wearing something simple and no doubt expensive.

He stood up once he reached the shallows and waded out, climbing up the steps to where she held out a towel. Grace didn't hold it open to wrap it around her father. No, not at all. She held it out at arm's length, by one corner, as if it was infected with something nasty, so he had to grab it and wrap it around himself before she dropped it by-mistake-on-purpose. He noted she had pink nail varnish matching her lip gloss and that her nails were long, symbol of the idle and wealthy bourgeoisie.

His daughter was a beauty.

'What are you doing here?' His tone was not welcoming.

Grace showed her teeth - in smile or snarl he couldn't say. 'I'm your daughter, or had you forgotten?'

Qin grunted. Very fucking funny it was how fast his good mood had evaporated, how he felt his headache stir in the depths of the addled grey matter in his skull, and how tired he felt all of a sudden from his morning exertions.

He sat down on his lounger like a man defeated, towel around his shoulders - he didn't bother with his cotton robe because he was sure Grace wouldn't be there long, not if he had his way. He noticed Grace was wearing heels - sky blue heels, no doubt from the latest Manolo Blahnik collection at a couple of thousand U.S. dollars a pair.

'What do you want, Grace?'

'Thanks for the warm welcome, Dad. I want to talk about my mother, your wife, and what you're doing to her.'

'I've done nothing to her she hasn't inflicted on herself.'

'You've had her staff detained, all her files and computers removed from her office. You've disrupted her business and caused her a lot of worry. You've terrified her. She's terribly upset. As soon as she heard, she went to bed. She wouldn't eat.'

Was that all?

Qin stared long and hard at his daughter's face. He saw both anger and fear. He saw resolve and doubt jockeying for first place.

'You think I've done this?'

'Who else?'

'I'll let you into a secret, Grace. I don't make every decision in the Party and the country. Many, yes. But not all. And let me tell you something else. Your mum's toy boy is being investigated for espionage. Your mum's lucky in that she's still free to come and go as she pleases, and yes, you can both thank me for that. She's under no restrictions.'

'She's entitled to a life, Dad.'

'Of course she is. We all are, within limits set by the Party.'

'She's entitled to a sex life.'

'Did I ever say otherwise? Did I?'

'She's afraid you're going to start a world war by invading Taiwan.'

So that was what this was.

'And what does she base this rumour on?'

'It's in the news almost every day. It's drip-fed in the China Daily among others. Mum follows the news, you know. You're not the only one who knows what's going on.'

'And she has family in Taiwan - to whom she has sent a great deal of foreign currency of late.'

'You bastard.' Grace flushed with anger.

Qin smiled then. 'Would you like some tea, sweetheart?'

That was the point at which Grace burst into tears. The term 'sweetheart' was enough.

The Emperor reached for a box of tissues on the poolside table next to him, pulled one out and held it up and waited for her to take it, the way she had given him the towel. She had to bend and lean forward to take it. Watching his daughter blow her nose, he thought how easy it was to bully people, to get them to react, especially those closest to him. It was just a matter of knowing which button to push.

Grace stood back and looked at him, her father. Really looked at him.

It was as if she was seeing him for the first time, as he was.

'This is like prison, you know.'

'What did you say?' He squinted up at her.

'This awful place. It's your prison, Dad. You built it, and you're its sole prisoner. I think it's called solitary confinement. Or maybe self-confinement in your case.'

Qin looked away. He wondered if his official daughter had heard about his son, her unofficial half-brother. If she had, would she say anything? She would know how highly the Chinese prized their male heirs, but all the same she'd most probably resent the fact that his affections were divided, that he had another family secreted away. That Grace had graduated from Columbia, spoke English with an American accent, had resident status, that she was now an important player in Party media and a member of the Red Aristocracy wouldn't count. It was a matter of how she felt, of what she believed proper or improper. She would consider herself his rightful, sole heir. Would she have heard the gossip spread by the Falun Gong - based on reality this time? The Emperor's parents had arranged the match to ensure Qin would have a male heir. Last Qin heard, the boy was studying at Beijing's People's University and was supplied with a bodyguard - organised by Wang - 24/7. The boy's mother, a former youth tennis champion from Zhejiang, also lived in the capital so she could be near her son. Qin had not been present at the birth, and had not seen the mother since, though he had made a generous settlement for them both. They would never want for anything as long as the Party was in power and he had the Security Bureau keep a watchful eye on them.

He received monthly reports on the lad.

The Emperor clambered to his feet, pulled the bathrobe around his shoulders. 'I have to go,' he said, and turned away.

'Dad?'

He stopped but did not look back. 'Yes?'

'I really came to tell you something.'

'What?'

'Mum's gone. She left late last night.'

'Gone where?' Now the Emperor did turn, surprised.

Why hadn't he been told? What on earth was Wang doing?

His head throbbed.

'She flew to Singapore, but from what she said before she left, she's headed to Taipei. You know. Our relatives?'

Yes, Qin knew about his wife's Taiwan relatives.

***

That evening, Qin had to explain something rather complicated in a simple way so the top cadres of the High Command would understand and appreciate its importance. He thought it exciting, even thrilling, but then not everyone would be of like mind. He realised that, so he had summoned his chief speech writer from the Propaganda Department to several overnight discussions - at short notice in the small hours - until the Emperor expressed satisfaction with the results while the exhausted chief speech writer took a few days' sick leave.

It had to be short and punchy to hold their attention. It had to be accurate, too.

They'd let their minds stray the moment he opened his mouth - to *er nai*, second milk, meaning the number one mistress, to the next bottle of vintage *maotai*, to the next *Zhongnanhai* brand cigarette, to the new Italian sports car, to the money they'd made from backhanders, the forthcoming holiday in the Seychelles or wherever. For most, nuclear weapons policy was a big turnoff.

Qin took his usual place of honour in the subterranean Strategic Command Centre.

Colonel Sun of the Intelligence Bureau was busy illustrating the General Secretary's talk with missile launches - sea, land and air - on the big screens. Missiles dropped and spun from bombers, burst out of the sea from invisible submarines,

117

roared off mobile launchers, rose priapic from silos buried underground. Fortunately, they did so in silence.

The Emperor tapped the microphone to check the sound was on.

It would be short, but then attention spans were shorter still among the doddery senior echelons.

'Comrades, China has, as you know, worked hard to strengthen our nuclear triad capability of land, sea, and air-launched missiles. We have pioneered new delivery methods, too, such as our hypersonic missiles, and I am happy to announce today that we are moving towards a launch-on-warning posture for the first time, a vital step in securing the country's rightful place in the world order and protecting our progress at home from the attacks of our enemies.'

Qin paused for effect.

'I want you to share this historic moment, for it bears directly on our reunification plans.'

Qin used the term *tongyi daye* - great project of unification.

'You'll recall that I announced the upgrading of the Rocket Forces of the People's Liberation Army from a military branch to a full military service some years ago, in 2015. The following year, I ordered the Rocket Forces to accelerate development and make a solid effort to bring strategic capabilities to a high level.'

Qin paused, drank from a glass of water and looked at the expressions of his audience, some of whom - especially the oldest participants - already seemed on the verge of nodding off. The top ranks of the Party resembled members of a millionaire's retirement home, with oxygen and nurses on tap.

'During an important Party conference in March this year, I again instructed the military to speed up the construction of a high-level strategic deterrent as part of our 14th Five-Year Plan.

'Let me be clear: China will not relinquish its no-first-use policy when it comes to nuclear weapons. It's an important principle on which the Party will not compromise. But this is the important point: the Party has become convinced that growing strategic rivalry with the Main Enemy makes our existing second-strike capability insufficient to deter a more hostile United States.

'In addition, we are concerned that the U.S. re-emphasis on low-yield nuclear weapons in recent years shows a lower threshold for nuclear use and that increases the real risk of nuclear conflict. This, too, we cannot ignore.

'As you all know, the People's Liberation Army has been building up conventional forces to deter - and defeat - any conventional U.S. military attempt to prevent reunification. Therefore, comrades, we have to be capable of conducting proportionate nuclear retaliation at the theatre level - in other words, over Taiwan - because this would deter Washington from escalating the conventional war to the nuclear level.

'We have to be aware also of the possibility that the Main Enemy could conduct a limited nuclear attack on China, while threatening a more massive nuclear attack should we dare to retaliate in self-defence with our own, much fewer nuclear weapons.

'Given overwhelming U.S. nuclear superiority, we might not be able to respond in kind, but we can mitigate or reduce the risk if we publicly adopt a launch-on-warning capability. Our enemies will then need to consider the genuine possibility that the Party might well order an immediate nuclear retaliation within minutes of detecting incoming U.S. missiles - and before any US threat of a massive follow-on nuclear attack could be issued.

'I hope you have followed this line of thought.

'It's a matter of China's survival as a first rank power.

'Because, comrades, I am happy to announce today, on behalf of the Party, the formal adoption of a launch-on-warning posture that will increase the survivability of our second-strike forces. I am also very pleased to announce that we have increased the number of nuclear warheads deployed by the Rocket Forces from 700 to a more credible retaliatory or second-strike deterrent of no fewer than 1,000 warheads.

'These are official announcements and they will be publicised by the usual Party organs, starting tomorrow.

'Thank you to all those who have, through hard work, skill and self-sacrifice, made this a reality. You have helped all of us Chinese sleep safer in our beds at night, protecting our loved ones, especially future generations, and our growing national prosperity.

'Thank you for your service to Party and Country.'

Qin bowed his head, counting a full half minute - if only for the video camera.

The usual scattered applause had followed, but he noticed it was more prolonged than usual, maybe because some of the elderly cadres had woken from their slumber and realised they should join in.

When the Emperor looked up, he saw the screens were blank, and the cadres had risen to their feet and were already shuffling off to the lifts, their faces wearing that blank Party mask that made it impossible to work out what they thought or felt about nuclear deterrence with special Chinese characteristics.

# 18

# December 11

Heavensgate was a funeral home on Pennsylvania Avenue that offered among its services one called 'direct interment', though there was no real interment that Ava could discern but cremation, the disposal of human remains without embalming or any other fancy embellishments - a euphemistic phrase, she thought, for relatively cheap and quick immolation.

Which led Ava to wonder who was picking up the tab. Was it the FBI? Or was it Pan's family estate, maybe as a trust? No-one had mentioned anything about it to her. Would some lawyer appear on behalf of the Ding Pan/Niki Kawashima estate?

The Heavensgate offices were bright and modern, the staff polite and helpful without being obsequious.

Calasso placed flowers on the plain laminate coffin, half a dozen white lilies, probably bought on FBI expenses. Kramer brought no flowers, but out of respect for the dead and the occasion, the DC detective had shaved, and wore a suit and tie for the occasion. Ava wore black from head to foot. It seemed they would be the only ones present.

An elderly man of some dignity - Ava thought he must be one of the directors of the firm - came forward to ask if he should proceed. Ava thought there would be a time slot and anything over that would increase the fee. There would be no service, no prayers - there was instead the faint sound of recorded music, which Ava thought she recognised as Bach's '*Lord, hear the voice of my complaint, To Thee I now commend me.*'

What would Pan have made of that?

The manager or director was interrupted by raised voices, a sudden commotion and, with the opening hiss of the automatic glass doors, the arrival of two more people, both male, both east Asian, both flustered. One was tall, in his twenties, in a dark suit with a black tie, hair parted in the centre. Ava thought he looked a little like Keanu Reeves.

The second was short, broad and bald in a rumpled, ill-fitting suit, the tie halfway down his chest, the collar open.

Agent Calasso joined the nervous young attendant who tried, and failed, to persuade the two latecomers to first sign the visitors' book, registering their names, but they'd rushed through reception and pushed in for fear of missing the event, the shorter of the two trying to elbow his way ahead of his rival. A stern Calasso blocked their progress, showed each of them her FBI badge and that seemed to nudge them into producing identification. She would not be rushed; she pulled out a notebook and pen and copied down their details.

It turned out later, according to Calasso, that the taller, younger man was a Japanese consular official, the shorter, older and pugnacious visitor his opposite number from the PRC mission.

The Communist Chinese wasn't happy. He rushed up the aisle to the coffin and, looking down, he tried - to the uplifting strains of Bach - to open it, hooking his fingers under the upper edge and straining to raise it. 'No, sir, please don't.' Three of the firm's staff intervened, pulling the Chinese back, restraining him while he shouted and twisted out of their grasp, throwing punches, or trying to do so.

'Wait!' Ava had to step in to stop the melee. 'Please, everyone, cool it, okay?'

They stopped, turned, looked her up and down.

'This official from the People's Republic wants to identify the remains,' Ava said. 'That's all. He insists he has the right to check that the body is that of the person we say it is. According to him, Pan is a Chinese citizen and that the consulate wants to verify her identity. He also protests at being manhandled and claims diplomatic status.'

Agent Calasso looked grim and shook her head - whether in disapproval or disbelief wasn't clear.

Ava translated what she'd just said in English into Mandarin for the Chinese official. He ignored her efforts and didn't seem impressed.

The senior staffer - the director, if that's what he was - raised his voice in a rich, southern baritone that suggested he was used to addressing a crowd - a crowd of five restive mourners, employees aside. 'Does anyone object if we open the coffin so the gentleman from the consulate can see for himself?'

He placed an emphasis on 'gentleman'.

No-one objected. Calasso shrugged, Kramer looked away. The Japanese smiled to himself, tapped a polished toecap on the floor, but he did not protest. Ava was silent.

The surly Chinese stood at the head of the coffin, waiting while a small electric hand drill was used to loosen the screws and the lid raised by the attendants. He glanced down, and, with no change in expression, nodded to the staff and stepped back, the honour of the People's Republic of China having been satisfied. The Japanese followed suit, only more circumspect in manner.

Ava also stepped up, glanced down at the battered, broken face of her dead friend.

*\*\**

Tears - of dismay, of shock, sorrow, of regret - didn't flow until Ava was out on the pavement. She turned away, so the others didn't see her weep. The Japanese and Chinese officials had hurried off on their own separate ways, without a word to anyone. It was freezing outside, with a cruel wind scything down the street, cutting through Ava's wool coat.

Calasso and Kramer came up on either side of Ava. 'Sorry for your loss,' was all Kramer could mumble.

'I know a place,' said Calasso, slipping a gloved hand under Ava's arm and giving it a slight squeeze. Kramer fell into step on Ava's right. He seemed to know whatever this was that they were going to.

'Where are you taking me?' Ava didn't protest or resist. She was not in the mood for further confrontations.

'My favourite dive bar,' said Agent Calasso.

'Mostly cops and congressional aides,' Kramer added.

The Tune Inn was on the corner of Pennsylvania and 4th - and was perhaps unusual in having maintained a laid-back ambience and in offering inexpensive food in such a wealthy, self-consciously political neighbourhood.

There were lots of pictures and dead animals on the walls. Roadkill, Kramer called the stuffed deer. The place looked old, but it wasn't especially grimy. According to Calasso, one reason for that might be because it had been rebuilt with a crowd-funder after a fire gutted it back in 2011. 'It's a different Capitol Hill around here,' Calasso said. 'You get the lawyers and the lobbyists, but you also get mechanics and plumbers.'

'And cops,' said Kramer. 'Lots of cops.'

'Plus the odd agent gone AWOL.'

Ava looked at the long bar, the booths, the pictures on the wooden walls.

'What is a dive bar, anyhow?'

'Time, grime and dime,' Calasso said. 'How long it's been around, how grimy it is, and how cheap. I read someplace this one first opened in 1947. It's not that grimy since the ban on smoking.'

Ava asked for a Bloody Mary and, feeling hungry, chose the daily special: meatloaf and mash. Kramer went for the Philly cheesesteak and a Bud Lite, Calasso a standard burger washed down with an iced tea.

When Calasso glanced with disapproval at Kramer's beer, he glared back at her. 'Hey, it's my day off, okay?'

Calasso shrugged.

'We can offer you protection, Avery.' Calasso had used the formal version of her first name. 'If you decide it's something you want, and my professional view is that you should take up the offer, you'll have to cooperate, and by that I mean we would need to know everything, otherwise we wouldn't know what we were getting ourselves into. Okay?'

'Okay,' Ava said. She had no intention of co-operating.

By the time their plates had been cleared away, the three had exhausted small talk and lapsed into silence, Ava thinking that each of them had their own immediate and particular worries and concerns - none of which had anything to do with Pan or the mysterious Beijing informant and his or her encrypted messages warning of war.

That was presumably the end of it with Pan's death.

The least Ava could do was to respect Pan's memory by sticking with her refusal to involve the FBI, NSA, CIA, or anyone else.

No, she wouldn't let herself cry again.

Ava's attention was taken by a tall figure who had just entered, a dark and blank silhouette against the light outside, someone in a long overcoat, who paused, taking in the place, saying something to the guy behind the bar, then moved down the long room towards them, wending his way with care between booths and tables on one side and bar stools on the other. Calasso turned to Ava,

'Hey, there's someone I want you to meet - or maybe I should say he wants to meet you.'

# 19

## 14:40 China Standard Time, GMT +8

The Emperor greeted the visitor in a low voice so that Wang wouldn't overhear.

'Lau Chong, how are you, Son?'

'Well, Father, thank you.'

Qin turned and called out, 'Leave us, General, please.'

Father and son stood together at the edge of the pool, looking across the still water as the chief bodyguard in his general's black *Gong'anbu* uniform withdrew.

'You'd like a dip? Water's not cold.'

'No thanks.'

'Suit yourself. You're the only person I've ever invited to swim, did you know that? I hope you feel honoured!' The Emperor meant it as a joke, but his son wasn't smiling. 'Please, take a seat. Right there, on the lounger opposite, yes, so we can talk together, in confidence. Let me pour you some tea. You know, you remind me of myself at your age. Tall, robust, not as fat as me, of course, haha, altogether stronger. Better looking, too, and a lot smarter!'

The Emperor found he felt nervous, an unfamiliar feeling, not unlike going on a first date with a girl, except this was no woman but his only son, his unofficial son. He poured the tea, that little crooked smile in place, head tilted.

'Tell me - how is your mother?'

'She's well.'

'Glad to hear it.'

They drank their tea.

'Is there anything you need? Anything that your mother needs?'

'I don't believe so. No, thank you. We're fine.'

Lau was also tense.

'Good. Good. I'm glad to hear you're both well. If there is something, speak up. You have only to ask. You have nothing to fear. I'll harm neither you nor anyone in your mother's family. They're quite safe, I promise. You all are. I'll make sure of it.'

The boy nodded, but he didn't look reassured. Boy? No, Qin thought, he's no boy. He's 20 and a man now, with a man's thoughts, dreams and desires. If I know a man's desires, then I know the man, the Emperor told himself. Only he had no clue at all as to his son's desires.

'You finish, soon, at university?'

Lau Chong nodded, sipped his hot tea, keeping his eyes on the pool.

'I hear good things about you, Chong. You have made me proud. You work hard at your studies. I am delighted that you attend Party meetings. Have you thought what you'll do after you graduate?'

Lau looked embarrassed, though the question could not have been unexpected. 'I thought I might go into business -' His voice tailed off.

He seemed to wait for the Emperor to disapprove, to tell him off, to blow his top.

Qin thought the young man - his unofficial heir and successor - had probably heard the most blood-curdling, monstrous tales of the Emperor's temper and his cruelty. Which was no bad thing, in Qin's opinion.

'That's fine - if that's what you want. Is it what you want?'

'I think so. I'm not sure, though.'

'Would you like to work here, in the *Zhongnanhai*?'

The young man seemed afraid to look his father in the eye, but he glanced up and looked away again, surprised. 'Doing what, Father?'

He likes money, Qin thought, not political power.

'You could work for me. Why not start off your political career in the Party from a sound position? You would learn much, and quickly.'

An unassailable position.

Lau frowned, then blurted out his response. 'Wouldn't that be resented? I mean, taking advantage of the fact that you're my father, kind of getting a Party job I haven't worked for and don't deserve?'

'It's how the system works, right or wrong. People will expect it of you as a matter of course. Don't worry - you'd work hard, all right. You'd have a lot of responsibilities, as well as power.'

'I'd work as what?'

'How would you like to be head of my security after a brief apprenticeship? You'd be my gatekeeper, screening visitors, looking after my personal safety on trips and public events. It involves a lot of organisation. It would mean some training in intelligence and security issues related to the task, though, because you'd have to liaise every day with ministers and Politburo members. You'd have to be both tough and diplomatic.'

'I see.'

Lau Chong nodded, his expression giving nothing away.

Qin realised that despite the dry and dull reports he received from the Security Bureau about his son, Lau was still a stranger. The Emperor knew nothing about him, nothing about his emotional life. Nothing about what mattered - his hopes, his fears, his inner self. He chased girls, well and good, and he liked to drink, as did millions of other young Chinese males. He was his father's son, after all.

Lau seemed to have a loose circle of friends, perhaps only a dozen fellow students, but the reports had failed to identify anyone close. As for girlfriends, he was said to play the field and had no single bedmate. Given the lad's age, Qin thought that sensible.

But what were his favourite films, music and books? How did he spend his free time? Did he follow football?

Was he loyal?

Was he the intellectual type?

Did his friends know who he was, whose son he was? It seemed unlikely. Not even the president of his university knew. Did he boast of it? Did he use his *guanxi* for his own benefit? Did his mother spoil him? Was he pampered? If the surveillance reports were to be believed - and Qin wasn't sure if they were because over-cautious officers were likely to be very careful in what they included in their assessments - then his son showed no particular interest in expensive toys such as Ferraris or fashionable brands of clothing. He was modest in his spending. He was no playboy.

In short, he behaved like any other somewhat privileged, card-carrying undergraduate.

He looked like one, too. He wore a white V-neck tee, blue jeans, white Reebok trainers and over the tee he wore a thin, unstructured black jacket. His coat, scarf and fake fur hat lay to one side - and they were ordinary, commonplace, and could be found in any high street menswear store. He hadn't needed winter boots today because Wang had sent a Public Security Ministry driver to collect him from the home he shared with his mother.

His hair was like his father's. It was black and thick and he grew it quite long, though today it seemed to have been gelled and combed back with a perfect parting - at least the lad didn't need pomade yet.

'No hurry, Chong. Think about it. Take your time. Just remember, you'd be a very senior Party cadre with a great deal of influence. You would have to be incorruptible and loyal to the Party. Loyal to me in all things. Once they found out who you were, who your father is, people would be envious. You'd inherit powerful allies - and enemies. People would also fear you. They'd try to influence you. They'd try all manner of temptations to win you over, to involve you in their schemes and plots to increase their wealth and power. You would have to be on guard, alert, and always discreet.'

'May I ask you something?'

'Go ahead.'

'How would I —'

'Yes?'

'How would I perform my duties with your official family around? I understand you have a wife and a daughter and they —'

'They don't come here. My daughter has done so a couple of times, mainly to pick a fight with me. My wife has her own interests - a life of her own - and she doesn't visit me here. There would be no reason for them to know you, who you are, or what you do. And you would have no reason to interact with them at all.'

Lau seemed to think about this. He didn't seem convinced. 'Qin is just a Chinese family name like any other, right? But for many people - maybe most Chinese - when they hear your name mentioned, Father, they think of the Emperor Qin. You know that, don't you? I'm not sure if it's an advantage or disadvantage as General Secretary. Maybe you can tell me. You would know better than anyone, but I'd like to know your view.'

He was right, of course.

Qin Shi Huang, or First Emperor of Qin, was the founder of the Qin dynasty, and the first emperor of a unified China from the age of 38, having conquered all the other Warring States. He gave up the title of king and appointed himself Emperor, and this self-invented title would be carried on by subsequent Chinese leaders for the next two millennia. He'd conquered 13 cities in seven years with a world-beating military machine equipped with state-of-the-art weaponry, but the enemies within proved far more dangerous than the armies without the Qin palace.

'You're right. I'm no relative of that particular Qin.'

'A good thing, wouldn't you say, Father, considering that Emperor Qin banned and burned many books and is said to have executed scholars?'

Qin laughed at his son's nerve. 'I don't know if the executions and book-burning happened. He standardised many customs and procedures and unified several state walls into a single Great Wall of China. He was a great unifier and nation builder, was he not?'

Lau smiled at his father for the first time, as if he'd forgotten who he was talking to. 'We mustn't forget the terracotta army used to guard his mausoleum, which was the size of a city. Did you know they've uncovered 8,700 terracotta soldiers so far? It seems he wanted immortality, or so we were taught at school, and he poisoned himself with mercury, which he'd been told was the elixir of everlasting life.'

'Don't worry, Son - I'm not that crazy. No mercury for me - only *maotai*.'

Lau Chong smiled at this, but was not deflected. 'To survive, Father, he learned very early on to be utterly ruthless and you no doubt know he perfected a totalitarian ideology called legalism, a kind of thought control governing every detail of every person's life.'

'Really?' Qin pretended to be shocked. His son had a rather serious side to him, after all.

'I must have missed that history lesson.'

Father and son laughed.

What was Lau saying - that his father was an autocrat, obsessed with control? Was he being accused by his own son - now wasn't that something? The CCP was a dynasty, so too the nationalist Kuomintang. But in the Communist system, sons could not inherit their fathers' wealth and power, at least they weren't supposed to. Perhaps, in time, Lau Chong would, as a Red Prince, adopt his father's name in place of his mother's — once he was powerful enough to do so.

Qin put all that aside. He had a serious point to make. He put his empty teacup back on the tray and leaned forward so that he stared into his son's face. 'The Party also has a glorious task of unification ahead of it, and I hope you will support our campaign. I am counting on your active support.'

Lau nodded but said nothing, waiting. Something told his father that he knew about the plans for Taiwan, or had heard of them. The young man looked down at his own feet, nodding. It wasn't clear to Qin if his unofficial son accepted the explanation about Qin's official family or not. It wasn't entirely accurate, of course, because Qin had said nothing of the perpetual rumour mill, the endless gossip, that permeated the Party's top cadres in the *Zhongnanhai* and beyond. The secret of the relationship, and of the unofficial son's preferment, would not stay secret for very long. Shit-stirring - Qin's phrase - was an inescapable, integral part of power politics. Just as that first Qin had learned in 247 BCE - or whatever year it was - to destroy his enemies in his own household with extreme ruthlessness, so this contemporary Qin and his unofficial son Lau would have to learn to deal with malicious gossip, master it, turn it to their advantage, and neutralise the threats close to home.

Lau looked up, serious again. 'This training course —'

'Oh, yes. It's a special university course for intelligence and security officers. Three months should be enough in your case, I would have thought. But you could opt for the full two-year postgrad degree if that's what you'd prefer.'

Qin was referring to the China Institute for Contemporary International Relations (CICR) - the State Security or *Guoanbu* analysis centre, in effect. It was one of about 2,500 think-tanks set up in the Deng Xiaoping and Jiang Zemin era. The CICR admitted genuine students as part of its cover; it offered a two-year Master's degree and a three-year doctoral program. It was supposedly one hundred percent academic, yet it was also one hundred percent an intelligence organisation, with its 'researchers' heading off into the field, whether this meant Taliban-held areas of Afghanistan or ISIS-held parts of Syria.

'One more question, Father, if you don't mind.'

He was quite respectful, Qin thought to himself, but not at all hesitant in asking pertinent questions, or in making fun of his father. He had balls, and that was splendid because he was going to need all his courage to survive.

'Yes?'

'You mentioned unification, Father. Is it true we're going to war over Taiwan in just a few weeks' time?'

# 20

## 12:30 Eastern Standard Time, GMT -4

'This must be Washington's Uber-cool coffee shop in DC's Uber-cool hotel, right?'

'Something of the kind,' Ava said. 'Thanks for picking this spot so close to my work. It's appreciated.' She didn't tell her companion she had taken the week off.

Samuel Turner was tall, even taller than Ava by an inch or thereabouts, but it was the winning smile she remembered from a three-day familiarisation tour of the Secret Intelligence Service in London that Sam had supervised during her secondment to GCHQ headquarters - the donut (or doughnut) it was called for its circular shape - in Cheltenham. Back then, she recalled he'd still had a full beard, piratical and appropriate for an SIS officer recruited from the Royal Navy. That was why, when he had walked up to their table in the Tune Inn earlier, she hadn't recognised the clean-shaven version immediately, at least, not until he smiled at her and she heard his clipped British voice.

But Cheltenham wasn't the first time they'd met. Did he remember? He must do.

*The Cup We All Race4* certainly seemed trendy, and so was its location, *The Line DC Hotel* in Adams Morgan.

'I'm going to try this Maple Latte,' Turner said. 'Sounds terrible, but I'll try anything once. And I'll have a bagel. What about you? Should I call you Ava or Avery or Ms Shute?'

So polite, this Brit. 'Ava will do fine.'

'And I'm Sam. How do you do?'

'Yes, Sam. I know who you are. I'll have mint tea, thank you. No bagel.'

He must be in his early 40s, she thought. Not unattractive, far from it, decidedly masculine, good at languages, a former Royal Navy submariner and career spy - an altogether interesting combination for a man with a penchant for green tweed. The SIS recruiters must have thought so, too, tweed aside, or they wouldn't have snapped him up, luring him away from the Special Boat Service after his tour in Afghanistan.

They found a quiet nook and sat opposite each other.

'It's been a while.'

'Sam, this isn't a social call on your part. So let's get to it, shall we?'

He grinned, put his head on one side, studying her.

'I remember your directness.'

At least he hadn't mentioned her red hair. That was a plus.

This opening exchange reminded Ava of her Friday evening meeting with Pan on Logan Circle, the cocktails, the meal, the chat about their school days. That hadn't been social either, not really, for Pan had had a specific purpose in mind when she had contacted Ava. So did Sam Turner.

'So.' It was Ava's way of saying, get on with it.

'So, Ava. I rather hoped it was a little of both.'

'Both what?'

'Both social and professional.'

'You did, did you? Didn't Agent Calasso tell you I'm no longer in U.S. government employment?'

'I was so informed, but not by Agent Calasso of the FBI, or Detective Kramer.'

'And?'

'You know how this works. I make my pitch...'

'And I say no.'

'Right. But show me the courtesy of pretending to listen to it, at least. My ego will be eternally grateful. Then you can rubbish it as much as you like.'

'Let's get it over with.' She tried and failed not to return the smile.

The former lieutenant-commander was breaking up his bagel and popping bits of it into his mouth. He didn't much care for the famous maple latte.

'Cincinnatus and its website are known to us. I read the recent articles on China's alleged war plans, which we, like the FBI, believe were written by your good self. The source is probably yours. I'm aware you're now an academic researcher in the private sector and you do write the odd journalistic piece. I have read some of your articles. I'd be interested to know if there is more where this came from, or whether that's all there is - following the murder of your friend Ding Pan, aka Niki Kawashima, who was - yet another assumption on my part

- in contact with the source. Did she pass the source over to you, and, if so, whether you are now the sole heir?'

Sam chewed more of his bagel and looked to see if his words had any effect on Ava. They hadn't, not visibly.

Turner's voice dropped so low she had to strain to make out what he was saying. 'You will know it's almost impossible to recruit people in hard target countries, what your fellow Americans call denied territories, such as Russia, China and North Korea. There are several reasons. First, any foreigner is under constant scrutiny - and any approach to a local puts the latter in great danger. Second, you may have noticed that we in the so-called West no longer hold the high moral ground - if we ever did, and even then, only briefly, thanks to the likes of Hitler and Stalin. So there's no ideological reason anyone would come to us of their own free will, given the risks, other than a loathing for their own system and a touchingly naïve regard for ours. So if we hope to recruit any hard target source, it has to be in a third country. Then we would run that source back on his or her home turf, using a succession of temporary case officers or TCOs to service dead drops. A hands-off approach, no personal contact except for rare meets in third countries. You know the drill.'

'Pretty much, though humint isn't an NSA concern.'

'The fact is, Ava, we rely on walk-ins. So does the CIA's Clandestine Service, and sometimes a walk-in can prove to be a highly effective agent who survives undercover for years - and yes, it happens, but it's rare. Gordievsky was one, Tolkachev another.'

'Your point?'

'When we first met, you and I, the very first time, I don't mind admitting my Service was going through a tough time. Our Requirements department was top dog. If I tripped over the equivalent in espionage terms of Putin's crown jewels, and I found it wasn't right there in the very long Requirements list for Russia, I'd have to shred and burn whatever it was and pretend it never happened. It killed initiative stone dead, believe me. Reputations were built by, and knighthoods awarded to, people who did absolutely nothing but shuffle paper and certainly never recruited an agent in a 25-year career. Thankfully, the worst is over and we have more wriggle room these days and we expect more from our people, too.'

'Sam, my heart bleeds for you guys and that's all very interesting, but again, I have to ask, what's your point?'

'I want your source. I want his or her material. Let's face it; what you have is as rare as hens' teeth. If the source is genuine. You'll have read of the destruction wrought by fake defectors.'

'Well, that's frank. Of course you do. You're not allowed to recruit American nationals, though. Didn't they teach you that at Fort Monckton - down south in Gosport, I think it is? You showed us around, in horizontal rain and a gale off the Solent, if I recall.'

'Who says we can't? You're no longer in government service. Do you really think Langley's National Clandestine Service would hesitate to entice, bribe, seduce or bludgeon some luckless Brit into its service if it saw its interests served by doing so - whether a civilian or an SIS asset? Do you?'

'I say fuck Langley.'

'Indeed. But please don't imagine the UK services aren't bought and paid for by the United States. You people pay for our geographic reach. Always was that way and still true today. Diego Garcia, Cyprus, Belize, and so on. What's your answer?'

'It's a no, Sam.'

'Is that because the source has dried up or is no longer accessible? Or is it because you feel that as an American you can't work with us?'

'Neither.'

'What, then?'

'Okay, Sam. You can have this for free. The source wants his material out there, in public, where he thinks it will have maximum impact and maybe - just maybe - stop the war from happening. What he definitely does not want is for some anally retentive spy to write it up in some eyes-only briefing paper for a half-witted prime minister or gaga president who doesn't know his ass from his elbow and then lock it away in a top secret file in the archives, to be forgotten for generations.'

Sam grinned and nodded - he seemed almost enthusiastic.

Ava realised that her little speech, however negative, had given away the fact she did control access to the material, that she could speak for the source, and that she was, or hoped to be, Pan's successor.

'What if I said - speaking, of course, as self-confessed, anally retentive spy - you could have your cake, Ava, and eat it, too? What if I said you could carry on writing it up for public consumption? Do what the source wants by all means.

Just let me have copies of the original Mandarin. I'm assuming it is in vernacular Mandarin - the simplified Communist version?'

Ava gave no sign of it being so or not, but she decided to return fire.

'I got to tell you, Sam. This source is risking his or her neck. The family too, if there is one. He's taking giant risks. He or she is a Communist, a Party member, for Chrissakes. One with access with a capital A. Not a peasant. Not a worker. If you ask me, I'd say he's probably Red fucking Aristocracy. Top drawer. He or she is doing this because she knows - knows - a war over Taiwan will destroy the country, the beloved Party, and kill thousands, maybe millions if it turns nuclear, and totally screw up the global economy. The source is a fucking patriot. God, how I hate patriots!'

'There speaks a true intelligence professional.'

Ava knew she'd said more - a lot more - than she'd intended, and to her surprise, she was completely sober.

Sam Turner looked down at his cold coffee. There was a long silence after Ava's outburst.

'Know what I think, Ava? I think we should adjourn, leave this painfully fashionable place and go get ourselves a real bloody drink. What do you say?'

*** 

Ava's cheeks stung from the sudden contrast between the cold outside and the warmth within. Leather and mahogany, subdued lighting, an atmosphere of discreet, private conversations and no intrusive muzak to spoil the ambience.

'I can see why you chose this place, Sam. It's a home from home, St James's and Pall Mall clubland and all that.'

Sam smiled, amused. 'Wrong. You've a stereotyped view of UK males, at least the middle class sort, but I don't belong to any club, Ava, and never did. Not my thing. It's discouraged, as a matter of fact. No Travellers, Whites or Boodles, not even Cavalry, the Army and Navy or the Special Forces Club. Not for serving officers. I should add, I don't play bridge or golf, and that's almost sacrilege in Whitehall. But I do like this place.'

He was referring to the Round Robin Bar in the Willard Intercontinental Hotel on Pennsylvania. They had found a comfortable corner where they could see all the comings and goings, and they both nursed double drams of malt whisky. Ava had insisted on going home first to change into something more formal. She'd showered, put on black tights and her one and only little black number, dabbed on lip gloss and a drop of scent and had tamed her wild red hair. She was, as far as she could tell, almost presentable by the time she found a taxi.

'There's just one question we have.'

'We?'

'Her Majesty's Government - that parcel of rogues.'

'And that is?'

'Will Beijing really go to war over Taiwan?'

'No doubt in my mind on that score.'

He gave her one of his cards, which described Turner as a first secretary, commercial.

'I need convincing. We need convincing. Your own government here in DC needs convincing. I suspect there isn't much time left in which to do so. On the other side of the fence, Beijing's *Guoanbu*, the foreign intelligence service under the aegis of the Ministry of State Security, has just one urgent question.'

'Which is — presumably — whether the United States will intervene militarily to defend Taiwan and stop Beijing's military offensive.'

'Right. Those two questions pretty much sum up the only ballgame in this town. Same goes for London, Canberra, Tokyo, Paris, Berlin. Millions of lives are at stake, along with the wellbeing and security of millions more.'

'I don't disagree. The source would wholeheartedly concur.'

'Glad to hear it. Tell me, did your source ever mention anything about China dropping, or changing, its nuclear weapons policy of no-first-use?'

'If he had, I would have written about it.'

'You may not know this, but your former service, the NSA, is reporting that Beijing has begun the deployment of launch-on-warning strategic nuclear missiles. Fewer than twenty, so far, in new silos. It's a big change and of serious concern.'

'I bet - but Beijing is responding to what it sees as possible U.S. nuclear blackmail. The Communist Chinese tend to react to events rather than initiate them. Your parcel of rogues might bear that in mind.'

'Possibly.'

Ava took a sip to mark this short truce.

'But Ava - please don't imagine that all you have to deal with here are the couple of dozen *Guoanbu* intelligence officers working under diplomatic cover out of the PRC embassy. They have illegals, too, along with their networks under deep cover. Our FBI friends tell us they've been mobilised these last few months.

They've brought in reinforcements - more surveillance teams, couriers and TCOs.'

'Presumably they killed Pan.'

'We assume so. But there are other players in this game.'

'You mean the *Naicho* - Japanese intel?'

Sam waved a hand, a dismissive gesture. 'Under General Secretary Qin's predecessor, Xie, the counterespionage role of the *Gong'anbu*, the security service of the Ministry of Public Security, was given a new lease of life. Its First Bureau people are here, too, also working out of the embassy and elsewhere. Essentially, the *Guoanbu* and *Gong'anbu* are at loggerheads, competing for the same prize - the attention of Qin himself and that means they too want answers. Huge kudos to whoever gets it right first.'

Ava ran a finger around the rim of her crystal tumbler. 'And what conclusions do we draw from that?'

'That both teams will do anything to get what they want, and that you're in genuine danger, Ava, as your friend was.'

He didn't need to add 'and look at what happened to her.'

Sam drained his glass, held it up and looked at Ava questioningly. She shook her head. Another and she wouldn't be able to walk in a straight line, let alone keep a clear head. She wasn't sure she could do so even now.

'Let's agree on some common ground, Ava. We both want to disseminate the source material in such a way that it has maximum impact. Right?'

Ava nodded. 'Damn right.'

'Then let's help each other. You do what you do best. I do what I do. You continue your work, but it will be at a location where we can keep a protective eye on you. No commuting every weekday, no rubbing shoulders with fellow office workers. No wandering out on your own to the shop to buy coffee. You won't know we're there most of the time, but we will be. Can you do that? In return, all I want is a copy of everything you source provides.'

'And you'll do what with it?'

'Do you have to ask? Really? Why is it that the NSA hasn't paid you a visit as yet, or called you in for a wee chat? Why hasn't the CIA snatched you off the street and taken you to one of their black sites? Do I really have to spell it out - to you of all people? This is how it works. I keep them off your back, you feed me the intel from your source and don't ask me what I do with it. A fair exchange, wouldn't you say?'

Ava was thinking about the elephant in the room and he seemed to know it, too, because he brought it up with perfect timing.

'Remember where we first met, Ava? It wasn't Cheltenham and GCHQ, was it? Not really. That's just what we tell people if they ask.'

It had been the Afghan Surgical Hospital run by Scandinavian volunteer doctors on the edge of Peshawar, over the frontier in Pakistan.

'I remember. I wish I didn't.'

Ava had been giving blood. She was AB negative, and they never had enough of it when the wounded came in.

'You were covered in dried blood, Sam. Your shirt and pants were stiff with it.'

'Not my blood, though.'

'You looked every inch an Afghan. I thought you were. You even swore in Pashto just like a native. Wonderful beard, too, even if it was filthy. OBL would have been envious.'

'I hadn't washed in weeks. I had crab lice, ticks, fleas, the works. The blood belonged to the kid I was carrying. I put him down, and they went to work on him right away. Remember?'

Ava ducked her head, didn't answer. She remembered and wished she didn't.

'Omar survived. He was eleven. Amazing, really, all things considered. It took us ten days to cross the frontier and get there on foot, but the boy lived. The others in his village weren't so lucky. The boy lost all his family. You remember, that too, Ava, don't you? One of the U.S. special forces "night raids", authorised on the basis of a single intercepted mobile call supposedly from that same village and intercepted by your colleagues in Bagram. Where you were based, actually.'

'Fuck you, Sam.'

'No, Ava. Fuck you. Thirty-five people died that night in that place for all the wrong fucking reasons.'

'Do you think I don't blame myself? Of course I do.' She'd insisted he take her there to see for herself, and she did. They were too late to see them bury their dead under mounds of stones. Ava had thought they might attack the Westerners, but they didn't. They were pleased, even grateful, that they'd taken the trouble, to ask questions, to show interest. The villagers had wanted to talk, to describe what had happened. 'They gave us all the names of the dead and wounded, remember?' Ava's tears were running down her face.

'It might even have been worth it in the long run if —'

'I know what you're going to say, Sam. If we hadn't pulled out in such a rush and left them to starve in their thousands. In our day the hospitals were full of wounded, but now they're packed with kids dying of hunger.'

Guilt. Anger. Sorrow. All of it mixed up and always bubbling under the surface.

He'd won. Sam's pitch had worked, and the single malt had torn open the old wound.

Ava sniffed loudly, wiped her cheeks with the back of her hand. 'You're assuming, of course, that there will be more intel.'

'Don't be such a pessimist, Ava. I have every confidence in both your source and in you. Also, please keep a small bag packed - and close to hand - for a fast getaway, should it prove necessary.'

Like the shoulder bag Pan had used, Ava thought.

What Ava hadn't mentioned to Sam was that she'd already heard again from the source, and this time he'd hit the jackpot.

# 21

# December 12

Qin had worked all night, editing the final version of a 40,000-word resolution to be unveiled in the Hall of the People. Some resolution - it was more of a book and it wasn't light reading. It reminded him of a biology textbook he'd had to study at school. Quite indigestible. He wondered if any person would ever read the entire thing aside from himself, and he'd done so because he'd had little alternative. It had been put together by a committee whose members didn't bother to even try, with teams of two or three Party ideologues working on each section and striving to make it as inaccessible as possible.

By 2 a.m. the Emperor's head was hurting, and the whispers had returned. After a nap of 90 minutes and something to eat, he had returned to his labours feeling refreshed, the headache gone, and he propped himself up with the pillows on his immense bed-come-desk. In brief, the resolution stated that the Party's historical course was the correct one. What a surprise that was. It said mistakes had been made. Everyone knew what those mistakes were - the Cultural Revolution, the Great Leap Forward. There was no need to mention the starvation of 36 million Chinese during the latter and other infelicities. Those bumps in the road to socialism aside, the Party was on the right track, of course, and Qin was superbly qualified to lead it into the future. Well into the future, a future bright with prosperity and rising living standards for all.

All thanks to General Secretary Qin.

General Wang appeared, looking more agitated than usual, just as Qin had completed 44 laps of the pool and was getting into his stride.

'What the hell is it this time?'

'A row has broken out during a meeting at the Joint Taiwan Attack Centre.'

'So? Let them sort it out. That's what the Central Military Commission and the Staff Department are supposed to do, isn't it - resolve differences, clarify policy, set the correct course? I deal with strategy. The JTAC thrashes out operational matters.'

'They need you. They're asking for you in your capacity as Chairman.'

'Bollocks. I'm not going. Fuck off.'

'Car's waiting, boss, plane's on standby. Crack the whip a couple of times, they'll fall in line, and you'll be back in the pool before lunch.'

'Damn you, Wang, I'll hold you to that.'

Wang briefed a disgruntled General Secretary en route. Qin sat back, closed his eyes and folded his hands across his belly as Wang spoke at length. He didn't react to anything that Wang said. Qin could have been listening; he might have been sleeping. It was impossible to tell, as his breathing remained steady throughout. He only opened his eyes again to climb out of the limo and board the aircraft, where the Wang briefing continued and the Emperor resumed his comatose posture for the two-hour flight due south to Nanjing, aside from a tea break.

'That's quite enough,' Qin said at last.

It seemed to be childish nonsense. Bruised military egos. Well, Qin said to himself, they'd pay for making him leave the *Zhongnanhai*.

Yet for all the warning he'd received from Wang, Qin found the service chiefs in an almost jovial mood, as if they enjoyed these occasional get-togethers. They seemed to treat these sessions as if they were social gatherings, not war planning conferences. The Emperor found them - twenty-two commanders and staff officers in all - chatting away in the conference room, only falling silent and adopting a serious mien appropriate to their senior rank when the Emperor appeared in navy blue suit and red tie.

They looked surprised to see him.

'I hear you have differences,' Qin said, sitting down. 'Please tell me, but I must remind you - in case you'd forgotten - that in 51 days we will be at war.'

'It's like this,' said Admiral Jia, who was never shy. 'Some of us believe we ought to bypass the islands. Others - myself included - believe it's essential we attack and seize them at the very outset of the campaign, that's to say, once we have isolated the enemy's communications with cyber attacks and have imposed an air and sea embargo - and that should be the moment to strike the first blow against their first line of defence.'

General Zheng begged to differ, the big man lumbering to his feet.

'We all agree, Comrade Chairman,' he growled, 'that our objective at the outset of hostilities is to gain local control of the airwaves, airspace and seas surrounding Taiwan. Our aim is to create a crisis - a crisis of great uncertainty for the Taipei regime. We'll already have intercepted all ships and aircraft approaching or leaving the island, because the vast bulk of goods they manufacture and use — their food and fuel especially — is carried by sea. By cutting off the internet and all other communications, we will cripple their supply chains.'

'Everyone agrees with that,' chimed in Admiral Jia.

'Very well. Thank you, Admiral. Our first military targets will be the early warning radars around the island. We will disrupt these by using jamming devices on PLA aircraft. We will also, with the Party's agreement —' Here Zheng glanced at Qin - 'use our electronic warfare assets to disrupt U.S. strategic warning satellites so that our enemies have little or no warning of our first missile strikes.'

Jia jumped up. 'We must address the issue of the islands, General.'

'Patience, Admiral. I'm coming to that.'

'I wish you would,' said Qin, fingers drumming on his podium.

'It's a matter of geography,' said Admiral Jia. 'Take Kinmen as our first example; fifteen rock islands that form a natural barrier and dominate the approaches to Xiamen harbour, one of our major ports and a vital jumping off point for our invasion forces. Artillery on Lesser Kinmen is just six miles from Xiamen's dockyards. There's also the fortress of Wu-Chiu, located 14 miles south of an important staging post, Nanri Island.'

'Bypass them,' said General Zheng. 'Or isolate them, but don't waste time and manpower trying to conquer them. They're Taiwan's version of the Maginot Line.'

Jia smiled broadly at his adversary and superior officer. 'Thank you for the historical analogy, General, but these islands form the tripwire that provides our enemies with early warning of our invasion and gives them time to prepare for our assault. We can't just go around them - they are a threat to our amphibious task forces, to both the assembly of our troops and to the crossing itself. No, we have to smash resistance and take these islands at the very outset, or at least some of them.'

'Trying to take all these islands could exhaust our forces before we've even begun the main effort,' said General Zheng.

Qin raised a hand. 'Comrades, you have talked about Kinmen and Matsu Islands, but what of the Penghu group? As I understand it, we're talking about 65 islands, some 35 to 40 miles or around 60 km off the coast of central Taiwan. What are your views?'

'We can't ignore them,' said Admiral Jia. 'They threaten the flanks of our invasion fleet.'

General Zheng blew out his cheeks, shrugged, and declared there was only one target in the Penghu group that mattered, and that was Magong, the centre of the Penghu archipelago, which could be neutralised with missile strikes, followed by air and naval bombardment.

Admiral Jia was pleased. 'So you accept Magong must be attacked at the start?'

'I do,' said the general, 'but not necessarily occupied.'

Qin stood. 'Comrades, I think you are closer to agreement than you seem to think. I don't believe an island-hopping approach would be wise. It would take too long, absorb too much in the way of resources, and exhaust our forces. I would suggest assaults on the most important island targets at the very outset and the isolation of those deemed less critical. Admiral Jia and General Zheng have both made useful points. They are both right and wrong. Destroying resistance and occupying enemy territory are not the same thing. Please continue your deliberations and let me know what you decide. Thank you.'

It was already 2 p.m.

Where was General bloody Wang?

\*\*\*

Qin strode over to the first of the three black Red Flag limos, veered away and, turning back to the second, nodded to the driver who was holding the rear door open, and climbed in.

The journey from the Joint Taiwan Attack Centre in Nanjing to Lukou International Airport was 4.7 kilometres, or a whisker under three miles - and given that they wouldn't stop at any intersections, it should take less than three minutes. The Emperor was glad he was alone, that Wang had apparently taken a seat up front in the first Hongqi H7 and wouldn't be bending the Emperor's ear about this or that. They were supposed to share the vehicle - that was the norm for the bodyguard commander accompanying the Emperor on Party or state duties - but Qin didn't care about the rules. He was grateful for the respite from Wang's nagging.

Qin breathed out, turned sideways, his back in the corner and against the door, so he could stretch out his long legs. He sat behind the driver.

Why had Wang told him there was an argument that needed his immediate adjudication? It hadn't appeared to be a quarrel at all; the participants had seemed to sort out their differences among themselves without the presence of the Chairman of the Central Military Commission in person.

Qin would not be back in the *Zhongnanhai* in time for lunch, though his stomach rumbled with hunger, but he reminded himself he could, and did, eat whatever he wanted when he wanted. He told himself not to kick up a fuss like some spoiled kid. They would no doubt offer him something on the plane, anyway.

The first he knew something untoward was happening was a thud, more a clang or clunk than a thud, and it was less the noise than a sense of something hitting the Red Flag's exterior, a reverberation as if someone had struck it with a bat, somewhere to his right and over his shoulder; just behind his head. He turned to his left to look back, but there was nothing to see. The noise was muffled by the bullet-proof glass of his window and the bomb-proof armour. Well, not bombproof, but blast and splinter resistant.

Nothing is ever truly bombproof.

All he saw was a trio of motorcyclists pass him at speed on the right, another two on the left.

They were in uniform and wore white helmets and big police gauntlets. Qin assumed they were members of the escort, racing to the rescue. It struck him as odd that they seemed to ride abreast.

When he saw the first motorcyclist throw something dark, the size and shape of a brick, at the rear of the first limo, Qin realised all was not what it should be.

Before he could react, there was a sound like a muffled explosion, but drawn out, like air being released under great pressure, a whoomf, and he turned again only to see through the rear window the third and last car in their convoy - 150 metres back, the correct spacing, it has to be said - rear up, nose down, until it almost stood on its front grill, then it turned over onto its side, bounced and rolled, once, twice, and ended up on its side again. There was a great deal of smoke, and in the midst of it, a bright stab of flame.

The sticky bomb, or whatever had been thrown at Qin's limo, failed to detonate (as he would discover later), so instead it was now the turn of the first car, which rose in the air, its trunk and back wheels rising as if trying to dive nose first into the highway.

Qin's driver screamed, 'Get down,' and Qin didn't need telling, having flattened himself almost full length on the backseat and then dropping onto the floor between the seats.

He heard short, staccato popping sounds he realised were bursts of automatic fire. Three or four rounds at a time, controlled, a disciplined shooter or shooters. Who was doing the shooting, and what the targets were, he had no idea, until he heard the incoming rounds rattle against the limo like pebbles tossed into a tin can.

Fuck! They're shooting at me!

The driver stamped on the accelerator and pulled hard on the handbrake, the limo shook, skidded and lurched sideways, a ponderous beast moving in slow motion, then crashed, accompanied by a screech of metal as the limo scraped along the roadside barrier as it slid to a final stop, facing the way they had come.

Eyes tight shut, Qin had both arms over his head, and he had drawn his knees up to protect his testicles.

# 22

# December 13

It was a bumper crop. Ava spent all day Sunday and much of Sunday night decrypting and translating the latest despatch, interspersed with nervous glances out of her window at whatever was going on out there in a world obscured by sleet and snow, then stiffening with alarm at the sound of footsteps outside her front door, along with frequent breaks for coffee, chocolate cookies and the occasional nap on her sofa. The mail had arrived at the Cincinnatus office in Friday's post and Louise, who worked the reception desk, had called to make sure Ava was home on the Saturday morning before sending it over by courier. The padded envelope bore a Dubai postmark, and the date and time stamp suggested it had been sent before Pan's death on the 6th - in fact, the day before her arrival back in DC, so Pan might have even sent it herself during one of her stopovers.

An odd precaution, one with its own risks, but no doubt intended to ensure Pan carried nothing incriminating on her person.

The latest envelope was stuffed with clippings, a couple of Chinese red and gold book markers and blank postcards of a gigantic seated Buddha on Lantau Island. As for the clippings, they seemed random and taken from the CCP's *China Daily*, Hong Kong's *South China Morning Post*, the *Financial Times,* and others. The thumb drive was right at the bottom, slipped inside the bubble wrap lining.

Was this the last, then?

It had been on the tip of Ava's tongue to tell Sam about the latest package, but something had held her back. What it was, she didn't know. Did she still not trust him? It seemed churlish to harbour doubt; he had been so kind, escorting her to her front door and making sure she was safe inside before leaving. A true gentleman, right?

Or a smooth bastard and skilful user of men - and women?

Oh, God, yes, Ava had to admit it to herself; she did fancy him - or would do so in different circumstances.

Standing at the living room window once again, to one side and back from the double glazing, she wondered how she was supposed to know if the two people sitting in the front seats of the nondescript grey Chrysler Voyager with DC plates on the far side of the street were *Guoanbu* operatives, *Gong'anbu* thugs or her SIS guardians - or someone else. At that distance, she could only make out the outline of their heads, the occasional hand movement — neither their gender nor ethnicity. She made a note of the registration, as Sam had advised her.

Ava recalled how observant Sam had been, how much attention he paid to other vehicles on the way back from the bar to her place, the way he paid off the cab two blocks short of her apartment, using the opportunity to get a good look at parked vehicles, then he'd asked her to take his arm, strolling right past the front door, chatting away but always alert, pausing on the corner, turning the corner, then heading back, again, using his umbrella to hide their faces, lifting it just enough to see other pedestrians' features and the car registrations. It seemed to be good tradecraft, but what did she know - a former NSA linguist? Not a hell of a lot, she had to admit, Bagram or no Bagram.

Was this some joint UK-US operation cobbled together overnight? Did he think that the original language would allow him to identify and locate the source? She could have told him the Mandarin the source used was the simplified version, the kind the Communist Party taught, not the Mandarin used elsewhere. Every intelligence service wanted control of its assets, and Sam - whether he represented SIS or had done some kind of deal with his U.S. counterparts - would be no different. Why would the Americans let a Brit act as agent handler with one of their own? Because the two of them got along, had something of a shared history, because they understood each other, because the Americans knew she'd refuse to cooperate with anyone else after her posting in Afghanistan?

In his lecture in the UK, hadn't Sam told his visitors that agent handling was a process of seduction that required both patience and a gentleness no James Bond would have recognised?

Ava told herself to stop daydreaming and to get back to work.

The latest batch had begun with another message from the source.

*My Friend,*

*I think they know there's a leak. Nothing specific, a feeling. Some colleagues seem especially interested in what I'm up to. Others are keeping their distance as if I'm infected with something unpleasant. Normally, they're quite indifferent, if not downright hostile.*

*I should explain. We Chinese Communists are not reared in a culture that stresses teamwork, empathy, mutual aid, tolerance. That may surprise you. We are brought up to compete for the best places in the best schools, the best universities, the best jobs - and we learn to fear those more privileged - hence powerful - than ourselves. We are driven by our parents to strive for success from the start, from play school onwards. Outward conformity is a ruse, a tool, a camouflage to achieve this. When I was in my twenties, my dates were only interested in three things. Did I have a good degree from a good university? Did I have an apartment of my own? Did I have a car? If I failed at any of those hurdles, the date in question would not consider meeting a second time. We call this the "three highs" — high education, high salary and high eyebrows. The last means snobbish. You can imagine the impact this has had on marriage and the birthrate, especially in a country where men outnumber women. Men living and working in rural villages have no hope of finding a partner. You'd think that being Communist we'd be different, right? A new socialist human: more cooperative, more humane, more understanding, more fair, less materialistic, less selfish.*

*Not at all!*

*Perhaps it's my sense of guilt turning into paranoia. It's made worse because right now I do not know if my efforts are having any impact at all. I watch the capitalist media but have seen nothing so far. I don't even know if you've settled in your mind the question — and it must have been a question, at least for a while — whether your source is crazy, whether this is a provocation, the start of some fiendish disinformation campaign, or fiction planted by some other foreign spy agency with an agenda all their own.*

*Perhaps concerns for your own safety have persuaded you not to take matters further. I quite understand because it would be rational — indeed, quite sensible — to want to survive. If that's the case, I'll not blame you or call you a coward, but I will not know where to turn. If you have decided not to pursue this, I still have to trust you not to betray me while I seek alternatives.*

*But I have changed the way this works. I am going to give you everything I have as soon as it comes into my possession and do so as quickly as I can. That will mean taking more risks, but on balance, I think it is the right thing to do.*

*My sixth sense tells me I'm in a race against discovery.*

Ava knew she wasn't the only link in the chain under pressure. The poor lonely bastard, whoever he or she was, was alone, and he was feeling the heat. If they found the source, he or she would face not twenty years in prison but a bullet - and that would come as a relief after weeks of torture and interrogation.

Ava hurried to translate the first message on military developments.

## OPERATION CHINA UNITY: AIR EXCLUSION ZONE

*1. An air exclusion zone will be imposed at the outset of the military assault on Taiwan, which the PLA has dubbed Operation China Unity.*

*2. All foreign aircraft - civil or military - which approach or enter the air exclusion zone will be intercepted and identified. They will be contacted on prevailing international radio frequencies in Mandarin and English and ordered to turn back.*

*3. PLAAF interceptors will warn intruders by 'painting' them with radar, by flashing lights and by aerial manoeuvres that threaten them with being forced down if they do not leave the zone.*

*4. Illegal third-party aircraft, civil or military, will be escorted to pre-selected PLAAF airbases where they will be forced to land, held in custody, searched and inspected. These would include reconnaissance aircraft from third parties such as the United States, Japan, South Korea and Australia. PLAAF interceptors will fire their cannon in front of and around the intruders to force their compliance.*

*5. PLAAF fighter-interceptors and surface-to-air missile batteries will engage and destroy any Taiwan military aircraft taking off within the air exclusion zone, which will encompass all the island and its adjacent territories and waters.*

*Note: These decisions were planned at a meeting of the Joint Taiwan Attack Centre (JTAC) in Nanjing and have been signed off by the Central Military Commission. The circulation list numbers 67 recipients, including Politburo Standing Committee members.*

Star jumps, and more coffee. Then Ava tackled a second, companion report:

## OPERATION CHINA UNITY: NAVAL BLOCKADE OF TAIWAN

*1. Control of the skies over Taiwan is a vital prerequisite for establishing a naval blockade at the outset of Operation China Unity because of the threat posed by Taiwan's air resources, both strike and defence.*

*2. Once Taiwan's air defence capability has been degraded, PLAAF and PLAN commanders will coordinate attacks on Taiwan's battle fleet on the assumption that the latter will have put to sea before the start of Operation China Unity.*

*3. Special efforts will be devoted to locating and destroying Taiwan's larger warships, its guided missile destroyers, employing satellite reconnaissance and surveillance aircraft.*

*4. The naval blockade will focus on deploying sea mines. Submarines will drop drifting contact mines close inshore at the entrances to Taiwan's major ports. PLAAF aircraft will then drop several curtains or belts of bottom contact mines two miles out. Belts of mines will be moored about eight miles further out.*

It all sounded so real to Ava. This wasn't something made up. They would do this. They had the means and the will to do so. She noticed her hands were shaking. Ava dropped to the floor and performed enough squats so that she was out of breath and felt hot. Then she went back to work.

*5. Foreign vessels may transit the outermost zone provided they agree to a PLAN escort and to being boarded for inspection. Any illegal vessel, or vessels carrying illegal materials, will have their cargo seized. Any vessels trying to run the blockade will be ordered to proceed to controlled areas for boarding and inspection. When necessary, foreign vessels will be fired on as a warning.*

*6. To ensure the effectiveness of the blockade, radar stations around Taiwanese ports will be attacked and disabled. Port infrastructure will also be attacked, weakening Taiwan's ability to harass PLAN minelayers and PLAAF patrol aircraft and safeguarding amphibious assault ships near the Taiwan Strait.*

*Note: This is based on another JTAC decision relayed to the CMC and Politburo Standing Committee. Distribution list the same.*

Those two reports would make an excellent feature, Ava decided, and for the next hour she worked on it, then copied her finished product from the air-gapped laptop to her own device, read it through one last time, and sent it on to James Halberton at Cincinnatus.

There was one more task on the matter of a Chinese blockade of Taiwan. She'd said she would copy the Mandarin version - decrypted, of course - and hand it over to Sam Turner. She would be as good as her word and Ava copied the Mandarin text to a clean thumb drive and pocketed it.

Sam had given her instructions; he'd repeated them twice, not that she would forget. He had handed her a burner to use just once in an emergency, along with a number to call. It too was a mobile device, not a landline - likely another burner. In all other non-emergencies, Ava was to use landlines, excluding her own, and preferably public phones from bars or hotels. The first time, she would let it ring three times, then cut the call, and on the second attempt, she should ask for Mrs Potter. Potter, as in Harry Potter, so she wouldn't forget. Sometimes this mythical Mrs Potter would answer, sometimes not, in which case Ava could leave a brief message without identifying herself.

It was straightforward and maybe too simple and old fashioned a system, but Ava imagined that Sam had had to improvise something basic but workable at short notice. The burner was already in her getaway backpack along with other bits and pieces.

Her mobile beeped. It was James, thanking her for what he called her fascinating report, attributed to the same, unnamed source 'close to the Chinese Communist Party'. He would run it, no question, and when was she coming into the office? He wanted to brief her on the new research project. Ava thought he sounded upbeat, cheerful and busy.

He should be. Cincinnatus had a new prominence, even notoriety, since the first article attributed to what some in the media were calling a Chinese whistleblower.

The NSA hadn't called again, he said.

Now that was interesting. Was Sam keeping them off her back?

With her cell to her ear, Ava looked down at the street while her boss was still talking. The grey Chrysler was no longer in sight. As she watched, and the conversation with James ended, Ava saw two dark green people carriers draw up opposite. They stopped, but did not park. The doors slid open, and she watched several people jump out, some of them crossing the street at a run - a street shiny with sleet - all headed towards her building, or so it seemed.

Her heart did some kind of somersault; that's how it felt, anyhow.

Ava didn't count them. She was too surprised to think. Were there three, four, six? She had the impression that they were similarly dressed - black running gear, she thought. A human swarm in black running gear and balaclavas, pulling them down to cover their faces as they approached.

One remained on the pavement next to the vans, talking on a mobile while looking up, appearing to scan the windows in Ava's block.

# 23

## 08:16 China Standard Time, GMT +8

The Emperor moved steadily through the water, not fast, not slow. He focused on coordinating his arms and legs and, once satisfied that he had the right rhythm, he concentrated on his breathing so that thoughts about the previous day's events weakened and vanished. After a while the anger was gone, so too the fear. He shut his eyes. His body did what it was supposed to do without conscious thought or effort.

He felt released, freed from himself and the habits of mind that make us what we are.

Qin was no longer Qin. He was no longer Emperor. He was swimming, that was all, a sensation of flying, of skin and nerves passing through a wind of water that cushioned him, parted, resisted again, and gave way - repeating itself as he repeated movements that required no conscious will.

He'd gone into the water just before seven, the pool undulating and silvery with artificial light because it was still black outside.

Qin closed his eyes and swam.

When he opened them again, he detected movement, but he did not look at the black uniform with its silver badges of rank.

Wang.

Qin sat on the lounger, robe around his shoulders, sucking hot tea from his porcelain cup. He said nothing, offered no greetings and did not respond to Wang's respectful good morning. Wang cleared his throat and made his report, and the Emperor listened. He did not interrupt. He let Wang speak without diversion or distraction. As Wang read his notes, breaking off to clear his throat, Qin sat still, expressionless, the only sound the sharp intake of air through his lips as he slurped the hot liquid.

No-one out there, beyond the red walls of the *Zhongnanhai*, not among the 1.5 billion Chinese citizens - aside from the select few with the security clearance to know - was aware of what had occurred. Qin had helped ensure this sense of normality by appearing, as scheduled, before Party delegates in person, wearing his navy suit, white shirt and red tie like a corporate executive; the Politburo ranged behind him in similar attire. The Party's board of directors, no less. He and they raised their right fists as one and swore allegiance to the Party at the same moment. This was shown on what was the largest video screen in the world, above and behind the Party leaders, and it was relayed on state television the previous evening, and recorded around the world. It was described as a live, event, which it wasn't.

'The attackers are thought to have numbered nine,' Wang read. 'All died in the failed attempt. Two of these died of their injuries before they could be questioned. The counter-revolutionary assailants wore the uniforms of the Peoples Armed Police and most carried PAP identification, though four had forged cards identifying them as officers of the Nanjing Security Bureau. They were equipped with standard military weapons, both submachine guns and pistols. The explosives comprised a type of military magnetic mine. It is not known how they gained access to the arms. The conspirators used false names, and so far none have been identified.

'Four bodyguards and two drivers were killed in the attack, three more bodyguards died of their injuries.'

Qin poured himself more tea and said nothing.

So far, the relevant departments have detained a total 1,469 people for questioning, including bystanders and potential witnesses. The head of the Nanjing Security Bureau has been suspended and is also detained for questioning. The regional PAP commander has been suspended, and he too is being investigated. Office 610 has rounded up all Falun Gong activists and sympathisers in the area, so far numbering 420.

'Special attention is being paid to possible foreign involvement, notably the special services of the splittist regime in Taipei.'

Wang stopped. He waited for a response. The way he used his fingers to fold the paper and ran them along the creases showed his nervousness.

The Emperor put his cup down. He pushed his arms into the sleeves of his robe, did up the sash around his middle and pushed his feet into the sandals he used when walking around the pool area. All this took some time. At length, he stood up.

The Emperor had reached a decision.

'Walk with me, General.'

Qin walked slowly, in silence, to the far end of the pool where the water was deepest, Wang at his side.

'Tell me,' Qin said in a low, confiding voice. 'Why weren't you in my limo yesterday after the conference?'

'I was in one of the chase cars.'

Qin's tone was conversational. 'Oh? That so? I must have missed you. I thought you'd been left behind or that you'd jumped into the first and I'd not seen you do so. Why was that?'

'I was late coming out of the conference and rather than keep everyone waiting - rather than keep you waiting, chief - I got into the first chase car because the three Red Flag limos were already moving and I wasn't certain which one you were in.'

'Oh, right. I see. That makes sense. Why were you late coming out of the JTAC meeting? Was there a problem with security?'

'I had a stomach bug, boss. I had to use the toilet, and it took somewhat longer —'

'Oh. Okay. I get it. Spare me the details. I hope you're feeling better today.'

'I am, thank you.'

'Great. I'm glad to hear it.' Now they stood side by side, facing down the length of the pool towards the steps at the shallow end and to where the loungers stood with the small table with the teapot and cups.

The water was settling after the Emperor's morning swim.

'I love swimming,' Qin said. 'Don't you, General?'

Wang was silent. Maybe he wasn't sure how to respond.

'You do swim, don't you, Wang? In the sea, in rivers or lakes, or maybe in swimming pools like this one. No?'

Wang shook his head.

'You mean you can't swim?'

Wang answered. 'No, I —'

Qin interrupted him. 'That's a shame. You know, I read somewhere that only twenty percent of mainland Chinese can swim. I imagine the figure is higher in Hong Kong, though. Isn't that extraordinary? Do you have any idea why that is, General? There was one news item that the life savers at one pool were themselves unable to swim.'

Wang thought for a moment. 'I imagine swimming pools still aren't that common in schools and most Chinese live too far from the sea to learn. And the Chinese prize white skin and don't like to get tanned as foreigners seem to.'

'You're right. I hadn't thought of that. Good points. We should do something about it, don't you think? Everyone should learn, even you. Every year people drown and it's such a sad waste of lives. And swimming is so pleasurable.'

The Emperor didn't wait for an answer. He leaned back a little, looked Wang up and down. 'Turn around, would you?'

A puzzled Wang half-turned.

Qin pointed at the holster on Wang's belt, close to his right hip. 'Is that thing loaded?'

Wang looked down, put a hand on the holster. 'All your security people are armed, chief, as a matter of course.'

'In the *Zhongnanhai* — sure. I get it. But not in here. Not in my working quarters, my office.'

Qin put out his right hand. 'Show it to me. I want to see it. I know nothing about guns, you know.'

Wang had no option but to unbutton the holster and take out the QSZ-92 semi-automatic pistol. Holding it by the barrel, he held it out to Qin, who took it.

'It's loaded?'

'Yes.'

'One up the spout?'

Wang nodded. To his surprise or alarm, or both, Qin slid the safety off and opened the breech to check if there was indeed a 5.86mm round in the breech. There was, along with what were presumably 19 others snug in the magazine underneath. These were not the actions of someone who knew nothing about firearms.

Qin weighed it in his hand. 'What do you think of it? Is it effective?'

'The military thinks so. I'm no expert.'

'How does it compare to our enemies' sidearms?'

'I'm not sure, to be honest...'

'Effective range?'

'Fifty metres.'

'That much, eh? But for practical purposes, its combat range would be what - half that?'

'About that, yes.'

'The rounds are armour-piercing, are they not?'

'Yes, chief.'

'That means they'd penetrate body armour, right?'

'Most types of body armour, yes.'

'I see. Did you fire your weapon yesterday in my defence?'

'I drew it, but it happened so fast and I had no targets.'

'Ah. You must have been too far back in the chase car, right?'

Wang was about to speak, but Qin pressed on. 'Do you practice marksmanship, General? You should.'

Smiling, Qin raised his right hand holding the weapon and before Wang realised what was happening, the Emperor pressed the muzzle into Wang's right eye socket. He increased the pressure, forcing Wang's head back.

'Don't move, General. Keep completely still, now.'

Wang could have tried to push the pistol away with a quick sweep of one hand or a punch. He could have jumped back, or forward. He could have ducked, fallen to his knees. He could have treated it as a joke and laughed it off. There were several possibilities, but Wang remained still, as ordered, one eye squeezed shut against the constant pressure on the eyeball.

'So you didn't fire this *Jiǔ Èr Shì Shǒuqiāng* at all yesterday during the incident?'

'No.' Qin saw the fear on Wang's face and he liked what he saw.

'How long were you planning yesterday's little episode for, General?'

Wang's one open eye stared up at the General Secretary in disbelief. Was he being teased, bullied, played with? Was the Emperor serious? Qin had moved slightly, shifting his weight over to his left so that Wang was between him and the edge of the pool.

'Who else was in on this, Wang? Just two simple questions. Answer me. How long had you planned this for, and who else was involved? Two simple questions, and I want two simple answers. I want them now - or should we test the trigger pressure on this toy?'

Wang opened and closed his mouth.

Qin withdrew the pistol from Wang's eye. He smiled as if this was all in jest. Then he pushed Wang hard in the chest, using both fists. It was part shove, part punch and it was so sudden, so forceful, and at such a close distance that Wang was compelled to take a step back to keep his balance, but there was nothing solid to step back on. Wang's arms flailing like a windmill's sails, he toppled over backwards into the water with an immense splash.

Qin wiped the Norinco pistol with his robe, especially the polymer grip, then flung the weapon into the middle of the pool.

Wang had surfaced, beating the water with his arms, gasping for air, and he managed a single word, 'help', then he went down a second time. The Emperor watched him struggle under the water, hit bottom, kick himself up, rising to the surface again. Wang tried to shout, pleading again for help or to raise the alarm, but even if he'd been able to do so in his advanced state of panic, there was no-one else to hear him or come to his rescue.

Only Qin could have responded.

When he surfaced for the third time, Wang made a supreme effort to heave himself up and snatch at the pool's edge, and he did so first with the fingertips of one hand, his left, then the right.

He was sputtering and coughing, whatever words he was saying remaining un-intelligible as he tried to breathe. He tried to pull himself up, but Qin placed a foot on Wang's shoulders and pushed down with all his weight so that he fell back.

Again, a gasping Wang grabbed the edge of the pool.

Qin leaned down close, hands on his knees.

'You should have answered me, Wang. But don't worry. Your family will be taken care of. I will take care of it personally. You have my word. No-one will know you were a traitor. Your death was an accident, that's all. You'll get your pension, and your family will still have their home. The Party regrets this ever happened. Please accept the Party's apology.'

The Emperor straightened up, then kicked at Wang's fingers. When that failed, he stamped on them with the hard heels of his sandals, as if performing a clumsy version of the flamenco.

Qin hissed at him. *Hun dan*! Bastard!

First the fingers of Wang's right hand, then the left. Qin had to stamp down several times, using his full weight again, hammering them until the nails bled. Wang was crying, begging to be helped up out of the water. He tried to snatch his hands out of the way before the heel descended, but almost lost his grip en-tirely. That's what finally happened; he lost his tenuous hold and slid back into the water. Qin watched for a few moments to ensure the uniformed figure now adrift, face down, under the surface of the pool, would not resurface. Once satisfied that Wang was dead or dying, Qin walked away, unhurried, back to his daybed. He had work to do.

# 24

## 09:57 Eastern Standard Time, GMT -4

Ava had to think - fast.

Her doorbell buzzed, and whoever it was buzzed it again, this time keeping a finger on the intercom. Ava heard muffled voices, the rush of passing cars.

She pulled on her coat, grabbed her backpack, locked her door behind her, and hurried along the corridor to the head of the stairs. She leaned over and heard voices - and yes, they were already entering the lobby.

Had a neighbour let them in? Did they have an electronic card key or the numeric code which they could have used to open its door?

Whoever they were, they were coming in, holding open the entrance for one another.

Ava would not wait to see who they were.

The bell buzzed again.

Using the lift was out. Ava had no intention of heading up onto the roof as Pan had done in her building, only to be thrown - or pursued - to her death.

She had dropped her keys into her backpack. It was heavy because it contained both laptops, all the flash drives and thumb drives, her chargers, two changes of clothing, including leggings and tights, a few essential toiletries, a hairbrush, her purse with credit and debit cards, her contact book, her own mobile and the burner James had given her along with around eighty bucks - all the cash she had.

Option one. Knock on a neighbour's door and ask for help - or don't ask for help, just smile, invite herself in on some pretext or other and leave once the danger had passed.

Option Two. Hide in her storeroom on the mezzanine. Every condo had its own store or walk-in cupboard. They weren't numbered. Ava's store had a key, a rather odd device, not unlike a small bicycle tool. She could take refuge in there

160

among the clutter and wait. Maybe she could call for help, as Sam had advised her.

She heard the lift doors close and the lift move up.

Oh, shit.

She would have to run down, race down, towards her pursuers, jumping three or four steps at a time, throwing herself down, and doing so as silently as she could to get there before they reached the mezzanine level and its storerooms.

There was no question of staying put.

She slipped the padded straps of the backpack over her shoulders, then took off her shoes and sprinted, one hand for balance, the other holding her shoes.

The stairs were functional and served as a fire escape. An iron balustrade ran down the edge of the stairs at waist height, and the steps were made of some composite material like stone - cold and smooth. Fire doors were at the top and at the bottom.

Ava dropped, using her shoulder and hands to take the impact of crashing into the wall at the bottom of each flight to break her momentum, then twisting around the corner to plunge down the next flight.

She flew down the two floors, expecting at any moment to collide with the people heading up towards her.

She heard the fire door below wheeze open and close.

Somewhere above, the lift stopped, and the doors opened.

Ava hit the mezzanine, knees bent, just as the strangers climbed. She heard a conversation and what sounded like orders. Male voices. They'd keep someone down in the lobby, send another out back, and a third down to the basement parking space. It was what she would have done.

She raced along the corridor to her storeroom, plunged the key into the lock. The doors were plain white and had no door handles. The inserted key, once turned, would pull the door open.

Ava couldn't bring herself to look back. She heard shoes scraping the stairs, the sound of those male voices going louder. Was it Mandarin? They didn't seem to hurry. Her fingers shook as she inserted the key, turned it, pulled the door towards her, slid inside, withdrew the key and pulled the door after her, tugging it into place.

The business of opening the door and closing it again seemed to take forever.

Complete darkness enveloped Ava. With great care, she bent her knees and lowered her shoes to the floor. She then felt her surroundings with her fingers.

She remembered the layout and contents - a big paint pot, almost empty. Behind it, three neat stacks of large square bathroom tiles, to her right a wooden sled on which were piled two silver and green patterned curtains from the living room, horrible in Ava's opinion, which had belonged to the previous owner. Nothing had changed in the store - but there was a lot more dust and a faint whiff of damp. Right in front of her, just inside the doorframe and at shoulder height, was the light switch. She decided not to switch it on because the light would almost certainly show under the storeroom door.

Ava stood still, mouth open so she could hear better. The murmur of voices seemed a long way off and fading. There were no footsteps heading towards her end of the corridor.

When they found her apartment, what would they do? Ring her bell and wait? Would they pick her two locks - or kick in the door? It was solid - they'd need one of those battering rams the cops used. Any attempt to force their way in would make enough of a racket to prompt a neighbour - any neighbour - to dial 911.

She sat down on the paint pot. She did so with great care to make no noise and to ensure it would support her weight.

Ava waited and time crawled by.

Five minutes.

Ten.

It was so cold that she couldn't feel her feet.

Ava slipped off the backpack, unzipped the smaller of the two compartments, and felt around inside until she found the burner. She held it in her hand, hesitating.

What would she say to Sam? That she thought there were several intruders in her building, that they seemed to be after her and that she was hiding out in a storeroom? What was Sam expected to do? What could he do? No crime had been committed, at least none she knew of, not yet, and she didn't know for sure who the alleged intruders were, or if they were intruders at all. Maybe they had sound and lawful reason to enter her building. She could be imagining the threat - the visitors might be legitimate workers from a utility company. It wasn't so odd for people to wear balaclavas in the cold or to run across the street in bad weather. The possibilities were endless.

Where was the protection Sam had promised?

Maybe she should use her own phone to call or text Agent Calasso - or Detective Kramer. Kramer had seemed more sympathetic than Calasso; he might help if he was on duty and not otherwise engaged, if only to send a squad car, but asking that pair for anything at all would only encourage them to pressure her still further to accept the FBI's offer of protection in return for full disclosure - something her source had asked her to avoid.

Ava dropped the burner back into the backpack and zipped it shut. She found her shoes and put them on, then pulled her coat tight around her and rocked back and forth to get the blood moving. She could always wrap herself in one of the ugly curtains. It might keep the chill at bay - but the thought of spider webs put her off. Ava had a horror of creepy-crawlies, spiders especially.

***

Ava had had no time to develop the third in the latest batch of reports from the mystery source. She had decrypted and translated it, but had to put it and everything else on hold to deal with the approaching threat. Sitting in there, waiting, shivering with cold, weighing her options and hoping the danger had passed, she recalled the details. It would also make an interesting, if somewhat speculative, report for Cincinnatus because it provided a window into Chinese military thinking - and according to the source, a difference of opinion emerged among top cadres.

## DIVISION OVER TIMING EMERGES IN IMPLEMENTING 'MAIN STRATEGIC DIRECTION' (主要战略 方向)

*1. Beijing's strategic priority is the conquest of the Republic of China (ROC), Taiwan, while deterring, delaying, disrupting or destroying any U.S. military response in defence of the island. This is what 'Main Strategic Direction' means, as used in briefings and operational orders.*

*2. As the countdown begins to the launch of Operation China Unity on February 1, a division has appeared among senior commanders and cadres within the Central Military Commission and the Politburo Standing Committee over the timing and duration of the strategy and the best means to deliver the desired outcome.*

*3. Both 'sides' in the argument await a final decision to settle the dispute from the Chairman of the Central Military Commission and CCP General Secretary, President Qin, who has the ultimate authority on all strategic matters.*

Sam would be delighted. His people would pounce on this. Inner conflict, differences of opinion among the ChiCom commanders? Ava knew from her own experience it would be seen as priceless, nothing less than pure gold to the spies and analysts on both sides of the Atlantic. The Brits could name their price after handling Ava's 'product'. They'd take the credit and dine out on it for years. Not that she minded. As long as collaboration with the source would halt military preparations for war.

*4. Top cadres are aware of the risk of the worst-case scenario: a war on two fronts, the first in the east against Taiwan and the United States, and the second in the south, a conflict with India. Tibetan separatist guerrillas might also seek to disrupt mainland communications and tie down PLA forces.*

*5. One military school of thought prefers 'Joint Firepower Strike Operations' against Taiwan, followed by a short, intense phase, the 'Joint Blockade Operations' against Taiwan. Once the island's defences had been weakened by intense missile and air strikes and the embargo, the PLA would launch 'Joint Attack Operations' against Taiwan, involving amphibious assaults, securing beachheads, and engaging in urban and mountain warfare to conquer the island.*

*6. In this 'zero warning' scenario, the United States is seen launching air and cruise missile attacks on PLA forces in the Strait and in PRC coastal areas, forcing the PRC to fight a campaign of 'Joint Anti-Air Raid Operations'. It is recognised by PRC war planners that Japanese, Australian, and other U.S. allies might also intervene on the side of U.S. forces.*

*7. A second school of thought - it seems to find favour with non-military cadres - is in favour of a gradual, intermittent campaign of increasing pressure, and is designed to win ROC concessions and test U.S. resolve. 'Boiling the frog' is one phrase used by advocates. Qin has himself used the phrase.*

*8. In the second scenario, Chinese military operations would be prolonged but intermittent, and would be characterised by low-intensity attacks, followed by pauses allowing for negotiations. The aim would be to avoid outright confrontation with U.S. forces while wearing down the resistance of ROC leaders and the general population, epitomised by the slogan 'winning without fighting'. Cyber attacks and air and maritime blockades would be the primary means, along with selected missile attacks on radar installations, airfields, naval facilities and government communications.*

*9. The first school of thought, favouring rapid, high-tempo missile and air attacks on Taiwan, coupled with an air and maritime blockade followed by amphibious assaults, accepts that simultaneous, pre-emptive attacks will have to be made against U.S. forces in the region to disrupt, degrade and even delay effective U.S. action. Anderson Air Force Base on Guam, the Guam Naval Base and Kadena Air Force Base and Futenma Marine Corps Air Station, both on Okinawa, are among several U.S. targets most likely to be attacked at the outset of the first scenario.*

*10. Commanders have expressed confidence that they have the qualitative and quantitative means to undertake pre-emptive attacks on both U.S. and Taiwan targets and sustain these attacks at a high tempo over a period of days and even weeks.*

*Note: The above is based on discussions overheard among senior staff personnel attached to the Joint Taiwan Attack Centre in Nanjing and having sight of draft memoranda on operational plans.*

Once a report had been decrypted and then translated, it became imprinted on Ava's consciousness. She picked up her bag and stood up. Ava checked she had everything. She listened. Nothing. She pushed the door - a little more, and, still listening and hearing nothing, she pushed it open far enough to slip out into the corridor, blinking in the abrupt change from dark to light.

The corridor was empty.

She must write this up, too, and send it off. The Mandarin version would have to be added to the reports already on the thumb drive in her coat pocket and a way found to hand it over to Sam. She had said she would do so, and she would. The notes or informal letters written by the source were another matter - Ava saw no reason she should share the contents with Sam.

Ava was on her own and she told herself she'd better get used to it.

She muttered the words under her breath.

*'Take care of yourself. Sure as hell no-one else will.'*

Ava climbed the stairs, moving slowly. At the door to her apartment, she found her keys for the two locks and entered. She closed, locked, and bolted her front door from the inside. An immense sense of relief swept through her. She dropped her backpack on the sofa and collapsed beside it.

She didn't bother with the lights. For what felt like a full minute, she put her head back, closed her eyes, and took several long breaths.

She was home, and she was safe, at least for now.

Had she imagined the whole sorry episode? How Pan would have laughed...

When Ava opened her eyes again, she saw the outline of someone, a man, sitting at her table, turned towards her.

# 25

Everyone who was anyone who knew — and they were very few, fewer than the fingers on both Qin's massive hands — agreed it was most unfortunate, a terrible accident. A tragedy, no less. Poor man — after a lifetime of loyal service, to drown in the Emperor's pool. A frightful business. Qin himself maintained a sombre expression, tight-lipped, eyes downcast and hooded, hands clasped in front of him. The slight, lopsided Mona Lisa smirk was banished and a black armband was attached to his sleeve above the elbow.

Wang's remains had been found that afternoon by one of his subordinates.

Sitting on his lounger, Qin had pointed to the far end of the pool as a bodyguard who doubled as a server set down a plate of cookies and a fresh pot of tea on the table at his side.

'What's that?'

The server-come-guard straightened up, turned.

'Over there. At the deep end. Something's in the water, d'you see?'

The server hesitated.

'Go see what it is, will you?'

The man walked over, stood at the edge and stared down into the water, then looked back to Qin, who was pouring himself a cup of tea.

The Emperor called out to him, 'Well?'

The server spoke into his walkie-talkie, then jogged back to the Emperor's lounger.

'I've called for help.'

'What is it?'

'It's a body… I think it's Comrade General Wang.'

'What? That's impossible!'

Qin put down his cup and stood.

Three bodyguards ran in, handguns drawn. The server pointed. Two of the officers jumped into the water and pulled Wang's corpse to the shallow end.

'Is he...?'

'Yes, it's him.'

They hauled him out, checked his pulse, then made clumsy efforts to revive him to no effect. Five bodyguards were gathered around the corpse while still more secured the entrances and exits of the pool area. One of the officers, whose uniform was already drenched, swam back to the deep end and dived down to fish out the pistol lying at the bottom.

The cause of death was quickly established. He had drowned. There were signs that the unfortunate Wang had tried to save himself by scrabbling out of the deep end of the pool where he must have fallen - a broken fingernail and traces of blood were found where he'd tried and failed to climb out. His service pistol had somehow become detached from its holster. It had not been fired. Had Wang tried and failed to fire off a round to draw attention to his plight because he'd been unable to shout? It was possible. More likely, though, in the view of the *Gong'anbu* investigator, it had fallen from his holster as he thrashed around in panic in water eight feet deep.

Tests showed no traces of alcohol or other chemical substances that might have accounted for Wang stumbling and falling into the pool were found in his blood, and it was confirmed by his family that Wang had never learned to swim.

Of course, Qin had heard nothing, seen nothing. He had been working. He recalled having exchanged a few words with Wang that morning, but had not seen him since. It was known that General Wang was conscientious and used to patrol the General Secretary's location in person, day or night. He took Qin's safety as his own personal responsibility.

That was it.

Death by misadventure.

There were no witnesses.

And there was no reason at all to link this unfortunate accident to the attack on the Emperor's car in Nanjing. Both events were classified top secret, and were known to members of the Politburo Standing Committee only, but there was nothing to link the two.

Wang's pension would indeed go to his family, who would, as Qin had promised, keep their Party home in the *Zhongnanhai*. Qin scribbled a short, personal note of regret at Wang's death and expressed both his shock and his profound appreciation for Wang's many years of selfless service to the Party, addressing his condolences to the widow and having it delivered by courier, though their home was barely three hundred metres away. Citing security reasons, Qin decreed the funeral would be a quiet affair, limited to the immediate family, and conducted in secret within the next 24 hours. The Party and the Ministry of Public Security would send flowers.

Qin had no doubt at all that Wang was the main perpetrator, the organiser, the brain behind the street ambush, and that the aim had been to assassinate him. There was no need for proof. Qin didn't want evidence. He knew. He would let things settle down, he told himself, then he would purge Wang's colleagues in the Ministry of Public Security, replacing them with his own *Gong'anbu* loyalists, tightening his grip on the top secret police cadres. That afternoon, he began putting a list of names together.

Qin also decided that his unofficial son would be brought in to play his part as Party enforcer and chief bodyguard. The lad was ready. He was expected to graduate in a matter of weeks. Whatever additional training he needed, it could be undertaken while performing his duties. He might work as 'white gloves' or *bai shoutao*, the Emperor's middle-man. From there, after a few months, Lau could move into the intended role of Qin's *Gong'anbu* chief bodyguard.

As for the pool, the Emperor ordered it emptied at once, then cleaned and refilled. He wouldn't be able to swim again for 24 hours, but the way Qin saw it, a little self-denial was preferable to the Emperor swimming around in any excreta Wang might have emitted in his last moments.

\*\*\*

The Emperor hated flying, but given the 'incident' in Nanjing, he couldn't refuse an afternoon flight south to Hainan Island as a guest of the PLA; the initial flight was four hours by an Air China Boeing 747, which he had to admit was a comfortable way to travel, followed by a transfer to a PLA helicopter, the locally developed, multirole Harbin Z-20. To Qin, it resembled an enormous black and red wasp. He wore a military combat uniform for the ride, without rank or any other insignia. A crewman strapped him in, placed an airman's helmet on his head, and he was shown how to use the intercom. The crewman communicated with hand signals, especially the universal thumbs-up. All Qin heard was a constant crackle of voices before he was shaken by the roar of the twin turboshaft engines and the vibration of the aircraft itself as it lifted off and surged forward, just feet off the ground, before lifting again without warning. His stomach seemed to jump right into his throat. The Emperor could do nothing but grit his teeth and close his eyes, and no, he did not want to look at the fucking view, thank you very much.

He felt seasick - or rather, airsick - and looked around for a sick bag, just in case.

Along with a brace of generals, Qin was freed of belts, buckles, and helmet and decanted into a sea of sand behind a beach. A track of duckboards had been laid down to the shore so that his shoes wouldn't fill with the stuff, and he was invited to take the place of honour, making his way down four steps into a trench reinforced by walls of sandbags and lined with the Chinese version of AstroTurf. It contained an armchair for himself, a carafe of water and a glass, flanked by mere benches for four- and five-star admirals and generals.

In front of him stood a pair of binoculars set up on a tripod and secured in place by a pile of sandbags.

The pallid, solemn faces on either side of him - grey hair or bald, heavy jowls, watery eyes - chattered away among themselves, but whenever he looked over at them to remember their names, their voices trailed away into silence and they dropped their rheumy eyes.

They're afraid of me, Qin said to himself, surprised but also gratified.

At least it wasn't raining, and the temperature was mild. There was even a hint of sun through the light cloud cover. The sea glittered all the way out to the southern horizon. It was all so calm and peaceful that Qin almost fell asleep, but for the screech of seagulls.

He stuck his legs out, raised his face to the watery sunshine and allowed himself a smile, his first of the day.

It was almost as if the PLA had been watching and waiting for Qin to drop his guard.

A long row of red flags rose in simultaneous warning along the line of trenches.

The rolling sand dunes behind the senior Party and PLA chiefs erupted like a series of volcanoes, founts of sand and smoke rising in columns thirty, forty feet into the air, then collapsing, followed by huge thuds, a thunder Qin could feel through the soles of his feet, all the way up his legs.

As heads shrank into their collars and a few bold spirits turned to witness the cataclysm, a dozen strike aircraft swept low overhead, coming in from the sea. This time, the beach in front of them erupted in geysers of smoke, flame and yet more sand and seawater.

These were J-10 and J-16 fighters as far as Qin could make out.

Then twelve H-6 bombers from the 8th Bomber Division were followed by another flight and yet another.

Above them drifted a flight of H-6K long-range bombers armed with CJ-20 cruise missiles.

Qin was almost overwhelmed by the experience - the deafening explosions, the cacophony of screaming aircraft, some of which seemed so low he felt he could almost put his arm up and touch them as their shadows streaked overhead.

Behind them came the first waves of troops, riding amphibious armoured vehicles firing their cannon. Above the marines' helmeted heads, airbursts marked the defenders' artillery fire - circles of smoke, white spirals shooting out in all directions as if they were discharging fiery projectiles among the approaching vehicles.

As they approached the beach through the shallows, the troops leapt down from the armoured fighting vehicles and stormed onto dry land, yelling their heads off, though their voices — hundreds of them at least — were drowned out by the explosions of artillery, landmines and heavy machine-gun fire.

More jet aircraft screamed overhead.

Qin had recovered from the initial shock to lean forward and use the binoculars to watch amphibious assault ships approach, discharging amphibious vehicles like ducks dropping their ducklings into the water.

At first he could see nothing at all until he found images and focussed on them.

Helicopters raced inland, helmeted troops sitting in the hatches, ready to abseil down to their objectives.

Transport aircraft dropped scores of paratroopers onto targets somewhere inland.

The VIPs turned to watch the parachutes open and drift down like upside down flowers in this next stage of a noisy military ballet.

During a lull in the sound of explosions and the rattle of automatic fire, a voice growled from a loudspeaker, explaining that the aim of the Hainan Winter Exercise was to practice command-and-control, orchestrating navy, air and ground forces in a live-fire island capture manoeuvre in the face of heavy opposition from counter-revolutionaries backed by foreign imperialist forces.

Of course - what else?

Few of those taking part — excluding the ancient spectators in the uniforms of generals and admirals on either side of the Emperor, their chests boasting rainbows of decorations and campaign ribbons (what campaigns was anyone's guess) — had any idea at all that in 50 days' time they would do this all over again, only for real, and for much longer. Then, Qin thought, it wouldn't just be sand, seawater and smoke in a glorified firework display to entertain the Party nomenklatura, but showers of white hot steel fragments and incendiaries. It would rain blood, lots of it.

Chinese blood.

He ran his right forefinger around the inside of his collar. The sand had found its way inside his camouflage smock and all the way down his back. It stuck to his sides because he'd sweated during the mock battle, the noise alone having terrified him. It had blown into his ears and his hair, too. While scratching himself, Qin saw that the once empty, placid surface of the South China Sea was filled with the grey outlines of warships. Puffs of smoke and the flicker of flame marked their bombardment of targets on shore.

Qin rose to his feet, a signal that, as far as he was concerned, the exercise was over. The chief of staff came over at once, smiled, and said,

'I hope you enjoyed the show.'

The Emperor glanced at him, nodded, and with no change of expression - he showed no expression at all - climbed the steps out of the VIP trench. He was about to call for Wang before remembering that he was dead.

*Get me the fuck out of here.*

***

The Minister of Public Security, Zhou Yi, was woken at home just before midnight and told he was wanted by the Party Secretary at his *Zhongnanhai* office. The driver and bodyguard who'd been sent to collect him waited outside the family home, a traditional courtyard house, stamping their feet on the icy paving while the Minister dressed, told his wife it was work and not to worry, and hurried out, pulling on a coat and woollen hat, to be driven the 450 yards where he was escorted on foot into the presence of the Emperor, who was sitting up on his bed, surrounded by piles of state and Party papers.

'Ah. There you are. Tea, or something stronger?'

Zhou wasn't fully awake, so it took a moment or two for the question to make sense.

'Tea. Thank you.' Not that he wanted anything at all but to be returned safe and sound to the warmth of his marital bed. That was no certainty, that much he knew.

Qin was all business. He shifted his weight to a loud rustling of papers. 'General Wang's deputy will take over his duties until a formal appointment is approved.'

'Of course. The officer has already been informed and will be here in the morning to report to you.'

'Brief me on the leaks, if you would. Do sit down.'

Zhou was a small, thin man, an old revolutionary in his eighties with a wispy white beard, rimless spectacles and the somewhat distracted air of an academic, even when awake. He reminded Qin of Ho Chi Minh in old age. Zhou hadn't had time to comb what was left of his hair over his otherwise naked scalp, and the strands stood on end once he removed his winter cap.

Zhou looked around in vain for a chair.

Qin watched him, that slight smile back in place. 'Sit there, on the bed,' he ordered, gesturing to a less disordered far corner.

Zhou's Adam's apple rose and fell as he swallowed hard.

'Well? Sit. You can take off your coat if you're too warm, Comrade Zhou. Make yourself at home, please.'

As if the *sha gua* — blockhead — could!

'Six reports in all so far,' Zhou began once perched on the immense platform, doing so without placing his posterior on the buff-coloured files and papers scattered everywhere. 'The reports - articles - appeared in swift succession on the website of a little known organisation in Washington, D.C., named Cincinnatus. They were picked up and published by mainstream media in the United States and Europe. The articles were not signed, though we suspect the author is an American female who speaks and writes Mandarin. Her name is —' He had to intone the foreign name to get it right — 'Avery Shute. The articles are brief and seem to be compilations of material leaked from top cadres, all relating to plans for the forcible unification of Taiwan.'

'So they're accurate?'

'Yes, as far as we can tell, but they are summaries, not verbatim.'

'And those original materials would have been classified secret?'

'Yes.'

'How did this woman —'

'Avery Shute.'

'How did this Avery, whatever-her-name-is, get hold of secret material?'

'We believe it was provided by a Japanese-American who worked here in Beijing as an academic. Her parents were Japanese, but she was born here and grew up here. Her Chinese name was Ding Pan and her true, Japanese name, Niki Kawashima.'

'And she's dead?'

Zhou was shaking, and it wasn't the cold.

'An oversight, Comrade, an error, the result of over-enthusiasm and impatience by members of our *Gong'anbu* team in Washington, D.C.'

Qin watched the quaking old man over the top of his teacup. 'Most unfortunate.'

Zhou nodded. His hands were shaking so much he couldn't pick up his cup.

'These were your *Gong'anbu* operatives working under diplomatic cover out of our Washington mission - or were they members of an illegal residency?'

'The former, Comrade Secretary.'

'What happened?'

'The woman was taken - abducted - from her father's apartment and taken up to the roof to be questioned. At some point, she broke free. She was intercepted, there was a struggle, and she went off the roof, falling four floors to her death.'

'She was pushed - or she jumped?'

Zhou was the colour of the secret papers surrounding him.

'Well?'

'There was a struggle. It seems a little of both. It's uncertain.'

'A little of both,' the Emperor repeated. His head was hurting again, but he kept his smirk in place. His voice remained soft, sibilant, as he sought to keep his rising anger under control. 'Please continue.'

'We know this Avery Shute and the deceased woman were friends from a young age. They were both linguists. They were both students of Chinese affairs. But despite the er, unfortunate death of Ding Pan, the reports have continued to appear, suggesting that somehow the material continues to reach Avery Shute.'

'What information was gleaned from this Ding Pan before she died?'

'None - nothing of significance.'

Qin sighed, followed by an awkward silence.

'I should mention, Comrade Secretary, that the American woman, Shute, is a former employee of the U.S. National Security Agency or NSA.'

'A spy. That explains everything.'

'A linguist and researcher, I believe. She was deployed to Afghanistan and was awarded a unit citation for her work.'

'Still a spy if she was an employee of the NSA. Once a spy, always a spy.'

Zhou didn't agree, but he wouldn't say so. He had calmed down sufficiently to drink his now lukewarm tea, or pretended to do so.

'Was the Japanese woman who died a spy also?'

'Not that we know of. We're still investigating.'

Qin's voice was soft, and Zhou had to strain to hear the Emperor. 'Tell me, Comrade Minister, has either the deceased Ding or her friend Shute at any point been in contact with U.S. secret services - the CIA, the NSA you mentioned, the Defense Intelligence Agency or the FBI?'

'Our information is that Shute was questioned by local police detectives in Washington, D.C., following her friend's death.'

'So the reports or articles based on leaks of sensitive material haven't alerted the American authorities - although they've been picked up by the major U.S. media and abroad? Don't they read their own newspapers?'

'Not so far, no, not to our knowledge.'

Qin laughed, a sudden, single bark of genuine but alarming amusement.

'Our enemies are many things, Minister Zhou, but one thing they are not - and that's stupid.'

Qin decided. Matters could not be allowed to continue as they had. This was an opportunity as well. He moved without warning and took his visitor by surprise, bounding off the bed and standing over Zhou, who looked away from the sight of a vast expanse of white flesh bearing down on him.

'What are you proposing to do now?'

Zhou looked lost, almost stupefied, as the Emperor loomed over him.

'And here - have you identified the source of the leaks?'

'Not yet.'

'Have you suspects?'

'We are investigating.'

'Investigating what?'

'Investigating those who had access to the original materials that were leaked.'

'And?'

'There are dozens of people on the distribution lists.'

'So?'

'We need more time.'

'More time? There is no more time. Use all the resources you need, but get a move on.'

In theory, everyone on the distribution lists could be rounded up, thrown in jail and interrogated, but given who they were, it would not merely create more enemies for the Emperor - who believed he had quite enough of those already - but disrupt Operation China Unity, setting it back months if not years and hence undermining his authority.

Mass arrests and vigorous methods of interrogation were not the answer.

Qin didn't wait for Zhou to work out a suitable, formulaic reply. He reminded himself that he should be restrained, civil, even kind; the old man was a hero, a survivor of the Revolution, of the Cultural Revolution, and the Great Leap Forward. He was like some ancient piece of delicate porcelain. He had suffered, but he had survived. The comrade minister was living history, and he was no threat to Qin. Not that he was much use, either.

'This is what you will do, Comrade. You won't wait for morning. You'll do it now, right away. What's more, you'll signal our people in Washington: The *Gong'anbu* head of station is recalled for consultations on a new promotion and you will ensure he takes the next available flight. Those involved in the questioning of Ding Pan and her death are suspended with immediate effect until they too can return to be investigated. They're incompetent. Got that?'

'Yes, Comrade.' Zhou was also on his feet, his head barely reaching the middle of the Emperor's broad and hairless chest, sensing perhaps that at last he could return to his bed. This was no master spy, Qin reminded himself, hero or not, but an aged Party bureaucratic whose *guanxi* had found him a comfortable, well-paid roost as head of the Public Security Ministry - with no previous expertise in security or counterintelligence. That, right there, was both the problem and an opportunity.

'One more thing, Minister Zhou. Tomorrow you will submit your own formal resignation in writing to the Standing Committee, citing ill-health and pressure of work. The usual thing - I don't have to tell you how this works. The premier will write back and, with regret, he will accept your resignation. You will clear your desk. The Party is grateful for your years of selfless and heroic service and wishes you a long and happy retirement. Please - the driver will take you home. Or would you prefer to walk?'

Zhou turned away.

'You can give back that teacup you're still holding.'

Qin put out a hand to receive it.

Qin's head ached, the pain coming and going in time with his heartbeat. He returned to his bed and lay down flat on his back among the secret files, not caring if he rumpled, creased or crushed them. He squeezed his eyes shut against the pain.

# 26

Ava was rigid with shock, so much so that her involuntary intake of breath sounded like a yelp of pain.

A moment later she sprang up — not towards the intruder, but back, rolling over the back of the sofa so it was between her and the stranger. She crouched in the dark, the streetlights far below providing a faint orange glow between the drawn curtains.

The tension and fright of the last few hours were back with a vengeance.

The figure rose to his feet, hands outstretched, empty.

'I'm so sorry, Ava. I didn't mean to startle you. You've got great reactions, though, I must say.'

She recognised his voice at once.

'Startle me? You bastard — don't patronise me — you almost gave me a freakin' heart attack!' Ava's posture relaxed as the tension seeped away and she stood straight, dropping her hands. But where there was fear a moment ago, there was now anger and perplexity.

She also felt foolish and embarrassed, and that added to her fury.

'What the hell are you doing here? How did you get in?'

'I was worried about you —'

'Oh? That so? I should be grateful? Like you break into my home, search through my stuff and hide in the shadows? It's an odd way to show your concern. I feel so much better, so reassured. Thank you.'

Sam Turner's response to the well-deserved sarcasm was unexpected. He put a finger to his lips, then pointed at his own right ear and up at the ceiling. He wasn't finished with the sign language. Once satisfied that Ava understood, he pointed at her, then at himself - and at the door. He walked over to it, beckoned to her, and gestured at her bag.

Ava understood, but she didn't move an inch except to shrug, raise her hands in a gesture that seemed to mean, 'what the hell for?' or 'why should I trust you?'

Sam rolled his eyes, put a hand to his forehead as if to say, 'for God's sake!'

'Okay,' Ava said in a loud voice. She picked up her bag, took out her keys.

***

Sam drove a battered Toyota Corolla, several years old, but from the growling sound of the engine in low gear, it had been souped up. Ava sat next to him, seatbelt fastened.

Fewer than five minutes into the journey, and Ava was sure they had a tail. 'I think we're being followed. Blue Honda Civic three cars back.'

'They're ours,' Turner said. 'Our babysitters, making sure we arrive in one piece, and watching the *Gong'anbu* comms.'

When they got out, she walked close to him so she didn't have to raise her voice.

'You've got some explaining to do, Sam.'

Turner said nothing until they'd settled at a corner table in the Emissary coffee shop on P Street NW, and being the spook he was, Turner's first task was to fix a time and place for their next meet: another coffee shop called Tryst in Morgan Adams, chosen for its location but two blocks from the Cincinnatus office.

He murmured, his eyes sweeping both the cafe and the pavement outside. 'Ava, they're using the condo next to yours to power their SF. It's being refurbished by the absent owner and they got access and set up overnight before the decorators returned this morning. They needn't have worried because whoever's doing the work hasn't come back at all today.'

'They? Who's they? And what's SF?'

'Our *Gong'anbu* friends. China's Public Security Ministry operatives working out of their embassy. SF — sorry — it's jargon for special facilities. They've wired your place for audio, visual and everything and anything digital, from your alarm system and TV to your washing machine. Very professional it was, too. They're taking enough power to light up a small city.'

'How do you know it's them and not the *Guoanbu*? Not that there's a hell of a lot of differences between Public Security *Gong'anbu* and State Security *Guoanbu*.'

'These guys have a definite signature. They're quite distinct.'

'The people I saw this morning, running across the street from a couple of unmarked green people carriers towards my building? Who were they?'

'Those were ours. They weren't discreet. Sorry. Our techies. They had a tight window to get the job done.'

'I thought that was the Chinese. So I panicked, made a run for it and hid in my store cupboard on the mezzanine floor for hours. Jesus, I was terrified. You could have warned me, or waited until I went out.'

'All I can say again is that I'm sorry. My people rang your bell several times and thought you were out.'

'What were your technicians, or whatever they're called, doing?'

'A thorough sweep of your place. They've also planted a couple of monitors in your building so we can relay and read everything the other side picks up. Everything they see, we see. Everything they hear, we hear. What happened to your friend Pan won't happen to you - at least, that's the intention. We didn't break into your place, Ava. I confess I picked your front door locks myself once our people had left. That Banham lock is a pushover, by the way.'

'So you could search my things? Was it fun poking around in my underwear?'

Sam's ears reddened. 'Not at all. I waited for you to make sure you were okay. I knew you hadn't gone in to work.'

'Their watchers will have seen you.'

'They'll have seen somebody enter, but not who. I was wearing glasses that reflect the IR they use, so for them it will have been like looking directly at the sun.'

'What now?'

'We finish our coffee. Then I take you over to meet the charming Mr and Mrs Potter. Oh, yes, they exist. I'm sure you'll like them. They run a safe house in the suburbs and they'll look after you. Not their real names, of course. They're Canadian.'

'I don't want looking after, Sam. I'm supposed to be at work and I don't need a nanny or a butler.'

'It won't be for long. We won't stop you working, far from it. But you'll need to take care because our Chinese friends will have got into your office by now. We have to assume they have, anyway. It'll either be wired or they'll have someone on the inside working for them. Or both. They are nothing if not thorough.'

'You certainly have a way of making me feel safe, Sam.'

He grinned at her. 'I'm telling you the way it is. It's your turn. Haven't you got something for me, as per our agreement?'

Ava took the thumb drive from her coat pocket and put it down next to her coffee cup. 'There's just one item missing, the last report - I was interrupted by your friends this morning and had to make a swift exit.'

'Can't you do it now?'

So she did, opening up the air-gapped laptop from her bag and copying the last Mandarin report onto the thumb drive, which she handed to him.

'Ava, you're not giving me everything, though, are you?'

'Sam, please. I agreed — reluctantly — to let you have copies of the Mandarin version of the stuff from the source once it was decrypted. That's what I've done.'

'But there's more, isn't there?'

'How would you know, Sam?' Ava gazed out of the window at the street. It was dark with that sinister orange light reflected from windows, street lights, billboards, headlights. People swaddled from head to foot in woollen hats, faces wrapped in scarves, bodies concealed in long puffer coats, went by, hands gloved or deep in pockets, city folk sunk in their own thoughts and worries - children, mortgages, holidays, the cost of living, jobs - all the stuff of real life. She thought she had spotted the Honda Civic parked on the other side, but she wasn't certain.

'I guessed.'

'You're not getting the source, Sam. No-one is. So any comments and notes are not for sharing. I'm already breaking one cardinal rule by dealing with you at all.'

'If you say so. What can you tell me about him?'

'Nothing you don't already know. I told you before he's a Communist Party member, a senior cadre, but he sees himself as a patriot trying to save his country and its people from what he believes will be a destructive war that will be in no-one's interest, not even the Party's. That's it.'

'Nothing about work or family? How about his place of origin, his family?'

'No. Nothing. Great coffee, by the way. Thanks. Shall we go?'

Ava packed away her gear again.

'Sure.'

'It's okay, Sam. I know you've a team in here. You looked over my shoulder a couple of times too often. That couple over there in the corner, behind me and to the left, and the guy at the counter in the plaid shirt reading the Post. I'm not stupid or blind, you know.'

'I never thought you were, Ava.'

'Are they staff from your SIS Station?'

Sam hesitated. She could tell he tried not to lie if he could help it. 'We call them contract labourers, Ava, people we trust and whom we pay for services rendered. In this case, technical specialists and watchers.'

'Tell me the truth, Sam. Are you working with the FBI?'

'No.'

'Langley?'

'No.'

'Not the National Clandestine Service?'

'No.'

'My former employers?'

'No.'

'Defense Intelligence?'

'No, Ava.'

'Don't tell me you Brits are running this all on your lonesome?'

Turner smiled. It was a wintry smile this time. 'I think we can just about manage it. It's always possible there may be some financial and operational arrangement agreed by London that I don't know about because it's above my pay grade.'

'I'd love to believe you, Sam. I would. Don't tell me the U.S. taxpayer isn't picking up the tab because they usually do.'

'Then maybe you should believe me. It might make it easier.'

***

The safe house was just off Wisconsin Avenue in Bethesda, an affluent suburb of DC. Bethesda was not only an upper middle class neighbourhood with large, detached homes and good public schools a fifteen-minute commute from DC, but it was also overwhelmingly white and, as Sam explained, it meant that people of minority ethnicities venturing into its quiet avenues stood out a mile, and although that might not be desirable or commendable in some important respects, it was helpful when seeking refuge from Communist Chinese spies.

'The ChiComs have their own contract labourers these days - freelancers who are not all Asian in appearance. They can afford to, what's more. They've used whites, Hispanics, African-Americans, too, for *jianshi* — surveillance — for just that reason, to fit in with the crowd.'

'Great house,' Ava said, impressed, gazing at the house from the front seat of the Toyota, the Honda having dropped back a couple of blocks. 'Must have cost a fortune.'

The property comprised two wings, one double-storey, the other single. With a pitched roof and big white shutters, it stood on a rise so that it dominated the road, and was surrounded by trees, mostly oak and beech. It had a country look to it, Ava thought. The front yard was open, as was so often the case with U.S. residential properties, but it was flanked by stone walls, and the yard fell in a series of rough levels marked by rocky outcrops, trees and flower beds down to the street. Snow clung to the uneven ground. There was a footpath with stone steps and a driveway ran around the side to what she thought must be a double garage somewhere at the rear.

'We've had it for many years, but you're right — nowadays it would fetch almost a million dollars. But it still makes sense to keep it, bearing in mind there are more spies per square metre in DC than anywhere else in the world.'

'More like a million four or five,' said Ava. 'The Potters live here?'

Sam avoided answering. He had the politician's habit of responding to questions he didn't like by offering answers to questions that hadn't been asked. He ignored questions he didn't like, as if he hadn't heard. It was evasive, but given his profession, not unexpected. Ava didn't hold it against him — she'd come across the manoeuvre all too often in her brief NSA life, and it was better than lying outright.

'You'll like them.'

They walked up the path, gravel with stone steps every few yards.

'Who? Who will I like?'

'The Potters. They won't ask questions, won't get in your way - but they'll be there when you need them. And Mr Potter is one hell of a cook, as you'll discover.'

'The British way - seen but not heard, right? Though I thought it applied only to the kids. They sound perfect. Sam, I'm going to need some clothes and other stuff from my place.'

'No worries, Ava. Make a list, give it to Mrs Potter and someone will get it for you within 24 hours.' He turned to smile at her. 'We aim to please.'

Sam put out a hand to press the doorbell, but he needn't have bothered because the front door opened at once and Mr and Mrs Potter stood there, smiling.

'Hi, you two. Welcome, Ava. Can we call you Ava? Is that okay?'

'Sure.'

'Come right in. You must be hungry. Supper won't be long.'

The house was warm and Ava could smell whatever was in the oven - and she salivated, realising that aside from coffee - too much coffee - she'd hardly eaten anything all day.

The Potters introduced themselves. Clive Potter was a tall, broad man in a plaid shirt, sleeves rolled up, blue jeans, and wearing a kitchen apron decorated with a Christmas tree. He had bright, smiling blue eyes set in a lined face - a face that looked as if it had spent a lifetime outdoors and in all weathers. Ava placed him somewhere in his 70s, but still vigorous and alert. His wife Kathy was much shorter, softer, with sliver-grey hair cut in a bob, a few years younger perhaps, and also robust.

Kathy showed Ava to her quarters on the first floor of the main wing, chatting as they went, saying Ava was the only guest and she had the run of the place, that there was a library of sorts on the ground floor which she could use. Did Ava have any particular requirements for food? Was she vegetarian? Ava's accommodation resembled a junior suite in an exclusive hotel - a furnished bedroom, a living room with an enormous television and a bathroom. A coded lock on the door, a safe in the wall, inside the built-in wardrobe.

She could close that special locker she'd rented.

Ava was left to herself to 'freshen up' as Kathy put it. When she went downstairs again, Ava saw Clive Potter setting the table while his wife Kathy was in the kitchen getting their evening meal ready. Sam was waiting for Ava in the hall. 'I'm off now - I wish you a good night's rest. I'll be back tomorrow to introduce you to your new team. Can't tell you what time, but it will be around noon.'

'My team?'

'Yes, Ava. Your team. You're going to be working together.'

# 27

# December 14

Qin shucked off the sandal from his right foot and, taking great care not to fall over, bent down and put his big toe in the water. It was as he suspected; they'd filled the pool, but it would take a while, perhaps a few days, for the temperature to reach an acceptable level so he could use it again in some comfort. He didn't enjoy swimming in cold water.

Forty-nine days to go.

The Emperor had reached an important decision. It came to him as soon as he woke in the small hours. It seemed as if his subconscious had been working while he slept, processing all the paperwork for him. He knew what he must do, what the People's Republic must do. Qin washed, shaved with an electric razor, brushed his teeth with his electric toothbrush, and dressed. He applied moisturiser to his face. This time he didn't ask for help but pulled out a charcoal suit, a well-ironed white shirt, found a leather belt, pushed his feet into black loafers. He was ready. He spent less time than usual combing his gelled hair. Satisfied from a brief inspection in his bathroom mirror, he strode over to the lift, checked his watch for the last time to ensure he was five minutes late, dropped down and in moments was at his podium in the Strategic Command Centre.

They were all there, of course, waiting for him.

'Comrades.' He paused, looked around at the familiar faces. He smiled, no smirk, but a genuine smile this time. 'Having read your reports, your briefing papers, your assessments, I congratulate you. I understand your urgent need for clarity, for direction. Everything you have said, the arguments for and against, and the persuasive logic of your deliberations, I note. I appreciate the time and effort you have put into this work out of love and loyalty for the Party and the people. I thank you all.

'So here it is. Some of you, I know, favour a massive, all-out strike against our enemies out of the blue, with total surprise, delivering such a crushing blow so that it's all over before they can react, catching their allies unawares and unprepared. I see the attraction in this option, I really do.

'However, I doubt this assumption about achieving surprise. Our enemies have many warning systems in place. We are watched. I believe it would be impossible to move without being detected. So,' he looked around, 'I have decided; I trust you, senior cadres of the Party, will ratify my decision. We will boil this frog by degrees. I have said this before, as some of you may remember.

'What does this mean in practical terms? It means we will begin with the Matsu Island chain. That is our first, limited objective. We will impose an air and sea blockade. It will not end there, of course, but proceed to our second objective: Kinmen's fifteen islands. We will learn a great deal from these island capture operations and improve our own performance in command-and-control while at the same time assessing every response of our adversaries.'

Perhaps he was imagining it, but Qin sensed not a stiffening of apprehension as expected but a sudden release in tension, a feeling of relief now that he'd announced the Party's decision or, at least, what would be the Party's decision.

They didn't want the responsibility, he knew. It was his alone - even if they had to add their names - which they would, of course. It was the Chinese way: to follow my leader and never, ever take personal responsibility for anything. There was a saying for this, quite commonplace in Communist China.

*Duoshuo duocuo, xiaoshuo xiaocuo, bushuo bucuo*

Which meant 'speak more, more mistakes, speak less, few mistakes, say nothing, no mistakes'.

He raised his right hand, a gesture of warning or perhaps caution.

'Please bear in mind that our enemies can at any point put an immediate halt to these proceedings by accepting our longstanding offer of unconditional talks on unification. The offer remains on the table. That would be the rational course, but then our enemies are neither logical nor sensible. Until they see sense, and accept that they cannot win, we will keep raising the temperature and turning the screws tighter and tighter. From the Matsu to the Kinmen, from the Kinmen to Penghu's Magong and on to Taipei itself.'

The Emperor paused. He was enjoying this. For once he knew his brief backwards, and he was certain he was making the right move.

'I know all too well what your primary objection will be, that we become bogged down in island-hopping operations that absorb too many of our military resources and for far too long, so that we exhaust ourselves before the ultimate objective. That is Taipei's hope, of course. Let me assure you now: this will not happen because the Party will not allow it to happen.'

Scattered applause followed. The Emperor's smile widened, and he turned his head, making eye contact with the members of the Politburo Standing Committee and the Central Military Commission - armed forces, intelligence and security chiefs, and key ministers.

'So - how will we attack the Matsu and Kinmen island groups?

'Some of you wrote the operational plans, so you know better than I. Let me just say, for the benefit of those not involved in military planning, that the bigger of the islands will be the primary targets. Why? Because our enemies will seek to use these as staging posts for their attacks on the mainland. We must deny them this option. Our forces have been indoctrinated on what they are likely to face - the weather patterns, the tides, the coastal sea depths, the cliffs, the landing zones and the suitable drop zones for our paratroopers behind, or on top of, enemy positions.

'This is how it will be: overnight missile and artillery strikes on the defenders, their radars and their defensive positions, will be followed at first light by our helicopters skimming the surface of the sea, below enemy radar. They will deliver infantry to neutralise enemy command posts and missile launch sites. Paratroops will seize key ground, airstrips and ports. Supported by heavy fire, our amphibious forces will storm ashore. Marines and paratroopers will clear the enemy out of pillboxes, bunkers and tunnels in close combat, blocking some entrances and using fire and explosives to force them into the open where they will be annihilated.'

\*\*\*

All those present knew the essential facts: that the Matsu - small groups of solid granite islands and isolated, single slabs of granite rocks totalling some 28 islets were home to about 13,500 people, and at their closest point only about nine kilometres or 5.5 miles, from mainland China's Fujian Province to the northwest of Taiwan. They had always been, in the eyes of the CCP, part of Lianjiang County. They formed an arc which dominated the entry to - and exit from - the mainland's large, international Fuzhou port, which faced the Taiwan Strait and would play a direct role in any naval operations, especially the deployment of amphibious invasion fleets against Taiwan.

Fuzhou was 155 miles, or 250 km, as the crow flies from Taipei, according to Google Maps, and it handled 35 million tons of foreign trade cargo every year.

The Matsu townships of Dongyin, Beigan, Nangan and Juguan were the centres of population. There were two small airports and there were garrisons of Taiwanese troops, which would, in the PLA's view at least, be crushed.

Qin stressed it was essential that all resistance be overcome. The Matsu Islands were part of Taiwan's first line of defence and formed an early warning system of an impending assault. They posed a direct threat to PLA invasion plans for Taiwan itself.

The Emperor had read the alternative proposals - to isolate and bypass the islands, but he wasn't convinced, and neither were the PLAN commanders. It would be like turning your back on a murderer holding a sharp knife to your ribs.

***

He saw her for the first time waiting outside his office and pool complex - feet apart, hands clasped in front of her, a posture relaxed yet alert. She wore a black suit and a white blouse or shirt, black boots. Her hair was pulled back in a ponytail, the tail itself dyed blonde. No makeup. No jewellery except for the sports watch.

'Mr President —'

She stepped forward.

Qin was president. That was true. It was a title without authority and symbolic, and while Qin would have preferred to be addressed as General Secretary, or even Chairman of the Central Military Commission, he couldn't object.

'I know who you are. You're Zhong Mei, my new close protection officer.'

She nodded — it was more like a quick bow.

'I'm only temporary. Until General Wang's replacement is appointed and he decides whether I should stay on as one of his staff.'

'We'll see.' The Emperor gave her his friendliest, though lopsided, smile. 'Can you swim, Ms. Zhong?'

'I can, yes.'

'That's good. I wouldn't want any more fatal accidents in my pool. One's enough.'

Zhong said nothing and her expression gave nothing away. Wang's death wasn't a joke, and she wasn't about to be tripped up by a wisecrack from the Emperor. It was an invitation to instant disaster, and she saw the trap at once.

'Why did you decide to become a bodyguard?'

'Hmm. Well, Mr President, there are some 800,000 graduates every year in the People's Republic, and as you will know, they all want good jobs. I suppose you could say that from a very young age I was inspired by the film *Shaolin Temple*. I was a kid. My parents were poor. I'm a realist, at least I like to think so. I'm capable and I'm not too stupid, so it seemed to me to be the right path.'

'And where is it you come from?'

'The south west. Zigong in Sichuan.'

'Ah, yes. I read your file, but I confess I've forgotten some details. I remember you're 25 years old.'

'Twenty-six now.'

'My apologies — I have so much to read every day and most of it is boring and bureaucratic, so by the time I get to the interesting stuff I'm asleep or crippled by a headache. Come with me now and we'll have tea by my pool. I want to ask you about your work.'

Qin saw she was careful, cautious, respectful - but not at all intimidated in his presence. That interested him. She sat opposite him on a lounger parallel to his own as tea was brought almost instantly and placed between them.

'So, Ms Zhong. I want to hear your story. Begin!'

She wasn't beautiful, Qin decided. This was no tall, long-legged Vogue model waiting for her billionaire lover to sweep her off her feet into the world of Cartier, Versace and a villa by the sea in Santa Barbara. She was desirable, he thought, as most healthy young women were at her age - and she was not as young or as attractive as the young Communists screened by the late General Wang, who had cavorted, sighed and squealed on his bed after dance nights. But she was interesting.

So what did he find so interesting? He nodded when she gestured at the steaming tea, expecting her to fill their cups. His first, watching her as she did so — with a steady hand and some grace, he noted.

First, she had an awareness, a maturity beyond her years. Maybe that was down to her modest but loving family background. And there was plenty of confidence, physical confidence. It amused him that she gave no sign of being overwhelmed or intimidated by his presence. His sheer size might have cowed her - but not a bit.

Good. Very good.

Once they both had their tea, she began. 'In 2015, I was accepted into Chengdu Sport University. I had good grades.'

'Your file records you had excellent grades, Ms. Zhong.'

'I graduated in *Sanda*.'

"Sometimes known in places such as Thailand as kickboxing?'

'Yes. I did three months' basic training in Chengdu and then came here to Beijing and attended special courses at the Genghis Security Academy. There were many subjects, such as advanced driving, unarmed combat, combat shooting, knife fighting, intelligence reconnaissance. The college then gave me a job training others in security and defence.'

'Aren't you at a disadvantage compared to your male colleagues, though?'

'First, only 20 percent of female trainees become guards because the training is tough and the security screening so stringent. As long as we train really hard, our employment rate is much higher than that for males.'

She had the Emperor's full attention.

'So, what are the primary criteria for being a successful bodyguard?'

Qin sucked at his tea.

'A high level of physical fitness and good close-quarter combat skills are basic requirements, but there are three levels to achieve. Junior grade bodyguards can drive, and they are proficient in fighting and anti-tracking skills. Intermediate level trainees have computer skills, can conduct business activities and understand official documentation.'

'You graduated at advanced level, didn't you?'

'I did. I had to show I could organise complex trips, make safety travel plans and understand foreign languages, as well as analyse risk.'

'Which languages?'

'Cantonese and English.'

'What else?'

'Also criminal psychology.'

'You are a champion at marksmanship?'

'I wouldn't say a champion, but I enjoy shooting.'

'You did internships in the private sector as part of your training. Why didn't you stay in the private sector? The pay is better and it's an expanding market. Maybe you'd find a young billionaire client to marry.'

She didn't find the remark amusing.

'I wanted to serve the Party. You see, I didn't like some of the rich and spoiled tai-tais or their rich lovers I had to protect during my internships. I wanted a greater challenge.'

'And now you are serving the Party, Ms Zhong. I hope you will be happy in your new role.'

She stood up and seemed to hesitate.

'Is there anything you'd like to ask me, Ms Zhong?'

'Anything?'

She looked shocked by the question.

He gave her his best smile.

'Anything.'

'You seem…' she searched for the word… 'so isolated here. Do people tell you the truth?'

Qin found it extraordinary that she seemed so unafraid.

'Truth? About what?'

'About China. About the people, the ordinary Chinese people. About what's going on out there, beyond those big red walls around you? Do they?'

'There are people whose task it is to keep me informed.'

'But do they tell you the truth, Mr President, or do they only tell you what they think you want to hear?'

# 28

## 07:25 Eastern Standard Time, GMT -4

'It's not much to go on. I'd hoped there would be more.'

The speaker was elderly. Ava put him somewhere in the eighties, with an English drawl, wearing a pullover under a baggy corduroy jacket that had seen better days. His hair was white and long. Sam called him 'professor' to his face and had introduced him to everyone as Dr. Clarke. He resembled a retired academic, someone who'd been interrupted pruning the roses in his garden in the Home Counties - or perhaps it was Montana - and dragged all this way for his opinion. All Sam would say was that he was an authority on Communist China with several well-respected books to his name. The professor just smiled at this, played with his empty pipe, said nothing. Ava felt she should know who he was.

'Is this it? I make it five reports,' added Jenny Tung, a petite woman around 50 or thereabouts, once again a work name, Ava thought, and introduced by Sam as a senior professor in strategic studies at a think tank in Taipei that Ava had never heard of. Well, it might very well exist without Ava knowing. Jenny was a compact, businesslike person, bespectacled, intense and not one for small talk. She sounded disappointed. 'Isn't there anything else? Nothing personal, no note of an individual nature, a letter perhaps, from the source - nothing at all to give us at least a clue?' She looked over the top of her glasses at Ava as if holding her responsible for this paucity of useful material.

The last member of the 'team' - aside from Ava - was another woman, also middle-aged, but tall and pale with a thin mouth - a slash of deep red lipstick - and a distinctive northern English accent. Her dark, auburn hair was cut in a severe bob, set off by a grey shift with no discernible shape, a coverall a painter might wear and a statement to the effect that she didn't bother trying to impress. Dr. Angela Philips was proud of her Lancashire roots, Sam said. And why not?

Ava thought she'd seen her face before - perhaps in the media - until Sam said she'd been a senior adviser on China to the UK Foreign Secretary at some point.

That was it - Ava recalled some details, along with some faint memories of controversy, but once again, Philips was an assumed name.

Their deliberations began in the basement of the safe house, a large, windowless space lined with acoustic tiles on walls, ceiling and floor, a giant Faraday cage of wire mesh in effect, dominated by a dining table with places set with writing pads, pencils, carafes of water, glasses and thermos jugs of coffee and plates of biscuits.

Whiteboards lined the room, mounted on wheeled frames.

A sign read, 'No smoking. Thank you!'

Sam sat at the head of the table, Ava opposite, at the far end.

'Ava, why don't you kick off by telling us what you know about the source?'

'I only know what he's said.'

'Fine, start with that if you would.'

'He's a Communist and a patriot, or so he claims. He's doing this because he believes a war over Taiwan would break up the CCP and the country, lead to huge loss of life and damage the global economy. If he can get his material out into the public sphere, he believes it will have more impact rather than feeding it to a foreign intelligence agency that would keep it secret…'

'He has a point,' growled Dr Clarke.

'He said in his latest note that he thinks they know there's a leak and people seem to watch him, but that it's just a feeling, nothing concrete.'

'Paranoia?' The interjection was from Philips. 'Pretty common to lone whistleblowers, I'd say.'

Ava plunged on. 'He says that because of this sense of being monitored, he's going to send us everything he can as quickly as he can, although it will increase the risk.'

Dr Clarke waved his empty pipe at Ava. 'He might well be right. They're probably searching through the distribution lists of the material he's sent us so far. That means scores of Party officials with high security clearance. They're hunting him down, but it will take time. They can't just pull out their nails or beat them all half to death.'

'I find the language interesting, if only for what it doesn't reveal,' said Tung. 'Both the PRC and ROC encourage people to read and write Mandarin in the vernacular. So not a lot could be gleaned from this - other than education, class, perhaps age to some extent. These aren't the original documents, but his recollection of them, his interpretation, right? But there are none of the usual terms or slogans you might expect of a senior cadre. There are no personal flourishes, no obvious giveaways. He keeps his egotistic impulses under firm control. Impressive.'

'Are you saying this is fake? A plant?' Angela Philips again.

'I didn't say that,' replied Tung. 'He's being careful, that's all.'

'So what can we make of it?' asked Sam.

'He or she is middle aged - anywhere from forties to high sixties,' said Tung. 'He or she is educated to postgrad level, maybe they - I'm going to use the pronoun to avoid upsetting anyone on gender - have been to a foreign university for at least some of it. They're very much aware of the outside world and its importance to China - something most top cadres don't, or won't, admit. Qin's view and that of the Party is that China doesn't need the West in any shape or form, though they spend a lot of time and effort stealing our technology. They're well-off and very confident of their own abilities. If they're not Red Aristocracy, then I'd say they are a senior functionary in the military-security establishment with wide access. They could be an administrator, a senior secretary in the Central Military Commission. They've got high security clearance. Just look at what we have so far. This is all guesswork, by the way.'

Sam was already writing the headlines on the whiteboards.

*1. JTAC holds the first session. Feb. 1 set as provisional date for invasion. Weather problems.*

*2. Plan of attack has three phases.*

*3. Operation China Unity. Air Exclusion Zone.*

*4. Operation China Unity: Maritime blockade*

*5. Timing of phased 'Main Strategic Direction'.*

It was time for coffee. Sam passed around the milk and sugar, Ava the biscuits. 'There is more,' Sam said. 'A lot more. This is just a taste.'

'A lot more biscuits or intel from our mysterious source?' Philips grinned at Ava.

Ava sounded apologetic. 'I haven't had time since it arrived this morning. I can make a start on it right now.' She looked at Sam, who gave a slight nod.

So she did. While the others drank coffee, nibbled Hobnobs, went outside in the frosty back yard for a smoke, visited the bathroom or scowled down at the five initial reports in the vain hope they'd somehow reveal more about the anonymous source, Ava got to work in her room decrypting the latest tranche, then set about translating them. She was careful to use her air-gapped laptop for the thumb drive - the temptation when faced with 36 separate items was to rush things.

She'd been woken by a call on her burner from James just after 7 a.m. Where should he send her mail, or would she collect it? Half-awake and confused in a strange bed in a strange house, she mumbled that she'd come in to pick up whatever it was.

But the Potters were having none of it. Cincinnatus wasn't safe, not for her. She was not to venture out unless Sam said she could, and he hadn't yet turned up. Clive would take her driving licence with him and pose as a courier come to collect it. In sweats, a high-vis jacket and a baseball cap, he'd done just that.

They weren't happy that she'd taken a call on her own mobile. 'Always use a burner if you can, or don't use a phone at all,' Clive admonished her. 'They could track that call right here.'

'I did. Use a burner, I mean.'

'Right. Good. Get rid of it. Use a new one for the next call.'

It was at this point that Ava had realised — over a croissant, coffee and an apple — that the Potters weren't just safe house minders but much more. They helped with SDR - route surveillance detection, that exhausting, time-consuming but vital procedure known to all intelligence services everywhere. Which was why Ava saw Mrs Potter leave the house carrying a basket and wearing a green coat, only to return in a yellow jacket, a navy woollen hat and a handbag. In denied territory, such as Moscow or Beijing, an agent could spend twelve hours in freezing cold weaving his or her way through the streets, on wheels or on foot, with maybe a hundred FSB Watchers and thirty or forty cars in pursuit, having already studied distances and angles of streets and street corners. And even here, in an open society, SDR was unavoidable. Yes, it was an open, 'free' society, but DC was infested with spies and their counter-intelligence counterparts.

Ava reminded herself that Pan's violent end was just one example of what could go wrong.

***

## PLA ORDER OF BATTLE UPDATE

*1. The PLA has been reorganised and restructured over the past four years, and this revised ORDER OF BATTLE has stabilised as follows:*

*2. Each of the five THEATRE COMMANDS (TCS) has 2-3 GROUP ARMIES*

*3. Each GROUP ARMY (GA) comprises:*

*4. COMBINED ARMS BRIGADES (CABS) and 6 SUPPORT BRIGADES (SBS) and/or INDEPENDENT BATTALIONS*

*5. THE 6 SBS COMPRISE 1 ARTILLERY, 1 AIR DEFENCE, 1 ARMY AVIATION or AIR ASSAULT, 1 SPECIAL OPERATIONS, 1 ENGINEER and 1 SERVICE SUPPORT BRIGADE.*

'Not much to add to what we already know,' said Tung.

'Still, an interesting corroboration,' said Dr Clarke, somehow keeping his pipe clenched between his teeth.

'Those four new marine brigades in northern and eastern theatres are news, at least to me,' said Philips. 'Taiwan has to figure large in that.'

'There's more to come,' Sam said.

So there was - a great deal more.

## TAIWAN JOINT ATTACK CENTRE (FORMERLY EASTERN THEATRE COMMAND) - ORDER OF BATTLE

*1. ROCKET FORCE 61 BASE*

*2. EAST FLEET COMMAND*

*3. PLA GROUND FORCES:*

   *a. 71ST GROUP ARMY (previous 12th GA)*

   *b. 72ND GA*

   *c. 73RD GA*

## PLAN:

## EAST SEA FLEET

## PLAAF:

*1. 10TH BOMBER DIVISION*

*2. 7TH FIGHTER BRIGADE (WUHU, ANHUI. SHANGHAI BASE)*

*3. 8TH FIGHTER BRIGADE (CHANGXING, CHEJIANG. SHANGHAI BASE)*

*4. 9TH FIGHTER BRIGADE (WUHU, ANHUI. SHANGHAI BASE)*

*5. 40TH FIGHTER BRIGADE (NANCHANG, JIANXI. FUZHOU BASE)*

*6. 41ST FIGHTER BRIGADE (WUYISHAN, FUJIAN. FUZHOU BASE)*

*7. 42ND FIGHTER BRIGADE (ZHANGSHU, JIANGXI. FUZHOU BASE)*

*8. 26TH SPECIAL MISSION DIVISION*

*9. 83RD ATTACK BRIGADE (HANGZHOU, ZHEJIANG. SHANGHAI BASE)*

*10. 180TH UAV (WIANGCHENG, FUJIAN. FUZHOU BASE)*

*NOTES:*
*ROCKET FORCE'S 61 BASE (formerly 51 Base) is one of the biggest bases for conventional missiles. Nuclear missiles will remain under direct control of CMC. EAST FLEET Commander will serve as DEPUTY THEATRE COMMANDER and COMMANDER OF ALL PLAN forces in EASTERN TC.*

'I take it all back,' said Tung. 'This is getting interesting. I hope there's going to be more of this - more detail. It's details I want.'

'So at last we see a deployment of the much-publicised PLA drones,' muttered Philips.

Ava thought they seemed a little happier now they had something to get their teeth into. She thought orders of battle - whatever country they applied to - were dead boring, even if they were secret. But not to everyone, it seemed.

She'd get two articles written for Cincinnatus based on this: the change of PLA designations and the expansion of marine units deployed close to Taiwan.

These academics would want to see the full breakdown. After an informal lunch lasting 25 minutes - pizza and white wine or beer - Ava had no choice but to retreat to her room to focus on the columns of names and numbers. What she really wanted to do was take a nap on the comfortable bed. No-one at Cincinnatus would think much of this material, of course, and her media outlets would like it even less. All they'd get out of it was the obvious: China had the largest standing army in the world, the world's largest navy in terms of hulls in the water, and the biggest, most powerful air force in the western Pacific.

And so it went.

## ORDER OF BATTLE: EAST SEA FLEET HQ

## FLEET TOTALS:

- *23 DIESEL-ELECTRIC ATTACK SUBS*
- *12 DESTROYERS*

- *9 CORVETTES*
- *17 TANK LANDING SHIPS*
- *11 MEDIUM LANDING SHIPS*
- *41 MISSILE PATROL CRAFT*
- *1 FIGHTER DIV.*
- *1 MIXED AIR DIV.*
- *1 RADAR BGDE.*
- *UNIT DESIGNATIONS:*
- *8TH FRIGATE FLOTILLA (SHANGHAI)*
- *3RD DESTROYER FLOTILLA (ZHOUSHAN, ZHEJIANG)*
- *6TH DESTROYER FLOTILLA (ZHOUSHAN, ZHEJIANG)*
- *21ST FASTBOAT FLOTILLA (NINGDE, FUJIAN)*
- *5TH LANDING SHIP FLOTILLA (SHANGHAI)*
- *NAVAL AVIATION UNIT (NINGBO):*
- *4TH NAVAL AVIATION DIV. (TAIXHOU, ZHEJIANG)*
- *6TH NAVAL AVIATION DIV. (SHANGHAI)*
- *1ST FLYING PANTHER REGT. (YIWU, ZHEJIANG)*

And on and on.

And still Ava decrypted, translated, printed and took the material down to 'her' team.

The ORBAT of the 72ND GROUP ARMY followed, and the 73RD GROUP ARMY was next. According to the notes provided by the source, the 72ND GA was tasked with an assault on Northern Taiwan and the 73RD GA for attacks on Kinmen, Matsu, and Penghu islands. This last had them buzzing with conversation, and arguments flared and died down and flared again, the faint sounds reaching her through her locked bedroom door as she worked.

It was midnight when Ava shut her air-gapped computer, gathered everything up - charger, pens, paper, thumb drives - and put it all away in her bag.

She walked down into the peculiar basement and gazed at them slumped in their chairs.

'Well? What do you guys reckon? There's more, but I need sleep.'

'So do we,' said Dr Clarke. 'But let's have a drink first, shall we, to celebrate your remarkable haul? I think you deserve our congratulations.'

His companions nodded and smiled. They even clapped a few times.

The mood had changed from resigned cynicism to enthusiasm and - if she wasn't imagining it - respect.

'Maybe more than one drink,' said Sam, who'd just returned to the house from somewhere or other and had stood outside for a few minutes, chatting to the Potters before entering. He brought in glasses and a bottle of Jameson's and put them on the table. Did anyone want ice? No-one did. Water? Apparently not.

'We also have an announcement to make,' said Tung, taking off her glasses and blinking up at Ava. 'This military material is genuine. There are some gaps, there are differences of opinion over some of it, but we all agree. It's the real thing.'

'It's priceless,' said Philips. 'A gold mine. The Ministry of Defence and US DoD will love it.'

'Glad you think so,' Ava said with more than a hint of sarcasm. She wouldn't say so, but she thought a great deal of it could have been put together from open source material available on the Net, given enough time and half a dozen researchers fluent in Mandarin. She knew from her own experience that people in uniform liked numbers and they liked things. They liked things they could see just over the next hill, across the river. To them, that was intelligence. To Ava - and no doubt Sam, too - intelligence was less about capabilities and more about hidden intentions, about what went on in enemy minds.

What she didn't mention to any of them, even to Sam, who was pouring out generous drams of whisky, were the latest notes and comments from the source himself.

Once the visitors had put on their coats and hats and said their farewells, the Potters ushered the visitors out into the night to the two cars - the Honda and Toyota. Ava, exhausted, still needed to talk to Sam before he, too, left and she could get her head down.

They stood in the basement, the most secure place in the house for a conversation, the table littered with scraps of paper, empty glasses, coffee cups and plates with the remains of pizza.

'Sam. I have something to tell you.'

'And I have something I've got to tell you, Ava.'

'You first, Sam.'

'Ok. There's been a spike in covcom traffic here over the last 24 hours.'

'Chinese?'

'Fraid so. At least it has all the hallmarks of Beijing transmissions. From here, in DC. Not associated with their local Station, either. Burst transmissions, and a new Numbers Station. Independent of any existing networks of theirs.'

'I thought Numbers Stations went out with Noah and the Arc.'

'Not at all. They're still very much in use because they're secure, especially when using OTPs.'

'One Times Pads? In the 21st century?'

Sam smiled, a patient, tired smile. 'Slow but reliable and quite unbreakable without the code - and we don't have that.'

'So?'

'They're closing in on you, Ava. On Cincinnatus. Maybe on us, right here. We have to assume they're watching our calls and other transmissions. We're going to have to take evasive action. You'll have noticed that the latest batch you've been dealing with was posted in Bratislava. Heaven knows why Bratislava, but at any rate, it's too insecure. It's just a matter of time before they intercept the packages in the mail and maybe whoever's delivering them to the post offices, and when they do that, we'll lose intel and they'll find the source. We have to change the way we - and the source - do our business, and we'll have to do so fast.'

'Change - how?'

'First, tell me what you've got for me. I hope it's good news this time.'

Ava sank into one of the chairs, shut her eyes, and tried to clear her head. She hadn't wanted to share this, not with anyone. She'd wanted to follow Pan's wishes and stay clear of all intelligence and security agencies, and here she was, getting sucked back into the world of state-funded deceit.

'I'm not sure if it's good or bad, Sam.'

Ava had noted that even at this late hour, Sam was looking smart, DC smart, wearing a well-cut navy suit, a wool and mohair mix by the look of it, a crisp white shirt and blue silk tie with tiny red dots. She had a sudden urge to lean her head on his dapper shoulder and weep - out of exhaustion and anxiety and, yes, also out of desire. It had been so long since she'd made love to any man, or even felt the desire to do so.

She told herself she was being ridiculous.

Fuck's sake, get a grip!

He waited, watching her, concern showing on his face.

Ava's tone was resigned. 'Sam, the source wants to make contact.'

# 29

# December 15

## 11:05 China Standard Time, GMT +8

Chen Meilin, chief of the foreign intelligence service, the *Guoanbu*, sat upright on the lounger, her back straight, hands in her lap, knees and ankles together. Her long hair, still black and shiny as a raven's wing despite her age, hung straight down her back. She wore what appeared to be black silk with a subtle reflective shimmer to it. Plain, but expensive - and her host, who sat opposite her, noted it fitted her slim figure perfectly. She'd accepted a cup of tea but hadn't so far drunk any because she'd been asked by Qin for an update and was about to speak.

She had to wait in respectful silence until he'd finished reading a report on an increase in air and naval deployments - something requested by the Joint Taiwan Attack Centre Command and which he'd just initialled.

The J-20 stealth fighters were to be transferred to the JTAC, along with the elite Wang Hai Flight Group, a unit originating in the 1950-53 Korean War. The J-20 had been deployed with the group since 2019, and the aircraft were already flying patrols in the airspace around the Diaoyu Islands, some 200 km or 125 miles from Taipei. As for the Miyako Strait between Taiwan and Okinawa, Qin had initialled orders for Y-9 anti-submarine warfare aircraft, Type 052 guided missile destroyers and Type 054 frigates to transit the sea passage for a fresh round of naval drills. Taiwan's waters, off its east coast, were deep and particularly suitable for submarine operations, so training the PLAN's subs and anti-submarine warfare elements there was vital, and the Emperor was pleased to read that they were mapping the seabed.

He glanced up. 'Almost done.'

The Emperor read through a wordy, officious report on live-fire drills of the YJ-62A medium-range, sea-skimming cruise missiles along the Fujian coast, facing Taiwan, a suitable response to Taiwan's imminent deployment of truck-mounted Harpoon missiles.

The YJ-62A had a range of 400km or 250 miles and could be launched by air, from the sea or land, and could reach all parts of Taiwan.

Pressure on Taiwan's separatist regime was building well.

Qin smiled at his guest, gestured with a hand as if sweeping his preoccupations with weaponry aside. 'Forgive me.'

Chen Meilin looked at him as she began. 'My *Gong'anbu* colleagues have made many arrests - aside from the suspects rounded up after the attempt on your life in Nanjing. As of this morning, 123 people had been detained in Beijing alone for questioning or had been invited in to be questioned, which amounts to the same thing. Most, if not all, are cadres, many of them senior with the highest security clearance. The Public Security Ministry is treading carefully, as it no doubt should. Friendly chats, along with warnings that failure to cooperate will have dire consequences, a loss of privileges, a downgrading in rank, a negative impact on their businesses, early retirement and it's pointed out their families will also suffer the consequences.'

'And?'

'They're trying to trace the plot back to its origins. They've found nothing to date, no leads. The change in ministers and rumours about General Wang's demise have affected *Gong'anbu* morale. We hear the investigators are anxious without clear guidance from the top. They don't want to take matters too far, but they also don't want to come up empty-handed by being too lenient.'

'So they're whining.'

'I wouldn't say that. They're concerned.'

Qin didn't seem in the least bothered. People always had something to moan about. He offered to fill Chen's cup, but she declined. He refilled his own, then took time lighting up one of his Dunhill cigarillos, drawing on it luxuriously, blowing smoke up at the ceiling where the light was reflected off the pool in wavy lines.

'And what's the situation in Washington, D.C.?'

This Chen was an attractive woman, and as was always the case with the women Qin found attractive, he speculated about her private life - especially her sex life, if she had one. Was she married? Did she have a regular boyfriend? Who was she fucking, and how often? Was she promiscuous? Was she sexually available? Despite her age, Chen still had an allure, something he put down to the elegant simplicity of her appearance, her dignity and confidence and the power she wielded as head of the foreign intelligence service. She was special, he decided, and desirable.

He told himself he must ask for her file again. Of course, he'd read it before, the last time just before her elevation to the very top of her service. He'd read it before initialling her appointment as the Ministry of State Security's spy chief, but he'd forgotten many of the details. There had been something intriguing in her background, he recalled, something that had caught his eye in the section on her family history, but he couldn't remember what it was.

She was still speaking. 'Our local Station knows about Cincinnatus and its staff. It knows the identity of the American woman receiving the material. It knows her address, and has installed the appropriate equipment in both her workplace and home. They are keeping both locations under observation. Static posts, walk-throughs. The COS - the chief of station - is working hard to recruit someone in Cincinnatus or to insert one of our people into the organisation - or he was doing so until his recall. The Station is aware of the primitive and somewhat amateurish modus operandi - use of the postal system, flash drives. They have traced parcels back - to Bratislava, Dubai, Hong Kong and so on, and they are trying to trace those links back to Beijing.'

Qin, wearing a suit for the occasion, leaned forward to sip his tea. 'But I take it they don't yet have the source or the identity of the source.'

'No, they don't.'

'Have they narrowed the suspects down to a dozen? Two dozen?'

'Not yet.'

She was honest. That was rare.

'What else?'

'The *Gong'anbu* and our own *Guoanbu* personnel in the Station are supposed to work as one team. That's obvious. It won't surprise you to know that they don't. They are at odds and spend most of their time working against each other. They are working as two rival teams.'

'The station chief?'

'On his way. Due in Beijing tomorrow.'

'Hold for questioning, and put him through the usual interrogation. No special privileges.'

'He's not very good at his job. Another political appointee, but he's no traitor as far as we know. Just ineffectual.'

'We'll see about that. He's not one of yours, is he?'

'He's a *Gong'anbu* appointment.'

'Good. So you won't feel offended, or embarrassed, if we press him hard? No loss of face.'

'What I feel or don't feel isn't the point. But I'm sorry our most important Station in the West has been crippled in this way and at such an important time.'

This Chen Meilin wasn't afraid to speak her mind. What was it about women that made them so bold and the men in the equivalent grade so weak?

'Of course, of course. I understand your professional viewpoint. But it's in a good cause, comrade. The damage isn't irreparable. We will fix it, straighten out the Washington end of things. But right now, these measures are necessary.'

Was she reassured? He couldn't tell. Her mask was in place and he couldn't read whatever lay behind it. That he had called her in for a chat should be a powerful signal that he placed special trust in her abilities, confiding in her to an extent not equalled elsewhere in the intelligence community, and that should count for something. They both got to their feet. Chen said nothing more about the attempt on the Emperor's life, and although she turned to look at the pool, she said nothing more about the demise of General Wang Zhenrong, either.

'And what are we doing at this end to investigate the leaks?'

Chen almost smiled. Yes, he could tell from that twitch of her lips that they understood each other.

'The Public Security Ministry - the *Gong'anbu* - are making discreet checks, trying to identify those secret reports that we believe were compromised, then focusing on the names on the circulation lists. The same names appear on several of the lists, so they are starting with those.'

'Have the leaked items been identified?'

'Not precisely, General Secretary, because they've been bowdlerised - simplified - to suit the needs of Cincinnatus and its clients. Sometimes, the material that has appeared seems to be compilations or summaries, with some omissions, to appeal to a wider audience, not to members of the Western intelligence community.'

'Does that mean the original classified material is not in the possession of Western intelligence and security services?'

'We assume that if the recipient - this Avery Shute - was under the control of any Western agency, they would not let her have the freedom to decide how to distribute her summaries - her news - to the academic world and the general media. They would want control over the leaked product and over her. They'd remove her, cut her out of it, and take over the source. As would we. She seems to be a free agent, at least so far, deciding herself what to publicise and how. That's interesting, if only because of the current debate among Western politicians about how to handle relations with Beijing over Taiwan. So far, they haven't shut her down - one has to ask how long they will let her write whatever she likes. Maybe it's because it suits them, or perhaps they don't know the identity of the source any more than our security service does and are letting her have her head to lead them to whoever it is.'

The Emperor didn't know what to make of this. 'Remarkable,' he said, not meaning it, just for something to say, though it was puzzling.

'There might be some rational method underlying all this, but our people haven't figured it out as yet. She doesn't appear to have any special protection.'

'Keep me informed, won't you?' An order, but politely put.

'Yes, chief. My *shao dui* - small team - are in place. They have formed a counter-surveillance team on the ground, alongside that of the Station's street surveillance.'

'So your people will work against your local Station's operatives?'

'I prefer to use the terms complementary to, alongside or parallel, not against - but capable of intervening, should it become necessary. The Station don't know - and won't know - that we're present.'

'How will we ever know who it is?'

'If the woman, or her employers, decide to share the leaked material with the Western allies' intelligence services, we will know more.'

'How come?'

'Because we have a penetration agent on the inside.'

'Who? Where?'

'I can't say.'

'Of course you can't. Is it the Japanese, the Australians?'

'Neither.'

'I see. Or rather I don't, but let's move on.'

'One other item on our list, General Secretary.'

'My wife, Meng Bin.'

'She's in Singapore, which is quite useful because we can keep a protective eye on her there.'

'And?'

'She's been buying life insurance for herself, her daughter, and other family members. Axa and Prudential are the foreign companies involved. It's one of the few legal ways to get money out of the mainland. Maybe you don't know this, chief, but in Hong Kong there are no fewer than 63,000 insurance brokers and they're servicing mainlanders who want to put some money overseas without breaking the law. It's a thriving industry. The only other way to do it for most people is through the Macao casinos, but things are being tightened up there and the window is closing, thanks to the Party.'

'What else?'

'She's met with members of her Taipei family a few times. Business and invest-ment seem to be the primary interests, but we have also monitored speculative discussion of a move to Australia, along with those same relations. They dis-cussed the relative merits of New Zealand and Australia at one point, without coming to any firm conclusion either way. Her visit to Taipei was very brief - one night, and a morning spent shopping — although our coverage there was less effective for obvious reasons.'

'Any mention on her part of rumours of conflict, of Chinese Taipei's unifica-tion, of war?'

'Nothing that we've picked up.'

'She's being careful. She knows we're watching and listening.'

'Perhaps she does.'

'No "perhaps" about it, Ms Chen. She knows the score. Anyone in her position and with her business interests would. She's not naïve, I assure you. Inappropri-ate talk of military preparations would amount to treason, and she knows that. She's also aware of the consequences of treasonous behaviour, even outside the mainland. Our laws apply to anyone, anywhere.'

'Of course. There's also your daughter.'

'What about her?'

'Your wife discussed your daughter's likely move back to the States. She studied there, right? It seems she has an American boyfriend, and that's a factor in the decision.'

'I've heard nothing about that.' Qin's face was grim.

'Well, I think you will soon. He just applied for a holiday visa for China. I checked. It suggests both he and your daughter might pay you a visit, so you'll be hearing from her. Maybe he wants your permission to marry her before he takes her back with him to America. Do things properly, our way, out of respect for her.'

Qin rose to his feet. He was annoyed, disconcerted and even embarrassed by the last item because of its personal nature. It was too close to home, though he tried to show nothing of how he felt. An American boyfriend? Marry? Live in the United States and just before the war for unification? How could she even think of such a thing? Was she doing this to spite her father?

*Fuck that.*

*This is my wife's doing. Bitch.*

They shook hands. He walked out of the pool area as far as the door with his chief spy, a courtesy he felt necessary for someone so vital to both his plans and his political survival. He needed her. Qin wondered if she knew how important she was - maybe that awareness was why she was so relaxed, even bold, in his presence. He liked her cool approach. It was impressive, though unsettling. Qin was used to deference, submission, even grovelling as the norm. He wasn't sure that he liked confident, self-motivated women in places of authority. He had enough of two already - his wife and daughter, and they were exhausting.

Chen spotted the new bodyguard hovering by the entrance, staring ahead, not looking at them but doubtless aware of them.

Chen turned to the Emperor. 'How is Zhong Mei doing? Do you approve?'

'Fine, so far. I like her. She seems bright and professional, a stable personality and of modest background and outlook. Perfect Party material, and I wish we had more like her. But I must ask you, Comrade Chen - do you think, in all seriousness, that she has enough experience - that she's old enough, mature enough - for what we have in mind?'

'I do. Her loyalty is absolute. I have every confidence in her abilities. If I wasn't convinced, I wouldn't have sent her over for your approval. She wouldn't be here. Zhong is well trained and skilled. She's capable. It won't be her first assignment abroad, by any means, should we decide to remove the American.'

'And experience -?'

'General Secretary, this won't be her first elimination. Ms Zhong has undertaken solo terminations before, and no doubt she will again.'

The Emperor returned to the pool in a pensive mood. He went to the pool's edge, going down on one knee, dipping his right hand in the water. It felt good, warm enough for a swim, but not too warm. Excited at the prospect of a dip after an absence of 48 hours, he decided to go inside, throw off the despised suit, kick off his loafers, pull on his bathing shorts, shuffle out again in his slippers. He had a few hours to spare and he would fill them with lap after lap, suspended in apparent weightlessness, in the nothingness in which he revelled. To hell with the Party. He loved the pool and the solitary, long swims. The effort would allow him to relax, to clear his mind, to focus on the forthcoming war, the Emperor's war to liberate - and unify - China's long-lost islands.

Victory was certain if he held his course.

The themes were simple.

First, win without fighting.

Second, resistance is futile.

What could go wrong?

# 30

## 08:25 Eastern Standard Time, GMT -4

From her guest suite in the safe house, Ava could hear the rain in the gutters, sloshing down the drainpipes, as well as gusts of wind hammering the windows. It was still too dark to see much outside. She met Sam in the hall and they went downstairs to the basement, carrying breakfast trays prepared by the Potters.

'So what do we have?' Sam was dressed for the office - Ava thought that must mean the SIS Station in the British embassy - and he had that freshly showered look, hair still damp, and smelling of cologne. Ava had to admit to herself the scent was both subtle and masculine and that she liked it, deciding it was something expensive and - for no particular reason she could think of - Italian. He wore gold links on his French cuffs, too.

They set down their trays and took their seats opposite each other at the table. Ava began. 'So far, a total 134 intelligence reports, most of a military nature, and two new operational notes from the source. I haven't been able to translate them all. It's a week's full-time work.'

'And?'

'He — or she — wants to change the way we do business.'

'May I?'

With considerable reluctance, Ava showed Sam the first, turning her screen around.

*DISMAYED DING PAN DEATH. MUST ASSUME IDENTITY BLOWN LOCA-TION HOME/WORK/COMMS COMPROMISED. ALSO U MUST ASSUME 24/7 SURVEILLANCE. YOUR SAFETY PARAMOUNT CONCERN. URGENT INSTRUCTIONS FOLLOW.*

'Now, isn't that kind? Sounds like he or she is panicking, don't you think?'

'Let's see what your source is proposing. It's hardly urgent considering he used the post to send it to you.'

And here it was, in the second:

YOU WILL RECEIVE EMAIL AC NAME MIKE DEVON555 AT PRO-
TONMAIL DOT COM. MSGE READS QUOTE LOOKING FORWARD TO IT
LOVE UNQUOTE PURPOSE TO SIGNAL ARRIVAL MATERIAL AT FOUR
SEASONS 288 PENN AVE CALL PUBLIC PHONE/BURNER ASK FOR CON-
CIERGE BENNY CHAN TO ASCERTAIN HIS AVAILABILITY/SHIFT. DO
NOT NOT COLLECT ITEM IN PERSON. USE COURIER IN NAME MICHAEL
OR MARY SPENCER. USE TAXIS/PUBLIC TRANSPORT. TO CONFIRM RE-
CEIPT SEND EMAIL EX LIBBY_ARRAN333 AT PROTONMAIL DOT COM
PSSWD A_HIGH_WINDOW2022 AS FOLLOWS QUOTE LOVELY TO SEE
YOU HUGS UNQUOTE. ENGLISH ONLY. PSE CHECK EMAILS DAILY.

'What do you think?'

Sam read it through twice without saying a word.

'The incoming signal isn't coming from the source, but at a guess I'd say it's someone else, closer to hand. That's what it implies.'

Ava drank her coffee and waited, watching him, feeling her tension grow.

She couldn't keep quiet or still any longer, shifting in her seat, putting her mug down. 'I mean, why doesn't he just send all his stuff as encrypted attachments using the email addresses he's set up? It would be so much easier.'

Sam put his hands behind his head and rocked back and forth on his chair.

'We've got to get inside his or her mind, see things the way he/she sees them.'

'Sure. Okay. Understood. But what does that tell us?'

'It tells me that your source is wary of sending anything encrypted via the Net and always has been. Your source knows Beijing puts a massive effort into track-ing emails and posts on social media. They capture and store everything - but everything - in bulk. As we do. Anything encrypted - anything at all - will send up a red flag and draw attention to itself. Even if the encryption means they can't make sense of it, they'll work on the metadata. The where and when, the who and what. They know how to attack messaging, how to break into servers and gut hard drives. They're aggressive and they're good at it, too. Their services have had masses of practice and they don't have to care about the law or ethics. Not unlike your former employers.'

'And we do care, you mean? About ethics? Really? Anything else?'

'Sure. Your source wants you to use ProtonMail because it has a high level of security. As a matter of routine, it wraps AES and PGB encryption around all emails. And that's the point, don't you think? Thousands upon thousands of Pro-tonMail email accounts sending messages every few minutes to one another and all encrypted by the ProtonMail servers in Switzerland - that's a headache. ProtonMail encryption isn't perfect, but then nothing is 100 percent perfect. It would take the PRC plenty of time and many people to select then unpick the messages they're interested in. Would it be worth it? And what do they get? Some guy called Mike sending his love to someone called Libby and getting hugs in return? Bravo, comrades!'

Sam had turned his attention to a warm croissant and a jar of strawberry jam.

Ava got up, poured herself more coffee from a thermos.

'Sam, is it so hard? The NSA collects telephone and email data about millions of Americans every day. In a thirty-day period, just one NSA unit harvested over three billion pieces of comms data from US communications systems alone. If we can do it, so can they.'

'Something else,' Sam said, about to conduct the delicate business of pushing a piece of croissant smeared with jam into his mouth without dropping any on his pristine white shirt. 'I think your source might have a network of sorts. People. The source is using people. Like this Benny, for instance. People to send material in the post, people to make deliveries, to receive goods, to pass them on, to work as cut-outs. The source has to have a network, a team. He or she isn't working alone. It must be a bunch of illegals.'

'Is that a good thing?'

'A network is only as strong as its weakest member. He must pay them, and that's expensive. Or they're doing it for love, and that means politics, ideology or kin. I'm not sure which is worse.'

'You know how to cheer someone up, don't you, Sam?'

\*\*\*

'Ava, you mentioned a third message?'

'Here. It's something I missed yesterday; an item written up as intel but more speculative, more subjective. It's kinda interesting.'

## TAIWAN WAR PLAN IS CCP'S BEST KNOWN SECRET

*1. PLA PLAN TO ATTACK 'CHINESE TAIPEI' (TAIWAN/ROC) NOW WIDELY KNOWN AMONG SENIOR CADRES - NOT SURPRISING GIVEN TIGHT-KNIT FAMILY TIES AND GUANXI.*

*2. GOSSIP TO THIS EFFECT RIFE AMONG ZHONGNANHAI RESIDENTS. WHILE NOT SPOKEN ABOUT OPENLY, NOW FAVOURITE TOPIC OF DISCUSSION WITHIN FAMILIES AS WELL AS 'BUSINESS DINNERS' ONCE MAOTAI STARTS FLOWING.*

*3. FALUN GONG MEDIA - BANNED ON PRC MAINLAND BUT STILL ACCESSIBLE IN CERTAIN QUARTERS IN HONG KONG - HAS PICKED THIS UP AND REPORTED IT. (NOTE SEVERAL HUNDRED SUSPECTED FG SYMPATHISERS AND ALLEGED ACTIVISTS REPORTED ROUNDED UP BY POLICE/GONG'AN BU/OFFICE 601 IN NANJING, SHANGHAI AND BEIJING AND HELD WITHOUT CHARGE.)*

*4. WIDESPREAD POLICE/GONG'ANBU/OFFICE 601 RAIDS IN URBAN AREAS ATTRIBUTED BY FALUN GONG TO ALLEGED ATTEMPT TO ASSASSINATE SECRETARY GENERAL QIN IN NANJING FOLLOWING HIS ATTENDANCE AT RECENT MEETING OF JOINT TAIWAN ATTACK CENTRE. TIMING NOT KNOWN, BUT ALLEGED HIT FAILED AND QIN SAID UNHURT.*

*5. UNCONFIRMED REPORTS SAY GENERAL WANG ZHENRONG, HEAD OF QIN'S BODYGUARDS AT ZHONGNANHAI, DIED SUDDENLY IN THE WAKE OF ALLEGED HIT ATTEMPT. MINISTER OF PUBLIC SECURITY, ZHOU YI, TO WHOM WANG REPORTED, SUBSEQUENTLY RETIRED AT OWN REQUEST, CITING ILL-HEALTH, SPARKING MUCH SPECULATION.*

*6. WAR RUMOURS NOT CONFINED TO BEIJING OR MILLION-STRONG PARTY. TECHNICIANS, CONSTRUCTION MANAGERS, ENGINEERS, RAILWAY WORKERS IN AFFECTED AREAS INCREASINGLY AWARE LOGISTICS BUILD-UP IN EAST AND SOUTH. PUBLIC SENTIMENT GROWING THAT TW ATTACK WOULD BE CATASTROPHIC. CHINA WOULD BE CUT OFF FROM THE WORLD—NO ACCESS TO GLOBAL CAPITAL MARKETS, NO OIL, COPPER, COAL, WHEAT, SOYABEANS ETC WHICH ECONOMY NEEDS ON DAILY BASIS.*

*NOTE: YOU MAY REGARD THE ABOVE AS WELL-INFORMED RUMOUR. EVEN SO IT SAYS MUCH OF INCREASINGLY FEBRILE MOOD IN CCP INCL POLITBURO. ONLY TIME WILL TELL IF THESE RUMOURED EVENTS ARE LINKED. I BELIEVE THEY ARE.*

Ava was excited by this last report. 'It'll make a great contribution to Cincinnatus and a general political feature for MSM. Maybe even a series. I have a feeling the Post and Guardian will lap this up.'

'It's good intel for us, too,' said Sam. 'We've been hearing similar reports through other channels. I'm impressed by your whistleblower.'

They were both seated at the basement table, breakfast trays pushed aside, Ava slouching rather than sitting. She needed more sleep.

'Not mine. He or she was Pan's source, remember? But I am going to need help, Sam. I've got a new project to work on for Cincinnatus and I can't delay it forever. James is already breathing down my neck. If I don't work, I don't get paid, and if I don't get paid I can't pay the bills... And it will take me at least a week full time to complete the translation of all this latest material from the source. It's not something that can be rushed.'

'We can help.'

'We? Who's this we?'

'Your team - the people you met yesterday. They're dying to get their teeth into this. They're excited and just waiting for you to ask.'

'SIS, you mean. Be honest.'

'No. They aren't SIS. They're not staff. In the past, they have helped us individually. From time to time we've needed an opinion, an analysis, a commentary. So they're on our books as useful contacts, that's all. But they're not on the payroll except as occasional freelancers - we call them contract labourers. You just have to say the word.'

'Freelance, contract labourers, staff - you're splitting hairs, Sam. It all boils down to the same thing. SIS. Or MI6, as it's sometimes called.'

What Ava didn't say out loud - because it seemed so obvious - was that the silence from the NSA and FBI was deafening. Both agencies had gone quiet - and their sudden loss of interest in Ava and her reports just happened to coincide with her partnership, or whatever it was called, with Sam Turner of SIS. It was no coincidence.

'Do you have a choice, Ava? They're willing because they think it's important and because they want to help. You don't have to pay them. I'll see to the compensation.'

'So you're saying I'd divide up the decrypted reports among them, they'd do the translations, I'd check them over, and you'd have the Mandarin version for your own purposes.'

'Right. And we'll pick up the tab for the time they spend on it. It's what we were doing before, you and I, only now on a bigger scale.'

That word 'we' again.

Ava glanced out at the rain. She wondered what the source would say if he or she knew what she was doing. But then again, the source was thousands of miles away, and Ava couldn't take this on all by herself, and if Sam was right, the source also had a team hard at work.

There were secrets on both sides.

'Okay, then. I'll go with that, if only because I don't see any other option.'

***

The heavy downpours had ceased, but Washington, D.C., was still shrouded in misty drizzle. Clive Potter drove the Honda, Kathy beside him in the front passenger seat, Sam and Ava in the back.

'You'll know about an NSA program codenamed PRISM.'

'I've heard of it, Sam, that's all. I wasn't cleared for it, nor was I part of it.'

'Just to refresh your memory, PRISM was classified TOP SE-CRET/COMINT/NOFORN, and it collected data - personal data - from the servers of the U.S. service providers Microsoft, Yahoo, Google, Facebook, Paltalk, AOL, Skype, YouTube, Apple. They signed up to PRISM though it was illegal and violated the Fourth Amendment of the U.S. Constitution. But let's leave that aside. The CCP has its own PRISM - bigger, faster, more intrusive. It isn't illegal and they don't ask their corporations to sign up - they don't get a choice.'

'Okay.'

'If you don't mind, Ava, I'd like to show you what you're up against - not in Beijing, but right here. It's a little adventure I thought you might appreciate. You could call it an experiment.'

'Terrific.'

Sam ignored the sarcasm. 'Your car is in the lot below your condo?'

'It is. In the basement.'

'Have you got your car keys and your normal mobile with you? Not the burner.'

'Of course, Sam. What is this about?'

'I'm going to show you the opposition - if the rain hasn't put them off. Clive and Kathy are going to drop us around the corner and we should exit on foot, then head over to your car. Ready?'

They were out and walking fast, hopping over potholes, skipping around puddles.

When they arrived at the basement parking space and Ava's blue Chevrolet Cruze, Sam went around to the passenger side. 'You drive, Ava.'

Once out on the street, Sam asked her to pull in to the kerb and call Cincinnatus on her normal cell and ask to speak to her colleague.

'Reception doesn't seem good right here.'

'Try.'

Sam had taken out what looked like an iPad, switched it on, and fiddled with it. It showed a grid of Washington, D.C., streets and as it focused in on the condo, there they were - Ava's Cruze represented as a blinking green square. After speaking for a few minutes on her mobile about her latest project - a study of the much-disputed Spratly Islands in Philippine waters, where Beijing has a semi-permanent presence in the form of 200 militia boats - she turned to Sam. 'Now what?'

'Head to Wisconsin, please.'

'Okay.'

After a couple more minutes, Sam asked Ava to slow and pull up at a filling station. 'Take a look.' Ava looked at his screen and saw there were two red dots winking behind the little green square, right behind them.

'Two cars are trailing us. Both from the PRC embassy.'

'Fuck.' Ava was more intrigued than scared.

'Drive.'

Ava headed up Wisconsin.

'Did you bug them?'

'No, it's their transmissions we're tracking. They have to communicate with each other and their base. The Chinese keep their people on a tight rein.'

'Are they still there?'

'Look now.'

Ava glanced at the screen. Now there were two more dots, yellow dots, this time over to the west and parallel to the first pair of trailing cars.

'Ava, I want you to cross Western Avenue, now, please.'

'Okay.'

'Great. Please turn south - right here. That's it. We're reversing direction through American University Park. We still have four cars trailing us, two behind, two parallel. Now head downhill to Canal Bridge into Virginia. That's it. Brilliant.'

'Got it.'

'That one's ours - the static grey SUV on the intersection of Arizona and Canal.'

Ava couldn't do more than glance in that direction. She was too busy concentrating - on the traffic, the poor visibility, her rearview mirror in case she could make out the tags, and on Sam's instructions. The mass of Christmas lights strung out across streets and building faces didn't help.

'Okay, so now the two cars parallel to the primary watchers are breaking away and heading north along the river, anticipating our course to Potomac village.'

'What do you want me to do?'

'You're going to disappoint them. Turn back, we'll head home, park at your place, walk out as before, and the Potters will pick us up and then we'll make sure we're in the clear before we return to the safe house.'

'That's it?' Ava had enjoyed herself, and would have liked more of this cat-and-mouse game, even if she was playing the mouse with four cats on her tail.

'That's it.'

'So what have we learned from this little outing?'

'What do you think?'

'That they are watching my mobile, that they picked us up fast, that there are two teams in four cars out there, and that we need SDR.'

'The question is, why?'

'I've no idea.'

'Two possibilities occur to me. One is that there are two rival teams, each trying to outdo the other in surveillance.'

'That sounds ludicrous. Why would they? And the second possibility?'

'That you had one surveillance team trailing you, and that the second was a countersurveillance team moving parallel to us.'

'Makes no sense,' Ava said as they drove down into the parking lot. 'Not to me. I know Jack shit about trade craft, but still —'

'It makes no sense,' Sam said, 'unless the second team is indeed countersurveillance, and it's there to protect you from the first team.'

Ava parked, switched off.

'You're kidding, right? Two Chinese teams of Watchers, the first tagging me, the second tagging the first? To protect me? Why? What the hell is that?'

'Wish I knew,' said Sam, unfastening his safety belt. 'It sounds crazy when you put it like that, though the Chinese system is very bureaucratic and they duplicate everything they do. They're using two separate networks for their covcom.'

'They've copied the Soviet system and added their own twist to it,' Ava said.

'Maybe that's it. But we'll monitor them by using the ANPR system.'

'That's —?'

'Automatic number-plate recognition. We can observe from the comfort of our office or the safe house.'

'They'll switch plates.'

'Maybe they will. Shall we go?'

Ava put her hand on Sam's arm.

'Wait.'

'What is it?'

'I know this isn't in the SIS training manual, Sam Turner, and it must be unprofessional for someone of your standing, but do this for me, would you?'

'What?'

Her hand moved to his neck, pulled him closer. 'Kiss me.'

And he did.

# 31

General Zheng was on the prowl, stalking restlessly around the Emperor's pool, glass in hand, while smoking a cigarette of his favourite brand, Double Happiness.

'Party members aren't allowed to smoke,' said Admiral Jia. 'Senior cadres are supposed to set an example.'

'Oh, is that so?' General Zheng turned on his navy counterpart with more snarl than smile. 'Thanks for the rebuke, Admiral. Party members aren't supposed to smoke in public. There's a difference, alright? And it's no use being holier-than-thou, Jia. I've watched you drink on many occasions. I have shared a bottle or two with you, remember? To excess, I might add, so much so that you couldn't stand on your own feet, if I recall, let alone set any kind of example. On one occasion, you had to be helped down the gangplank of your own destroyer, or have you forgotten?'

Jia laughed, but it wasn't a laugh of amusement, more of a jeer, and the much younger man went on, for reasons best known to himself, to lecture his elders.

'It might interest you to know, comrades, that China National Tobacco Corporation, or CNTC, produces 40 percent of the world's cigarettes - more than anyone else, in fact, and that we have 300 million adult smokers. We're a cigarette superpower. And more than half of all Chinese adult males smoke, but only two percent of women.'

'That's why I have so much difficulty getting my people fit,' grumbled Zheng. 'They love the *Hongtashan* brand most of all.'

'Don't forget *Baisha* and *Red Golden Dragon*,' replied Jia. 'My sailors smoke these a lot. You know what the Chinese tobacco industry is worth?'

Zheng turned away, shaking his head. 'Do we need to know?'

'You should. In US dollars, 136.2 billion, up 76 percent in five years.'

Candles - nightlights - had been placed on several small tables around the pool and had been lit, providing a soft and flattering glow, reflected in undulating waves of light on the surface of the pool and on the ceiling. Three bottles of vintage *maotai* stood on one pool table, along with glass tumblers. The bottles were nearly empty. Zheng's meanderings threw huge, bear-like shadows on the walls, rather spoiling the romantic atmosphere.

Three loungers had been set out at roughly equal distances in a semi-circle, facing the pool at the far end. The Emperor lay on one, bare feet up, the slight smile in place, not more than a couple of paces from where he'd kicked and pushed General Wang into the deep end and watched him drown.

Qin looked up at Zheng. 'If you're going to smoke, General, why don't you smoke something decent? Try the *Zhongnanhai* brand. Or have one of mine - here, help yourself to a cigarillo.'

'Foreign muck,' said Zheng, glancing at the Dunhill packet and making a face of disapproval. 'No thank you, General Secretary, no offence intended.' He tipped up his glass to get the last few drops, then headed over to the remaining *maotai* for yet another refill.

Jia sighed. 'Let's get back to what we were talking about, shall we? It's serious, and no laughing matter.'

'Of course it's serious,' boomed Zheng, his bass voice reverberating off the walls. 'My friends, let me give you just one example of how important it is. I was on one of those Zoom calls, or whatever you call them early this morning, and I talked to my great-granddaughter in Shanghai. You can't imagine what she said. Really, you can't.'

'But you're going to tell us,' said Jia, rolling his eyes.

Zheng was not deterred by Jia's response.

'She said to me, "Great-grandfather, please don't die." I asked her what she meant and reassured her I had no immediate plans of doing so. She's only 10, you know. I thought she might be referring to my advanced age. Then she said, "Great-grandfather, I know you're old, but I love you and I don't want you to die in the war." I asked her what war she was referring to. I mean, I thought that maybe she'd been learning about the war against Japan or the Nationalist bandits. But no. She said, "Everyone knows there will be war soon and I know you are a general and that means you will have to fight with your soldiers. Please don't die in Taiwan." So I said there was no war, and not to worry, that she shouldn't listen to rumours, but she replied everyone was talking about it, that there was going to be a war because of the problem with the bad people in Taiwan. Her friends at school even talked about it in the playground and she said they were scared. Their teacher had got angry and told them off, but it had made no difference.'

'There's been a leak for sure,' said Jia. 'Somebody has leaked our war plans to the imperialist media in America, and now it's found its way back here. It's a poison on social media that's being spread to demoralise our forces. There are only so many people with the access to have got hold of this.'

'I agree with you on this one,' said Zheng.

'That's something, at least,' responded Jia. 'I'm touched by your story.'

'It's a mole,' Zheng said. 'Got to be a fucking mole. Right at the top of the Party. Some filthy bastard has sold out his country and his countrymen. My question is, what are we doing about it, and what can we do that we're not already doing? I say line the suspects up, beat the living daylights out of them until you get a confession - it's the only way.'

'I might point out,' said Jia, 'that you, General, have your name at the top, or near the top, of all those distribution lists as commander of the Joint Taiwan Attack Centre, and my name is right below yours as your deputy and commander of the Eastern Fleet. So when it comes to beatings, we'd get priority at the head of the queue for interrogation, and I don't want my balls fried to satisfy your lust for violence.'

'Very fucking funny,' spat Zheng.

Both the general and the admiral looked at Qin, waiting for his response, but the latter had somehow kept his apparatchik's mask firmly in place and stopped himself laughing at these two drunken clowns - clowns in charge of the war machine.

'Not just the Party leaders,' said Jia, waving his arms about in excitement. 'It could be anyone with clearance to read secret documents. Administrators, secretaries - you name it - anyone working in the CMC, the Politburo and handling sensitive material, including both the Command Centre right here and the Joint Taiwan Attack Centre in Nanjing.'

The Emperor sat up, swung his legs off the lounger, found his sandals with his feet and slipped them on. He stood, shuffled to the edge of the pool, and looked down at the water. It looked so inviting, especially so in candlelight.

Tonight Qin and his drinking buddies weren't in uniform, but open-collared black suits, and they'd spent the best part of the day in a bruising discussion at the Command Centre right below them, under the several feet of steel reinforced concrete.

Qin thought he would like to bring his next dance partner out here one evening, have the candles lit, clear everyone else out, and fuck her right here on one of the loungers to see what it would be like. It should be fun - well, different anyway.

In the meantime, he wanted another swim. The urge was upon him again and he almost salivated at the thought, though why the desire to swim made him salivate, he had no idea. He wished his two cronies would take a hint right now and shove off back home, sleep off the effects of the booze, and leave him alone.

'We're investigating,' Qin said at last, a weary note in a voice that slurred slightly, having been well lubricated with *maotai*. 'The Ministry of Public Security has invited several people in for questioning, and we'll find whoever's responsible. The procedure is thorough. No-one is excluded on the basis of rank or position. We're hunting for the mole. Don't worry. Focus on our unification project. We'll find them and uncover the conspiracy. Leave it to me, comrades, and the *Gong'anbu*, please. Please.'

The second 'please,' meant 'you'll do this or else.'

Jia finished his drink and set down his glass.

'That's good enough for me. I'm heading home to bed. Excuse me.'

'You're excused,' barked General Zheng.

'Thank you both for your company,' the Emperor said, still looking down at the water, his back to his guests. 'You can go, too, General. You're excused.'

\*\*\*

The meeting at the Strategic Command Centre earlier that day had been a mess. Instead of talking strategy in a measured and thoughtful way, which was what the centre was supposed to do, the participants - including Qin - had got bogged down in operational matters, in particular the choice of landing zones for the amphibious forces of the PLA.

Fourteen beaches were on the table - literally, as Colonel Sun dashed about the model in the centre of the room, poking at it with a long pointer to show the various locations: five in the south of Taiwan, nine in the north.

Satellite images on the big screens showed each one in bright, clear sunshine: Luodong, Zhuangwei, Toucheng, Fulong in the northeast, Green Bay, Jinshan South and Jinshan North in the very north, Linkou and Haiku in the northwest.

Finally, the south-western cluster: Budai, North Tainan, Tainan Gold Coast, Linyuan and Jialutang.

White sand and surf, rocky cliffs, grey and blue water, villages and harbours.

Just like a holiday video for tourists, Qin thought.

Join the PLA and enjoy China's best beaches!

There was a lot to consider, so much, in fact, that some officials didn't want to get involved in the discussion because of the complexities or because they had nothing to contribute or gain from the proceedings. They doodled on their pads, gazed into the middle distance or dozed where they sat, and one or two even had the audacity to snore to everyone else's irritation.

The primary aim - and no-one disagreed because it was so obvious - would be the swift capture of the capital, Taipei, or as General Zheng put it, 'cutting off the head of the snake.' Promising areas for a landing, in his view, included the Chuoshui River delta in central Taiwan, the southwest Chianan Plain and Taoyuan in the northwest. Why? He answered his own question, his accompanying glare meant to deter anyone from challenging his views. Because they offered potential beachheads close to roads to enable attackers to push inland quickly, that was why. But the briefing officers had pointed out that water depth, sea bottoms, gradients, tidal conditions, beach composition, nature of the surf, the frontage and width, and the availability of beach exits were just some issues to be considered. As these were mentioned, so the participants' snores multiplied and reached their crescendo just before the lunch break.

Who cared about this shit except the old men in uniform playing soldiers?

The Emperor tried not to show his annoyance at the lack of interest by some octogenarians present. He kept his apparatchik's smirk in place while noting names and faces. By the end of the working day, three senior officers would receive notices that their letters requesting retirement had been received and approved (the fact they had written no such letters was neither here nor there - the format was a standard three lines, and they wouldn't do themselves or their families any favours by protesting).

Qin turned his attention back to the war gaming. As for the Taiwanese, it was explained that they weren't making things easy for their Communist foes. They had built seawalls, breakwaters, artificial reefs and wind farms and all these modifications to the coastline helped the defenders, while there were networks of irrigation canals and fishing ponds in low-lying areas that also presented many obstacles to the invaders.

In short, some of the most suitable landing areas were in the middle of nowhere - while some of the least suitable were near Taipei, the most important target of all.

And that paradox served as the trigger for a bruising argument between Zheng and Jia.

Admiral Jia started it. 'The Green beaches - those most suitable for our amphibious operations - are: Jialutang beach in southwest Taiwan at Fangliao township in Pintung County, then also Jinshan South beach in New Taipei's Jinshan district in northeast Taiwan.'

'I know where they are, dammit,' grumbled General Zheng, lumbering to his feet. 'I don't need a lesson in geography from the Navy. And I tell you now, Admiral: Jialutang is far too distant. It would take weeks, possibly months, to fight our way up the island in hostile terrain. Can't be done. Impractical. Linkou, in the northwest, close to Taipei port, makes a lot more sense for the knockout blow. Haihu beach, also in the northwest, is next to Taoyuan International Airport. Couldn't be better. It's almost purpose-built for landing our troops and we could fly in reinforcements. A beachhead and an airhead would be mutually reinforcing once the initial resistance is overcome. One quick, massive thrust at Taipei, and it's over.'

'But those are some of the best defended sections of coastline,' Jia protested. 'The ones you mention are coloured red, classified as the most unsuitable beaches. We'd be inviting disaster before any boots hit the ground. My landing ships and their escorts wouldn't survive.'

'So what would the Admiral suggest?' Zheng was at his most sarcastic, swinging his considerable bulk around to face his adversary and subordinate.

Jia wasn't intimidated. 'We need to establish and build up the beachhead in the south, break through into the hinterland and work our way north.'

'Work our way north? We'd have to fight for every inch of territory under a hailstorm of enemy fire from high ground and well-prepared defensive positions. They'd demolish bridges and tunnels and attack our flanks from the high ground. We need ports and airports to bring in armour and artillery quickly, or risk our paratroops, light infantry and marines being cut off, isolated, and overrun without heavy fire support. Taipei's proximity to our forces is critical and I must remind you, Admiral, that we should not underestimate the shock value of striking at the capital at the outset.'

So it went, back and forth.

Qin kept out of it, watching, listening, nodding, smiling.

The argument was a useful apéritif for the *pièce de résistance* of the day's proceedings before the Emperor called it quits: a briefing paper on the PLA's definitive intelligence assessment of Taiwan's defences in time of war, presented by military intelligence.

If anyone thought Taiwan was going to be easy, they were in for a nasty shock.

# 32

# December 16

## 07:28 Eastern Standard Time, GMT -4

The first of the ProtonMail emails arrived at 04:00 local time. At 07:28 Ava called Sam on her burner only to discover he already knew - after all, he did have access - and he told her he had briefed his personal assistant in what was presumably the SIS local Station - a position that used to be called a secretary back in the old, politically incorrect and 'unwoke 'days - to make the run to the hotel and pick up the goodies once Sam had established that Benny the concierge would be on duty at 8 a.m. The assistant was trained for it, apparently. He or she wasn't just someone who answered his calls, took down shorthand, typed letters and made the tea. S/he was a spook in her own right. First, though, the same, nameless assistant had to carry out an SDR through Washington's streets, the Potters providing her with cover fore and aft from mobile posts - no doubt their cars parked on corners and intersections.

Sam had done all this without consulting Ava. She thought that he'd make the excuse that he hadn't wanted to wake her so early, and he did.

Their verbal exchange this morning had been brief, if only for security reasons. Sam sent back an email confirming receipt - with love from Libby, as instructed. Ava ate breakfast alone in the safe house, listening for the approach of any cars on the driveway or on the street below the house. It was quiet, eerily so. Outside, the drizzle had given way to thick mist, which could only be seen once it got light. It seemed to have a similar effect as snow by cloaking the world in silence, wrapping suburban homes, trees and street lights in ghostly, unreal shapes.

Thinking about Sam's actions that morning made her realise how easily she could be squeezed out of the operation and how easy it would be for Sam and his SIS colleagues to take over and manage without her.

Ava was nervous. It was neither the buildup to war, nor the deliveries of top secret Chinese intel from the source, still unidentified, that made her jumpy.

It was whether her impulsive behaviour in the car - now regretted - would affect her professional relationship with Sam, and if so, how.

She'd done it on the spur of the moment, with little thought. With no thought. Oh, god. How stupid.

She ran it through her mind again and again like a video clip. Ava reminded herself that Sam needn't have responded to her advance, but respond he did, in spades, even though they were on duty as it were, or to use Sam's word, 'operational'. The 'operational' kiss was not a one-sided or half-hearted affair, at all, but it had lingered long and had been well, passionate - yes, passionate - on his part as well as hers.

Or at least lustful. It was as if he'd been waiting for a signal from her.

That thought made her feel better and a little less guilty.

After all, she told herself, she was a young, fairly normal adult female, and she had needs just like everyone else. That was all. There was no need for either of them to read too much into it.

She paced back and forth through the rooms on the ground floor - sitting room, library, kitchen, hall, study - and back again. Over and over. Ava wore black tights, black flats, a short grey skirt, a long-sleeved cream blouse. She didn't need a cardigan or jacket. The house was warm, too warm, thanks to the heating system. Americans seem to overheat their homes in winter, in contrast to Europeans, who appeared to resent having to pay to heat them at all.

Ava wanted to see Sam again, but then again, she didn't want to see him.

She must have stalked around the safe house at least a dozen times when the Honda arrived. It was Clive Potter. A few minutes later, the Toyota, driven by Kathy Potter, parked in the driveway at the rear of the house.

Ava could feel her own heart beating hard and fast when Sam strode in through the front door. He didn't appear to be carrying anything - no envelope, packet or file. Kathy came out of the kitchen with a cloth in one hand. 'Hi, Sam. Had breakfast?' Ava was grateful to Kathy for having been the first to speak, to break the ice - if indeed there was any ice to break.

They said good morning to each other, and Sam threw in a conventional query which Ava didn't feel she had to answer. 'Sleep well?'

That was that. They got down to work, and there was a massive amount of it.

Kathy brought in coffee and warm croissants wrapped in a kitchen towel, too, just in case.

The kiss seemed forgotten, as if it had never happened.

Two thumb drives, the contents to be decrypted, translated.

The decrypting was easy enough, and fast, now that she was familiar with how the disk provided by the source worked, but it was the translation that was going to take up so much of Ava's time.

'I'll take these files,' Ava said, having numbered them all. She'd picked what she thought would be the best, the most interesting, and the shortest messages that appeared to be the source's own notes. It was also the smallest list, 32 items in all. There were limits on what she could and couldn't do; Ava had to work up some of the material for posts on the Cincinnatus website, aside from her overt Cincinnatus project on the Spratly Islands.

Sam didn't argue with any of that, and he didn't seem to expect an explanation.

Ava went upstairs to her suite, her share of the intel on her air-gapped laptop, and she left Sam and the Potters to divide the remaining reports, sorting them into roughly equal quantities in time for the team to collect them that evening. Sam's assistant had already alerted them. Ava's team, so called.

She had a long day's work ahead of her.

Ava started with one of the shortest, and it was a shock.

## MOLE HUNT UNDERWAY, 1200 DETAINED

*1. MINISTRY OF PUBLIC SECURITY OR GONG'AN BU HAS DETAINED 1,243 OFFICIALS, ALL PARTY MEMBERS WITH TOP SECRET CLEARANCE, FOR QUESTIONING OVER ALLEGED 'MOLE' RESPONSIBLE FOR LEAKING SECRETS RELATED TO 'OPERATION CHINA UNITY'.*

*2. IN ADDITION, APPROX 400 CADRES HAVE BEEN 'INVITED' TO MEET GONG'AN BU AT SECURITY BUREAU OFFICES TO 'DISCUSS' LEAKS OF SENSITIVE MATERIAL TO WHICH THEY HAD ACCESS.*

*3. INTERROGATIONS AND 'DISCUSSIONS' ARE 'ROLLING' IE. ONCE SOME SUSPECTS ARE PROCESSED, THEY ARE RELEASED AND REPLACED BY OTHERS. REASON GIVEN IS THAT CMC DOES NOT WANT ANY DELAY IN PREPARATIONS FOR TW ATTACK SCHEDULED FEB ONE. THOSE RELEASED CONTINUE TO BE CLOSELY MONITORED.*

*4. NO TRIALS, CONVICTIONS, SENTENCES OR DISAPPEARANCES RE-
PORTED TO DATE.*

*5. INVESTIGATORS WORKING SYSTEMATICALLY THROUGH DISTRIBU-
TION LISTS OF THOSE SECRET REPORTS THEY BELIEVE TO HAVE
BEEN COMPROMISED, BASED ON MEDIA REPORTS PUBLICLY ACCESSI-
BLE OVERSEAS. SOME LEAKED REPORTS HAVE BEEN MISSED AS A RE-
SULT, BUT INVESTIGATORS EXPECT TO DISCOVER WHICH ONES
WHEN THEY OBTAIN FULL CONFESSION FROM GUILTY PARTY IF AND
WHEN IDENTIFIED AND APPREHENDED.*

*6. THE FIGURES ABOVE EXCLUDE APPROXIMATELY 300 PEOPLE DE-
TAINED ON SUSPICION OF HAVING PLOTTED/SUPPORTED FAILED AS-
SASSINATION OF SECRETARY GENERAL QIN. THEY INCLUDE UN-
KNOWN NUMBER OF PEOPLE'S ARMED POLICE, NANJING STATE SECU-
RITY PERSONNEL AND ALLEGED FALUN GONG SYMPATHISERS. 'ROU-
TINE' INTERROGATION METHODS ARE USED.*

*NOTE: I EXPECT TO BE DETAINED OR CALLED IN FOR QUESTIONING
ABOUT LEAKS AND YOU SHOULD EXPECT INTERRUPTION/CESSATION
IN MY REPORTING. I AM THEREFORE INCREASING QUANTITY OF MA-
TERIAL AS QUICKLY AS POSSIBLE.*

A lesser mortal would stop altogether and go into hiding.

Did the source have some kind of death wish? What about family? Parents,
siblings, partner, children?

It made Ava feel nauseous just thinking about the source and his or her pre-
carious life, and what could go wrong, what would go wrong, given time. Was it
really a genuine love of country and his fellow Chinese, a hatred of war and
loathing of authoritarian rule?

What was it that made the source so special, so aware - so sensitive - to the
impact of full-blown war when everyone else party to the war plans seemed accepting, indifferent or perhaps, in the case of the diehard CCP members, even
enthusiastic? Or was there something else, something they'd missed? Was this a
believer, Christian or Buddhist? Wasn't the source afraid all the time? How did
she/he sleep? How did she/he ever relax? Ava wondered about his or her job
for the Party or the state, the nature of his or her work, where the source lived.
Had something happened to the source, to the source's family, that had made
him or her especially prone to blowing a whistle on the bastards?

Where did the courage and defiance come from?

Now the security police were out hunting, wouldn't the source accept an offer to defect, a generous resettlement package, a job and change of identity if Sam offered it? It was the only decent thing SIS could do, given the enormous quantity and quality of the intelligence already provided. Langley might share the costs. They'd done so with Soviet defectors to the British.

Yet they had lied — Ava had lied, keeping up the fiction that she wasn't feeding the intelligence to Western intelligence services, which was what she was doing. She was deceiving the source, putting his or her life in great jeopardy, maybe guaranteeing an early and violent end, a bullet in the back of the head in some filthy prison yard after weeks of torture. Sam could hardly offer exfiltration and resettlement without an admission that the source's reports were indeed being seen by the Five Eyes intelligence partners. Five Eyes — plus others. Maybe Taiwan's intelligence service, the National Security Bureau or *Guójiā Ānquán*.

Ava turned her attention to translating what seemed to her to be the cream of the latest crop of high-grade CCP intel.

Only then did the thought occur to her: the reason the source had been so emphatic in insisting that he or she did not want the material placed in the hands of western intelligence services was because the source must have found out at some point the Chinese had penetrated one or more of the allies' services.

Why hadn't she thought of this before now? It was so obvious.

Beijing knew.

\*\*\*

## PLA ASSESSMENT: TAIWAN DEFENCE PLAN ASSUMES WORST SCENARIO

*NOTE: THE FOLLOWING IS THE PRC CENTRAL MILITARY COMMISSION'S SECRET ASSESSMENT OF TAIWAN'S DEFENCE STRATEGY*

*1. TAIWAN'S GU'AN (SOLID AND SECURE) DEFENCE PLAN ASSUMES ALL-OUT AMPHIBIOUS INVASION COMPRISING AT LAST ONE MILLION PLA TROOPS. THIS WOULD BE COUNTERED WITH A DEFENSIVE STRATEGY BASED ON A LONG WAR OF ATTRITION. SUCH A DRAWN-OUT CONFLICT IS SEEN BY TAIPEI'S ENEMY RULERS AS A DETERRENT BECAUSE OF THE NEGATIVE POLITICAL AND ECONOMIC COSTS TO THE PRC - COSTS WHICH THE ENEMY BELIEVES WOULD INCREASE WITH TIME AND WOULD BECOME UNSUSTAINABLE.*

Was this Communist Chinese intelligence assessment of Taiwan's defence strategy accurate? Ava didn't know, but it seemed plausible.

*2. TAIWAN CITES AS AN EXAMPLE OF ITS INVASION READINESS THE 2015 'FORMOSA FUN COAST' DISASTER WHEN A DANCE PARTY EXPLOSION CAUSED 500 CASUALTIES. THE BLAST TRIGGERED DEFENCE EARLY WARNING SYSTEMS, WITH EVACUATION AND TRIAGE UNITS SET UP IN RECORD TIME.*

*3. THE GU'AN PLAN NOTABLY DOES NOT DEPEND ON THE ENEMY HOLDING OUT LONG ENOUGH FOR A HOPED-FOR U.S. AND JAPANESE MILITARY INTERVENTION. THE PLAN ASSUMES TAIWAN WILL HAVE TO FIGHT ALONE, WITHOUT DIRECT EXTERNAL HELP.*

*4. SECRET LEGAL PROCEDURES ARE IN PLACE FOR MOBILISATION AND WAR DEPLOYMENTS TO BE LAUNCHED BEFORE HOSTILITIES, TRIGGERED BY UNAMBIGUOUS WARNING OF AN IMMINENT ASSAULT. MARTIAL LAW WOULD BE DECLARED AND THE ENEMY GOVERNMENT WOULD MOVE TO UNDERGROUND SHELTERS AHEAD OF EXPECTED MISSILE STRIKES.*

*5. THE ENEMY'S GU'AN PLAN IGNORES AIR AND NAVAL BLOCKADES OR THE PROSPECT OF 'LIMITED WARFARE'. TAIPEI'S CURRENT LEADERSHIP INSISTS TACTICS OF INTIMIDATION WILL NOT FORCE TW INTO SUBMISSION OR INTO NEGOTIATIONS LEADING TO UNIFICATION WITH THE MAINLAND. PLAN GU'AN IS BASED ON AN ALL-OR-NOTHING SCENARIO.*

If this was the case, then Beijing would have to give up the notion that it could intimidate Taipei into surrendering its autonomy and democratic way of life without fighting.

*6. THE TW ENEMY SEES 'FORCE PRESERVATION' AS CRITICAL ASPECT OF NATIONAL SURVIVAL IN WARTIME, STARTING WITH THE ENEMY LEADERSHIP. THE PRESIDENT, CABINET AND PARLIAMENT LEADERS WOULD BE MOVED BY CONVOYS OF ARMOURED VEHICLES TO DEEP UNDERGROUND BUNKERS, ESCORTED BY TW MARINES, MILITARY POLICE AND SPECIAL OPS TROOPS. TUNNELS HAVE BEEN BUILT UNDERGROUND TO ALLOW MOVEMENT OF KEY PERSONNEL ACROSS THE*

*CAPITAL. ENEMY GOVT WOULD NOT MEET IN A SINGLE LOCATION,
BUT WOULD BE DISPERSED TO AVOID A SINGLE 'KILLING BLOW'.*

*7. TWO AND A HALF MILLION TW CITIZENS ARE REGISTERED FOR RE-
SERVE SERVICE AND THEY WOULD MOBILISE AT THE OUTSET, MANY
OF THEM AS CIVIL DEFENCE WORKERS. TRADE UNIONS, CHURCHES,
TEMPLES AND PRIVATE CONTRACTORS ARE INTEGRATED INTO THE
ENEMY'S CALL-UP SYSTEM. ANNUAL MOBILISATION TESTS SET RAN-
DOMLY IN DIFFERENT AREAS OF TW INDICATE 97 PERCENT WOULD
MUSTER ON TIME IN AN EMERGENCY.*

*8. ENEMY RESERVISTS WOULD DEPLOY AND FIGHT LOCALLY ON
THEIR HOME GROUND WHICH THEY WOULD KNOW BEST, DEFEND-
ING THEIR OWN VILLAGES, TOWNS AND COMMUNITIES.*

Ava walked up and down, trying to imagine what the conflict would be like.
Nasty and protracted, of course, and extremely bloody. Civilians on both sides
would be trapped in the middle of it. She stared out of the window, made herself
yet more coffee, and returned to the task at hand.

And this, Ava realised, was just the introduction, the preface, to an entire set
of 22 Central Military Commission reports profiling Taiwan's defences, right
down to a detailed order of battle. The details of Taiwan's defences would be
well known by the Americans and its other allies, but what wasn't known - until
now - was how the CCP interpreted those plans.

It would take all day and much of the night to translate all of it.

Oh, joy!

# 33

## 13:05 China Standard Time, GMT +8

'Hi, Dad.'

'Hello, Son.'

Lau Chong was smartly turned out. Qin thought he looked like a young man starting a job after graduation, which he was. He appeared keen and well-scrubbed, an energetic and well-groomed puppy. Even his shoes had been shined. A rising star of a business executive, perhaps, the kind portrayed in Hollywood films set in Wall Street. Naïve and ambitious until he realises how ruthless capitalism is, how harmful it is to the general wellbeing of society. The impression was underlined by his first peeling off his outer, cold weather clothing, then taking his suit jacket off, rolling the sleeves of his blue shirt up to his elbows and slinging the jacket over one shoulder. Smart-casual. Casual-chic. Or something of the kind.

'Sit. Tea?'

'I'm fine, Dad, thanks.' Lau perched on the edge of a lounger opposite his father, its plastic frame squeaking as he settled on it, gazing at the pool, not meeting the Emperor's eyes, he pinched the creases of his trousers, then undid his collar, pulled down his tie, draped his jacket next to him over the back of the lounger. What was it? Armani?

'Everything okay?'

'Sure.' The lad nodded several times, as if trying to convince himself. 'Isn't that how you get questioned by security? They invite you to tea. That's the euphemism they use, right?'

'I don't know. Do they? Here, tea means tea and only tea. Nothing to worry about.'

'I'm sure you must know, given all the thousands of people being detained without charge or trial right now. Some of my friends have been invited to tea.

What have you got there?' Qin's unofficial son was referring to the sheaf of papers in his father's lap. He must have realised that invitations to tea was not a suitable subject, so he'd changed the subject and pretended he cared what his father was doing when they both knew he didn't give a toss.

'People's National Congress. We hold the annual sessions in the spring, but there's quite a lot to organise well ahead of time, given that we have around 2,800 delegates, and it lasts for up to two weeks. I have to attend, too.'

'Yeah? I thought it was just two weeks of pressing the flesh and rubber-stamping minor stuff the Party had already decided. No serious decisions are ever taken there, right?'

'That's what you think?'

So young, yet so cynical and with a wagging tongue - and a Party member to boot.

'Am I wrong? I mean, what's the point?'

'For a start, Chong, they'll vote for my 4th term in office. It'll be a record.'

Lau smiled at his father, showing his perfect teeth. 'No-one would dare oppose it, right? It'll be unanimous, not least because every delegate is hand-picked by the Party.'

'It's called a consultative democracy; a chance for people to take part in the way we run the country, to have a say in how we do so. It's important, Son. They're volunteers, patriotic volunteers, they do it part time and they don't get paid. I'm grateful to them.'

'I stand corrected. Why then, does Wikipedia call it authoritarian?'

'Depends which Wikipedia you read. That's not what the mainland Chinese version says. In fact, the Congress is going to propose appointing me president for life. Not even Mao Zedong managed that.'

'Congratulations again, Dad. But that will be after the unification project, right? Once you've won your victory on the corpses of hundreds of thousands of people. That's when you'll announce it, amid the general rejoicing. No doubt there'll be victory parades, too, while the gravediggers work overtime at night, unseen and unheard.'

No-one outside Qin's circle of relatives would have dared say such a thing.

'You don't approve?'

'Of what? War? In wars, everyone loses, except the politicians and the arms manufacturers. But I say again, congratulations.'

'Thanks, Son. Not that I think it's sincere on your part. Your sarcastic tone leaves much to be desired and will only get you into trouble. You'll stay for lunch? It's always refreshing talking to you, even if you seem cynical and defeatist.'

'Sure. Lunch would be good.'

'There's someone I want you to meet.'

'OK. But tell me something. What's the point in planning a National People's Congress when you'll be in the middle of a war? Not you. I mean we. We'll be in the middle of hostilities. All of us.'

'By March or early April it'll be over.'

'You sure about that?'

'Of course I am.'

'How can you possibly know? It won't be easy. They're not going to run - there's nowhere to run to. They won't give up; you know they'll fight. If anyone tells you different, they're lying. They're telling you what you want to hear. The Taiwanese will drag it out as long as they can to draw in foreign powers so that it becomes a Pacific-wide war. The U.S. for a start, along with Japan and Australia. Maybe South Korea and the Philippines. With the usual token support from the Europeans. A French destroyer, a British frigate, a Belgian fighter squadron, a Polish infantry battalion. The longer it goes on, the bigger and wider it gets, the worse it will be, and the more dangerous it will become, given the nuclear weapons on both sides.'

'You seem to have thought it all through, then. No point in my saying anything. Maybe you should run things. I could appoint you commander-in-chief right away. Does that appeal to you as a career move?'

'That's right, Dad. Listen to me, Lau Chong, and I'll solve all your problems.' He gave his father a big grin.

'I wish. Cheeky sod. It's ok to call me "Dad" when we're talking in private, but don't try it on when we've got company.'

'You know, I suppose, that people in Taiwan don't see themselves as Chinese. Not any longer. All the opinion polls show they prefer to call themselves Taiwanese. That's also how they want to be regarded by outsiders. It's no good the Party spokespersons talking about how we're all one people, one culture, one language, blah-blah-blah. It's Party bullshit and everyone knows it. The Taiwanese don't see it that way. They live the way they want. They've got a real democracy and don't want to lose it. Their economy is booming, and they've got great educational, medical and social care policies.'

'Thanks for the lesson and the vote of confidence in my leadership.'

'Something else.'

'I thought there might be.'

'I'm your son.'

'You are, yes, which is why you should guard your tongue.'

'But I'm unofficial. Your official offspring - your daughter, my half-sister - can't inherit in Communist China. Not legally, anyhow. You know the saying, you men, front door, zheng men, back door. The front door is always locked, the back door always open. But I can inherit because I'm unofficial and come in through the back door. At least for now. Once I've made my own way in the Party and inherited your estate at your death, I could then change my name to Qin, right? It's been done before and there's no reason it shouldn't be done again. What do you say?'

'I don't believe in inheritance. There's nothing to leave anyhow, aside from a few pots and cups and a picture or two.'

'That's not true. Families stay in their Party homes when the patriarch dies, right? And you'll have accumulated stuff — art, furniture, savings accounts, books, jewellery — just like everyone does, even if not meaning to do so.'

'If you're asking for my blessing, Chong, then I say you'd better get your stubborn head straight, mind what you say, swallow your brave words and follow the Party line - on Taiwan, on all our major policies.'

'Hong Kong, too?'

'Of course.'

'Dad, the Party is killing the Hong Kong goose and there'll be no more golden eggs. Hong Kong is the only way China has to service its enormous debt. It's ok if it becomes more like any other mainland city, of course, but if you continue to strangle their way of life, if you suppress whatever they have left in terms of a democracy, if you try to replace Cantonese with Mandarin, and flood the place with mainlanders, it will fuck our economy, not just theirs.'

Chong rubbed his eyes before continuing.

'Did you know there are 80 million empty flats on the mainland? That's a conservative estimate. And that's in a country where there's a desperate shortage of affordable housing. Our state economic sector is growing at the expense of the private sector thanks to your policies but is only half as efficient, and because of that, Hong Kong will only grow in importance.'

'Thank you for the lesson is economics.' Qin's head was hurting again.

'That's ok, Dad. You're an old-fashioned Marxist, and I've nothing against that, really I haven't, but you don't begin to understand global markets. How could you? You should hire a real economist to advise you, someone who knows what he's talking about and has seen it for himself, or herself, not spent years buried in books approved by the Party but someone who has run a proper business...'

Qin was surprised that he wasn't upset or offended by this tirade.

Cheeky young bastard. But my bastard, after all.

'One thing you might help me with, Chong. The *China Daily* want to do a profile on me - a double-page spread, they said. It would be an interview and feature. How should I manage this, do you think?'

'If the Party hacks at the *China Daily* do it, it will be dull and no-one will read it.'

'What do you advise?'

'Make yourself seem normal.'

'Aren't I normal?'

'Dad, I think you know the answer to that.'

'Then how do I change my image?'

'By talking about normal stuff.'

'Such as?'

'Hobbies, pets, family, favourite food and music, your last holiday, that kinda thing.'

'I don't have hobbies, pets, holidays or much of a family.'

'You like swimming, though, don't you?'

'You know I do.'

'That's it, then. Focus on the swimming. Have a headline right across the two pages, such as "The Emperor Loves to Swim" over a good action photograph of you in the pool.'

'Are you joking? They wouldn't dare call me "emperor".'

'Everyone calls you that. Your enemies, your critics, your admirers. Even your own children. It'd be a great headline if only you can get the *China Daily* to loosen up a little.'

Qin wasn't sure what to make of that. Chong seemed serious.

'Let's eat, shall we?'

***

The bowls and chopsticks came and went.

Qin felt a little better by the time the tea arrived. Lau Chong preferred coffee.

'One thing I don't understand, Dad. Maybe you could help me.'

'What?'

'Why does the Party leadership prefer to deal with Taiwan's Nationalists — the KMT we fought all those years ago and which fled to Taiwan and took over the island, slaughtering the indigenous inhabitants — and not the current government on the island?'

'Regime, not government. We don't recognise them. No-one does.'

'Regime. Whatever.'

'Words are important.'

'So it would seem. I think we should get past the words, deal with what's important. After all, this regime you refer to won the Taiwan elections fair and square.'

'Such as?'

'We should get down to the genuine issues that are making us — and the Taiwanese — such bitter enemies.'

'Let's deal with your question. Simply put, the KMT Nationalists accept the "One China" policy of ours. They also accept that Taiwan is Chinese and part of China. They dominated politics on the island for over 70 years and we recognised them as a Chinese political party. In 2005, they sent an official delegation to Beijing for talks — the first time since their 1949 defeat. With our help, they opened up the island to the mainland in travel, investment and so on.'

'Sure, I get that, but they still lay claim to all of China.'

'I think they recognise the futility of that anti-Communist position by now. They are anti-separatists and are opposed to any move to establish an independent Taiwan republic. They themselves crushed Tibetan and Uyghur rebellions, if you recall. If both sides accept "One China", it's a good basis for unification talks, don't you agree? A good starting point, something we in the Party can work with.'

'So if the Nationalists — the Pan-Blue coalition I think it's called — were voted back into power, we'd negotiate, not go to war.'

'Pretty much, yeah.'

'Whereas the Pan-Green coalition that's now in power and very popular - specifically the Democratic Progressive Party - wants a separate Taiwan state.'

'Right.'

'What's so bad about having China, one China, Communist China, as a world superpower - and a small, independent Taiwan with a thriving economy as a neighbour? Isn't it time we accepted their new reality as they must accept ours? Why hark back to the civil war — which we Communists won? Taiwan today is a very different place. As is our country.'

'It's in our constitution. It's right up front in the preamble. Maybe you should read it.'

'I have, Dad. Several times.'

Qin drank his tea, Lau his coffee. In a silent truce.

***

The man Qin wanted his unofficial son to meet did not stay long.

Colonel Zhang Junfu, the late General Wang's former deputy, and now his temporary replacement as acting head of the *Zhongnanhai*'s thousand-strong bodyguard under the Ministry of Public Security, was a short, pudgy figure with a round face, small eyes, a squashed and wide nose, thick lips and a bald head. He was not a pretty sight. He swaggered into the pool area as if he owned it, Qin thought, but then the Emperor recognised this was his way of overcompensating for his nervousness, his shortness of stature, his ugliness. His face was shiny with sweat.

Zhang glanced at Lau and away. 'General Secretary, I apologise for intruding.'

'Not at all, Colonel. I invited you. You're most welcome, too. May I introduce my new secretary, Lau Chong? Chong, this is someone you will see often, Colonel Zhang, once you yourself start working here.'

They nodded at each other, the young gift to Wall Street and the ancient enforcer looking each other up and down. Neither seemed to like what he saw.

'So this,' Zhang said, turning his attention to the pool, 'is where —'

'Yes,' said Qin, before Zhang could finish his sentence. 'It is. Over there. Do you want to see for yourself where it happened?'

The Emperor was offended that Zhang had brought this up at all, especially at the start of their meeting.

'No, no, that's alright, thank you.' Zhang looked flustered.

The Emperor rose to his feet, towering over his new and temporary chief bodyguard. 'Come, I'll show you myself. I insist.' Qin took Zhang by the arm and led him to the deep end. 'He seems to have gone in over here, at the deep end. You see?' Qin tapped one sandalled foot on the spot where he'd stamped General Wang's fingers. 'It's deep, around eight feet, and he didn't swim - couldn't swim. No-one saw or heard anything. He tried to get out. They found blood and torn nails where he tried to save himself.'

Zhang said nothing.

'Do you swim, Colonel?' Qin smiled when he asked the question.

No answer. Qin tightened his grip on the colonel's arm.

'Can you swim?'

'A little.'

'Well, that's good. Better than nothing. Perhaps you'd like to take a dip yourself?'

Qin didn't mean it, of course. He was teasing the man, who would read into it an implied threat. Qin had no intention of letting anyone else swim in his pool.

'Are you armed, Colonel?'

'No, I —'

'Let me see, if you would.'

Qin turned him around.

'No sidearm?'

'No.'

'Nothing hidden in your pocket?'

A vigorous shake of the head. 'No.'

'Great. I'm so glad. I don't appreciate weapons being brought into my work and living area, not even by the temporary head of my close protection people. You understand. It's best if all offensive weapons can be left outside, in the entrance.'

'Of course.'

Colonel Zhang didn't stay long after that, which Qin regretted because he'd wanted to discuss arrangements for his weekly dance nights - out of Lau's hearing, of course. Maybe Colonel Zhang didn't know about the Emperor's taste in young, female, Communist bodies, music and vintage *maotai*.

Once he'd gone, Lau offered his opinion without being asked for it.

'He's scared shitless of you, Dad. Did you see? It's interesting to see the fear in his face when so many people must have been petrified of him over the years.'

'I think you're imagining it.'

'He's so old. Maybe the Party's oldest torturer. He has a face like a wet pudding. I can picture him skulking in the basement cells of our prisons, dreaming up the nastiest and most painful techniques and applying them to the prisoners and laughing as he does so. A real knuckle-dragger and sadist.'

'He's only a few years older than me, Chong, and I'm 73. Are you going to tell me I've a face like a wet pudding?'

Lau could not fail to notice the edge that had crept into his father's voice.

'Of course not, Dad. I was kidding, okay? You look so much younger, fitter than most men your age. You seem to thrive on power. Or maybe it's the swimming — or both.'

'He's a widower, poor fellow. No children. Most unfortunate.'

'I guess that's it, then. All he can do is sit alone after work in front of the television or computer screen of an evening, watch porn and *dǎfēijī*, beat the aeroplane. If he can even do that.'

Qin knew what Lau meant. It was nasty. But he said nothing. He had this feeling that Lau Chong enjoyed mocking him, the sarcasm never far below the surface.

# 34

## 12:17 Eastern Standard Time, GMT -4

Someone tapped on Ava's door. She got up from the desk, leaving the laptop where it was. Having sat for so long without moving, her feet had gone to sleep and she stumbled. She had to lean against the wall and wriggle her toes until the circulation returned.

'Who is it?'

'It's me - just checking in,' said Sam.

She unlocked the door, opened it, stood back.

He didn't move, but looked past her at the laptops, the cables, the discs.

'Hi. Sorry to interrupt. How's it going?'

'Fine. I need a break, though.'

'Have you had lunch?'

'No.'

'Fancy a short walk? Then maybe a bite?'

'Sure.'

He waited in the corridor while she put her gear away. Ava was careful to stash the disks and drive in a wall safe. Once they were outside the house in coats and gloves, borrowed boots and scarves, Ava, feeling the sting of cold air on her face, turned to Sam.

'Are we black?'

Black meant free of surveillance.

'We are.'

'You're sure.'

'Sure, I'm sure.'

'Ok, then. Let's do this.'

They ambled side by side for several minutes without speaking, circumventing the block. A man was outside, clearing snow from his driveway. He paid them no attention. Outside another house, a dog barked at them in the yard as they strolled past.

Ava broke the silence.

'I know now why he was so eager not to involve you people, or people like you.'

'You mean intelligence services, right?'

'Yup.'

'So why? What's the reason?'

'You know, Sam.'

'Do I?'

They paused together on a corner, looked both ways. No cars. No pedestrians. No Watchers.

They crossed together in step.

Ava spoke again when they reached the pavement on the other side. 'Because the source knows one of the partners in the Five Eyes club has been penetrated by one of theirs. Our mole knows they have a mole. That's why he's using these low-tech methods - the post, the parcels, the thumb drives. It takes a mole to know a mole.'

Sam didn't respond.

'Come on, Sam. The NSA is the biggest intelligence agency in the world. Forty-three thousand employees. Along with their British pals in GCHQ tapping into undersea cables, they scoop up everything - GCHQ alone boasts of 50 billion of so-called events every day - every call, every email, every radio message, every bank account deposit, every grunt and every whimper, every cry, every fuck. Everything, and you and they pay very close attention to everything Chinese. You guys must know if the source knows.'

'I don't know that.'

Ava threw up her hands, opened her eyes wide, playing shocked. 'What? It's above your pay grade? Really, Sam?' He was playing the cool, stiff upper lip British bullshit, and it was irritating.

'Humint is my business, Ava. Not Sigint. I'm not routinely cleared for Level 3 STRAP.'

'So ECHELON stuff doesn't cross your desk or your screen? How about material from what Langley calls upstream operations with code names such as BLARNEY, FAIRVIEW, OAKSTAR, STORMBREAK? No? Nothing? Don't ring a bell? You don't match your humint agent reports with sigint captures on your computer back in your Station? I'm surprised, Sam. I'm appalled. Disappointed, too. Let's not forget the very close, cozy relations between the NSA, GCHQ and Israel's ISNU, either.'

He stopped, turned to face her. He was pale with anger. Or just hunger.

'Will you stop this? Now? Please?'

'No. I don't like being lied to. You people can fuck up our privacy, destroy the internet, screw the democratic process and break the law as much as you like with your illegal bulk snooping. I can't do much about it. But don't lie to my face, Sam.'

He stepped back, looked up and down the road, nodded as if he'd got back his self-control or made his mind up about something.

About her. About the source. Who the hell knew what he thought?

'Ok,' he said at last. 'I think we should eat. Which do your prefer? Mexican or Thai?'

'I don't care. Mexican.'

They'd almost reached the house when Sam ventured to speak again.

'Your source now has a code name, Ava. It's GREMLIN.'

'Nice. As in gremlin in the works. Most apt. Gender neutral, too. I suppose there's a computer algorithm that churns these out.'

'It's no different from the system you used to use.'

'I want to get in touch with GREMLIN to ask if he knows if there's a mole in our midst and if he can identify who it is.'

'GREMLIN might well refuse. Our source seems to have a clear and single purpose: to expose Beijing's war plans. Anything else GREMLIN might reject as a threat to his security and his special project. GREMLIN will also suspect you're working with us, or people like us, and your question would confirm it.'

'It's a risk, I agree. But if there is a mole we need to know.'

'Let's get together to talk about it later, after your team has been and gone.'

'Sure. I do owe you an apology, Sam. For yesterday. I'm sorry.'

'Why? No need. I wanted to, just as you did.'

'You did? No shit?'

'I did. I still do.'

'Me too. Did we agree on Mexican?'

'We did. Let's give the shop talk a rest while we eat - if that's alright with you.'

'No problem.'

They had lunch, a quiet affair because they stuck to their agreement not to talk about work, and that meant not talking about anything, and also because they drank nothing alcoholic that might have loosened their tongues. Back at the house, the 'team' was on time; the members were shepherded in on arrival — no waiting outside the front door — and down to the basement by the indefatigable Potters. Amid much chatter and the occasional burst of laughter, the reports were divvied up; the participants seemed to enjoy their meetings, at being brought back into play, honing rusty skills and socialising among fellow sinologists and linguists. They soon got down to work; they could remove nothing from the steel mesh Faraday cage and its lucite tiles. Two hours later they were on their way out again, moving singly or in pairs, divided between the Honda and Toyota and dropped off in the dark at whatever point they'd left their own cars.

'All black,' Clive said.

'Black,' said Kathy.

'I must get back to work,' Ava announced after helping Kathy clear up the dinner things and putting them in the dishwasher.

Sam stopped her in the hall as she was about to head upstairs. 'No, not yet. We've things to discuss, remember?'

'Here - now?'

'No. My place.'

'I didn't ask to see your etchings, Sam.'

'I don't have any, don't worry. Come on.'

It was snowing again; big flakes drifted and swirled out of the night sky.

Sam Turner lived in a Georgetown condo, not much larger than her own. There wasn't much stuff, books and dust aside. The books were everywhere, though, both fiction and non-fiction; they climbed the walls, tottered in perilous stacks on the floor, and even sprawled about the minute bathroom. The living room had a light blue, loose-cover and spavined sofa, a red Tajik carpet and a colourful Mongolian cabinet - Sam said it was a cheap Chinese copy - upon which stood, or rather sat, a big Chinese vase. Tang dynasty. The bedroom had a double bed and books and nothing else.

'No television? For real?'

'Can't stand the bloody thing. It's all too easy to flop down in front of it after work with a beer and a packet of pretzels and lose what's left of my brain watching crap - so I don't have one. I mean, I don't have a television. I hope I still have a brain, or some part of it.'

'Budweiser and pretzels aren't you, Sam.'

'You're wrong. I'm totally acclimatised to the American way.'

'That's not my impression.'

Sam picked up a paperback.

'Look at this, Ava. Tell me what you think. It's from a poem by Du Fu, Tang Dynasty. This edition would not be hard to find in a Beijing bookshop, I imagine. I thought these lines might provide our OTP code if it comes to that.'

*bamboo sways in the wind*

*graceful as any court beauty*

*rain makes the lotus flowers*

*even more red and fragrant*

*but I no longer hear from friends*

*who live on princely salaries...*

'It sounds better in Chinese,' Ava said, and she recited it aloud in Mandarin. 'Perhaps GREMLIN would prefer to choose.'

'To be honest, Ava, he's had things his way all along. It's time we put a name to him, don't you think?'

'He's not a dog needing a collar and lead,' Ava said. 'But we need to know if there's a Chinese penetration of the services receiving GREMLIN'S product.'

There were a few pictures on the walls, after all. Oils and watercolours, a huge and lascivious pen and ink abstract drawing Ava recognised as the work of a young Glaswegian with a studio in New York who was very much a la mode.

Ava drifted past Sam, turned, drew him towards her, put her arms around his neck.

'I just love your etchings, Sam. Now take me to your bed.'

***

Ava listened to his breathing, so quiet and even.

She stood by the window, naked, peeking out.

'What are you doing?' came a gruff question from under the bedclothes.

'Watching the snow.'

It was still falling, silencing the world of Bethesda, and its Christmas trees winking in front rooms.

'Are you ok?'

'Yes. Are you?'

Was this a mistake? Would she regret it later?

'Come back to bed.'

'In a minute.'

They'd been in too much of a hurry. The whole thing had been conducted with great urgency and energy. It hadn't been the best experience she'd ever had, by any means. Not that it wasn't enjoyable - it was. But they were still near-strangers, a strangeness that had fuelled her want and his, but it had prevented greater intimacy. Not that Ava could ever claim to know how these things worked between men and women. They'd taken what they'd wanted from each other, but it could have been better. Perhaps it would improve with practice. If there was to be more practice and if they were to grow closer, and if there was more give, less take. Lots of 'ifs'.

'Come on. You'll freeze. It's the middle of the bloody night.'

'I'm coming.'

Ava thought that although they worked together in one sense, they were at odds in others. Sam was in the intelligence game. She had an intelligence background of sorts, but Ava believed she saw it for what it was. Sam worked in the rarified world of human intelligence and possibly he felt himself to be part of some elite above the squalid business of mass electronic eavesdropping. Ava hadn't had that luxury. It was also the case that their objectives differed. Sam wanted source GREMLIN for the intelligence he provided to his employers, the SIS headquartered in Vauxhall, south London. It might be described as a boutique intelligence service compared to the giants, such as the NSA, CIA, SVR and *Guoanbu*. Ava wanted GREMLIN's product because it warned of a war in the making, and she intended to spread the message as widely as possible, to help GREMLIN prevent the slaughter ever taking place. A lofty ambition that wouldn't succeed, she knew, but she had to try. Sam would see her as a hopeless idealist, a jejune activist, someone he could use, exploit for his purposes.

And she was sleeping with him.

Had she no self-respect?

Ava returned to the bed, slipped under the duvet, glad of the warmth. He turned to her and they held each other. She felt him relax as he slipped back into sleep and again she listened to his breathing.

# 35

# December 17

## 10:43 China Standard Time, GMT +8

The Command Centre was all of a flutter. There was a nervousness in the air, and only the Emperor seemed unaffected by the mephitic atmosphere. Head tilted, Mona Lisa smile in place, his hands like a bear's paws rested on his *juemi* or top-secret papers. He looked especially inscrutable.

Only he knew that was because he'd woken at a few minutes after four that morning and changed into his swimming trunks and gone for a long swim in the pool, finishing up by lying inert on his back in the water, watching the play of artificial light reflected off the water in wavy lines on the high ceiling.

He was so relaxed he had let his tea get cold and had eaten nothing.

He would far rather be back there now in the water, but he would have to wait.

PLA3, responsible for Signal Intelligence, which reported to the Army General Staff, which in turn reported to the Central Military Commission, had urgent, overnight information of a U.S. Strike Force leaving its anchorage at Yokosuka and heading south, bound for the South China Sea, with the apparent intention of breaching the first and second island chains. It had embarked its usual complement of 64 aircraft - most of them F/A-18 'Hornets' from the Carrier Air Wing 5 based at Iwakuni, also in Japan, on board the strike group's flagship, the nuclear-powered Nimitz-class supercarrier, the USS Ronald Reagan.

The aircraft carrier aside, the group comprised ten surface warships: three Ticonderoga class cruisers and seven Arleigh Burke class destroyers. The first of the latter, the USS Dewey, was headed for the Taiwan Strait and behind it a second destroyer from the same group, the USS Howard, was on the same course.

Unusually, the conference participants were whispering to each other, even moving out of their seats to huddle in small groups, discussing the latest developments.

Admiral Jia unveiled the news with a flourish that had everyone's attention. He was in full uniform and he stepped up to the speaker's podium, looking very serious. This time, his immediate superior, the pugnacious General Zheng, did not interrupt.

'I'll be as brief as possible. This is a powerful strike group, and the only one that is permanently forward deployed by the United States. A U.S. Navy spokesperson in Hawaii stated overnight the usual bland and misleading explanation to cover this outright aggression: that the United States is exercising its right to navigate international waters, and he said that this was a routine deployment prior to joint U.S., Japanese and Australian naval exercises in the Pacific. We all here know that what the United States regards as international waters in the Western Pacific, notably in the South China Sea, does not accord with our definition, and that in fact, this deployment is designed to intimidate us in our very own waters.'

Colonel Sun was already busy with his usual video show: images of the massive, 100,000-ton Ronald Reagan appeared, then shots of the F-18/A Hornets landing and taking off from a carrier deck, and standard stills of US Navy missile destroyers.

'The latest deployment should be seen in the context of a news report which appeared in the latest edition of the New York Times, citing unnamed sources in the White House as saying that the President of the United States is discussing with America's allies a formal Pacific mutual defence agreement to which Japan, Australia and other countries may be parties. The report omits mention of Chinese Taipei.

'We are monitoring these hostile activities. The PLAN has two intelligence ships shadowing the strike group, along with PLAAF electronic warfare aircraft. Seven of our diesel electric submarines are in the vicinity. We also believe a second U.S. carrier group may join the Ronald Reagan. I'll take questions.'

Was it time to panic? Sell the shares, buy Swiss francs, sew gold into coat seams, catch the next plane to anywhere outside China, dive into the bomb shelter? Some participants glanced up at Qin to see how the Emperor was reacting. He wasn't. He looked sleepy or bored, or both, resting one cheek on his open hand.

Jia continued, 'You may have seen media reports to the effect that two Japanese carriers, platforms for anti-submarine warfare helicopters, are headed for manoeuvres in the East China Sea, accompanied by eight surface escorts. You may draw your own conclusions.'

Colonel Sun was showing off more images, this time of the PRC's shadowing aircraft and ships. Two of the PLAN's nine intelligence vessels of around 6,000 tons, the Type 815 *Beijixing* with three big radomes and a helicopter hangar - along with the more recent Type 815G *Tiansangxin*, both of the Eastern Fleet, were seen on the big screens pushing through moderate swells under clear blue skies.

Next, two J16-Ds, twin-seater fast jets carrying radar jamming and electronic surveillance pods as well as air-to-air missiles screamed across the screens, prompting several dozy members to jump in their seats. Even Qin dropped the hand propping up his head and sat up straight.

'These are some assets we're employing to monitor hostile activity by the U.S. carrier strike force,' said Jia. 'Questions?'

A hand shot up. 'What about satellite reconnaissance?'

'You can bet on it,' said Jia. 'Both low-orbit signal intelligence and photo-reconnaissance satellites have been repositioned and are watching both the U.S. strike group and the Japanese carrier group.'

Another arm was raised.

'Is the enemy preparing a pre-emptive strike before we're ready with Operation China Unity?'

Qin was alert. The question was close to the bone, and he tried to identify whoever it was who had asked, but he didn't know the colonel's name.

'Intentions are hard to predict,' said Jia. 'We see this as naked aggression. We're keeping our eyes peeled.' Jia had avoided a direct answer.

'I might add that the forecast in the area is for gale force winds and rough seas. And more snow. Neither the Americans nor the Japanese will have a comfortable ride.'

Heads turned, faces looked up at Qin as if expecting a definitive answer.

The Emperor did not react at once. His eyes were closed.

Then he spoke, eyes still shut.

'Anything's possible,' he said. 'We must be ready for any and every eventuality.'

A military aide tiptoed up to him and passed him a note.

***

What preoccupied Qin this morning was not the activity of the U.S. Navy in China's backyard at all, but matters much closer to home. The note said his daughter - his official daughter - was back and had just landed at Beijing International Airport as the Command Centre session drew to a close. Grace was not alone, but was accompanied by her boyfriend, an American named Dale Ratner. She had referred to him as her fiancé and she now invited herself - and the American devil - to lunch.

Her companion would not be welcome at the *Zhongnanhai*. He would be refused entry on security grounds just like any other foreigner wandering off the tourist trail. Grace had said in her last phone call she wanted the *waibin* to meet her father. The Emperor did not want to meet the boy, but he reasoned he couldn't avoid it - and Grace knew it - not if he wanted to maintain any kind of relationship with his only official daughter, so he told himself he might as well face up to it and get it over with.

Qin knew it would be an ordeal, of the kind he assumed every father with daughters must face up to at some point if they are ever to marry. But an American? What was wrong with her? There had been no time to inquire into his background, check his family origins, his education, his political affiliation, and that made it worse. Qin was dealing with an unknown quantity and the Emperor disliked everything that was unknown.

Orders were given to the staff to prepare the official Qin home. The courtyard villa on Jade Hill would have to be cleaned and heated because it had been left empty while his wife and daughter were absent. Special food would be brought in from the Emperor's own kitchens. The tasters were alerted. It would not be a simple lunch, but would have to express the generosity and largesse expected of the country's leading political family.

This Dale somebody-or-other should have a foretaste of what life was like for top Communist Chinese cadres. Didn't he want to become a member of the nomenklatura himself, albeit somewhat detached in view of his foreignness? Of course, he did. He must have seen huge potential for himself and his family back in Wyoming or Kentucky or wherever the hell he was from. A gold digger, the little shit. Qin grinned inwardly — maybe he'd subject Grace's suitor to a ritual glass or two of *maotai* which most *da bizi* - big noses - regarded as little better than raw diesel fuel, highly combustible and a dangerous fluid that would strip the tissue from unwary foreign throats and explode their brains. Yes, a few toasts in *maotai* were a splendid idea and the guest would soon stumble back to whatever backwoods hole he'd crawled out of to rethink his plan to marry the illustrious Grace.

Qin was confident he could find a better match in China, even if Grace was of a shrewish and outspoken nature. Who would not want to marry the General Secretary's daughter? It was almost unlimited power on a plate, along with access to all that the business world had to offer. His access to the top cadres alone would be worth millions of American dollars without him lifting a finger. Whoever it was would have to be very wealthy, that was all, in order that he deploy the stream of expensive trinkets essential to improving the worst of her bad moods.

The Emperor would be late. It was deliberate. The staff had been instructed to let Grace and her paramour enter and to invite them to make themselves comfortable in the rather stark and seldom used library of Party works. Maybe Dale would find something on the shelves to interest him, even inspire him.

An hour seemed a reasonable time for keeping his lunch guests waiting.

Chen Meilin of State Security had sent him a personal note classified as top secret. It listed the names of three Hong Kong banks in which his wife held accounts, along with the account numbers, sort codes, and the bank cards' pin numbers. There was a Singapore bank, too, and even one in Taipei. Qin smiled. If she put a foot wrong, she'd be left with nothing except for whatever she had in her purse.

Qin whiled away the remaining minutes by initialling the latest list of those tried, convicted and sentenced to death for a range of capital offences: sabotage, espionage, aiding and abetting the special forces of a foreign power. There were a few criminals on the list; most were political: in a word, terrorists.

He didn't read the dockets or check the signatures of the judges. He didn't need to. It was all legitimate. It was legal. These were security courts, military courts, secret tribunals. The Ministry of Public Security knew its job. Qin never interfered or objected.

Two hundred and thirty-seven names in all.

The names of most of those condemned to death - by lethal injection or a bullet in the back of the head - had foreign-sounding names. Quite attractive, Qin thought, some of them at least, both male and female.

Aynur, Patigül, Reyhan, Yusup.

Of course. These were Uygurs.

Moslem bandits, the lot of them. A dangerous scourge to be wiped out. Almost half the Uygur population of China was confined to labour camps of one kind or another.

What was this?

Ceba.

And this?

Chodrak, Dorje, Garab, Jangbu, Kalsang.

Tibetan traitors. Armed separatists, religious fanatics, subversives, CIA paid assassins.

Whatever. He left the sordid details to his Party subordinates.

He initialled each one, added his stamp.

The driver stood at the door.

Qin flung down the papers and pushed himself to his feet. He checked his watch. It was time for a modest 15-course lunch, a bottle or two of best quality *maotai*, and a crate of beer. Let the American see how the Chinese entertain guests! The Emperor told himself he was not a man to do things by halves.

\*\*\*

Tall and thin, was Qin's first impression of Dale Ratner. Whiskers, big ears, an enormous nose, large even by the standards of the *waibin*. He'd jumped up from a sofa as Qin strode in, shrugged off his black winter coat and flung it at a hovering flunkey.

'Welcome,' he boomed in English. 'Welcome to China, and welcome to our family home.'

The Emperor even beamed at the visitor, though he felt the beginnings of another headache coming on. Hopefully, the *maotai* would help cauterise the fucking thing in his brain that was killing him.

Whatever the foreigner murmured in response was lost in the general hubbub of the Emperor's arrival. Did he stutter? Was he that nervous?

'Grace, how are you?'

'Okay, Dad, thanks,' she responded. They did not embrace.

'Out,' he said, gesturing at the bodyguards who'd accompanied him. He gestured at them as one might shoo away a housefly. The protection team wore two-piece black suits and ties, white shirts, and they carried semi-automatic handguns under their jackets. Qin had 17 of them outside the villa, some working in pairs and always on the move, others single and stationary.

They'd arrived in three black, Red Flag limos flying the red flag, the chrome grills in the front of each like the wide grins of great white sharks. Qin had been in the last of the three.

Two bodyguards remained in the hall and corridor, one in the kitchen.

Qin, Grace and Dale Ratner took their places at the round dining table. The *waibin* was next to Grace, but not too close, and opposite and at an equal distance from them, the Emperor shook out his crisp white napkin and dropped it in his lap.

'*Xiānshēng* Dale, I propose a toast.'

A server darted forward and filled Qin's cup, then slipped around the table and did the same for the guest and Grace, who groaned when she saw the bottle of vintage *maotai*.

'To our guest, a long, happy and prosperous life!'

Qin raised his hand, holding his cup above his head.

Grace translated.

'Drink it in one go,' said the Emperor. 'Now shout after me, "*Gānbēi!*"'

Grace glared at her father. Dale Ratner leaned towards her. 'What did your father say?'

She translated it as 'down the hatch', her eyes on her father. Grace wasn't happy. She was furious. She hated drinking rituals. But the visitor was game; he threw his head back, and shouted, '*Gānbēi!*'

Qin looked on with approval as the honoured guest did not choke or splutter.

Grace did not touch the powerful spirit.

The dishes were being brought in rapid succession and placed on the white tablecloth. Undeterred by his first gulp of aviation fuel, Ratner climbed to his feet. 'I would like to offer a toast to our host.' He raised his cup, already refilled by the attentive server, and called out, 'To the General Secretary of the People's Republic of China, a long, happy, healthy and prosperous life! *Gānbēi!*'

Qin nodded, quizzical half-smile in place. He appeared to have understood.

He thought to himself, we'll see how long you last, my clever young American.

'To the American people, peace and property - *gānbēi!*'

'To the Chinese nation. All wealth and happiness - *gānbēi!*'

'To peace, everywhere - *gānbēi!*'

'To peace and development - *gānbēi!*'

Grace broke in to explain to her boyfriend - who by now looked pale and sweaty - the nature of the dishes before them, pointing at each:

'Lotus root soup. Kung Pao chicken. Ma po tofu. Yangzhou fried rice. Chow mein. Peking duck. Spring crayfish. Lamb hotpot. Fish with Sichuan pickles. Steamed fish head with diced hot peppers. Sweet and sour ribs. Scalded shrimp.'

Qin said something to a server behind his chair, who darted forward, snatched up a clay pot, marched over to where Ratner sat, removed the lid and placed something in his bowl.

'Eat. It's delicious,' Qin commanded.

Grace shrugged and translated.

'He says it's delicious and that you must eat it.'

'But what is it?'

'Do as he says or he will be offended.'

Ratner did so despite the novelty of using chopsticks for only the second or third time in his life. He took a morsel, chewed, swallowed, did so again, repeating the process, nodded at Qin.

'Yes, delicious,' he declared.

'It's sea slug,' said Grace. Then she said in response to the appalled expression on the face of her fiancé, 'Stick with the duck and fried rice and you'll be okay.'

Cold beer was brought. Qin insisted Ratner try every dish, and servers kept leaning forward and filling his bowl and plate with more. Grace tried her best to protect him from her father's attentions, pushing some offerings away, pulling others closer. She chose for Ratner, dismissing the over-zealous attendants, and Qin wondered how long such a marriage - if there was to be one at all - would last. Grace was very much in control.

It was if she knew what he was thinking.

'We're going to get engaged, Father. Then in a few months we'll marry in the States, not here. California, near his parents.'

Qin hadn't travelled abroad for a decade. Then it had been to Moscow - to visit the swivel-eyed, poisonous ferret otherwise known as Putin - and then on to North Korea, China's very own satellite state.

He wasn't going to any wedding in the United States. They knew it, too, and it would be pointless for the Emperor to encourage them to hold the ceremony here, in Beijing. Grace wouldn't have it, so there was no point in trying.

The meal was brought to a sudden conclusion. At 14:00 local time, the three diners heard four massive blasts right overhead, or so it seemed, followed by four more ear-shattering explosions. Ratner ducked, his head and shoulders vanishing below the table, and Grace put her hands over her ears and hunched forward.

Qin knew what it was and showed no physical reaction.

In the kitchen, someone dropped a pot and there was a cacophony of shouts and curses in Mandarin.

'Jesus H Christ,' yelled Ratner, his own cry muffled. 'What the fuck?'

Qin remained unperturbed. He held up his small and chubby hands. 'Nothing to worry about, please. No need to be frightened, *Xiānshēng* Dale.'

Ratner's face re-appeared above the table's edge, but he was not reassured. 'Are we under attack? What is this?' He pushed himself up and back onto his chair.

Six more thunderous cracks, more distant this time.

The white-clad servers, who'd fled the dining room, returned, looking sheepish.

'Our military forces are practising air defence drills in Beijing, that is all. Sonic booms I think they're called in English. Nothing to worry about. You're perfectly safe. Grace, please tell him not to be upset. It's just a PLA exercise, and it will soon be over. I should have remembered. So sorry.'

'PLA? What's PLA?'

The foreign devil must know. 'The People's Liberation Army,' said Grace.

What Qin did not tell his fellow diners was that the air defence exercise involving the air force, the army and civil defence workers was in part aimed at the foreign community in Beijing, especially the diplomats, a loud signal (and one they could not ignore) that China was girding itself up for an armed confrontation with Taipei and its western allies.

# 36

Ava was taken aback. She thought little of cars and wasn't interested in them. But this was unexpected. Sam had struck her initially as stuffy, uptight, a typical English diplomat. She did not expect him to drive a red Chevrolet Stingray.

'Wow. I'm impressed by your boy's toy,' she said when she climbed into the passenger seat.

Make fun of me, Sam's smile seemed to say, it's quite okay.

'She's the love of my life - present company excepted.'

Ava thought that if Sam regarded her as his agent, or an asset, then he would know only too well that becoming physically or emotionally involved with her — and he seemed to be both — violated the fundamental laws of agent handling. If found out, he'd be summarily dismissed from his current post and sent home - to the SIS equivalent of the salt mines - a post in registry, the archives or in research. He'd be condemned to a desk for the rest of his tenure with his Service unless he took the hint and quit.

They were going to have breakfast, read the papers over coffee, fruit juice and French toast - or whatever - just like any other couple. Maybe that's what he wanted them to be - just another couple. It was a dry day, overcast but much warmer of late, around 9 Celsius.

The Potters had driven out ahead of them from the safe house and had set up static posts as part of their SDR. It was very relaxed; there were no agent meets, no plans to visit either of their residences or offices. Ava and the team had almost completed the translation of all the latest intel.

Whether there was a mole - and whether GREMLIN knew of its existence - was left aside, at least for now. With Ava's approval, Sam had written out, and Ava had encrypted, a short message asking GREMLIN if he was aware of any security breach in Western services that could compromise his identity or the source of his material. It stated Ava's concern for his safety, but even so it was an admission on Ava's part that she was collaborating with Western intelligence services. They'd sent it that morning from the safe house and all they could do now was wait.

'Are we black?'

'Let's have a look. It seems very quiet.'

Sam drew into the kerb, pulled out his TALON device and switched it on.

Ava leaned over to look.

There were two red dots, one on either side of their own blinking green spot. And two blue - one ahead and one behind.

'Looks like we have company. Two teams tagging us again.'

'What shall we do?'

'Let's keep going. We'll keep an eye open, but I don't think we should try to throw them off. We'll have breakfast. I'll signal Clive and Kathy, so they're aware if they're not already.'

'Sounds good.'

They drove on. The general rule of tradecraft was not to throw a tail unless it was deemed essential.

'Did you see the news?'

'No,' Ava said. 'What news?'

'In this morning's Washington Post. We'll look at it properly when we eat.'

There was a copy of that morning's edition behind their seats.

'What is it?'

'I'm always amazed by the extent to which Washington media depend on leaks for their existence. It's how the game works - it's how the administration fights its turf battles.'

'I know this, Sam. So?'

'If it's true, the Security Council is to hold an urgent session in New York on Monday. The subject: Taiwan. According to unnamed diplomatic sources, the U.S. Secretary of State and her opposite number in Moscow have agreed to co-sponsor an emergency resolution.'

'Holy shit. Saying what?'

Sam didn't have time to answer.

They were crossing the infamous intersection on Wisconsin Avenue and M Street North West. They were in the correct lane, and the lights were green. Neither Ava nor Sam saw any of it coming. There was no warning - other than converging dots on Sam's screen which, at that precise moment, neither of them were watching.

A blue SUV — it turned out to be a blue Mazda 'Kicks' model — struck the 'Vette broadside at high speed, spinning it around and throwing it aside the way a fighting bull tosses a matador.

A tremendous crash, a crunching of metal and splintering glass, a massive shock that threw them bodily forward and back.

Fortunately, the point of impact was just behind their seats.

They both had their seatbelts on. The Chevvy came to rest against a pavement bollard, releasing both airbags, and as it did so, another utility vehicle, a Ford 'Maverick' pickup, came from the opposite direction, turned and swerved to a stop alongside. What appeared to be the barrel of a pump-action shotgun poked out of the window and the driver pulled the trigger. He fired at least three rounds before he was shot in the neck by person or persons unknown.

The entire intersection erupted in gunfire, a blizzard of popping sounds, single and double rounds. Neither Sam nor Ava were fully aware of it, not at first. They were too busy trying to survive. Sam helped Ava free herself from her safety belt, and out of her seat. He grabbed the TALON, kicked his own door open, and pulled Ava out, his one arm around her. Ava, who was conscious but dazed, was kicking her way out as well.

They fell into the street, the 'Vette wreckage now between them and the gunman, who had been joined by the driver, who fired his weapon - one that turned out, according to a subsequent police report, to be a Glock 19.

Both attackers were of east Asian appearance.

The driver of the Mazda played his part in the ambush. He jumped out of his vehicle, ran towards Ava and Sam, pointing a .38 Ruger revolver in their direction as they struggled to crawl out of the crumpled 'Vette, but he didn't get off a shot. Before he could do so, he was thrown forward, falling flat on his face in the street, struck in the back by a round from another weapon.

***

Ava and Sam, arms around each other, staggered onto the pavement and around the corner, Sam taking most of her weight. They were aware of the gunshots, but after another brief exchange, the detonations ceased altogether. Then a friendly but urgent voice. 'Come on, you two, into the back. Quick, before the police arrive.' It was Clive with the Toyota, door open, helping them in. 'Stay down'. Sam groaned with pain as he climbed in after Ava.

Kathy was right behind in the Honda.

They passed two police patrol cars, lights flashing, sirens wailing and heading the way they'd come.

'Sorry about your car,' gasped Ava. There was blood on her clothing, all down her front, on her blouse and skirt, on her hands, on her face. It seemed to have flowed into one eye, her right, and she was having difficulty seeing out of it.

Her head ached and throbbed.

'It's okay,' Sam said. 'It's insured. Or was.'

Sam looked at her. 'Christ, you're bleeding.'

'I think it was a near miss,' Ava said, her voice hoarse. 'A graze.'

'A very near miss, I'd say.'

Clive glanced at them in the rearview mirror. 'Looks like one lot tried their best to kill you, and another bunch intervened. Quite a crossfire. Three bodies down, at least as far as I could tell, and all Chinese by the look of them — on both sides.'

This wasn't the time to ponder the mystery.

'We don't want the cops asking awkward questions. You were never there.'

'Where are we going?'

Clive had found a first aid pack in the front glove compartment, broke out a dressing and passed it over to Sam, who was using tissues to wipe blood off Ava's forehead and ear but doing so with great care. He opened up the dressing and pressed it on what looked like a scalp wound, just above her hairline. Ava shuddered but said nothing more.

Clive replied. 'We're heading to our friendly clinic. Kathy called ahead on a burner. They'll be expecting you and will check you both out, no questions asked.'

For Ava, the wound stung like merry hell, and she felt dizzy. All she wanted was the bleeding to stop, to take something to kill the pain, then lie down and sleep forever.

They were alive. That was the main thing.

***

Clive stopped the car in an alley in Anacostia, a neighbourhood of DC most tourists don't see, a mix of low and high-rise buildings populated mostly by low-income households. He helped Sam with Ava, leading to a walk-up where Kathy was already waiting on the first floor alongside a small, swarthy man in his mid-thirties in a white coat. Ava would have described him as being of Mediterranean appearance. He looked at Ava, smiled, and told her to lie down on a gurney in a small, white room with a dusty window and bare floorboards that apparently served as a clinic or examination room.

'You were lucky,' was all he said as he helped Sam into one of two chairs. Sam was holding himself across his torso with both forearms and he was pale with pain and gritting his teeth against it.

The doctor cleaned Ava's wound, stitched it up. 'Only four stitches, don't worry.' Then he added a fresh dressing. 'You can take off the dressing tomorrow if there's no more bleeding. You know, head wounds look worse than they really are because they bleed a lot with the blood vessels so close to the surface of the skin. Oh, and if there is a scar eventually, it won't show because it's above the hairline.' The advice came with a reassuring smile.

'That's good,' Ava said. Her words felt thick and awkward on her tongue.

'How do you feel now?'

Ava said her head and neck were painful.

'Whiplash,' said the unnamed medic. He seemed friendly with a pleasant bed-side manner, but he didn't ask what had happened, where or why. Presumably because this was off the books.

He spoke rapidly in Spanish to Kathy. They seemed to know each other.

He asked Ava to sit up, helping her to do so, then took her blood pressure, examined her eyes, felt her head and neck all over with light fingers, and examined her back and legs, feeling his way along bones and muscles, checking with her if she felt pain anywhere.

'Other than the scratch and whiplash, you're in good shape. But you must rest. Stay in bed for a day or two. Avoid stress if you can. Stay off work and the booze for a week and you'll be fine. No beer, no wine, right? And lots of sleep.'

He helped Ava move to a steel and leather armchair.

He turned to Sam.

'Now you. Can you get up and sit here? Nothing broken?'

'Don't think so.'

'No contusions, either. But you're hurting, right?'

'Bruised down my left side - that's what it feels like.'

'Open your shirt and let me see.'

Again, with gentle, latex-coated fingers, he traced the line of the ribs in Sam's chest. Sam winced twice.

'You're right. Nothing broken - but you'll have some spectacular colours soon - as if you've been beaten with a baseball bat. You've got three badly bruised ribs and maybe a hairline crack or two in the fourth. You haven't complained about the pain. I don't think I could walk with that without screaming my head off. I'll strap you up, so it will be a little easier and less painful to move. Okay?'

'Okay, doc.'

'I'll give you something for the pain, too. It will be enough for a couple of days. After that, you can use whatever you usually buy over the counter without a prescription.'

He pulled off his latex gloves and said something else in Spanish to Kathy.

Kathy explained. 'He'll give you painkillers himself - he doesn't want to give you a prescription that can be traced. Only four tablets in 24 hours.'

When they got back to the safe house, there was an encrypted message waiting for Ava from GREMLIN.

Whatever it was, it would have to wait. Ava swallowed one of the painkillers, then crawled into bed and slept.

# 37

## 19:43 China Standard Time, GMT +8

After a slow swim of 64 laps and an hour's nap, the Emperor was ready to deal with his lieutenants of the Politburo Standing Committee. They were to come to him rather than he to them, if only because a rapid decision was required on the U.N. Security Council initiative.

First, though, he went out on foot in his black overcoat, leather gloves, woollen scarf and flat cap and stood by the lake for a special rendezvous. It was layered in mist and there was no sign of the ducks. No sooner had he stopped and picked out one of his Dunhill cigarillos, than he saw the slim figure of Chen Meilin striding towards him in her suede ankle boots, a long, pleated wool dress in navy and a black puffer jacket. A Russian *shapka* hid her black hair.

At 73, there was for the Emperor little left in this world that prompted an immediate hard-on, but Chen was one of them, even without *Wei-ge*. That mystique of femininity, the enigma of espionage, the power she wielded as head of his foreign intelligence service, her apparent indifference to the cruelty he was capable of in the name of the Party - it added up to a swift physical frisson of excitement. All too brief, though.

As ever, she was direct. 'They were clumsy, and the results are messy. Mid-morning, broad daylight, the *Gong'anbu* team from our DC Station used two cars to ram the sports car in which American woman Shute was a passenger, forcing her vehicle off the road and then blazing away with firearms. Thanks to us, she got away, but whether she's hurt, I can't say. Her foreign male companion, identity not known, also escaped.'

'And?'

'Of course, my team intervened. There was no alternative. They exchanged fire. Two *Gong'anbu* operatives died at the scene, a third in hospital. My people got away and are making their separate ways out of the country. They prevented Shute's death — if we knew then what we know now...'

Chen didn't finish her sentence. Qin knew what she was getting at. She was referring to the Security Council move, the invitation to talks on Taiwan.

She looked at him. Those bold eyes made his legs quiver. 'What will you do?'

'Talk,' Qin said, pulling up his collar and adjusting his scarf. It was cold out there. He wasn't used to it. 'We're the peacemakers, remember? There's nothing to lose by talking so long as the discussions are what the Security Council says they will be: with no preconditions. We give up nothing, demand everything. One China, unification, no recognition of the splittist regime's existence, let alone sovereignty.'

'Good. I'm sure that's right, chief. And the mole, the traitor in our midst?'

Qin smiled - actually smiled. 'What do you think our whistleblower should do?'

They walked a little. The frozen snow crackled under their feet.

'Throw in the towel,' she said. 'He's done his duty. Pension him off with the Party's thanks and a warning to keep his traitor's mouth shut.'

'Let this Avery Shute know then, will you, Ms Chen? A last message, yes? I hope she's grateful that we saved her life.'

'She'll never know,' Chen said.

***

If Chen and the Emperor were on the same political wavelength when it came to both foreign and domestic affairs (Taiwan falling into the latter category), nothing could be further from the truth at the meeting of the Politburo Standing Committee.

Encased in his camouflage uniform, General Zheng was performing his role as the proverbial bull in the China shop. On his feet, barely able to contain himself, he stormed up and down, half the pool's length one way, then back again. At one point, it seemed as if he might fall into the shallow end. Qin thought it might cool him down if he did.

'Talk? Of course, we won't talk,' he bellowed. 'Fuck the United Nations! We've got the bastards on the run and now they're trying to wriggle out of it with the help of their pals on the Security Council. The American bandits are behind this, of course. It's another conspiracy, an anti-Chinese plot.' He shook his fist. 'We should attack at once, now, catch them with their dicks in their hands. We're ready!'

Qin waited for the tantrum to subside.

There were five members of the Standing Committee, including Qin. The constitutional rules stated that the Committee reported to the Politburo, the Politburo to the Central Committee. Practice, however, ensured it was the opposite. Qin told the Standing Committee what to do; it told the Politburo what to say and do, and the Politburo dictated the Central Committee's mandate.

Certainly not General Zheng.

But opinion was divided today, something not especially unusual, but feelings ran high. General Zheng wasn't the only one at risk of losing it.

The foreign minister was in favour of accepting the invitation. Speaking quietly, his tone shaky, he said China was giving nothing away by talking. To accept was not to lose face. On the contrary, it would be seen to live up to its status as a Security Council permanent member. The People's Republic would be seen by all as a world leader, a superpower that sought only peace, that sought reconciliation to avert a terrible war provoked by the imperialists. The talks would be an opportunity for Beijing to restate its One China policy, and to call for peaceful reunification.

Perhaps Beijing could put forward a detailed proposal to establish a new code of conduct for navigation in the Taiwan Strait, something their enemies had long said they wanted but had failed to produce. It would take the imperialists by surprise and steal a march on them in the diplomatic sense.

Zheng groaned. Screw diplomacy! Qin smiled, head tilted. His headache had returned, and so had the whispers in his head. At first, he thought he was hearing the voice of Grace, and he resisted the temptation to look around the pool area to see if she was present.

The remaining two Committee members kept their eyes down, waiting, pretending to take notes. They were Party cadres who liked to suck their fingers, stick them up and try to discern which way the wind would blow. They waited for Qin to come down on either side of the argument, and whatever he decided, they would agree to. That was their role in life - to smother dissent at the highest level. Whatever they really thought, if indeed they thought all, they'd keep it to themselves.

'We accept,' Qin said. 'Is that understood? We are not warmongers.' He glowered at the smouldering hulk of General Zheng. 'The Party has decided. We will join the talks in Geneva. Inform our permanent representative. Our esteemed comrade, the foreign minister, will lead our delegation in person. It's done. One China. Unification. That's our agenda. Nothing else.'

The meeting broke up, General Zheng, his face blotchy with resentment, still muttered profanities to himself.

*** 

Dr. Lo lived with his family in the *Zhongnanhai* complex. He didn't have to travel far after dark from his three bedroom flat to see the General Secretary, although an icy wind made the journey on foot especially uncomfortable.

In his fifties, he was a cheerful man with a comb-over, a wife and four children, and a distinguished U.S. medical background. He was a latecomer to the Party and a man lacking in a sense of his own importance. He had no ego, or so it seemed, and treated everyone equally, from housemaids and labourers to billionaire Party chiefs. All three were among his patients. This made him popular, and his reputation had received an immense boost when he was assigned as the Emperor's personal doctor two years before. Qin he treated with the respect any General Secretary was due, but Dr. Lo did not grovel, lie or offer false praise.

Sitting on the side of Qin's bed-come-desk, he held the Emperor's wrist and took his pulse, then his temperature, using an instrument he inserted into an imperial ear.

'How many of those cigarillos are you smoking every day?'

'It depends.'

'On what?'

'On how I'm feeling. Obviously.'

'And how are you feeling?'

'The headache's bad.'

'How long have you had it - this one now?'

'A few hours, ever since I chaired a session of the Standing Committee.'

'Was the meeting stressful?'

'I guess it was.'

'How often do they occur, these headaches?'

'Once or twice a day, depending on —'

'Stress,' offered Lo.

'Yes.'

'You're taking your medicine?'

'When I remember.'

'Which isn't often, right?'

Qin grunted.

'Your swimming has helped, Mr President. It's an excellent way to exercise, but you must stop smoking those cigarillos. Are you still drinking?'

'Sometimes, while entertaining.'

'Try not to smoke or drink. Avoid spirits if you can.'

'Is that it, doctor?'

'No. I must insist that you have another scan. As soon as possible. It's long overdue, as you well know. This isn't a request. We can arrange it right now rather than upset your schedule tomorrow. Is that okay? I'll alert the staff and we'll go together. How does that sound?'

# 38

# December 18

## 10:38 Eastern Standard Time, GMT -4

'Good grief, is that the time? Oh, no!'

'Hey, you're staying in bed - remember what the doctor said?'

'I'm supposed to be at work. James will be furious…'

Her head felt better. No actual pain, only a slight tenderness.

'Ava, it's Sunday. Come and have some breakfast if you feel up to it. Or we can bring it to you here…'

'I'm feeling better. I'll come down. With this bandage, I just look and feel stupid. I thought it was Monday. How are you? You look as if you're still hurting.'

'May I sit?' Sam sat on the edge of Ava's bed, keeping his back unnaturally straight because of his bruised ribs. 'Never mind the ribs. I'm deep in the shit, Ava. What's left of my car was traced back to me. The Feebies and the DC cops are asking questions of the State Department, and State is demanding answers from us. The ambassador has thrown his teddy in a corner. In fact, I think His Excellency enjoys having something to rant about. He hates SIS and what we do, and Sir Richard resents the fact that we exist at all and take up any space in his precious embassy, so now he has a stick to beat us with. He's a right royal pain in the arse. The old fart thinks spying ungentlemanly.'

'I'm so sorry —'

'The COS isn't chuffed, either, putting it mildly, but all the plaudits he's been getting from Vauxhall Cross and Langley make up for it. I'm talking about our mole. We've three brief messages from him and I don't know about you, but I'm dying to know what they say. At least my boss is pushing H.E. to complain to the PRC for its armed thugs assaulting an accredited diplomat.'

'I'll come down. Get out so I can make myself presentable.'

Half an hour later, they had the answer. The three intelligence items had been sent over 14 hours, using Benny as the drop, and it was clear much had happened between the first and the third messages.

*CCP SECY GENERAL QIN HAS DECIDED CHINA WILL REPEAT WILL JOIN UN SEC COUNCIL DIRECT TALKS WITH TAIWAN LEADER WITHOUT PRECONDITIONS. PUBLIC STATEMENT IMMINENT. POLITBURO DIVIDED. MILY LEADERS TALK PRIVATELY OF TAIWAN QUOTE SELLOUT UNQUOTE BUT OVERRULED BY QIN, FORMIN AND INTEL CHIEFS. FUTURE OF HARDLINE WAR PARTY LEADER GENERAL ZHENG IN DOUBT. NO SIGN INVASION FORCES BEING STOOD DOWN.*

'Changes everything,' said Sam.

'You mean no war?'

'We can't tell, not just from this. We'll have to wait. Could be they're just using the talks as a cover for continuing the buildup. A diversion. Maybe.'

And the second item:

*CCP SECRETARY GENERAL UNDERWENT BRAIN SCAN OVERNIGHT REVEALING TUMOUR HAS GROWN. PERSONAL PHYSICIAN DR LO ATTRIBUTES INCREASING FREQUENCY AND INTENSITY OF HEADACHES TO THIS BUT REFUSES TO SAY IF CONDITION LIFE-THREATENING IN SHORT TERM. DR LO INSTRUCTED QIN TO GIVE UP SMOKING AND DRINKING SPIRITS.*

'I wonder if Qin listens to his physician,' Sam said. 'Somehow I doubt it.'

'I didn't know about a tumour.'

'No-one did, but there were rumours. Falun Gong publicised them a year or two ago. Seems they were right, after all.'

'Maybe this is why he's been pushing so hard for an invasion,' Ava said. 'He knows he doesn't have much time, and he wants his legacy assured. Any views, Sam?'

'You could very well be right. Let's see the third and last.'

'I need another coffee first. You?'

'Sure.'

Twenty minutes later the third and last message from GREMLIN had been decrypted and translated:

*UNABLE ASSIST MOLE QUERY. NO.NO COUNTERINTEL ACCESS. PRO-*
*CEED AS FOLLOWS: TIMES SQUARE NEW YORK 1900 HRS EST TODAY*
*SUN DEC 18. LOOK UP. HAPPY XMAS/NEW YEAR.*

Sam was unimpressed. 'No access to counterintelligence after all that he's already given us? He's making excuses. And a happy festive season to you, GREMLIN, whoever you are.'

'What's GREMLIN on about? Is he serious? What does he mean by "look up", do you think? Let me check my translation. No, it's correct - that's what the message says.'

Sam was taking the Mandarin versions off her air-gapped laptop screen, photographing them with his TALON and, Ava assumed, transmitting them in encrypted form again to the local SIS Station - or London. 'I'll make the arrangements, Ava. You good to travel?'

'If I have to, then yeah, sure. Are you okay?'

'There's a United Flight at 13:30. Flight time one hour twenty. Plenty of time.'

'Sounds good.'

'Return same day, or shall we have a night on the town?'

'Now you're talking.'

'Oh, I forgot something. When Kathy collected the latest batch, she was told our hotel contact, Benny, had quit as concierge. Gave in his notice, picked up his final cheque and left. No forwarding address. Looks like GREMLIN is shutting up shop.'

***

Midtown Manhattan after dark and its Christmas preparations hit them like never before. For a start, the massive, brightly lit spruce at the Rockefeller Center towered above the merry crowds of shoppers and tourists, the skaters on the ice rink, the families, the kids. It took Ava's breath away; she'd been isolated from the festive season for far too long in the safe house with its minders, the Potters, the enigma of GREMLIN, the anxiety over an impending war engendered by the flow of intel, the mad rush to decrypt and translate, the Saturday ramming and gunfire, the pain and running scared. The episode had somehow set Christmas back, almost cancelled it.

Until now.

She felt childlike — delighted, stirred, uplifted.

Ava clung to Sam's arm. She didn't know if she was doing so to steady herself or the Brit beside her, who still winced at the pain in his side.

They kept walking south.

'Are we black?'

'We are black,' he said.

'Where are we supposed to look?'

'Up.'

'Sure, but up at what? There are so many enormous billboards.'

There were, too.

The biggest digital display showcased what seemed to be a succession of beautiful actresses and models from across Asia.

Two minutes.

C'mon, GREMLIN, don't screw around.

Ava turned, turned again. It wasn't doing her whiplash injury any good.

Sam was saying something she couldn't quite catch about a billboard ad costing 5,000 bucks an hour. Or had she misunderstood? It must be more than that over the festive season, surely.

Thirty seconds.

'See anything?' she shouted to Sam to make herself heard.

He shook his head, head back, also turning, staring upwards. Whatever it was going to be, it couldn't be more public.

Then she saw.

Right above them.

Alternating in English, Pinyin and Mandarin in huge letters.

*Ava. Thank you very much.*

Ava. fei chang gan xie 非常感谢

*Ava. bài bài* 拜拜

The last line needed no translation.

For a few seconds, the three vanished, then returned. Enormous digital characters were displayed again and again; after several more minutes of the same, the screen went blank.

'I think we got the message,' Sam said.

'GREMLIN played us, Sam. Whoever he, she or they might be.'

'He, she or they did a pretty fine job of it, too.'

'You think?'

'Oh, yeah. The intel was genuine, well, most of it. I'm sure of it.'

'But GREMLIN never did supply his bona fides, which is what agents are supposed to do, right?'

'The intel was his or her bona fides.'

'But you would believe that, Sam. It's in your interest to do so. You're not going to tell your chief of station or London it was all made up, now, are you? Agent-runners always believe their agents, isn't that so? They leaked a stream of their own top secret material to persuade us they were serious about an invasion, even to the extent of inventing their own whistleblower, a fictional mole, and initiating a hunt for the notional traitor. Have I got that right?'

'Not us. They didn't want to persuade us. Not SIS. Not Langley. The media, yes, and world opinion for sure. I think they've succeeded - with your help, Ava.'

'Whether fake or real, is it over? Can we all go home now?'

Sam put an arm around Ava's shoulders.

'It's never over. Never.'

# 39

# January 27

## 14:23 China Standard Time, GMT +8

The Emperor swam. On his front for the first twenty laps, then he rolled over onto his back, arms out, legs and hands moving in unison. He watched the sinuous waves of light, bending, flowing, dancing on the ceiling, matching his disturbance of the surface water, little waves that slapped and tickled him.

Qin ploughed forward again, pushing himself, using his powerful upper body to propel himself through two more lengths, and performed a racing turn underwater, then drifted again, arms out. He felt playful, relaxed.

All things considered, life for the Emperor in the *Zhongnanhai* was pretty good.

Grace had married her American in California. It was sad, but not unexpected. As for his wife, she'd written to say she wasn't coming back. She was going to live with her family in Taipei. It was done to spite him, of course. Who would want to live on some awful little island populated by pretentious reactionaries and their half-baked religious notions? What kind of life would it be for the estranged wife of the president-for-life of Communist China? He'd cleaned out her overseas bank accounts, but he knew she would survive. She would almost certainly have assets salted away where even Chen Meilin's efficient *Guoanbu* agents couldn't find them.

It hurt. She'd damaged his stature. That was at least part of the reason she'd done it - to weaken him in the eyes of his Party comrades, to make him seem vulnerable on the personal level. It was a deliberate wounding.

He drifted, feeling the water lifting him, lowering him, lifting again.

Lau Chong was coming on. He was a rising star in the Ministry of Public Security and was now in charge of the Emperor's safety. They saw each other almost every day, though they didn't discuss political developments because they seemed to disagree on most things. Taiwan, for a start. But the boy was loyal, no doubt about it.

General Zheng had retired at the end of the previous month, for health reasons. That was the official reason. It was sad that an old warrior like Zheng should then die in a mysterious fire that swept through his home late at night. He had been alone at the time and no-one else was caught in the furnace. The Emperor had sent a huge wreath to the state funeral. Everyone said it was a most impressive tribute.

Investigators declared faulty wiring had been to blame.

As for Qin himself, his health wasn't good, but since his last scan he'd made a real effort to stop smoking and drinking maotai. Dr Lo had assured him he still had years in him if he led a healthy life and avoided stressful situations.

He still swam every day, attended the occasional dance night, enjoyed the company of healthy young Communists in his bed now and then, and he stuck to beer and the occasional cognac. What more could anyone ask of him?

The prospect of war had receded. The PLA was stood down, the Joint Taiwan Attack Centre suspended. To everyone's surprise, the Taiwan talks had gone well. That was the Party line. They'd agreed a new code of conduct for the Taiwan Strait; all warships from whatever navy were obliged to notify authorities on both sides of their intention to transit the Strait, giving both course and time-scale. Airforce planes from one territory would stay out of the air defence zone of the other. Beijing had made no concessions on the 'One China' policy, but hardliners protested in private that no progress had been made on the key aim of unification, though some argued - and Qin ensured the Propaganda Department did so - that the agreement to hold direct talks every year promised more substantive moves towards unification.

Qin saw the talks as bringing Taiwan back into the Chinese fold, as a tacit admission by the island's leaders that the only peaceful resolution lay within the framework of a greater China, and that the discussions in themselves provided the United States with a let-out, an excuse to back off, to treat the dispute as a Chinese matter to be resolved by the Chinese alone — something Beijing had always maintained.

The Emperor declared his strategy a success, and a big step towards unification.

No longer seen as an aggressive warmonger, Qin himself was cast by international media - with a little help from well-funded pro-Beijing influencers - as a world statesman, a champion peacemaker.

He liked the sound of that.

The Party hardliners didn't agree.

They argued - among themselves - that Taiwan's so-called president had refused to budge on the island's autonomy, that her so-called government was not convinced by the 'One China, two systems' approach. They spread the rumour that Washington was encouraging a return of Taiwan to the U.N. General Assembly, something Qin could never allow, and he had let it be known he would exercise China's veto in the Security Council to kill any resolution to that effect.

PLA commanders were restless.

His spies told him Party hardliners were unhappy, including members of his own Politburo - though they'd never say so to his face. But he knew who they were. He had read their files. The phone and email intercepts were delivered to him every day. He knew. They spread the notion that his nerve had failed, that he lacked courage, that he'd backed down in the face of international pressure, that he was gravely ill - in short, that he'd lost it, and through weakness had provoked an international backlash. All lies. They smelled blood - his blood - and now sought an opportunity to bring him down, take his place and divide up the imperial spoils.

They blamed him for the stalling of China's growth, the collapse of the property market and the huge spike in personal and government debt.

The Emperor stood up in waist deep water, ran a hand through his hair.

Time for lunch.

He waded towards the steps.

These things would pass. He'd taken a few hits, but he would come out fighting. The great unification project was on hold, that was all, until the weather improved. Maybe next October would be the best time for the invasion - after the typhoon season and before winter. Meanwhile, the shipyards would still be hard at work. There would soon be four aircraft carriers at sea, with two more nuclear-powered super carriers planned. More nuclear subs, too, along with more advanced aircraft in the pipeline.

Under Qin's leadership, the PLA was unstoppable in its march to unity.

They were waiting for him, his reception committee.

Old, lined faces above black suits and red ties.

The Politburo Standing Committee, now expanded to seven members, including Qin, stood in a respectful and silent semi-circle at the poolside, facing the Emperor as he emerged, water streaming down his well-fed body.

He grabbed a proffered towel, wrapped it around himself. Lau Chong stepped forward, expressionless, holding the white bathrobe open for his father and helping him pull it around his shoulders.

Qin read treachery in their six faces, the six fake smiles, the pathetic fawning, the ridiculous bowing. They'd been conspiring behind his back, whispering to one another, spreading the dirt, preparing whatever it was - a palace coup, another assassination attempt. He knew it all, and he knew them.

Greedy for absolute power.

Behind the cadres and against the wall stood Zhong Mei - silent, inconspicuous, lethal.

Little did they know that Qin's suspicion, his innate ability to preempt whatever his enemies might have in mind, had already done its work. They would not pull a fast one on him. There would be no repeat of Wang's botched assassination. Three of the faces in front of him were of men who would lose their liberty that very night and face charges of sedition and corruption. They would not be seen again, not alive anyway. Two more would learn this very afternoon that they were to be 'promoted' - moved to posts far away from the capital with immediate effect.

The Emperor smiled his half smile, head on one side.

They had the air of conspirators; they wouldn't even look him in the eye.

He could smell their guilt on them like sweat.

I'm ready for you, dear comrades!

# Acknowledgements

Three people in particular made this novel possible. Ian Easton of the Project 2049 Institute has carried out brilliant research into Chinese military writings. A Mandarin speaker with years of experience living and working in China, Japan and Taiwan, Easton's non-fiction 'Chinese Invasion Threat: Taiwan's Defense and American Strategy' was my bedside reading while writing Emperor. His work provided much of the raw material for my fictional intelligence reports, while military writer and analyst Jaidev Jamwal generously helped me update the PRC's Order of Battle. Not least, a good friend who lives under the shadow of a 'certain department' and who cannot therefore be identified, helped put matters into perspective, encouraged me to persevere and assisted with Chinese phrases and anecdotes. I am most grateful to all three, and I should add that any errors of fact or judgement in this work of fiction are entirely mine.

# Select Bibliography

Allison, Graham, *Destined for War, Can America and China Escape Thucydides's Trap?*Scribe, London, 2017;

Brown, Kerry & Wu Tzu-hui, Kalley, *The Trouble With Taiwan, History, the United States and a Rising China*, Zed Books, London, 2019;

Clissold, Tim, *Mr China,* Constable, London, 2004;

Davies, Philip H.J., *MI6 and the Machinery of Spying,* Frank Cass, London, 2005;

Easton, Ian, *The Chinese Invasion Threat*, Eastbridge Books, Manchester, UK, 20017;

Faligot, Roger, *Chinese Spies from Chairman Mao to Xi Jinping,* Scribe, Victoria, 2019;

Li, Dr. Zhisui, *The Private Life of Chairman Mao,* Random House, New York, 1994;

Shum, Desmond, *Red Roulette: An Insider's Story of Wealth, Power, Corruption and Vengeance in Today's China*, Scribner, New York, 2021;

Yang Jisheng, *Tombstone, The Untold Story of Mao's Great Famine*, Allen Lane, London, 2012.

**Free first chapter of Fullerton's next novel and first of a new series of spy thrillers, Bloody Snow: the making of a wayward spy**

# 1

The gunmetal sea glinted under a drifting blanket of drizzle. Paul Snow registered a stench of diesel and seawater, the hollow thump of sea boots on sweating steel plates, the shriek of gulls wheeling like Stuka dive bombers, the razor's edge of winter wind scything off the North Sea. Hulls of submarines lay tamed, moored like captives to the Rosyth dockside, and above them, revealed in breaks in the mist, the alien skeletons of cranes appeared in twos and fours, stalking their prey on long, spindly legs.

Peace. Unfamiliar, uncertain territory.

Lieutenant Paul Snow, R.N., put out a gloved right hand and tapped the forward hatch with his knuckles, his own private, unspoken farewell to *Thor*, a thousand long tons of complicated machinery, all 84 welded metres of her, with her two diesel engines and electric motor, 11 ballast tanks and her eleven, 21-inch torpedo tubes and the 20mm Oerlikon gun mounted aft of the open bridge.

A killing machine, but one that had by skill and good fortune escaped being killed herself on more than one occasion, along with her complement of 48 officers and men packed together in this tin can under sentence of death for months at a time.

Chief Petty Officer Maguire shook Snow's hand in passing. 'We made it, sir. Best of luck.'

Lieutenant Snow surprised himself with a momentary surge of affection, not for Maguire but the boat; Snow would not see her again, not in this form. *Thor* might be placed in reserve for a year or two, be sold off to the Australians or the Chileans, refitted or broken up and turned into bicycles, buses and train carriages. Maybe she'd linger on into the 1950s. He was glad he would never know her fate. He told himself not to be sentimental. It was all in the past. Best thing was to look forward.

Some men he'd served with were going ashore, laughing, joshing one another as they moved up the gangway, bulky kitbags on their shoulders. Pale and spotty faces, badly shaved, they were 'hostilities only' service people, the best of them and the bravest; they were off the hook and returning to their civilian lives. Demob happy. They might still wear a uniform, but there was a jauntiness, a cocky self-assurance now it was over. Most were going home for good. They had survived. They were heroes, in a manner of speaking. These men had families, wives, kids. Some grinned at him, emboldened by newfound liberty, others waved or came up to him and out of shyness shook his hand without a word; a few saluted his rank. They wished him well with easy familiarity now hostilities were over, their accents Scouse, Irish, west Yorkshire, Glaswegian, Welsh, Cockney, the West Country, and more. Able seaman, leading rating, warrant officer, petty officer, chief petty officer, commissioned officers. The last came up, said something with a smile, two suggested a last drink together, and when they saw he was deep in thought and disinclined to respond, moved on.

It was almost over, too, for the Royal Navy Reserve (RNR) and Royal Navy Volunteer Reserve (RNVR) officers. Paul had heard a number of them remark in one mess or another as hostilities drew to a close that Britain wasn't going to revert to being the same old dump it had been before the war; it was going to be a decent place to raise a family. Better housing. Better health. Better schools. Better jobs. That's why they'd fought, for a better world. No return to class, to deference based on birth, to inherited wealth. Snow listened in his quiet, attentive way; he knew little about it, except that he didn't approve of politics being discussed by officers in His Majesty's ships. It didn't seem to him good manners. No talk of sex or politics in the mess was the unwritten rule and it was a sensible one at that.

He was reminded of a tired, worn-out generalisation: the RN comprised officers and gentlemen, the RNR officers trying to be gentlemen, and the RNVR gentlemen trying to be officers. Unfair as it was snobbish, yet there was a possible grain of truth in it.

He'd said his farewells to the bearded captain. Lt. Commander 'Dick' Travers, DSO and bar, over a couple of pink gins in the tiny wardroom. Travers was over six feet, and there wasn't room for his legs; he'd learned to fold them up like a deckchair and stow them under the wardroom table. Not that they said anything to each other, both shy in the absence of hostilities, other than the banal 'good luck.' At 28, Travers was considered to be ancient, and known throughout the

Service for sinking an Italian destroyer with a single shot from the stern tube, and a little later for entering Bari harbour on the surface at night and sinking a troopship with three fish at close range before enduring 14 hours of intense Italian anti-submarine attacks, surviving to laugh about it, though Snow thought there was precious little humour to be had; the Italians were especially effective at anti-submarine warfare and the Submarine Service had sustained horrific losses to prove it. The Italians had sunk more British submarines than the Germans, in fact. Travers was staying on board, waiting for his replacement and the replacement crew who were due the next day. Then he, too, would have three weeks' shore leave to look forward to. Snow wondered what on earth the 'Old Man' would do to keep himself occupied for three weeks of sullen winter weather and food rationing.

The Navy was Snow's home. It was all he'd known since the age of 12. As a regular officer, it was still home. He had no other. If he was determined to quit, he would need their Lordships' permission to resign his commission. It was something to which he'd given much thought of late, and it filled him with both excitement and dread.

What would a peacetime Navy be like? He assumed promotions would be slow and based on years of service rather than bold initiative; there'd be cut-backs in both men and ships. Life ashore or afloat would become routine, an endless cycle of training and occasional foreign deployments with little or no chance of action to speed matters along. Dull men, sticklers for regulations, would do well in times of peace. Not so Paul Snow.

There was also the no small matter of a junior officer's inadequate pay, not enough to keep a man in tobacco and gin, let alone pay the rent.

What was the alternative? How would he cope on the outside, on his own, in a colder, less hospitable world with its unfamiliar rules and social mores? Here he was at least someone with a reputation of sorts and a career if he wanted it; out in the civilian world no-one knew him or cared who he was and what he'd done.

Lieutenant Paul Fergus Andrew Snow was just 21, with two mentions in despatches in his four years of active service. Snow had the look of a veteran of at least 30, and his tired face revealed something of his character. Now an experienced submariner, he could no longer be mistaken for a boy. Snow knew how to impose his authority, by force if necessary; he knew, too, how to inspire respect and exert command over the lives of others, to bend the will of people older, more experienced and often more skilled than himself. Snow had earned their trust.

His appearance wasn't much; he didn't cut an impressive figure. He was preternaturally thin, of medium height, broad in the shoulder, narrow hipped, clean-shaven, with blue eyes, blond hair and a mouthful of teeth worn down to the gums on one side of his jaw by his ubiquitous pipes and all of them stained a yellow-brown by tobacco. His narrow face was etched with exhaustion and prematurely lined. Snow's favourite tipple was pink gin, which he drank in vast quantities whenever the opportunity presented itself. He knew himself to be no intellectual — but no fool, either. He sensed that the world that lay ahead of him would require courage, but of a different kind, less physical than moral. It would also require cunning, a rare quality among guileless sailors.

Lieutenant Snow had his orders. In one week he was to report to the School of Slavonic and East European Studies (SSEES) at Coulsdon, a place he'd never heard of, but the rail warrant showed it was in south London. In the meantime, he could do as he pleased, though with little money in his pocket there wasn't much he could do. Snow could only hazard a guess why he'd been selected for SSEES, and he reasoned it was because (a) Uncle Joe and his Reds weren't turning out as friendly to British interests as so many of Stalin's useful idiots said he was, and (b) His Majesty's Government was short of fluent Russian speakers in time for the next war. Having been fluent in French as a child, Snow had picked Russian as his required European language while a cadet at the Britannia Royal Naval College at Dartmouth in Devon. The only reason had been his penchant for Russian poetry and Chekhov's short stories. He assumed some junior clerical person at the War Office must have pulled his file. Lucky him.

***

Snow's mother, Catherine, cried out his name when he appeared on the doorstep, took his hands in hers, delighted to see him. 'My son!' He'd warned her of his impending arrival by telephone, giving her the chance to escape or make her excuses. He would not impose himself. She was tall and blonde for an Englishwoman. The Swedes would have mistaken her for one of their own, a looker at 42 who turned heads and would continue to do so for two decades more. Dressed by Chanel, she was the eldest of four Branscombe sisters and had money of her own. These days, she lived in a villa in Guernsey with a fine view of the sea from her own terrace, having repossessed her property after the German occupiers surrendered in May, '45.

'You'll stay a few days, won't you?' Her question sounded like a command. 'You look exhausted and half-starved. You poor child. Rest and some decent food will put you right. Now I've something to show you, Paul. Follow me, then do join us for drinks.'

He obeyed. He'd would have preferred a drink before indulging his mother's latest hobby, or whatever it was. He followed her down stone steps and around the side of the house to what looked like a double garage.

Catherine was not alone. Paul knew she was enjoying the friendship of a Canadian general, a decent soldier who'd been shattered by the bloody debacle at Dieppe in August '42. More than half of the 6,000 mostly Canadian attackers were killed, wounded or captured. It was said Major-General John Roberts, MC, DSO, had been robust in expressing opposition to plans for the amphibious assault, dubbed Operation Jubilee. It was rumoured that Churchill neither forgot nor forgave him. Roberts had been shattered by the sight of his wrecked brigades struggling back to the waiting ships. It was said that he'd sobbed at the sight. But it was his allegedly inept performance in coordinating artillery and infantry during a war-game codenamed Operation Spartan the following year that had ended his operational career. Broken man, some said. Churchill's' revenge, said others.

Only General Roberts would know the truth, and he wasn't saying.

'What do you think? Do you like it?'

Snow was not someone who showed surprise or gave voice to it. On this occasion, he was speechless.

In the garage stood every young adult's dream of a sports car: a brand new, low-slung, Guards Red, two-seat MG TC convertible with a canvas roof. In the afternoon light, and with the garage doors open, it seemed to glow.

'Good grief, Mother. Like it? I love it —'

'It's yours, my darling. Here are the keys.' She opened her palm and held them out to him.

'It's time you got rid of that horrible old bike of yours. It's far too dangerous. I've been keeping this as a present for your missed birthdays. You earned it. Just don't drive too fast. Promise me.'

Snow was still dazed. Catherine smiled, pleased that it surprised him, made him happy.

She'd always hated his Norton, which his father had given him for his 12th birthday, convinced he'd kill himself riding it.

For just a moment, the usual decorum between mother and son was forgotten. They hugged each other, and for the first time since he went off to Dartmouth in his officer cadet's uniform, complete with dirk, he breathed in her scent and remembered what there had been of childhood.

She put an arm around his shoulders. 'Welcome home, dearest Paul. When you're ready, do come up to the terrace and have a drink with us. I'm so proud of you, I want to show you off. Then we'll change for supper — if it's warm enough, it'll be alfresco.'

Snow went up to the terrace and his mother introduced him to the General, who struck Paul as a genial, robust man, big and broad with a toothbrush moustache, the kind of officer Snow thought soldiers would look up to, whatever people might have said about his generalship. Snow helped himself to a large pink gin and settled on a chair opposite them both. Within minutes, it was clear that there was considerable affection between his mother and the Canadian. They didn't hide their smiles, laughter and fond glances. Why should they? Paul wasn't embarrassed; he felt happy for his mother. She deserved a decent life.

In 1941, after Snow had begun active service in the Mediterranean as a 17-year-old midshipman in the battleship *Elizabeth*, he'd been summoned to the captain's cabin. Not a little perplexed by the order, he knocked, entered, stood to attention.

'Midshipman Snow, sir.'

'Snow? Ah, yes.' The captain picked up what appeared to be a radio signal and glanced at it as if to remind himself of the details.

'I am requested to inform you that your father died four days ago.'

He looked up at Snow, still at attention, eyes fixed on a point above the captain's greying head and whiskered face.

'Sir,' said Snow, thinking that this information must require some acknowledgement.

'That's all, Snow. Carry on.'

'Aye-aye, sir.'

Snow saluted, turned about, and marched out.

No leave was offered, none was requested.

The next day, a note appeared in the officers' mess calling for volunteers for the Submarine Service. Snow was the first of the *Elizabeth*'s officers to respond. It had nothing to do with his father's death, and everything to do with the illusion that the old dreadnought and her sister ship *Valiant* were operational. In fact, 'combat swimmers' riding manned torpedoes of the *Decima Flottiglia MAS* had penetrated Alexandria's allied naval base on December 19, 1941, and planted limpet mines on the hulls of both warships. The blasts caused considerable damage, though there was no outward, visible sign. The daring frogmen were taken alive. Snow was already impatient for action and while on watch, had kept an envious eye on the sleek, predatory hulls of Royal Navy submarines moored alongside a mothership at the base. 'That's for me,' he thought. Now was his chance. As it so happened, it would be 18 months before HMS *Elizabeth* could leave Alexandria, by which time Snow had been promoted to sub-lieutenant and, at 18, commanded the five-man gun crew and boarding party of an S-class boat, *Sea Hound*, based at Trincomalee and tasked with hunting and destroying Japanese vessels in the Malacca Strait.

Relaxing on the terrace, watching the sunset, gin in hand, sucking on his pipe, Snow thought about his father, Alexander. He compared him to General Roberts sat opposite. Paul couldn't imagine his father - stiff and pompous at the best of times - in a short-sleeved shirt with an open collar, baggy yellow golfing shorts, canvas and rope soled sandals without socks, sitting back, relaxed, drink in hand, showing an equanimity and pleasure in the company of others. Impossible! The old man had been 73 when he died. Snow senior had always been a distant figure - unsurprising, given that Paul was his fifth child and fourth son, by a second marriage, what's more. In practical terms, it meant Paul wouldn't inherit a penny from the Snow family estate. It was 'entailed', which meant it would pass down the generations along the male line, from eldest son to eldest son. The current eldest — Charles, Paul's much older half-brother and someone so far without issue — would not get his hands on the capital, only the earnings and interest, in itself a considerable fortune.

Snow's father had been an odd chap. He'd insisted that the change he carried on his person for tips be boiled every night and placed on his dressing table. When he was seven, the child broke a cardinal rule: no dog was allowed inside either of his father's two homes, one near Doncaster in south Yorkshire, the other at Boothby Graffoe, across the Pennines in Lancashire. But Paul's excitable young King Charles spaniel had done just that, leaving a fresh turd on prominent display on a fine Tabriz carpet in the hall. Without a word, Snow's father had fetched one of a pair of James Purdey 12-bore shotguns, loaded both barrels with buckshot, then hauled boy and dog outside, and among purple hydrangeas, blew the dog's head off.

'Learn to obey the rules,' he'd growled at the stunned and trembling Paul.

Alexander Fergus Herbert Snow met his second wife - Paul's future mother, Catherine - when he was 54 and she 18. He spotted her on a hunt and enquired of the Master who she was. He had noticed her figure, her fine seat, her willingness to take on any jump without hesitation. Her bold nature aroused his interest and his libido. The heiress to the estate next to yours, came the answer. Paul's father broke off the hunt at once and rode home, informing his then wife and mother of three sons and a daughter of his intention to divorce her, and began without delay his pursuit of Catherine. They both had money; it was deemed a good match notwithstanding the immense age difference, his indecent haste and a divorce that scandalised what passed for Yorkshire and Lancashire society. Not that Snow senior cared one jot about society, whatever it might be. It seems people will forgive and forget anything and everything if there's enough money in it.

During World War One, Paul's father had led his yeomanry cavalry regiment, the 500-strong Yorkshire Dragoons, to Palestine. He'd also taken along the regimental silver, the rugs and much of the furniture at his own expense. He paid for his pack of foxhounds to accompany them so officers might amuse themselves hunting jackals when not fighting the Ottoman Empire. Anything with a bushy tail or a tarboosh was fair game. Colonel Snow insisted his officers change into mess dress for evening meals - regardless of season and weather.

He was an accomplished killer of foxes, Palestinian jackals and Turkish troops. By the age of 40, he was reported to have accounted for 70 brace of foxes. He was blooded before his fifth birthday, a ritual of marking the forehead with the fresh blood of a severed foxtail. There was no time when he did not hunt as man or boy, except when boarding at Harrow School or when the ground was frozen too hard for his favourite hunter, Signal. Alexander Snow, TD, JP, owned and managed a stud of 56 hunters. First Master of the Badsworth and then Master of the York and Ainsty Hounds, he also hunted on his own estates. Snow senior saw himself as something of an authority not only on breeding hunters, but foxhounds, too. He didn't care for the creatures' looks; all he cared about was producing hounds with strength, stamina and the instinct to scent, track and kill foxes. His habit was to carry a bucket of scrambled eggs to the kennels and feed the hounds himself every Sunday morning. It was supposed to be a treat.

***

General Roberts seemed to like Paul; he showed it by teasing the young man over sole meunière, accompanied by a delicious white Bordeaux.

'What's your nickname in the Navy, son?'

'It varies, sir, depending on who's doing the naming, and the circumstances, of course.'

'Such as?'

'I inherited one of my father's names. Fergus. My fellow officers call me Fungus when they can't think of anything better.'

'That's pretty tame. Can't you do better than that?'

'Bloody Snow is common among the other ranks, especially when I have to supervise disagreeable tasks such as loading stores and on occasion, insisting they do it all over again if they don't get it right the first time.'

'Could be a lot worse.'

'Indeed it could, sir. No doubt there are worse, only I haven't heard them as yet.'

For no apparent reason, two momentous exchanges with his father came to mind. Perhaps it was the General himself, his natural authority and his age, which was probably around 60 or so. The soldier reminded Snow of some aspects of his own father despite the obvious differences.

The day Paul turned 11, he was told his father wanted to see him in the latter's study.

Snow had wondered what he'd done wrong this time, what rule he'd broken, and whether it would merit a thrashing. That it was his birthday wouldn't matter to a father everyone had taken to calling The Colonel.

He need not have worried.

'Church or Navy?'

'Sir?' He'd never called his father anything else.

The question was repeated, louder. 'Church or Navy?'

So this was it. Snow knew that according to the family tradition, the eldest son went to the Royal Military Academy Sandhurst and spent a few years in the Regular Army before returning to manage the family estates, while younger sons had a choice. It was not much of a choice. Snow was not a believer in any divinity so far as he was aware, and while that might not be a bar to taking holy orders (to judge by the activities and morals of some senior churchmen) living and working as an impoverished country parson had little to commend it.

'Navy, sir.'

'Very well.'

That was an end to it until the following year when 12-year-old Snow was measured by his father's London tailor for his first uniform. Once again, he was summoned by the Colonel, who gave his youngest son his standard lecture on the conduct expected of an officer and a gentleman, which Snow would become the moment he stepped aboard the Devon train in his officer cadet's uniform.

Life was simple when there were orders to be obeyed. In war, the way forward was straight; there was always duty to be performed, hazardous or not. Peace was a different matter entirely, complicated and confusing. Snow wasn't at all sure what he wanted and even less what he needed as man. He was of the opinion that people seldom got what they wanted, but that if they were determined and worked at whatever it was, they'd sooner or later be rewarded with whatever it was they needed.

The train had halted at Exeter for a good half hour, as Paul knew it would. Eager to test his elevated role in life, he marched into the lounge bar of a pub opposite the station, went up to the counter and demanded a pint of bitter. The barmaid or publican's wife - it wasn't clear which, but either way she was a *jolie laide* - looked him up and down, then leaned on her forearms on the counter and appeared to give his request her full consideration, inadvertently offering Snow the opportunity to admire her cleavage.

'We don't serve children in here, sonny. Come back in a few years and you can have your pint.'

Neither of them knew it of course, but six years on, just after midnight on May 3/4, 1942, the woman, Miss Angela Simmons, along with her mother, would be among 156 people killed when 20 bombers, flying low and in good visibility, visited Exeter's town centre uninvited and flattened it, destroying 1,500 homes and starting several huge fires as part of what were known as the 'Baedeker blitz' — the deliberate targeting of cultural sites across Britain. Most of the raiders made two sorties that night.

Neither of them could have foreseen that the precocious child in Edwardian fancy dress, standing before Miss Simmons and solemnly demanding his first pint, would personally kill seven enemy soldiers with bayonet and pistol that same summer, or that unlike Miss Simmons, he would survive the war to find himself rising through the ranks of His Majesty's Secret Intelligence Service, to become a senior if somewhat errant spy.

For more details about the author and his books, please visit his website at https://johnfullertonauthor.scot

If you have enjoyed Emperor, please leave a rating and review on Amazon, Goodreads, Waterstones or any other book seller's website. It helps enormously. Thank you.

Printed in Great Britain
by Amazon

43121380R00169